MILDRED'S RESISTANCE

THE NETWORK SERIES
by Katie Cross

Mildred's Resistance

Miss Mabel's School for Girls

The Isadora Interviews

Antebellum Awakening

MILDRED'S RESISTANCE

Katie Cross

Antebellum
Publishing

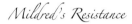

Mildred's Resistance

Young Adult Fantasy

Cover designed by Jenny Zemanek at www.seedlingsonline.com
Typesetting by Chris Bell with Atthis Arts LLC at www.atthisarts.com

Published by Antebellum Publishing.
Visit www.antebellumpublishing.com for more information.

ISBN (paperback)   978-0-9915319-5-0
(ebook)   978-0-9915319-7-4

Visit the author at www.kcrosswriting.com

Visit The Network Series at www.missmabels.com or on
Facebook at www.facebook.com/missmabels

To my Mildreds.

You know who you are. Love yer guts.

Acknowledgments

To write a novel is to harness the power of a village.

I truly relearn this lesson every single time, but never so much as I did with Mildred's Resistance. MR is a work of many, many tears. My heart's blood went into figuring out and finalizing this story. No work of mine has required such sacrifice so far, so it's with great joy that I turn it into your hands.

I have a few Mildreds in my life. Learning how she/they think was insightful, exhausting, and sometimes hysterical. So first I must thank the Mildreds for tolerating my endless questions and personality explorations. Love yer guts.

To the most incredible publishing team in the world: Catherine (and all the other fabulous editors you provide me), you make my words pretty. To the beta readers who suffered through early drafts of MR when the going wasn't easy (Kelsey, Brandi, Kirstin, Holly, Stephen, and any others I may have forgotten), I think you've earned a personal swimming pool in heaven for putting up me. To Kella, Chris, Jenny, and all those who put this beast together and made it what it is: you guys rock.

To my friends and family: I'm so grateful for all the support and love.

To my fans: love yer guts too, guys. MUAH.

Husband, Lucas, Ryker, Bridger: I sure like your handsome faces.

Here be Monsters

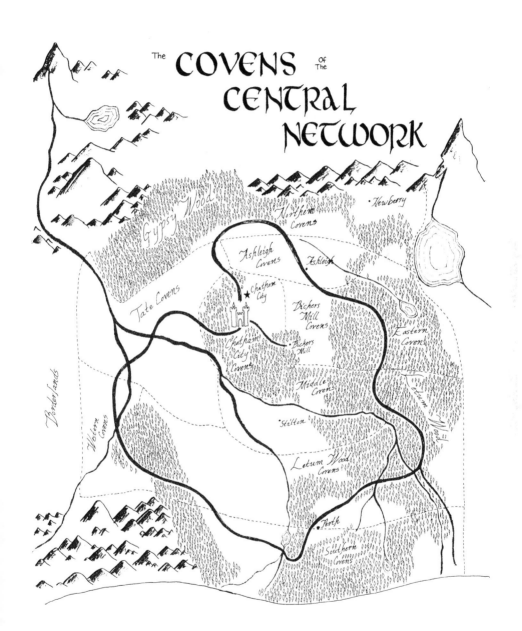

The COVENS of the
CENTRAL
NETWORK

Dear Reader,

This book is written by an unknown author. That's the name I've chosen and it's the only name you'll ever know. My identity is not nearly as important as yours.

Suffice it to say that you may trust me; everything in this book is true. I tell the story about the people of the Resistance and all that it meant at the time. Perhaps it means something to you now, but it will never mean anything to you like it did to us.

The Resistance wasn't an explosion. Rather, it was a slow burn that turned to flame, and then to fire. As to blame, I ask you to draw your own conclusions, for you now hold the truth in your hands.

Sincerely Yours,

The Unknown Author

The Beginning

Mildred was a young girl, but she didn't know it.

A typical six-year-old girl didn't spend her evenings hiding in a closet, protecting her little brother, while trying to block out the sound of her drunk father with magical spells. Most young girls dressed dolls, went to bed with a full tummy, and had time to play.

But not Mildred.

"Look at the picture of the dragon, Jorden," Mildred whispered to her little brother, wincing when shattering glass crashed outside the small closet. "What color is it?"

Father screamed something at Mother, but Mildred couldn't make out the words.

"Gween," Jorden promptly replied, but his wide brown eyes strayed back to the door when the bellowing ceased. Mother's calm voice responded, soothing some of Mildred's worry. Mother would calm Father down; she always did. Then he'd apologize and be kind for a day or two before falling back into a sullen silence.

"Very good," Mildred said, turning the page. Her right cheekbone throbbed every time she spoke, but she ignored it. Jorden was watching her warily, so she acted like nothing was wrong. "How about this dragon?"

A candle trembled in the air next to them, held there by Mildred's weak ability to do magic. Beads of wax rolled down the candlestick, whose flame flickered eerily in the dark. A dollop of hot wax fell onto the back of her hand, but she ignored it.

"This dragon is red, isn't it?" She pointed to a painted scene in the book, but Jorden wasn't looking.

"Milly," he whined, pressing his hands to his ears and leaning into her side. "Make the yelling go away."

A slam sounded. Father had thrown a chair this time, no doubt. They'd never have the currency to buy new furniture. Mildred pressed her hands to Jorden's ears and tried to think of an incantation that would block out sounds, but her mind had gone foggy. Her hand strayed to the tender skin covering the pulse in her cheek. Father had never struck her before tonight. She hoped Mother wouldn't have to spend the next day in bed, like last time.

"We can't make them stop fighting, Jorden."

"I want Mother!"

She slapped a hand over his mouth. "Quiet!" she hissed, listening for the sound of approaching footsteps. Father often forgot about them during his ipsum-fueled rage, but sometimes he remembered. Even Mother's protection spells couldn't stop him if he really wanted to open the closet door. She softened her voice when Jorden's lower lip trembled.

"I'm sorry, Jorden," she said, gathering him into her lap. "I didn't mean to scare you. But we can't see Mother right now. She locked us in here, remember?"

He nodded. A long tear ran down his cheek from a wide brown eye.

"Let's keep reading about dragons," she said, holding the book a bit higher. "Want to keep reading?"

He hesitated but finally nodded and ran an arm underneath his drippy nose.

"Good," she said in a tremulous voice, wishing she could cry. "I'll sound out the words, and you tell me what color the dragon is, okay?"

Halfway through the book, Mildred paused when the yelling stopped, followed by a heavy thud. Silence fell. Jorden held his breath as his eyes returned to the crack under the door.

Not a sound.

Mildred's heart pounded in her throat. Was Mother okay? Had

Father left? Perhaps he'd passed out, and they would escape over to Mrs. Tattleton's across the street until the next morning, like usual. Jorden grabbed Mildred's hand and held so tight it hurt. She wrapped her arm around his skinny body and waited.

The silence seemed to last forever.

A quiet murmur of voices eventually came. She strained to hear but found only hums. Mother's voice, then Mrs. Tattleton's, and then the deep reverberations of a male witch she didn't recognize. It wasn't father.

"Milly," Jorden whispered. "What's happening?"

"I don't know."

A long time later, the voices left, and Mildred heard the sound of feet approaching the closet door. Mildred hastily blew out the candle. It fell to the floor with a thud when she shoved Jorden into the corner and put herself in front of him just as the door opened a crack.

"Mildred? Jorden?" Mother's voice called as light spilled into the closet. "It's just me. You can come out now. It's safe."

Jorden scrambled from behind his sister and threw himself into Mother's legs. Mildred clambered out behind him and followed suit with a cry of relief. Mother crouched down and hugged both of them, her brown hair shining with red highlights in the candlelight.

"It's okay, children," she said in a soothing tone, though her hand trembled against Mildred's back. "We're safe now."

Mildred glanced over Mother's shoulder to the kitchen, surprised to see their heavy iron frying pan sitting on the edge of the table. Mrs. Tattleton was kneeling on the floor, scrubbing the wooden boards with a heavy brush. The soap bubbles reflected a distinctive pinkish-red hue.

"Where's Father?" Jorden asked. Mother pulled away.

"He's gone," she said resolutely. She touched Mildred's swelling right cheek with the tender caress of a parent. "He's never going hurt any of us again, I promise."

Jorden buried himself deep in Mother's arms, letting free all his pent-up sobs. Mrs. Tattleton glanced up, saw Mildred watching, and blocked the stain on the floor with her body.

No matter how six-year-old Evelyn looked at it, the High Priestess was *old*.

Her graying hair puffed out in cloud-like curls, and she spoke with the measured, even tones of a grandmother. Evelyn sighed. Why had Mama insisted she meet the High Priestess? She didn't care about an old witch, even if she did help rule the Central Network and act as Mama's boss.

It wasn't that Evelyn was afraid; *nothing* scared Evelyn. Not even the chants of the gypsies wandering through Chatham City at night. But the High Priestess smelled like talc, and it made her want to sneeze. Evelyn put her hand under her nose, already feeling the preliminary prickle.

"Bring her in here, Marcia," the High Priestess said. "I do love children. You speak so much about her. I can't wait to see her red hair."

Evelyn leaned away from the doorway and back toward the hallway. She didn't want to have tea with an old lady! What would they talk about? Mama turned to the door and waved.

"Come in, Evelyn."

Evelyn shook her head of bobbed red hair. No *way* was she going in there, no matter how much she loved Mama.

"Evie, come on!" Mama's voice sounded encouraging, but the stern listen-to-me-right-now press of her lips appeared, so Evelyn stepped away and leaned against the wall. She contemplated running down the hallway, past the Guardians standing by the stairs, and into the kitchens to beg Mrs. F to hide her. Then she wouldn't have to smell the dry talc powder and pretend to be friends with a raisin.

"What are ya doing?" Mama asked, stepping into the hall and snatching Evelyn's wrist before she could run. Mama's thick Chatham City accent was even more pronounced when she was angry. "Ya can't play these childish games."

"Mama, please!" Evelyn whispered, trying to tug her hand away. "She smells funny!"

Mama's eyebrows, so light they almost didn't exist, lowered until her eyes became skinny lines.

"She doesn't either. Now, ya will be on ya best behavior tonight and be kind ta the High Priestess, or ya father will hear about it."

Evelyn stiffened. Mama never threatened to involve Papa unless she meant business.

"But Mama—"

"The High Priestess is a very busy witch, Evie," Mama said, her voice softening as she lowered into a crouch next to her. "Sometimes she gets very sad. So sad she can't even get out of bed. I thought that bringing ya here might cheer her up and stop her from getting so sad because ya so young and happy. Just try? For me?"

Evelyn stared deep into Mama's sea green eyes. She adored Mama and would do anything for her. "Fine," Evie mumbled, picking at the bow on the front of her dress. "I'll try. For ya."

"Thank ya," Mama said, batting Evelyn's hand away from the half-bow, re-tying it, and then straightening. "Do ya remember what I taught ya ta say?"

"Yes."

Evelyn followed a few steps behind Mama, dragging her feet as she went so it was clear this was *not* on her agenda for the night. She stood in front of the old woman with her eyes downcast.

"Merry meet, High Priestess," Evelyn mumbled, studying the white velvet slippers that covered the High Priestess's veiny feet. "I'm grateful ta meet ya."

"Merry meet, Evelyn," the High Priestess said, peering down at her from where she sat at a vanity table filled with powders, ointments, and potions that older witches used to keep wrinkles away. "How are you?"

"Good," Evelyn said, taking Mama's hand and glancing over the contents of the vanity table. "Are ya putting ointments on ya face ta stop the wrinkles? Because it's not working. You should try a different one."

The High Priestess's eyes popped wide open the same instant Mama grabbed Evelyn's shoulder with hands of steel.

"Evelyn!" Mama hissed through her teeth. "Apologize right now!"

To Evelyn's astonishment, the corners of the High Priestess's lips twitched. Her eyes went from kind to surprised clearly enough that Evelyn knew she wasn't mad. At least, not like Mama, whose vise-like grip had tightened.

"Mama," she whined. "That hurts—"

"Ya Highness, I deeply apologize," Mama said, bowing, her face a flaming red that matched her hair. "I never imagined that she would—"

The High Priestess waved a hand, smiling. "Don't worry, Marcia. She's right. I do need new cream for my skin. I shall write the apothecary tomorrow. I've been meaning to for several days now; she's simply provided the motivation. You have very pretty red hair, Evelyn. I've heard much about it."

"Thank ya," she responded promptly, as Mama had taught her to do. "Mama said it matches my personality."

Red hair in the Central Network was rare, so witches in the markets flocked to her with comments and questions. "There's that little red head," they'd say to their friends, waving. "I see her here all the time. Don't ya just love her freckles?"

Evelyn basked in the attention because there was nothing she loved more. Except, maybe, all the pretty trinkets in the castle. They had a few trinkets at home—*to prove we aren't poor, we're middle class*—as Papa always said. None of their trinkets were as pretty as the ones here.

The High Priestess smiled. "I'll bet your hair does match your personality," she said. "I think you're a very bright, energetic girl."

"I am."

"We're working on her humility," Marcia said, brushing the hair out of Evelyn's eyes. Evelyn leaned away with a scowl.

"Don't," the High Priestess said in a whimsical tone. "She's perfect just the way she is."

Evelyn stared at the High Priestess with new eyes. Perhaps this old lady wasn't so bad, even if she was saggy.

"Mama says I was born talking," Evelyn said. "I like ta talk ta other witches. Sometimes I get in trouble for making Mama late, and then Papa gets angry and yells so that—"

"Yes, well, I'm sure the High Priestess has things ta do," Marcia said, interrupting her daughter with a nervous smile. "Say merry part ta the High Priestess, Evelyn."

"Oh, don't go yet!" the High Priestess said. "You haven't even had tea."

"Oh! Do ya have cookies? I love cookies with tea, but we only get them at home on birthdays and special holidays." Evelyn leaned toward the High Priestess and whispered, "Sugar is bad for ya teeth."

A call came from the hallway before Marcia could admonish Evelyn for asking.

"Marcia?"

The High Priestess smiled at Evelyn, but this time her eyes twinkled. "Yes, we have lots of cookies," she said with a little hop in her voice that reminded Evelyn of a jumping game. "You can eat as many as you want."

Evelyn's mouth dropped. "What?"

"Are you sure you want her ta stay, High Priestess?" Marcia asked, glancing at the door. "I—"

"Yes, of course. Evie is a delightful little girl. She's made my day bright just by being here. Go take care of what's needed. We'll be here in the meantime."

"You can call me Evie because I said it's okay," Evelyn piped up, lest the High Priestess think she was above getting permission. "I only like some people calling me that, like Milly and Stella, but ya can be one of them because ya nice. I thought ya'd smell like talc, but now ya smell like cookies."

The High Priestess chuckled. Marcia hovered, glancing from her daughter to the hallway.

"Really, Marcia," the High Priestess insisted with a dismissive wave of her hand, "just for tea while you sort things out. It shall make me very happy. I think Evie and I are going to be great friends."

Evelyn smiled so wide at Mama that her cheeks hurt, but Marcia finally relented, so the discomfort was worth it. Evelyn jumped with a cry of joy—what could be more fun than tea in a castle?—and tugged on the High Priestess's soft hands.

"Let's go!" Evelyn cried impatiently. "I'll pour the tea because I'm afraid ya won't do it right. Mama taught me how, and I'm really good at it. I'll teach ya. I'm a good teacher."

The Witches' Oath

Mildred carefully dunked a stack of wooden plates into the steamy bucket of dishwater bubbling with soap. Next to her stood her best friend Evelyn, perched on a similar stool, in front of a similar tub, with her own stack of dishes to wash.

"What happened?" Evelyn asked, eyeing Mildred's right cheek, which had a faint black and purple bruise. Unlike Mildred, who didn't have a splash of water on her apron, Evelyn was half soaked.

"I fell," Mildred said, "and knocked it on the stairs."

Evelyn shot her a knowing look. Both of them had fathers driven to drink ipsum because of poverty, or in Evelyn's case, bad memories from his job as a Guardian.

"Didn't hide fast enough?" Evelyn asked with a sympathetic look. Mildred hesitated, then nodded. Evelyn gestured to the side of her head with a grimace. "Me neither."

Mrs. F, the head cook for Chatham Castle, bustled up from behind them to set three more plates on their pile.

"There are my hardworking girls," Mrs. F cried with a warm smile. Tufts of hair peeked out from underneath her round white hat, and a frilly apron hung all the way to her knees. Recipe cards hovered around her head in a circular dance, reminding her of dishes to be cooked. Mildred was glad Mrs. F had shown up; now she didn't have to explain to Evelyn that Father would never come back. It made her stomach hurt just thinking about it.

"Thank you for helping with the breakfast dishes, as always," Mrs.

F said, already moving on again, recipe cards in tow. "Don't be late for class now!"

They continued their soapy chore in silence. Evelyn's mother was an upper-floor maid at the castle, which meant she could afford the uniforms and had some education. Mildred's mother Vanessa worked in the kitchen; she didn't have currency or much official education, so she worked with bread and pastries. Both Evelyn and Mildred cleaned dishes every morning to pay for their breakfast at the castle. Jorden was too young to work as a fireboy, so he stayed with Mrs. Tattleton.

"I found a spider in my bedroom last night," Evelyn said, her nose wrinkling with delighted disgust. "And I pulled his legs off, the way Papa taught me. It was so gross! The legs kept moving!"

Mildred grimaced. Pulling the legs off spiders didn't seem very kind. She opened her mouth to reply, but Evelyn kept talking.

"And I stayed up late practicing for Miss Sonia's lesson today."

To demonstrate, Evelyn used a magical spell to lift several bubbles from the suds. They hovered in the air ten seconds before popping. Evelyn's bright red braid flopped around her neck like a fish when she turned to Mildred.

"Well?" she asked, eyebrows lifted. "What about ya?"

Mildred had been practicing how to raise objects with a levitation spell for the past week. Whenever she did it at home by herself, she managed. Most of the time. Whenever she had to do it in front of others, well . . .

"It's fine," Mildred said, grabbing a few more plates. "Come on, we have to hurry, or we'll be late for class."

The idea of being late to anything sent a shiver of fear through Mildred, and she went back to her work with singular determination. Evelyn played with the bubbles instead, chattering about the Guardians who had complimented her bright hair that morning. Mildred ending up washing and drying far more than her fair share.

"Hurry!" Evelyn commanded as they scampered down the hallway. "We're going ta be late!"

Their classroom was tucked into a deep corner of the servants' quarters. Fifteen pupils attended, all children of other castle employees. Stella, the final component of their trio, met them in the classroom with a bright smile. Stella's father was the Assistant to Council Member Porter, and they lived at the castle because her father worked all the time. Like Evelyn and Mildred, Stella's birthday was also during the third month of summer, which meant all of them would turn seven in two more months.

"Merry meet!" Stella said. Her blue dress, which matched her lovely eyes, was illuminated by the light from the tall windows.

"Merry meet, Stella!" Evelyn replied. "I can't wait ta show ya what I can do with magic! Papa taught me a new spell last night with—"

"There she is!" called a young fireboy from the other side of the room, his dirty arm pointing at the three of them. "It's Mildred Graeme: the witch who can't do magic!"

"She can't even buy new shoes."

"She's so poor, the dirt stays away from her!"

"She thinks she's so much better than us, though," called another. "She doesn't even talk with an accent!"

Mildred's cheeks burned hot with shame when the rest of the students exploded in tittering laughter. Stella stepped up to Mildred's side with a gasp of shock. Evelyn whipped around to face the bullies, fire in her eyes, hands stacked on her hips.

"Hey!" Evelyn yelled back. "Ya don't know anything, Charlie! Ya can't even remember ya letters, can ya? Mildred's my friend. My best friend. Ya want to make fun of her? Ya gotta go through me."

Charlie, whose cheeks were smudged with charcoal, hesitated. The others' chortling died down.

"I'm not scared!" he said, swallowing.

"Ya should be!" Evelyn took a step toward him. He leapt back. "I'll hex ya until you're cross-eyed for the rest of ya life, ya obnoxious cow! I know ya daddy, and he's the worst drunk in Chatham City."

Charlie recoiled when she moved closer, then stopped and tried to square his shoulders. But even his friends shuffled back, leaving him standing alone before Evelyn's wrath. He shrank away.

"That's what I thought, coward," she muttered, then moved her sharp gaze to his friends. "If anyone has a problem with Mildred, ya take it up with me, got it? She's got a Mama who doesn't have an accent, but that doesn't mean she's putting on airs."

They nodded haphazardly, scrambling when Miss Sonia soared into the room. "Take your seats, everyone!" she called, clapping three times. "To your seats!"

The three girls slipped into their shared bench at the very back of the room without another word, though Evelyn tracked Charlie and his friends all the way to their desk. Mildred sat in the middle of the bench and reached for Evelyn's and Stella's hands with a firm squeeze.

"Thank you," she whispered, and Evelyn winked.

"No one makes fun of my best friends."

"I trust all of you practiced over the weekend," Miss Sonia called in a sing-song. A scroll flew from her desk and into her hand. "We shall demonstrate our levitation spells after I finish roll."

Dread dropped into Mildred's stomach like a heavy stone. Now that Charlie had humiliated her, it would be even more difficult to do magic in front of other witches. The words always froze in her mouth like a chunk of ice. Too soon, Miss Sonia set down the attendance scroll.

"Evelyn Ringer, you shall demonstrate first."

Evelyn strode to the front of the room, the ends of her dress swaying around her legs. Instead of levitating the feather that Miss Sonia had provided on the table at the front, she lifted Charlie's stack of books, using magic to move them to the far end of the room, where they flew out the open window.

Miss Sonia shot her a disapproving glare. "Evelyn," she drawled.

"Oh, very well, Miss Sonia," she said and summoned the books back with another spell, one that Mildred wouldn't have been able to do if she'd tried endlessly for days. The books returned with a plop in front of the sulking Charlie. Evelyn gave him a triumphant smile and flounced back to her seat

"That'll show him!" she muttered when she fell back into the chair with her usual gusto.

Mildred swallowed hard, already sensing that Miss Sonia would call her next. Her mind fluttered like a rising flock of birds. What would she do now? A simple levitation spell was beyond her ability. Now that Evelyn had embarrassed Charlie, he'd really make fun of Mildred for not being good with magic.

"Mildred Graeme," Miss Sonia said. "How about you go next?"

"You'll do great, Milly," Stella whispered, squeezing her hand one last time. "Just concentrate like we practiced after class last week."

The walk to the front of the classroom felt interminable. Mildred looked to Miss Sonia, who gave her an encouraging smile, and down at the feather, avoiding the quiet taunts of Charlie and his friends.

Easy, she reminded herself, gathering the words for the incantation. *It will be easy.*

But the words for the incantation had fled, dissolving into the teasing voices of her peers.

There she is! The witch who can't do magic.

Mildred's the dumbest student in class.

She's so poor that she uses sticks to eat her porridge!

She tried to shove their voices into the back of her mind, but it didn't work. Oh, why couldn't she remember the words?

"Put your back to the classroom," Miss Sonia said when silence prevailed for too long. "Sometimes that helps."

Mildred mumbled a few magical words under her breath. Instead of lifting into the air, the feather caught on fire.

"Oh no!" Mildred cried, scrambling forward. "I didn't—"

Miss Sonia cast another spell and the feather snuffed out before Mildred could get to it. The smell of singed hair curled in her nostrils. The smell of failure.

"It's okay, Mildred," Miss Sonia said with a patient smile. "I get nervous in front of other witches, too. Come see me after class and we'll try again."

Mildred gratefully returned to her seat, eyes averted. Charlie and his friends remained silent, watching Evelyn's clenched fist from the corner of their eyes. They let Mildred pass without bothering her.

"You did great, Milly," Stella whispered with a comforting smile.

Evelyn patted her on the back. "You'll show them one day, Milly," she said. "I just know you will."

Relieved to be amongst friends again, Mildred pushed her embarrassment from her mind and focused her whole attention on the lesson.

"It's all right, Mildred. Keep working. Magic isn't easy for every witch you know."

Miss Sonia patted her on the back as Mildred's simple illumination spell failed to light a candle yet again. The cold wick seemed to mock her.

"Thank you, Miss Sonia," she whispered, sliding off the bench and gathering her books. A week had passed since her last embarrassing failure in front of the class, and though she'd remained behind every day for more instruction, she still struggled with levitation and illumination.

"I'm sure Stella and Evelyn are waiting for you outside."

Mildred nodded, then slipped into the hall, books in hand. Her friends weren't there like usual, so she kept walking until she found them just down the hall. Stella and Evelyn were huddled together, their ears pressed to Mrs. F's office door. Evelyn moved to the side to give Stella more room, her face scrunched into a worried expression.

"Stella?" Mildred asked. "Evie?"

Evelyn glanced up, then seeing Mildred standing in the hallway, waved frantically for her to join them. They wore solemn, intent faces.

"What are you doing?" Mildred whispered. Evelyn put a finger against her lips. Stella pulled Mildred in close.

"We overheard your name when we were walking by," she whispered, "just when your mother walked into Mrs. F's office. Evelyn put a listening incantation on the door so we could hear what they were saying about you."

Mildred wedged herself between her two friends and pressed her ear to the door.

"What will you do with only one income, Vanessa?" Mrs. F asked, her voice muffled through the heavy wood. "You know the rest of the kitchen staff will help you in any way you need."

Mildred's heart leapt into her throat. Did her family need help? Was something wrong?

"Without two incomes, we can't afford rent where we live now," Mother replied. "I'm going to find a place on the outskirts of the city that won't be so expensive."

"You should try York," Mrs. F said. "I grew up there. It would be a lovely, safe place for your kids while you're at work."

"I suppose I can transport here every day."

"York is in the country, so there isn't as much crime as Chatham City, but it's still in the suburbs. It's a quiet, quaint little place. No doubt Mildred will like being away from the city."

Mildred glanced at her two friends with equal anxiety. Move to a place called York? Her stomach roiled with the thought of leaving her friends.

"Mildred will be happy to get away."

"She won't be able to come to work with you like she does now," Mrs. F pointed out. "She's so happy here, and Sonia said she's just starting to get over the worst of her shyness."

Mother sighed. "I can enroll Mildred in a common school in York. She'll continue to learn magic there, even if she's not with her friends. The good gods know she needs practice. I could bring her in every now and then to see Stella and Evelyn."

Stella reached out and grasped Mildred's hand. All three girls pressed harder into the door.

"Will you be able to afford food on your own?"

"I think so. We'll have to scrape by for a while."

"I'll make sure to send any scraps home that you may need. Everything will be all right, Vanessa, now that he can't hurt you anymore."

Mildred felt that cold feeling in her stomach. *Now that he can't hurt you anymore.* Mother and Mrs. F's conversation faded into a discussion over warming dishes that needed new incantations. Evelyn pushed away from the door, and all three girls tiptoed to a hidden alcove down the hall.

"What will we do?" Stella wailed, wringing her hands together. "We can't let Mildred leave!"

"I can't stay if Mother is leaving," Mildred said. Evelyn's lips were a hard, thin line that meant she was thinking. She would come up with something, surely. She always had good ideas, ideas Mildred could never have dreamed up on her own.

"Ya could transport!" Evelyn cried. "Just transport ta see us everyday."

Mildred shook her head. "I'm only six! I can't learn that until I'm older. Besides, I can barely levitate a feather."

Evelyn's shoulders fell, and her lips slipped back into their narrowed lines of thought. "Ya could move in with Stella?"

"Oh yes!" Stella cried. "Then you could see your mother while she's at work."

Mildred shook her head. "Mother wouldn't let me. Besides, I'd miss my brother."

A full ten minutes of agitated silence passed. "We can't stop it," Evelyn concluded, as grim as Mildred. "Ya will have ta listen ta ya mother and go where she says."

Mildred could hardly comprehend a change so drastic. Not see her friends each morning? Not laugh with Evelyn while washing dishes? It didn't make any sense. First Father left, and now she had to leave. She just wanted all the changes to stop.

"I'll write you all the time," Stella promised, her eyes filling with tears. "You won't even feel like you're gone."

"Me also," Evelyn said. "Just because ya aren't here doesn't mean we can't still be best friends. I'll make sure we stay friends!"

"Your mother said she'll bring you to visit every now and then," Stella said, trying to find something happy because that's what Stella always did. "Everything will be okay."

Evelyn glanced at the bruise on Mildred's cheek. "Now that ya mean father is gone, it'll be okay."

Mildred absently touched the sensitive skin, reliving the moment she saw the back of Father's hand flying toward her. She shrank away from the memory with a shudder. She'd miss both of her friends desperately. Their soothing presence brought such comfort into her confusing life.

"I know!" Stella cried. "Let's make a Witches' Oath. Together we'll be strong enough to seal it!"

Evelyn's bright green eyes lit up. "Yes! We'll promise ta write each other at least once a week. Then, when I get older and better at magic, I'll transport ta ya all the time Milly! We'll never *really* be apart if we have the Witches' Oath ta seal us."

"Yes!" Mildred squealed, and the three of them giggled. Evelyn stuck her little finger into the middle of their group.

"We'll promise to always be best friends to the very end!" Stella said as she hooked her finger with Evelyn's. Mildred looped her finger around the others. They all grinned and began the incantation for a simple Witches' Oath with hushed, childish whispers.

"We make an oath on the honor of all witches who have come, who will come, and who shall ever be," they chanted in unison. "We shall be friends to the very end!"

A thin gray line appeared around their left pinkies: the symbol of the Witches' Oath. They inspected their hands and fell into each other's arms, laughing as if nothing bad had ever happened to them, nor ever would again.

Changes

The fire crackled merrily in the hearth one fall evening, illuminating Nell's personal chambers with a bright light for Evelyn to play by. Remnants of her seventh birthday party littered the table: a new tea set, crumbs from the cake of which she'd greedily consumed two slices, and the brown wrapping paper that held most of her presents.

Nell had never enjoyed a mess more.

She glanced at the clock. Evelyn's mother Marcia had been called away from the celebration hours before and hadn't returned. Evelyn spent most evenings with Nell now, keeping the usual dark depression Nell suffered from at bay with her witty comments and bossy attitude. But never had Marcia been so late picking her up.

"Are you getting tired, Evie?" Nell asked, looking on the girl with fondness. Her red hair was so luminous and her skin so pale. Playing quietly on the floor, she looked like the porcelain doll Nell had just given her. Even her blue silk dress matched the doll's frock. Evelyn wasn't a naturally beautiful child, but her impish smile held plenty of sway over most witches.

"No," Evelyn said, "I just want ta play with my dolls."

Nell chuckled and stared half-heartedly at the tottering pile of envelopes awaiting her response. Playing with Evelyn was much more enjoyable than working because she could, for just a moment, imagine that Evelyn was her daughter. A blessing that could never be.

"Have you finished your homework?" Nell asked.

"Yes, Nell."

"And responded to Mildred's letter?"

Evelyn nodded with a long-suffering sigh. "Yes, Nell. You need to work," she said, sending Nell a ripe look of authority with her green eyes, standing with her hands on her hips. "You've been playing with me all day. Mama says I'm a distraction and shouldn't bother you. She won't let me visit you after school every day if I get in your way."

Nell smiled. Paperwork scattered her lap desk; she had much work to do, as usual. "You're the best distraction, Evie. And your accent is improving. You aren't changing o's into a's as much."

"I know. I forget sometimes, but most of the time I'm perfect."

A knock sounded on the door. "Mama's here!" Evelyn cried, then ran to Nell's side with a frown. "Nell! I don't want to go home," she whispered, her lips falling in the same irresistible pucker that too often earned her cookies for dinner. Evelyn lowered her eyes to the ground and finished with a mumble, "Papa was in a bad mood this morning. I don't want ta see him again."

But it wasn't Marcia. A tear-stained maid opened the door just a crack and motioned for the High Priestess to come into the hall. A worrying thought tickled Nell's mind. The maids would never beckon unless . . .

"It's not your Mama yet, pretty girl," Nell said in a bright, cheery voice. "Looks like the maids need me. How about you go find your new tea set and give your doll a drink before she goes to bed? It will help her sleep."

Evelyn hesitated, her young eyes calculating, and for a second Nell worried that she hadn't hidden her concern well enough. Then Evelyn gave in with a sigh.

"Good idea. But she can't have any cookies this late!"

"I agree," Nell said, standing. "I'll join you when I've finished."

"Don't be gone long!" Evelyn retorted with high-handed command. "I'll wait for you here. Come right back."

Nell smiled to set her at ease. The maid paced back and forth outside the bedroom, wringing her hands.

"What is it, Agatha?" Nell asked, closing the door behind her.

"There's been a terrible accident," Agatha whispered, tears welling in her eyes.

"What happened?"

"Marcia is dead."

Nell grabbed the table in the hall to steady herself. "Explain," she said.

"Marcia transported into a riot in Chatham City when she went to the apothecary. I-I don't even know why they were rioting. I just know that she was killed in the melee, and they just found her body."

"Tobacco," Nell whispered hoarsely, the color draining from her face. "The poor and the gypsies threatened to riot over the new tax Donovan placed on tobacco. I told him not to do it, the fool."

Agatha sucked on her front teeth, the way she always did when nervous. "The Guardians are dealing with the riot now, but it sounds like nearly twenty witches have died. I-I just found out and came up here right away."

"Where is her husband, Xavier?"

"Still very sick at home." Agatha shook her head. "He's taken the plague that's swept through Chatham City, so Evelyn can't return home yet. The apothecary said it's not likely Xavier will survive the night either. He didn't get the right potion in time because Marcia didn't return."

Nell paused, listening to Evelyn playing inside, speaking for her doll, imploring for cookies. The doll's hopes were dashed when Evelyn refused her.

"What about Evelyn?" Agatha asked, tearing up again. "We'll have to send her to an orphanage if Xavier dies."

"No!" Nell snapped. "We'll not do any such thing."

"But, High Priestess, she—"

"Needs a family. Let me handle her. I'll tell her the bad news myself. It needs to come from me. We'll work out all the other details later." Nell pressed a hand to her forehead. "Goodness. How shall I say it?"

Agatha said nothing.

Nell composed herself by taking several long, slow breaths. "Thank you, Agatha. Please remain out here for further instructions."

Nell steeled herself as she returned, trying to predict what Evie's reaction would be. How could she tell the girl, who believed the sun revolved around Marcia, that she would never see her again? Could a seven-year-old comprehend so final an end? Was the grave little more than a nightmarish chasm?

"You took too long," Evelyn said, sticking out her pink bottom lip in a pout and folding her arms across her chest. She gave Nell her back in a familiar move she employed when she didn't get what she wanted.

"Evie, darling, come here. I have something to tell you."

"No."

"Let's not be like that." Nell's heart swelled with compassion and fear. Was she up for this? Could she care for and adequately love this fire-driven child? Evelyn peered over her shoulder, her lashes fluttering with an angelic look that destroyed all Nell's hesitations. "Can we talk?"

The little girl let out a dramatic sigh before walking to Nell. Evelyn's eyelids drooped, and her jaw quivered as she fought back a yawn. Nell brushed a stray red curl out of her face.

"I just had some news of your mother, Evie." She faltered but pressed on. "There's been a terrible accident."

Evelyn stood stock-still, staring at Nell through her round, freckled face. Like Marcia, Evelyn's eyebrows were so red and faint they almost appeared translucent.

"What happened?" she asked. "Did a horse die in a carriage crash? I saw that happen once."

"No, darling. Marcia was in an accident today. She . . . she won't be coming back to get you tonight."

Evelyn's nostrils flared in fear. "She doesn't want me?"

"Oh, no!" Nell said. "That's not it at all. Marcia was caught in a very bad place tonight, and she . . . she died. Your Mama is gone, sweetheart."

Evelyn blinked three times. "What about Papa? Is he still sick?"

"Yes. So sick that you can't see him right now."

Evelyn's face went blank. She turned around and walked over to her dolls. "Mama'll be by later," she said. "You'll see, Nell. She'll be back tomorrow."

Nell opened her mouth to protest, but stopped. Evelyn wouldn't comprehend what her mother's death meant, not yet. Nell sat in a silence that was broken only by the clink of Evelyn's doll trying to take tea. The quiet continued until Nell stood up, swallowed her tears, and held out her hand.

"Come, Evie. Let's get you to bed. We can start a new day tomorrow."

To her surprise, and for the first time, the child offered no resistance. She tucked her doll under her arm and solemnly took Nell's hand.

Nell set Evelyn into her own sprawling bed, made sure she had a fuzzy blanket, and sat at her side until Evelyn dropped into the wispy breathing of sleep. She stared at her chubby cheeks, her scattered freckles, and swore a silent oath.

Even if Xavier lived, which seemed unlikely, Nell would take the girl. She would give Evelyn the education she deserved. She'd have a family here at the castle, and above all, she'd have Nell to dote on her and personally see to her comfort.

In lieu of her parents, Evelyn would have Nell, and everything.

1st Month of Fall

Dear Stella,

Sorry I haven't written much lately, we've been very busy. My new house in York is very small. All of us sleep in the same room, and the floor is dirt, but Mother seems happy, so I'm happy. I miss you and Evelyn. Mother says I can come to work with her before winter sets in. We'll have to walk the whole way, which she says will take a couple of hours, but I won't mind.

How is the castle? Is Evelyn still very sad about her Mama and Papa? I've written her five letters but haven't heard back. It was boring turning seven without you.

Mildred

Changes

2nd Month of Winter

Dear Mildred,

Evelyn and I miss you very much. The castle is the same as always. Evelyn doesn't do dishes ever since the High Priestess adopted her, but she comes to class with Miss Sonia still. Evelyn doesn't talk about being sad, even though I know she is. I don't see her after school as much anymore. She spends most of her time with the High Priestess.

Miss Sonia told me to tell you that she says 'merry meet.' I miss you in class.

Stella

3rd Month of Summer

Milly,

Happy birthday! Can you believe we're eight years old now? Nell gave me a brand new dress made of silk and so many hair ribbons that I can't wear them all. I'm sending a few to you for your birthday present. I hope they arrive. Stella has matching ones, so we can all wear the same hair ribbons. You won't look as pretty as me because you don't have red hair, but I think you'll still like them.

Are you afraid to start the new year of school? I'm sure this year will be better for you. You won't be the slowest student, Milly, like you think. Just keep working hard. I know you can do it. Nell tutors me, and it's hard sometimes too, especially when I miss Mama, but I keep learning. If anyone tries to tease you, just let me know. I'll take care of them. Maybe Nell would let me send Guardians after them!

I must go have tea with a few Council Members. Nell lets me follow her everywhere because I don't like to be alone. I don't go to the boring meetings, though, because I'd rather just play in the gardens. Everyone likes talking to me. I love it.

Evie

23

3rd Month of Summer

Dear Stella,

Happy twelfth birthday! Have you and your family moved to the Northern Covens yet? I'll bet you're excited that your father is going to be one of the Coven Leaders over Newberry. Were you very sad to leave Evelyn? I'm glad we were able to do another sleepover at the castle before you moved. It was so much fun to play in the gardens when it was dark outside. When Evelyn fell in the fountain I thought I'd laugh until my sides burst.

Life in York is quiet like always, which I love. I hate going into Chatham City now. It's so loud. Good news! I just finished summer school. My teacher says if I keep working this hard to learn magic, I should be able to get into a Network school. Wouldn't it be nice to go to classes together? I wouldn't be so frightened if you or Evelyn were there. What if we all made it into Miss Mabel's School for Girls? It seems like too much to hope for.

I must go. I'm working at the grocer's to earn currency. I'm saving it all to pay for tuition (if I can actually get in), but I must plan ahead, or we won't be able to afford it. Mother says I can learn to transport next year, which means we'll be able to see each other more often.

Now that I'm not in school, I promised Jorden I'd climb the apple trees with him more often too, so maybe I'll send you a few from the top.

Your friend,
Mildred

2nd Month of Spring

Dear Evelyn,

The Northern Covens are lonely without you around. Papa is always busy as a Coven Leader now, but we live in such a big house, and the orchards here are so fun, that I don't mind so much.

Sometimes I miss the castle, but I like the fresh air and quiet. Mildred came to stay the night last week, and she loved it here. When are you coming?

We turn fourteen this summer, which means we'll be able to interview with the Watcher next year to see if we are accepted into a Network school. Mildred is working so hard to earn currency. She's cleaning houses now, I think. Do you think all of us could make it into school together? I hope for it every night. Our Witches' Oath always brings me comfort that we'll eventually be together again.

Tell me more about all the dances you are going to with Nell. Do you get to wear a ball gown? Do you dance with anyone? I'm very jealous! Please, tell me everything. Your life at the castle is so much more exciting than mine.

All my love,
Stella

Finding the Future

No matter how many times Evelyn stamped her foot in objection, Nell remained firm.

"You must go to a Network school, Evelyn. You simply must. You're fourteen years old now, and it's already the first month of spring. You'll turn fifteen in the summer, which means you'll be ready to go when school begins in the fall."

"But I don't want to leave the castle!" Evelyn said. "I'll be so lonely without you. I loathe partings. Remember how sad I become when Stella and Mildred leave after their visits?"

Unbidden, a memory of Mama's face shuddered from the depths of Evelyn's mind. She shook it away, forcing her thoughts from the bleak depths of fear. Mama had left once, and she never came back. What if she went to school and Nell died? Evelyn knew she was too old to throw such a fit, but it didn't matter. Leaving the castle to live somewhere else was downright terrifying.

Not to mention she'd be leaving her many adoring friends behind. Most of the Council Members and Coven Leaders cherished her here at Chatham Castle. What if they forgot about her? Worst of all, what if she wasn't popular and didn't make friends? She'd die. She'd simply die.

"Both Milly and Stella have appointments with the Watcher already," Nell pointed out. "They said so in their last letter. Maybe all three of you will be placed in the same school."

Evelyn hesitated. If there was anything good about going to school, it would be Stella and Milly's company. "Well, I *do* want to see them again. But there's no guarantee the Watcher will put us in the same school! I shall be alone."

"Don't you want to learn and become a great leader?"

"Can't I do that here?"

Nell's maid, Leslee, interrupted by knocking on the door and peeking inside. "Your three o'clock appointment is here to see you, Your Highness."

Nell sent a quiet warning glance at Evelyn.

"Send her in, Leslee, and please prepare the tea." Evelyn gave in with a resigned sigh. It wasn't often that she couldn't sway Nell over to her side in one way or another, but today Nell's face held that stern look that meant Evelyn wouldn't win.

A slender witch with raven black hair and a slight underbite introduced herself with a perfect curtsy. "My given name is Mabel, but I go by May," the stranger said in a quiet voice. "I am the Head Witch of Miss Mabel's School for Girls."

Nell bestowed a silent nod of approval, but Evelyn acted as if May weren't there. Instead, she ordered Leslee about unnecessarily, instructing her on duties she had already performed. That way, May would know who was *really* in charge. Despite not wanting to leave Nell, Evelyn had an inner desire to have—and be—the best of everything. Miss Mabel's School for Girls was certainly the best the Network education system had to offer. If she must go away, it would be the only place she'd go.

"Please have a seat, May." Nell gestured to an elegant chair with light green backing and rolled arms. Leslee set the tray on the table, curtsied, and moved to the other side of the room. "Evelyn, you may now pour the tea."

Evelyn watched May with unusual attentiveness. She was thin and attractive but not extravagant, with bright blue eyes and pale skin. Her maroon dress was exquisite but tasteful, and the delicate lace along the edges testified to a wealthy background. She seemed aloof, which piqued Evelyn's interest.

"Merry meet, Evelyn," May said, settling on the chair across from her. "I'm always glad to meet a possible future student."

Evelyn smiled.

"I understand how unusual a meeting like this is for you," Nell said to May, sitting next to Evelyn on the couch and straightening her skirts. "We both appreciate you being here."

"I don't mind coming to discuss a student beforehand," May said. "It's an honor that you are considering my school above all the others. Of course, you know that Isadora has to give her final approval to any student attending my school."

"Yes, we know about Isadora," Nell said, glancing at Evelyn. "I'm very hopeful that she will see the potential in Evelyn. I give Evelyn only the very best, you see. She was born to be a leader, and with the proper grooming, I believe she shall change the world."

May smiled, but it didn't quite reach her eyes. "I'm sure there's great potential."

Instead of feeling annoyed, Evelyn wondered why this witch didn't immediately give reassurances regarding Evelyn's certain success, the way everyone else did.

Rare indeed.

Evelyn used an incantation to pour the tea into the cups, then sent May hers on a cream colored saucer. May received the cup without a single acknowledgement or thank you. Evelyn next sent a tray of tea sandwiches, but May refused, and said nothing about Evelyn's magical skills.

Evelyn's interest deepened.

How unusual.

"I want Evelyn to have the best education possible," Nell said. "Which is why I brought you here to ask if you'd be willing to tutor her personally."

If May was surprised by the request, she didn't show it.

"I'm always open to requests," May said. "But I will not give private tutorship the first two years of her stay."

"Not even as a personal request from the High Priestess?"

Nell didn't often throw her title around to get what she wanted, but this unexpected situation must have called for it. Evelyn held her breath.

"Don't take my refusal personally, High Priestess. I really must say that, in fairness to the other students, Evelyn needs to prove herself worthy. I don't coddle to privilege unless talent and education justifies the work."

Nell set down her teacup and gave May her whole attention. A flicker in her eyes suggested surprise, perhaps annoyance.

"How so?"

"For one, Miss Mabel's School for Girls still participates in the Competition, so I can't tutor just any student," May said after another sip of tea.

Nell's mouth rounded in an understanding circle. "I see. If Evelyn is to have a one-on-one education with you, she must first enter the Competition as a third-year and win."

Regret seemed to creep into May's mournful tone. "Yes, that would be my exact expectation. I can't make any exceptions. There are many gifted witches out there, and I wouldn't want to diminish their experience for one who isn't as committed. What I can do, however, is promise to keep a special eye on Evelyn during her third year if she doesn't win."

That did it. Evelyn could handle May's lack of blatant adoration but refusing Nell was too much. Her curiosity turned to flame. How dare May insinuate that Evelyn wasn't intelligent enough to win?

"You think I'm not clever enough to win the Competition?" Evelyn asked, eyes blazing. May stared at her with an aloof, studious glance.

"Are you prepared for my honest reply?" May asked. Her tea drifted back to the table when she folded her hands on her lap in an easy gesture.

"I'd expect nothing less!"

"Then no," May said. "You seem like a spoiled little girl that doesn't have any emotional control. Such a student would not do well in my private lessons. I have very high expectations of my pupils."

Evelyn clenched her fists, barely able to contain her fury. The nerve of this witch! Evelyn might have things that others didn't, but she had lost everything before she gained it. What could May know about her life?

"Consistently strong magical control does not occur without emotional control," May continued, her voice rising into an instructive tone. "Most teenage girls have neither emotional nor magical control."

She turned to Nell. "If I take her as a student, I will demand that she go through the first two years of school to learn those skills. At that point, I would permit her to enter the Competition and win her chance to be my pupil. Otherwise, I should be doing all three of us a disservice."

Nell leaned back in her seat. "I'm not accustomed to being refused, but I respect your reasons. A lesser witch would have given me what I wanted simply because of my political position."

"It may not be what you wanted to hear, High Priestess," May said. "But it would be disrespectful for me to be involved in anything that wasn't for the best of the Network. If you truly want Evelyn to be a leader, she'll have to earn it."

Evelyn blinked, slowed her breathing, and settled back in the chair. Her anger abated, and her face cooled.

I'll do it, she thought with impressive resolution. *May doesn't think I can win the Competition? I'll win it, and I'll be her pupil. I know I can. I'll give her a reason to like me. By the time I leave, she won't be able to refuse approving of me.*

"If I'm chosen for your school, I shall be happy to learn whatever you want to teach." Evelyn picked up her cup of tea and sipped it like nothing had occurred in the meantime.

May asked the High Priestess a question regarding the new Head of Education and ignored Evelyn for the rest of their tea.

"You can't fool a Watcher," Mother said in her usual clipped tone as they passed York's red brick bakery and the grocer's stall filled with fat winter squash and cool weather greens. "Don't try to inflate yourself."

Mildred rolled her eyes. "Really, Mother."

"I'm just saying what I must," Mother said, elbowing Mildred into an alley. "You don't have any control over whether you are accepted into Miss Mabel's School for Girls with Stella and Evelyn, so don't even stress over it. The Watcher will put you where you belong."

"What if the Watcher doesn't accept me?" Mildred asked, her stomach curling in fear. Watchers had the rare ability to perceive personality traits. The most powerful Watchers could view glimpses of the future. The Network paid them to decide who had the talent and skill needed to attend a Network school.

Mother glared. "Don't even say it. You've worked twice as hard to perfect your magic as anyone else. I'm sure you'll be accepted."

A gust of early summer wind escorted them to the schoolhouse, rustling Mildred's shoulder-length hair. She batted it out of her eyes in frustration, wishing Mother would let her chop it all off. She didn't have time to fuss over her looks.

"The thought of so many girls in one school scares me," Mildred said.

"You'll have to learn how to deal with it." Mother dodged a horse-drawn carriage and nodded to the driver. Mildred scowled. What would it be like to live away from Mother's steep expectations and constant demands that she improve her magic and overcome her shyness?

Perhaps a school full of strangers wouldn't be the worst thing.

"Teenage girls are confusing and emotional," Mildred muttered.

"You are no exception to confusing and emotional, Mildred. Just remember your goal. That'll make it easier."

Her goal, yes. There was nothing Mildred wanted more than to have the power to create change. To be somebody. To get out of poverty. To achieve as much as Stella and Evelyn, although she had started with so little. But above all, she just wanted to make Mother proud.

"Besides," Mother said, "you'll never be a Council Member if you don't earn your circlus at a Network school."

Mildred looked down at her wrist and thought about the circular tattoo received at the beginning of the school year. Knowing she might attend the same school as Stella and Evelyn gave her strength. She rubbed the pale skin on her wrist as if the circlus were already there, then realized she'd fallen behind and scrambled to catch up. Mother could never simply *walk* anywhere. She always moved with purpose and determination, even just to cross the room. They continued in silence until they arrived at the school to find Mildred's teacher, Miss Sarah, speaking to an old woman with graying hair.

"There you are," Miss Sarah said, glancing at the clock. "Right on time, as usual. Mildred, Vanessa, this is Isadora. She's the Watcher for all the Network schools right now, so she's quite busy."

Isadora smiled. One of her eyes was hazel, the other, olive green. Mother nudged Mildred with a sharp jab of her elbow. Mildred curtsied.

"Merry meet, Isadora."

"Merry meet, Mildred." Isadora patted the desk next to her while Mother and Miss Sarah withdrew from the room. "Have a seat."

They sat side by side in separate wooden desks but didn't look at each other. Mildred let out a breath of relief. It would be easier to answer the questions if she didn't have to look Isadora right in the eyes. Mildred waited for Isadora to start for several minutes.

"You intrigue me, Mildred," Isadora eventually said. "Of all the students I've ever interviewed, I've never met one with such a quiet personality. I didn't even detect you until you were already at the door."

Mildred kept her eyes on the chalkboard. The familiarity of the classroom eased her initial nervousness.

"Perhaps that's because my mother's personality is so strong," Mildred said. Isadora's laugh startled Mildred. Another stretch of silence passed before Mildred turned to find Isadora staring at the fire, musing.

"Aren't you supposed to ask me questions?" Mildred asked.

"Yes, but I find speaking to strangers to be very draining."

"Are you saying that to set me at ease?" Mildred asked, convinced that Isadora had an angle behind the comment. No witch came right out and admitted that they didn't like social requirements.

"No, do you think I'm obligated to put you at ease?"

Not knowing how to respond, Mildred remained quiet. Perhaps this wasn't a witch she could frighten away with her usual abruptness. The thought didn't comfort her.

"Talking to strangers is part of my career," Isadora said. "But that doesn't mean I enjoy it. It exhausts me."

"Then why do you do it?"

"It's what I was meant to do. Sometimes we fight our destiny because of our fears, when what we really need to do is learn how to make destiny work for us."

The words fell like barbs in the fleshy part of Mildred's heart. A flood of shame, of insecurity, and then uncertainty swept through her. She hadn't expected Isadora to infiltrate so deep into her mind after only a brief exchange.

"Besides," Isadora continued. "I learn the most about someone by what they do not say."

Mildred, unwillingly, fell into Isadora's conversation.

"What do you mean?"

"You don't like small talk," Isadora said, as if she had a private vein into Mildred's mind. "You speak only if required, regardless of whether there's an awkward silence. That tells me that you don't care about social conventions, which tells me that you have a strong sense of right and wrong."

"If you have such an insight into my mind, then you must know that I'm uncomfortable with attending an all-girls school without my two best friends with me."

"Yes," Isadora said. "I do know that."

"And?"

"And what?"

"Would you put me in the same school as them?"

"No."

Mildred straightened, bristling. "Even though I'm not comfortable being with so many other girls my age?"

"I think you're very smart!" Isadora said, laughing. "I wouldn't want to attend school with that many girls either."

"Oh. I didn't expect you to agree."

"Attending an all-girls school is the only way to get what you really want," Isadora said with a twinkle in her eye. "You know that already, which is why you're here."

Mildred's heart began to pound.

"What exactly do you see that I want?"

"To be somebody," Isadora said easily, as if they were discussing what type of tea Mildred would take. "You want to make a difference in the lives of witches like you so they don't have to grow up in the same poverty. You also want to make your mother proud. But beneath all this stoic bluster, and perhaps your greatest motivation of all, is a girl that just wants to measure up to her friends who always had more than she did."

Isadora's easy reading of her mind was unnerving. Mildred turned away, annoyed by this wily witch, despite her lack of discernible ill intent. Isadora kept her observations so neutral that Mildred couldn't even distrust her.

"In fact," Isadora continued amicably, "you have such a strong desire to lead—to prove yourself to a silent audience that doesn't exist outside your head—that you're going to attend Miss Jane's School for Girls, even though you're deeply frightened. You have stronger emotions than any witch I've ever met. You just hide them behind your arrogance exceptionally well."

"Miss Jane's?" Mildred asked. She'd heard of it before. Respectable, but it certainly wasn't the top of the list. "But what are my chances of—"

"Miss Mabel's is not the right school for you," Isadora said, anticipating her question. "Trust me. Your magical ability is not good enough yet. Sending you to Miss Mabel's would alter the course of your life, and possibly the Network, in ways you can't imagine."

Mildred deflated. "Oh."

"Now," Isadora said, slapping the desk with a sprightly clap of her hand. "I have some advice for you before you start Miss Jane's: Do not nurse your weaknesses as you do now."

Mildred opened her mouth to protest, but Isadora cut her off.

"You're not at all gifted socially. You never will be. Find one or two witches with whom to be friends when you start school—it will help. Take alone time when you need it, but don't let it become an excuse. Also, keep working on your magic. I know it's difficult for you, but eventually, with dedication, time, and patience, you'll be very powerful. Does that sound manageable?"

Very powerful with magic? No one had ever said that to her. "Yes."

"Wonderful. I'll tell Miss Jane that you shall be a member of her school starting in the fall."

Isadora hopped up—she was impressively spry for her age—and called for Miss Sarah and Mother to rejoin them. By the time their chatter faded, Mildred had filed all of Isadora's advice into a special place in her mind and managed to smile and curtsy in parting. The surge of relief she'd felt at being accepted ebbed away.

The good gods, she thought shakily. *What have I gotten myself into?*

Ambitions

"I'm so relieved, Nell! I'm positively the most popular girl in school!" Evelyn declared, throwing herself onto the couch in a flurry of red hair and petticoats.

Nell laughed from her seat near the fire, where she had been watching the snow fall outside while impatiently waiting for Evelyn to return for the Yule holiday. The edges of her depression had already begun to fade, dissipating in the wake of seventeen-year-old Evelyn's rambunctious energy.

"Of course you're the most popular!" Nell said, not the least bit surprised. "You won the Competition, and you were the most popular first-year and second-year, weren't you?"

"That's true," Evelyn said. "Some of the girls hate me, like the maids here do, but they're just jealous because I have more currency than them. The poor girls are always complaining about my tea parties because I don't let them attend."

"How could they hate you?" Nell asked, unable to fathom another witch not approving of her red-haired ball of sunshine. Evelyn waved it off with a careless flap of her hand.

"It's mostly May's granddaughter, Mabel. She thinks she's so much better than the rest of us just because she's pretty. Well," Evelyn huffed, her chest expanding with pride, "I've shown her plenty of times who is in charge. I won the Competition, and I keep winning the best prize of all."

"What's that?"

Evelyn flashed a grin. "May's attention outside of class. May has tea with me and takes me on special outings. Mabel hates it!"

Nell didn't like the thought of Evelyn vying for any other witch's attention but pushed the thought away. Evelyn's education was of the utmost importance. If May gave her a little extra time, all the better.

"You must have been very busy," Nell said, trying to keep her tone neutral, unable to make eye contact with the vibrant young girl. She smoothed the wrinkles out of her lacy handkerchief. "You've hardly responded to any of my letters."

"Very busy!" Evelyn agreed, missing—or ignoring—the subtle accusation. "There were baking competitions, game days on the weekends, and Stella and I snuck in a few secret sleepovers. One night, we went out into Letum Wood and pretended to be ghosts! You should have seen the first-years, Nell. I almost died from laughing. Mildred transported over during a few of the long weekends, and we had a picnic. It was wonderful!"

Nell smiled. *This* sounded much more like the lovely girl she'd sent off to school. "It appears you are having a wonderful time. Have you enjoyed your teachers?"

"Studying is such a bore, but May is a wonderful teacher. She seems to know everything," Evelyn said, banging the back of her feet against the couch in a very unladylike way. Nell couldn't bring herself to reprimand her yet.

"Oh?" Nell asked. Surely May didn't know everything.

"Yes, she's very smart. Most of the other students don't like her, although I can't figure out why. They say she's too strict, but she's never seemed that way to me."

Leslee set a tray of cookies and tea on the table and stepped away. Evelyn hopped up and grabbed one in each hand, biting into them before Nell had a chance to ask her to pour.

"I'll pour," Nell said with a glance at Evelyn that quickly faded from its severity. "But just this once."

Evelyn smiled her crumb-littered gratitude.

"I can't wait to visit the Council Members," Evelyn declared, spewing crumbs on the table. She brushed them onto the floor and resumed eating the cookie.

"I thought we might spend the evening together," Nell said. "I asked Mrs. F to send up your favorite dinner, and I purchased a new puzzle from the shops in Chatham. Leslee and her sister Lavinia picked it out."

"We'll spend time together, Nell," Evelyn said, popping the rest of the second cookie in her mouth. "Right after I make the rounds of the castle. I have so many friends I want to talk to!"

Nell paused, uncertain how to proceed. It would take no less than three hours for Evelyn to jabber with all her friends, and Nell had been waiting for this night for weeks.

"Are you going to go to the kitchens to see Mrs. F?"

"Perhaps," Evelyn said with a shrug. "I'm not all that interested in talking to servants. May told me not to waste my time because they can't really advance my career, and everything I do from here on out needs to benefit my future in some way. But I do so look forward to seeing Council Member Gloria."

Nell poured her own cup of chamomile tea, a bell of alarm ringing in her mind. *Not all that interested in talking to servants?* Mrs. F had always been a role model for Evelyn. When had that changed? Instead of pursuing the topic, Nell asked the next most pressing question.

"What do you and May talk about during tea?"

"Oh, everything!" Evelyn said breathlessly, leaning back against the couch with a sigh. "Life here at the castle, mostly."

Another tremor of suspicion ran up Nell's spine. "Oh? What kinds of things does May ask?"

"Normal stuff, I guess. What the Council Members do all day. What they think of the educational system. How many meetings they attend. How many servants work here."

"Why would she want to know so much about the Council?"

"Because she lives in a small little country estate, I suppose, and doesn't get to enjoy the benefits of wealth and prosperity that you and I do. Who doesn't want to know more about the castle if they don't live here? Anyway, she asks a lot about you and Donovan as well."

"About me?" Nell asked, pressing a hand to her heart in surprise. "Why me?"

"Doesn't want me to get homesick. She says that the more I talk about you, the less homesick I'll feel."

"What do you tell her?"

Evelyn must have caught on to the sudden anxiety in Nell's tone, for she rolled her eyes in a dramatic but amused way. "Silly Nell! It's nothing important. She was just curious about how long you've had depressive episodes, if you advise Donovan in his choices, if you resent that Donovan is Highest Witch and not you, if you've seen the Esmelda Scrolls, that kind of thing. General stuff. Last night we talked about the article in the *Chatterer* reporting that Donovan's old knee injury is getting worse. Is it true?"

"Donovan is none of your business," Nell said. "You need to focus on studying, not taking tea with the Head Witch and discussing idle gossip."

"It's not idle gossip, is it?" Evelyn replied indignantly. "Donovan's so fat now!"

"I haven't seen any signs that he can't perform his job at his current weight," Nell snapped.

"It certainly is my business if the High Priest of my Network is sick. I'm learning a lot about politics and how things work, you know. May knows everything there is to know about the Network, and she discusses it with me like I'm an adult because she knows I want to be a Council Member. She even told me about the Tobacco Riots that killed my mother!"

Nell stifled a gasp. "What?"

"I know all those poor people trampled Mama to death, that Papa died because he didn't get the potion he needed soon enough. The poor rioters and the gypsies just didn't want to pay a fair tax on tobacco, and my parents died because of it. They didn't even know that the tax money was going to help fix the broken highway. Stupid gypsies."

"Evelyn, I never withheld that from you. We simply never spoke of it," Nell said, leaning forward. "Darling, we have no secrets."

Evelyn relaxed slightly. "Well, it's no secret that Donovan has become lazy ever since he fell off his horse ten years ago and injured his knee."

"That's enough of that!" Nell cried, setting her tea saucer down so forcefully the cup rattled. "While you live in this castle, you will show respect to those in power. I've never in my life heard such a high-handed opinion from a teenage girl that can't even sit up straight and eat with her mouth closed! My goodness. I believe your manners have gotten worse since attending school!"

Nell shot to her feet and turned her back on Evelyn, ignoring the indignant flash of anger on Evelyn's face. Oh, this wasn't going at all like Nell had planned! Evelyn replaced her tea cup and drew in a long breath.

"You're absolutely right, Nell," Evelyn said in a repentant tone. "I suppose I just get so tired of maintaining perfect posture and decorum the way May demands that I just completely relax when I'm around you. I apologize."

Nell bit on her bottom lip and swallowed hard. She wanted to go back to the beginning of the evening and start over. Perhaps she'd been too hard on Evelyn. After all, wasn't she just a social, excitable young girl?

"I didn't mean to snap at you," Nell said, turning around with a frustrated breath, feeling guilty for not asking Evelyn about her poor behavior before reacting. Evelyn's new world had wrapped Nell in a heavy coat of bitter jealousy. How she longed to be at the school with her little darling! To have weekly chats with her over tea, to watch her mature and grow. The jealousy in her heart burned like a fire. She tried to quench it but found depression creeping up in its wake instead. "I suppose I'm just tired."

Evelyn gave her a warm smile. "Me too, Nell. Coming home from school may have caused more excitement than I planned on. Let's eat dinner and put the puzzle together. I'll visit Gloria later."

Graduation

"You earned all four marks, Mildred, I'm sure of it."
Deborah spoke with a confidence that meant she wasn't
actually confident at all. Mildred didn't even try to smile to
thank Deborah for the attempt at comfort. Oblivious to Mildred's
tense response, Deborah continued prattling to herself with a verbosity that set Mildred's nerves on end.

"You've been living and breathing homework and magic all year, haven't you? Me? I'll just be happy if I earn the usual three marks. I'm not nearly as ambitious as you. Yes, yes. I know you'll have earned them. How could you not?"

Very easily, Mildred thought.

The two of them sat in the second row of third-year students in the lush yard of Miss Jane's School for Girls in the heart of Chatham City. Despite being surrounded by three- and four-story buildings, the school was set back in a grassy plot and guarded by tall trees. Noises from passing carriages and scrollboys didn't extend past the fence, which magically protected the school from errant noise.

Mildred rubbed her fingers together and drew in a deep breath.

I earned all four marks. I didn't fail. I'll have something wonderful to show for my Council Member's Assistant application, just like Stella and Evelyn. I earned all four marks. I didn't fail. This time, I won't be behind my friends.

Miss Jane stood on the platform wearing a lovely pink dress and a white hat, glancing over the growing crowd of parents and family members. The past three years of Mildred's life culminated in these moments. All the nights of studying until her candle burned out, the weekends holed up in her room, and her ambitious plans ended here.

I didn't fail.

The Advanced Political History test she'd finished yesterday had been a scroll an inch thick. She'd written into the wee hours of the night, which meant she wouldn't find out if she'd passed until the graduation ceremony. If Miss Jane called her up for a special honor, that meant she passed.

If not . . .

Mildred glanced at the empty circlus on her wrist. The marks that indicated which classes she'd successfully passed during her third year would appear when the school year officially concluded.

"Relax," Deborah said in exasperation, nudging Mildred's shoulder with her own. "You're so wound up, you look like you'll snap any minute. Look, Coven Leader Irene just took her seat on the stand, and there's Miss Jane. I think we're going to start, so you won't have to wait much longer."

"Good," Mildred said, and folded her trembling hands in her lap. "I just want to get this over with."

Miss Jane raised her arms for silence.

"Thank you for coming!" she called. The excited hum from the families seated behind the students faded into hushed whispers. "We'll begin the ceremony today with a special treat. Coven Leader Irene will give the invocation of blessings."

Irene stepped forward, closed her eyes, and invoked good powers and hard work on all the graduating students. When she finished, Miss Jane thanked her and stood with a scroll in hand.

"First, I have three very special students I want to acknowledge today. They've worked hard to achieve difficult goals. Today we honor their dedication and commitment."

Deborah grabbed Mildred's forearm and squeezed. Miss Jane skimmed the crowd, ensured she had everyone's attention, and opened a small scroll.

"Ann Delany, Melanie Tripp, and Kate Jacoby. Please come to accept your special certificates of recognition."

The names rang in Mildred's ears. She kept her eyes down, glued to the spot where the grass touched the tips of her shoes.

I failed.

"Oh, Mildred," Deborah said through a sigh. "I'm so sorry."

Mildred said nothing, unable to speak around the thick clog of tears in her throat. The rest of the ceremony sped by in a blur of faces and words. Mildred smiled, congratulated, applauded, and finally accepted her diploma scroll without meeting Miss Jane's searching gaze. Once finished, she joined in the traditional juice drinking ceremony that signaled the end of their third year.

"Ouch!" Deborah squealed, dropping her glass. "It burns!"

A hot sensation started on Mildred's right wrist. Moments later, three marks appeared in her empty circlus. The two triangles of the Esbat mark, the podium of Public Speaking, and the stars of Advanced Silent Magic.

But not Advanced Political History.

While the girls compared marks and the kitchen staff set out a feast, Mildred slipped away, escaping to a hidden spot in the lush gardens around the back of the school. She sat on a chilly stone bench, enjoying the cool kiss of something solid on her flushed palms. A rustle of feet in the grass approached from behind.

"Mildred," Mother said, setting a hand on her shoulder. "Do you want to talk about it?"

"Isadora told me not to nurse my weakness," Mildred cried, stuffing her face into her hands. "And now look what it's gotten me! I failed. I could have graduated early, but I stayed! Now I won't have anything to make me stand out amongst other witches trying to become Council Member Assistants!"

Fat tears leaked fast between her fingers. Mother sat on the bench next to her while Mildred vented all her frustration through hiccups and sobs. Once she showed signs of calming, she accepted Mother's offered handkerchief to mop her wet face.

"You've experienced a real failure and disappointment for the first time," Mother said. "You have every right to be sad, but hope isn't lost."

"I might as well become a librarian," Mildred snapped. "I don't stand out!"

"What's wrong with being a librarian? It's an honorable job. You still have three very commendable marks."

"Stella earned four marks! Evelyn won the Competition and is graduating with highest honors. They each have three possible jobs lined up, while I have none. I—"

"Am not Stella or Evelyn," Mother said quietly. "Are you?"

Mildred stared at her with teary eyes. "No," she whispered. "I'm not."

But sometimes I wish I were.

"You've come a very long way, Mildred," Mother said, tucking a stray length of hair away from Mildred's face. "You completed three of the hardest marks and worked for four, despite how difficult magic is for you. Failure is part of life. The important thing is that you pick yourself back up and keep going. You're going to face many disappointments, my girl, and you'll probably fail many more times. But if you keep going and don't let it defeat you, no one is going to remember what you *didn't* get done."

Mildred hadn't wanted comfort, but she couldn't help but feel it. "You really think I'll still be able to become Council Member?" she asked, sniffling.

Mother chuckled. "I think you'll do more than that. You'll change the world. You're made of steel, you know. This is just a little bump on a very long road. Don't let it get you down, okay?"

Mildred wiped her face again, blew her nose, and placed the handkerchief in her pocket. "Okay," she whispered.

"Now, I know an incantation that will take care of your splotched face. How about we go to dinner, and you enjoy your last night with all your friends?"

Mildred's face cooled and the heavy puffiness faded out of her eyes when Mother completed the spell. With Mother at her side, Mildred turned back to the graduation celebration with renewed resolution and a willingness to face a new—if not somewhat unexpected—future.

No expense had been spared on the celebration of Evelyn's graduation.

The dining room was an intimate space with pale yellow walls, white drapes, and a gleaming, cherry wood table large enough to seat fifty. A delicate linen swan napkin, the color of subtle sunshine, sat atop each china plate. Crystal goblets and wine glasses twinkled in the copious candlelight that kept the room stuffy but bright.

Nell kept a vague ear on all the conversations around her. Most of it was small talk about Donovan, the unfortunate drought in the Eastern Covens, the plague of locusts on a summer crop, and gossip that the Almorran *Book of Spells* had resurfaced somewhere in the Southern Covens. Nell chuckled. Rumors swirled about the ancient book of black magic at least once every ten years, and still it was never seen.

"I gave a lovely graduation speech," Evelyn was telling Donovan, the glassy-eyed High Priest, who tapped the edge of his empty wine glass to indicate a refill. "The Head Witch, May, attended, and I heard rumors that she rarely goes."

"Sure," Donovan muttered, his lips squeezed shut in a failed attempt at suppressing a belch from his cavernous belly. Evelyn's nose wrinkled, but she maintained an ignorant expression and continued to regale her own prowess. Nell silently applauded her girl, who finally displayed appropriate manners, but still frowned. Thanks to his haze of wine and ipsum, Donovan's traveling eyes on Evelyn's elegant gown were not well concealed.

"Evelyn," she called. "Please come have a seat. We shall begin soon."

Donovan was the Highest Witch, the top power in the Central Network. As High Priestess and second in command, Nell consulted with him on most things but held responsibility for education, highways, and any other issue Donovan chose to delegate to her. He and Nell had agreed that she would host all their joint social events, as he didn't particularly enjoy speaking to crowds.

Nell indicated for the Head Butler to begin with a nod.

"Witches," the Head Butler called in a toneless drone, his voice rolling over the loud conversations with unusual clarity. "Please be seated. The dinner shall begin."

"Thank you," Evelyn whispered when she lowered herself into the chair next to Nell. "Donovan is so difficult to talk to when he's relaxing with his wine."

Evelyn sent Nell a private little wink. It was a small token of affection, but it made Nell's heart swell. Evelyn had been fickle and distant since her return from Miss Mabel's School for Girls. She spoke of May at least every hour, and it felt like a dagger in Nell's heart each time. How had she been replaced in Evelyn's life in three school years? The impressionable young girl idolized May with such strength that at times she seemed nearly obsessed.

Not any more, Nell thought resolutely. *Not after tonight.* Evelyn would forget all about her precious teacher and remember Nell as her favorite once she received her graduation gift. Gaining strength at the thought, Nell stood and tapped the edge of her spoon on her flute of champagne. Every eye at the table gave her its attention.

"I'd like to be the first to raise a toast to our dear Evelyn tonight. She has accomplished something very difficult. She won the Competition, was Head Witch of the debate team, received three very difficult marks, and sits before us today as valedictorian graduating with highest honors!"

The congregation clapped politely, smiling at Evelyn's radiant figure at Nell's side, where she belonged. Evelyn's success sent a thrill of pride through Nell.

"To commemorate such a grand event," Nell continued, "and as a graduation gift, I would also like to make an announcement. Because of our dear Evie's dependability, as well as her intricate knowledge of the castle and everyone in it, I've decided to appoint Evelyn as my new Assistant."

A cry rippled through the dining room, but no one was as genuinely surprised as Evelyn. Aside from Assistant to Donovan, there was no higher position with which she could begin her career. Her mouth bobbed open and closed in mute shock. She pressed a hand to her chest, and her sea green eyes filled with tears.

"Nell," she whispered. "I don't know what to say!"

Nell lifted her champagne, and all followed suit, sending a low murmur of *to the new Assistant* through the dining room. Nell clinked glasses with a stunned Evelyn and took the smallest sip of champagne, shuddering at the uncomfortable way it sucked all the saliva from her mouth.

Another round of applause moved through the crowd when Donovan grabbed a fresh bottle of champagne from the butler behind him.

"To the new Assistant to the High Priestess!" he called and poured himself a tall glass. Nell settled back in her chair as the cries of laughter died down, turning into the constant, easy hum of conversation.

"Nell!" Evelyn leaned close, her eyes as wide as saucers. "Do you really mean it?"

Nell smiled with a warm tingle at her spine, soaking up every moment of Evelyn's unmasked affection. Not even the indomitable May could have given Evelyn such a fabulous gift, and it felt wonderful.

"Of course!" Nell cried, taking Evelyn's warm, delicate hand. "You've earned it. I'm so very proud of you and love you very much."

"Oh, thank you!" Evelyn said in a breathy voice. "I shall do my very best!"

Nell squeezed her hand. "I know you shall. I trust you, my heart. Now, enjoy your evening. All of us are here just for you!"

Evelyn lifted her almost-empty glass of champagne to signal for another one—Nell didn't stop her, for she was of age now—and seemed to enjoy the excited chattering that revolved entirely around her. Nell squeezed Evelyn's hand.

"Just wait until I tell May," Evelyn murmured, watching the delicate bubbles float through the amber champagne and to the surface with an impish grin. "She'll be so proud of me."

Eighteen

The tea shop smelled like glue.

It had always been like that, so the odor didn't really bother Mildred when she walked in on her eighteenth birthday, grateful to get away from the stench and sound of Chatham City. Porcelain tea sets decorated three cupboards on the side wall, interrupted only by shelves filled with glass jars of assorted tea from the Bickers Mill Covens.

"Merry meet, Charles," Mildred said, nodding to the slender witch behind the counter. The wrinkles around the corners of his eyes peaked up like bat wings when he smiled.

"Good to see you again, Mildred. Evelyn's upstairs waiting. She already chose the tea set and tea, of course. Just like every year."

Mildred laughed. Even if she hadn't been the first to arrive, Evelyn still would have chosen the tea. She always did. *My tastes are the most refined,* she said every year. *I'm just doing you a favor.*

"Thank you. I'll head upstairs. Stella should be here any minute now."

Mildred climbed the stairs at the back of the room to find Evelyn sitting at a table looking very morose. Fading sunlight streamed into the room, illuminating her red hair with strands of orange and yellow.

"Merry meet," Mildred said, approaching the table. Evelyn started, then smiled and straightened.

"Merry meet, Mildred. You're just on time, as always."

Mildred glanced at the tea set spread across the table. It was a deep green, with gold and white leaves painted into the delicate china, the same tea set they'd chosen since their thirteenth birthday when the tradition began and all of them could—and did—transport in for the first time. Three of the cups were chipped, and the lid didn't quite fit on the pot, but Mildred loved the consistency more than anything.

"You look very tired, Evie," Mildred said, settling into her chair and looking at her with concern. Evelyn shook herself awake.

"I am tired."

"How are things with Nell? Is being an Assistant everything you ever wanted?"

"Quite boring, Milly." Evelyn set her chin on her palm with a renewed slump of her thin shoulders. Her forehead ruffled into lines. "I thought being an Assistant would be much more exciting, but it turns out it's little more than meetings and paperwork."

"Don't you go to soirees and social events all week? Surely you love that."

Evelyn waved that off impatiently. "Yes, yes. The social events are wonderful, of course. You know how I've always loved parties. But the rest of it?" She shrugged. "I could do without."

Mildred nearly choked. What she wouldn't give to trade positions! Evelyn could keep the social events, and Mildred would take all the work, no matter how boring. It was much better than her current job, anyway.

"You seem very frustrated."

"I am!" Evelyn cried with ruthless honesty. "Assistants can't really *do* anything, you know? So many problems, and thanks to May I have good ideas on how to fix them! But it doesn't mean much because I don't have the power yet. Believe me, I've tried. But Nell only gets after me and says that my ideas are tyrannical. She's very . . . it's just different now, that's all."

Mildred leaned back in her chair. "What solutions do you have?" she asked eagerly, seeking the thrill of a stimulating conversation. There was nothing Mildred wanted to speak of more than the many issues the Network faced and how to combat them. It's what she thought of at night before she went to sleep. Determining how to best serve the Network would establish the course of her life once she became a Council Member.

"There's already a division of classes forming lately," Evelyn said, leaning forward and catching Mildred's fervor. "I think we should encourage it more. Allow the poor to be poor and the rich to be rich."

"What?" Mildred asked, recoiling. "Evie, separation of classes is the last thing the Network needs right now."

Evelyn rolled her eyes. "You sound just like Nell. The poor are threatening to riot in Newberry, aren't they? It's because they want a life they don't deserve. They haven't worked as hard as the wealthy have to achieve success, so why should the wealthy, who have worked, give up their currency to lazy sluggards who turn to violence and throw fits like a petulant child? No, it's all backward, Milly, and has been since the Tobacco Riots that killed Mama and Papa. I'm determined to make more witches see it, and even *more* determined to stop it from happening again. The constant riots are evidence enough. When they don't get what they want, they turn to fire and violence."

Mildred didn't know how to respond. Evelyn's sudden spouting of doctrine reeked of Elitism, the belief that separation of the classes led to a more stable economy. The rich remained in their sphere and the poor in theirs. It stood opposed to the doctrine of their current law, as outlined by the Esmelda Scrolls, and was a terrible basis for a government. Surely Evelyn could see that!

Mildred was about to say so when Stella walked up with a beaming smile, breaking off the depressing conversation. Charles followed close behind, chortling over something Stella had said, bearing a cake in his large hands.

"Merry meet!" Stella called, and the room felt brighter for her presence.

"A birthday cake for my three favorite ladies," Charles said, setting it on the table in front of them. It was a lovely two-layered cake with light purple frosting decorated with swirls of white. Mildred's mouth began to water. Charles and his wife made the most delicious confections.

"Thank you, Charles," Mildred said as he backed away. "This looks wonderful."

Evelyn stared out the window and said nothing.

"It's so good to see you again," Stella said, lowering herself gracefully into her chair. "Here we are! Celebrating our eighteenth birthday. Can you believe that we're out of Network school like a bunch of adults?"

Evelyn wasted no time before using an incantation to cut into the cake. A generous piece landed on her plate, and her fork lifted into the air for her hand to snatch.

"Upset today?" Stella asked with a teasing note in her voice.

"Yes, I am. Milly and I were just discussing how boring being an Assistant has turned out to be. Not to mention how busy I am in the evenings with May—"

She stuffed a piece of cake in her mouth, preventing her explanation of whatever else she was busy with. Evelyn groaned with delight and seemed to melt into the chair. Mildred cut a more realistic slice, set it on her plate, then served Stella, who had finally settled and poured a steaming cup of blackberry tea. All concerns over her conversation with Evelyn left Mildred's mind for the time being. No doubt it had all been the frustrated musings of a young Assistant.

"The job of Assistant can be boring sometimes," Stella agreed, hedging her words as if she were afraid to put them out there, lest someone catch her in a less-than-grateful state. "But I do love being the Assistant to Coven Leader Irene. She's a wonderful witch. I hope to be just like her one day. She handles her portion of Chatham City beautifully. It's been a true honor to work for her."

"What about you, Milly?" Evelyn asked, forking another fluffy bite of cake into her mouth, effectively destroying the frosting that had once said *18*. "Do you like your job?"

Mildred hesitated. Technically, she'd only just started last week. It wouldn't be right to form a decisive opinion yet. "It's fine."

Stella glanced up in surprise. "You found a job, Milly? Tell us all about it!"

"It's not that exciting."

"You searched for a job all summer," Stella countered, cutting a small mouthful of cake onto her fork. "Anything is exciting after as much work as you put into it!"

Evelyn took a sip of wine—though it was an odd pairing with cake—and studied Mildred with curious eyes. "Out with it, Milly. What's your job? You're not a librarian after all, are you?"

She giggled, and so did Stella, but they both quieted when they saw the troubled expression on Mildred's face.

"No, not a librarian," Mildred said, pushing her frosting around the plate. She cleared her throat. She wasn't a librarian, thank goodness, but she wasn't much higher either. "I'm the Assistant to the High Witch of York."

"But that's a wonderful position," Stella countered, though her voice had lost its gusto. Mildred shot her a perturbed glance.

"It most certainly is *not* a wonderful position," she said, feeling rigid with shame and disappointment again. While grateful for a job, she couldn't help feeling a sense of desperation. High Witch was very last on the list of political positions, and the High Witch of York oversaw a measly one hundred residents. Most days Mildred couldn't find enough work to fill her time. How would she ever advance her career in such a state?

"You must start somewhere," Stella replied. "And at least you're making currency again. I know your Mother must be happy about that."

"Yes," she agreed, forcing false bravado into her tone. *I'm still living at home, unlike both of you who found prestigious positions and have moved forward with life.* "I'm grateful to help pay the rent."

What Mildred didn't tell them was the full truth: She'd been passed up as High Witch for a scaly-skinned man named Tom Flannery. He'd taken her as his Assistant out of sheer laziness; he didn't want to interview other witches for the job. To say she was disheartened would understate her feelings dramatically. How had it been so easy for her friends? Why did she have to fight so hard for *everything*? It felt ridiculous.

To her relief, Stella turned the conversation by digging into her purse and extracting a well-worn envelope.

"I received a letter from Dale today!" she said with a smile. "He's just finished the first half of Guardian training and is doing well. I should be able to see him again in just four months."

"That's nice," Evelyn said, perking up. "Did you hear the rumor about the new Assistant, Jayne?"

Stella and Evelyn fell into a light prattle about gossip they couldn't discuss at the castle while Mildred turned to her own thoughts, content to be quiet, as usual. The shops below had already lighted their candles, illuminating the approaching darkness with warm yellow light. She hardly saw any of the slow bustle of Chatham City, nor felt the hot summer air fade into a sweet breeze through the open window. Instead, Mildred let the memory of Mother's words comfort her, for they ran in a circuit through her mind most days now.

You're going to face many disappointments, my girl, and you'll probably fail at something many more times. But if you keep going and don't let it defeat you, no one is going to remember what you didn't get done.

Assistant to a High Witch was as forward-moving politically as a librarian, but at least she had a start.

Feeling resolved to work twice as hard, and eventually catch up to her friends, Mildred took a bite of cake, turned away from the window, and started to track the merry conversation between Stella and a contented Evelyn who had eaten her fill of sugar and sweets.

Even if she didn't have an ideal job, she always had her best friends, and that counted for a lot more.

Evelyn watched the bustle of Market Street in downtown Chatham City from the safety of Piccadilly Pub. The tall windows edged with stained glass gave her plenty of opportunity. She sat in the shadows of the last booth, still visible from the front door so May would see her right away.

The smell of Piccadilly Pub's famous pumpkin soup wafted from the ovens in the back. She ignored the heady scent and kept her eyes on the close, wintry streets of Chatham City. A queue of witches bundled up against the cold loitered near the little trinket shop across the street, where the slow accumulation of dirt stained the brick, and the cobblestone street had worn smooth. She tilted her head to see the sky, but the close buildings admitted only a grimy light. Still, downtown Chatham City was a charming place.

As soon as she saw May's loose black curls, Evelyn smiled. How good it would be to see her old teacher again! It had only been eight months since graduation, but she already missed school and all her adoring friends.

"Merry meet, Evie," May said, walking up to the booth with a blithe smile. "You wore your favorite dress. It looks lovely on you."

Evelyn glanced down at the light blue day dress with its full skirt, lacy sleeves, and gauzy overlay. It was certainly overdone for a pub of this sort, but it gave her a dignified presence. She was, after all, a gentlewitch.

"Politics is presentation," Evelyn said with a warm smile, ecstatic to be alone with May again. "Just as you taught me, I always look my best."

"A pot of lemon ginger tea," May commanded the moment a buxom waitress with flyaway hair walked up. "Two cups with spoons and saucers. Don't pour the tea yourself; I don't trust you to steep it correctly."

The waitress faded away without a word.

"Tell me, Evie darling, how have you been?" May asked in a warm, maternal tone, folding her hands on her lap. "We've missed you terribly."

"A little bored," Evelyn admitted, propping her chin on her hand. "Being Nell's Assistant keeps me busy, but the work isn't very exciting."

"Did you expect it to be?"

"Perhaps," Evelyn admitted, feeling sheepish. "But I'm learning a great deal about Network business, which shall help our mutual purposes in the end. Donovan holds so many parties and balls that I'm rarely bored in the evenings."

"In matters such as these, you can't rush your career," May said. "If you do, it will seem like you're too impatient, and witches will get suspicious. Build up trust. You cannot change the world overnight."

Evelyn sighed. "I wish I could." She studied Chatham City again. Carriages and horses walked past in a continual stream, cutting tracks through the cold slush. Two scrollboys dropped their scrolls into a puddle for a fistfight, and a baker chased down a haggard man with a loaf of bread tucked under his arm. Thanks to a weak Network structure, theft and violence weren't even a surprise. So much unchecked poverty only led to lawlessness and despair. Evelyn's lips curled down at the thought, recalling a flash of her Mama's bright red hair.

All those rabid, poor people just trampled your Mother to death during the Tobacco Riots, May had told her once. Evelyn drew in a deep breath. That would never happen again. Not if she had anything to say about it.

"It's chaotic out there, isn't it?" she asked.

"Even chaos has a purpose," May said, leaning back in her chair, but still maintaining perfect posture. "It will be up to witches like you and I to control it once it gets out of hand."

It was nothing short of incredible that May hadn't progressed further in the Network political structure. Such poise and diplomacy were difficult to find in one witch, not to mention her quick mind in such matters. May always had an answer. Evelyn feared she'd never become even half the witch May was. How could she lead the world when she knew so little? May had grand plans, and sometimes they frightened Evie. She didn't know if she could live up to them or fulfill all that May intended for her. But she had to try, for she wanted May's approval above all else.

The waitress returned, setting a steaming pot of tea and two cheap porcelain glasses in front of them.

"I want a slice of Newberry pie," May said. "If the crust is burned or browned on the bottom, I shall send it back without paying."

The woman nodded, then glanced at Evelyn. She refused with a wave, and the woman scurried away.

"You aren't going to order any lunch?" May asked. "I thought we came here to eat."

"Miss Celia aside," Evelyn said, pouring the pale yellow tea into their cups, "I've never found any food outside of the castle that was worth eating."

"You're a snob."

"There's a difference between snobbery and refinement," Evelyn said. "As a witch that works in the castle, I always err on the side of refinement."

"I find that refined people are more suited for leadership. To lead requires a certain respectability that is difficult to find. You have it, Evelyn."

Evelyn absorbed the rare compliment, tucking it into her heart to remember later.

"You mentioned that everyone at the school misses me," she said, eager to hear more about herself. "Certainly that doesn't include your granddaughter, does it?"

"Mabel doesn't like or miss anyone." May lifted the petite silver spoon next to her cup and stirred the tea, releasing vapors of ginger and citrus. "Don't worry about her. She'll come to a bad end on her own."

"She never worried me," Evelyn replied coolly. Mabel had infuriated Evelyn at every opportunity during their classes. None of the girls in the school liked her haughty superiority, and most were afraid of her perfect looks. Evelyn had stood up to Mabel in a heroic way, which made Mabel the villain. May had simply laughed when she heard of their eternal war.

"I asked you to meet me here today because I wanted to see how your transition from school to Assistant to the High Priestess was going," May said after taking a sip and setting her cup down. "Don't try to pull the wool over my eyes, either. Tell me how it's really going. Starting in the workforce, even when the High Priestess is your special confidante, is never easy."

Evelyn hesitated, her stoic resolve faltering. May was right—it hadn't been easy. Of course, it hadn't been that hard, either. The increased arguing with Nell had been downright painful. It was like they were two old friends reuniting to find they were totally different witches. She felt like they were drifting apart and she had no way to stop it.

"Let me guess," May said, leaning back and studying her with an unnervingly keen eye. "Nell doesn't understand your new views on politics and the world around you?"

"Yes!" Evelyn said with a sharp intake of breath, relieved that she understood. "It's not the same. Nell insists I befriend the staff and admonishes me when I speak up regarding the importance of encouraging class separation."

Katie Cross

"They won't understand," May said in a calming voice. "We are far more educated than the poor, and so we must kindly lead them to a better life because they won't choose it themselves. Nell would just say we're oppressing them, when really we're helping them succeed in their own separate sphere."

Evelyn let out a sigh, feeling a great burden had been unleashed from her chest. "I've tried explaining this to Nell—"

"Don't!" May leaned forward so quickly that she jarred her tea, and it sloshed onto the saucer. Evelyn recoiled, startled.

"Why not?"

May's lips twitched at the corners. Her voice calmed. "She won't understand. Poor Nell, stuck in the old ways, and not able to wield as much power as Donovan. She's too old to change, Evelyn. That's a responsibility that will weigh on your shoulders instead of hers. Let her continue as she is."

"But she's wrong, and she doesn't even know it!"

"Giving away our plans to improve the Network will only make her more suspicious. Perhaps she would even take your ideas and profess them as her own. Let her go. She's not one of us."

Evelyn rolled the taste of that idea round in her mind, and it was bitter. She didn't like the idea of excluding Nell, but May was right. May was always right. Evelyn trusted in that above all things. Hadn't May been the one to tell her about her parents' real death? Hadn't she correctly predicted Nell's response to Evelyn's return?

May is right.

She resolved to do just as May had taught her: slowly gain political power and trust. Together, they would lead the Network to a better end, just as Evelyn had always dreamed. No more unfair deaths. No more violent protests.

"I'll let it go," Evelyn promised. "I trust you, May."

May lifted her tea with a smile.

"I'm very glad to hear that, Evie. Now, let's talk about how you are going to lead the Network, for I have an idea I think you'll like very much."

Reunions and Farewells

Mildred stared at the frozen ground in a stupefied daze. Her hand rested on Jorden's shoulder while he wept, imparting no real comfort, but linking her to the darkness of her new reality.

"I'm not ready," Jorden whispered, his head in his hands. "I'm not ready for Mother to leave us."

Winter snow banks drifted over the cemetery and the fields beyond it. Ice coated the wrought iron fence rails and dripped from bare tree branches in long fingers. Mildred stared at them, feeling an odd kinship with their cold, frozen nature. Gray clouds loomed above, overtaking York with the threat of snow and the promise of uncertainty.

"I know you weren't ready," she said woodenly. "But that doesn't change the facts, Jorden. Mother had a heart problem. We couldn't have done any more for her."

He covered his eyes with his bare hand, cold and nearly frozen in the winter light, and gave in to a fresh round of grief, one hand resting on Mother's closed casket. He'd built it from the walls of the lean-to because they didn't have the currency to buy a coffin. A pang of guilt stabbed Mildred's aching heart.

I should have given her a better funeral, she thought. *She deserves better. I've been working as Assistant to the High Witch of York for almost a year and a half now. Why couldn't I afford it?*

Because taxes were too high. Food was too expensive. Mama's

apothecary bills too large. Mildred remained lost in her thoughts, finding a certain safety in their expansiveness.

I need to prepare an audit. We're out of Mother's favorite tea. I must tutor tomorrow. Mother's gone, I don't need her tea. The house hasn't been swept if anyone stops by. Mother will be angry if the house isn't swept. I must write Stella and Evelyn to tell them the news.

"Mildred?"

Her old school teacher, Miss Sarah, shook her gently, startling her back to the present. "It's time to go home," Miss Sarah whispered, setting a warm hand on Mildred's arm. Mildred pulled away, unable to bear the touch.

"Thank you, Miss Sarah. Come, Jorden. Let's go."

Jorden had gained his feet again but stared mutely at the casket, his eyes swollen with tears. "Merry part, Mother," he whispered.

Mildred remained behind as Jorden and Miss Sarah departed. She stared at the frozen earth, her heart bleeding with every beat. She hadn't been ready for Mother's death either, and she feared what life would be like without her steady presence.

I'm only nineteen. How can I make you proud if you're not here to guide me? What will I do without you?

"Merry part, Mother," she whispered, an icy tear trailing down her cheek. "How I shall miss you."

Four weeks after Mother's death, Mildred woke to an unnatural silence in the house. She shuffled into the main room to make a pot of tea and found a note sitting on the table.

Milly,

I've joined the Guardians. I can't live here amongst the ghosts and the quiet. I'll write when I can.

—Jorden

After finishing a soothing cup of tea, Mildred dressed, leaving early for work. The spring morning held a nip in the air, but an undercurrent of warmth promised better days. She stopped at Miss Sarah's house, a pair of shears in her pocket.

"Cut it off, please," Mildred requested calmly. "I need it gone."

Miss Sarah hesitated, then motioned to a chair.

"Have a seat."

Mildred's long locks of auburn hair fell to the ground in gentle wisps. When Miss Sarah finished, she stepped back.

"It looks better, actually," Miss Sarah said, running her fingers through the short strands to loosen any stray hairs. Mildred's hair feathered her face now, framing her full cheeks and small eyes.

"Thank you, Miss Sarah," she said, touching her bare neck with a sense of relief. "That feels much better."

Mildred transported to the stair landing just outside Tom's office. A late spring slushstorm had descended on quiet little York, flying past the windows in a vague wall of gray. A fire crackled in the hearth, and several lighted candles dotted the bookshelves and desk. Mildred stopped short. Tom never came early, nor started the fire. Who had started the fire? To her great astonishment, Coven Leader Irene sat behind Tom's desk.

"I fired Tom last night," Irene said with her usual abrupt, business-driven air. She wore her long blonde hair away from her face with ivory combs.

"Oh." Mildred set her heavy armload on a side table. "I see."

"The Chatham City Covens have a Network audit coming up, and I need a new High Witch." Irene signed a document before looking right at Mildred. "I want you to take the position."

"Me?" Mildred asked, straightening. "You want me to be High Witch of York?"

"The position will be for two years. I'll double your pay, extend your influence to cover the neighboring village of DuPont, and approve funds for you to hire an Assistant out of Coven currency."

Mildred hesitated. "DuPont is twice the size of York."

Adds a bit more credibility to the position, she thought. *Managing only a hundred witches isn't all that hard, even at nineteen. Three hundred will sound better.*

"And twice the mess," Irene said with a sigh. "Their High Witch just died, and I don't trust anyone else to clean it up. I'm not blind, Mildred. I know who *really* did the work around here. Will you take the job?"

"Forgive me a moment," Mildred murmured, reaching into her bag to pull out a scroll and begin a list of all the pros and cons. Irene waited with a vague impression of curiosity.

Five minutes later Mildred stared at her hasty list. The experience as High Witch would be invaluable, with a chance to build a professional friendship with Irene. Besides, she'd become quite fond of the witches of York. In truth, she wasn't ready to leave Mother behind yet. While the job didn't offer the same prestige as Assistant to a Coven Leader or Council Member, at least she'd have time to grieve.

"I'll accept the two-year contract," she said, allowing the scroll to roll back up. "But only for two years."

Irene stood, her arm extended. Mildred followed suit and they clasped forearms.

"Agreed," Irene said with a hint of a smile around her steely gray eyes. "Now have a seat. I'll go over the details of DuPont since you already know York so intimately."

Council Member Rand resembled a rat with his long, twitchy nose, narrow face, and skinny limbs. The only reason he held a position in the Council was his childhood friendship with Donovan; the two of them were oafish chums. Rand ruled over the sprawling, but sparsely populated, Southern Covens.

Evelyn didn't particularly care for Rand and his buggy eyes, but she treated him like a friend all the same. There was no telling when she and May could use his influence, for he had contacts that they didn't.

He stood behind a statue in the middle of the long hallway on the main floor of Chatham Castle, whistling as he picked at his fingernails. Stone walls lined either side, soaring into buttresses several stories high, accentuated by the stained glass windows on the far wall.

Evelyn gritted her teeth. She knew *exactly* why he lounged around. He'd hired Stella as his new Assistant—based solely on her attractive face and feminine features, as he'd told Donovan during a party—and she didn't want him pouncing on her the moment she arrived. Evelyn's usual protective instinct toward her friends swelled in her chest.

"Merry meet, Rand," Evelyn called as she approached, bracing herself for the fishy scent of his breath.

"What are you doing here?" he asked, wetting his lips with a flick of his tongue.

"Meeting my friend, Stella. Your new Assistant, I believe."

Rand smiled, revealing a mouth of crooked, rotting teeth. "That she is," he said, sticking four fingers in his vest pocket. "Friend of yours, eh?"

Evelyn narrowed her eyes with threatening promise. "Best friend," she said, smiling archly. "And someone I'd protect with all my considerable influence and power."

He recoiled with a frown. In truth, Evelyn wasn't sure that her power and influence were *exactly* considerable yet. But Rand would recognize Evelyn only for her position: adopted daughter of, and Assistant to, the second most powerful witch in the Network. He took a step back, appearing to be properly hesitant. She smiled, gratified.

The scratching sound of the main door halted their conversation. Stella entered, carrying so many valises and suitcases that she looked like an overburdened donkey.

"I think it's time for you to go back to work, don't you?" Evelyn asked Rand with a saccharine smile. He glowered for a moment but left, mumbling in disappointment. She waited until he'd rounded the corner to start for Stella.

"Merry meet, Evie!" Stella dropped all her luggage to embrace Evelyn. Her bright cheeks felt cold from the spring winds raging outside.

"Goodness, but you packed enough for both of us," Evelyn said. Noticing a familiar maid a few paces away, she called, "Matilda! Take Miss Stella's things to her new room."

"Oh, no," Stella said, snatching a white valise from the floor. "I can manage. I just need a moment and then—"

"Nonsense. Matilda isn't doing anything important right now." Evelyn waved for the maid again. "Come, Matilda. Don't just stand there like a dead tree. I gave you an order."

"M-miss Evelyn," Matilda said, stepping forward, "I'm on an errand for Council Member Porter. If I don't—"

"I didn't ask what you were doing."

"I have a message for Council Member Porter that must be delivered immediately, Miss Evelyn and I—"

"Then transport it to him."

Matilda's eyes turned down. Evelyn shook her head in disapproval, much the way May had often done when Evelyn first started as her pupil. Evelyn had found the disappointment motivating and hoped Matilda would do the same. Transportation was such a simple magic to learn but so few staff members did so. Why not? Because poor people didn't *want* to change their stations or improve, just as May had always told her. Seeing it in person disheartened and infuriated her. Wasn't this the same ignorance that killed Mama?

"There's no one to teach me that magic, Miss Evelyn," Matilda whispered.

Stella stepped forward. "Let the poor girl finish her errand, Evie. You and I can take these bags to my room together."

I must be firm with them, Evelyn reminded herself with a deep breath. *The poor need a strong leader.*

"Matilda, take Stella's bags this instant, or I shall fire you on the spot."

"Oh please, Miss Evelyn!" Matilda cried, her eyes filling with tears. "I'm already going to be in trouble as it is! Council Member Porter is waiting. Please have mercy! I've two children at home. If I don't deliver this right away, Council Member Porter will have me fired!"

"Yes, good. Let's use logic to solve this problem. No matter what you do, you're going to lose your job," Evelyn said. "Since you are already here, you may as well take Stella's bags. If you don't mess anything else up, I'll put in a good word for you with Porter. As Assistant to the High Priestess, I have considerable sway with the Council Members."

Matilda froze.

Stella extended her hand. "Hand the letter to me, Matilda. I'll transport it for you since you've been stuck here speaking with us. Porter will get it on time."

Matilda hesitated, glancing between Evelyn and Stella, then finally relinquished the envelope. It remained in Stella's hand for only a moment before it disappeared. Evelyn let out a long-suffering sigh. How could she ever enact change for the good of the Network when witches like Stella catered to the needy laziness of the servants?

An uphill battle, she thought, recalling something May had said. *I shall have to fight it one day at a time.*

"Well, you're a lucky girl, Matilda. Come with me, Stell." Evelyn grabbed Stella's arm in a move that brooked no arguments. "We have catching up to do. Matilda will take your bags."

"No, Evelyn. I shall take my own bags, thank you."

"I don't mind, Miss," Matilda said, curtsying, one wary eye on Evelyn. "I-I'd love to be of service, especially after you helped me."

"Oh, no. You don't have to—"

"Come, Stella."

Ignoring the look of apology Stella sent the idiot maid, Evelyn took her by the elbow and steered her to the grand staircase.

"I'm sorry you had to see that little disagreement," Evelyn said with genuine regret. "If you don't keep the servants in line here, they walk all over you. Trust me. I've lived here my whole life, and it's an increasing problem. Let's not talk about Matilda. I need to talk to you about Rand."

"Rand?" Stella asked, appearing startled by the swift change of subject. "What about him?"

Evelyn smoothed her velvet green bodice and tossed her flowing red hair over her shoulder. "He's a bit of a lech. I can guarantee that it's not your experience as Assistant to Coven Leader Irene that got you this job."

Stella smiled ruefully. "It's my looks."

"How did you know?"

"Irene told me. She also had my contract drawn up by her own legal witch. It says that Rand can't fire me for five years unless he has physical proof or at least three witnesses stating that I've been lax and not done my job. That way he can't fire me for not letting him feel me up. So, as long as I work hard and watch his hands, there's no reason that this won't be a wonderful opportunity."

Stella's eyes sparkled with mischief. Evelyn tilted her head back and laughed. "I should never have doubted! Is Dale very upset that you'll be here at the castle with Rand?"

"Not at all! In fact, he taught me a few incantations to keep Rand's wandering hands away should he try to take liberties. Dale just finished his Captain of the Guardians training and is assigned to a contingent in the Eastern Covens."

Evelyn smiled wide. "Wonderful, Stella. Just wonderful. It is so nice to see you again. Shall we go visit the kitchens? Mrs. F promised me she'd set aside a little treat to refresh you once you arrived."

"Yes!" Stella cried. "It won't be the same without Milly, but it will be wonderful to see Mrs. F again."

"Now let's talk more about your job and how I can help you in it," Evelyn said, taking her arm and steering her toward the back staircase. "Being Assistant to a Council Member isn't too far below what I do, is it? I'll make sure your life at the castle is wonderful."

Poor Form

Council Member Porter ran Chatham City and Chatham Castle with unusual temerity.

He began every day at five and retired at midnight. He never needed much sleep, and he never appeared tired. Although he inspired respect, many on the Council found him overly opinionated and prone to favor only the witches that agreed with him.

They were right.

He stopped at a mirror to ensure that his silver hair hadn't moved, straightened his frock coat, and turned to his Assistant.

"I've an early appointment with the High Priestess. I'm unavailable until then."

The floor-length windows behind his desk lit the office in an early morning light, illuminating drifting dust motes. Stacks of old tomes lined his walls, hiding his special collection. His *very* special collection.

Porter approached the farthest bookcase on the left, murmuring a rare incantation under his breath. The entire shelf swung forward, revealing an extensive collection of wine. He ran his fingers over the smooth surface of a bottle, selected one, and withdrew to his desk to pour.

"Delicate," he murmured, closing his eyes with a deep sigh and enjoying the lingering bouquet on his tongue. "Just a hint of lavender."

Drinking such an expensive wine in the morning dulled his constant frustration with his career. Thoughts of meeting with the High Priestess eased some of the strain. Nell had always seen eye-to-eye with him. They'd had something of a silent partnership for many years now, preventing Donovan from implementing some of his dumber ideas.

But knowing that Nell's troublesome Assistant was the topic of their meeting tempted him to enjoy a full glass before their arrival. Evelyn, a spoiled teenager with too much power, was going to throw a fit.

"No." He replaced the wine with a feeling of regret. "Just a sip."

He'd just settled in to reply to his weekly correspondences when a knock interrupted him. "Come in."

The High Priestess stepped inside wearing a muted gray dress, her matching hair tucked into a high bun.

"Your Highness," he said warmly, executing a perfect bow. "I am so grateful that you agreed to come to this meeting. Please, have a seat."

He pulled his best chair close to the fire, and she settled in with a smile.

"I'm always happy to meet with you, Porter. And of course I would come to anything that involves my Evie," she said with a note of worry in her voice. "You said that you had an issue about her to discuss?"

"Yes," he drawled, not wanting to alarm her. "If you don't mind, I would like to wait until she arrives."

Nell nodded. "Of course. In the meantime, tell me how things are going in Chatham City."

Evelyn slipped inside five minutes later, wearing an extravagant dress with emerald beads and a silky blue skirt that sparkled in the sunlight. Porter grimaced. Such an expensive gown on a weekday morning? Poor form.

"You wanted to see me, Council Member?" Evelyn asked, stopping a few paces in. Porter motioned her to the chair opposite Nell.

"Yes, Evelyn, have a seat."

She paused, catching sight of Nell's familiar bun over the top of the chair, and slid her eyes back to him in calculated question.

"Thank you," she said, as calm as pond water as she sashayed to Nell's side. "I prefer standing. Good morning, Nell. I didn't know you would be here."

Nell waved, but neither of them had taken their eyes off of Porter. "Go ahead," Nell said. "What do you need from us?"

"I'll get right to it," Porter said, leaning back against his desk. "As Council Member of Chatham City and Chatham Castle, I make sure that everything here runs smoothly. I'm in charge of the staff, the Coven Leaders, the upkeep, the kitchens, and anything else you could think of, right down to the smallest garden and the employment of librarians."

"What's your point?" Evelyn asked. "I'm already aware of what you control."

Porter stopped to stare at her in undisguised annoyance. Evelyn did not back down, though a light flush in her cheeks indicated she had some awareness of her horrible manners.

"*Are* you aware of what I control, Evelyn?" he asked with cool surprise. "Because you like to order the servants of this castle around as if you were in my position."

Evelyn's eyes went distant for a minute.

"What does he mean, Evelyn?" Nell asked.

"I'm sure I don't know," Evelyn replied innocently, folding her hands behind her back.

Porter gave her a flinty grin. "Then I'll be happy to fill you both in. It just happened last week, so I'm sure you'll remember soon."

Nell's eyes widened as Porter regaled her with the story of Evelyn, Stella, and Matilda.

"According to the two butlers who reported it independently of each other, Matilda begged to be allowed to complete her errand, but Evelyn refused to listen. Do you need me to recount more?"

"No," Evelyn muttered, teeth clenched and cheeks bright red. "I remember now."

"Oh good. I thought you would."

"Evie, is this true?"

"Yes," Evelyn whispered, leveling a glare of fire at Porter, who received it with an easy smile. Seeing Evelyn so uncomfortable was delightful. "I threatened to fire Matilda if she didn't do as I said."

"I see. Then you shall apologize to Porter and to Matilda," Nell concluded, rising to her feet to look Evelyn in the eyes. "I'm very disappointed in you. It seems to be a recurring theme lately."

Evelyn swallowed, enduring a long stretch of silence. Her cheeks flared a brighter red.

"I apologize, Council Member Porter," Evelyn finally muttered, bowing her head in reluctant subjugation. "I shall also seek out and apologize to Matilda."

"Accepted." He turned to Nell. "In the future, Evelyn may request favors of the staff in a courteous manner, but they are under no obligation to follow her commands. I've met with the staff, and they are aware."

"That seems fair," Nell said. "It's no less than the rest of us should do to respect our staff. What came of Matilda?"

"I've reassigned her to avoid any . . . unpleasantness."

Evelyn stalked to the door without a dismissal, letting it slam in her wake. Nell stood with a weary smile.

"Thank you, Porter. I appreciate your honesty. The good gods know it hasn't been easy since she returned."

"Maybe she'll come around."

Nell stared at the door. "Maybe."

Porter waited several minutes after they left before he chuckled, congratulated himself on successfully putting Evelyn in her place for the first time, and plucked his wine off the shelf again.

Miss Mabel's School for Girls was in full swing when Evelyn transported there in the middle of the first month of Fall. The smell of Miss Celia's bread wafted through the deadfall of Letum Wood with the beckoning promise of buttery crusts. Evelyn sauntered up the path to the front door and slipped inside. The low murmur of voices, once so familiar to her, now wrapped her in a distant memory. How she missed her days at school! Things were much simpler then. Did adulthood become more complicated with every step?

Students walking by gave her an odd stare, but Evelyn ignored them and started down the hallway to the left, following it until she found a familiar set of spiraling iron steps and began to climb.

"I'm here, May," she called the moment she set her slippered foot on the landing. A lone student—the winner of the Competition and

May's only pupil—sat at a desk in the middle of the attic classroom, where she'd spent many days herself. The girl glanced up, then turned away.

"Come to my office, Evie dear." May's voice drifted down the hallway. "Tea is waiting for you."

Evelyn found May sitting behind her desk, a small disaster of scrolls and parchments scattered on top. She wore a pair of glasses on the edge of her nose and controlled three quills writing furiously on different scrolls. The room was neat but cluttered with trinkets, a small tapestry on the wall, and a few paintings. Evelyn smiled to herself. Nothing had changed since she left. Steady, reliable May! Just being in her presence soothed Evelyn's frazzled nerves.

"Have a seat," May said, giving Evelyn her usual smile. A small scroll at her elbow closed and zipped past them, sliding under the door that led into May's personal quarters. "Miss Celia just sent up the tea tray."

Evelyn lowered herself into a wooden chair. A circular table held a gold-lined tea set. Steam rose from the spout, filling the air with the smell of warm vanilla and sugar. Tea sandwiches and rose-shaped meringues filled a silver tray next to the tea, almost too lovely to eat. May continued to write, so Evelyn arranged her skirts, folded her hands on her lap, and waited.

"Go ahead and pour," May said, setting down the quill. "Tell me about things. Your letters have been so long lately that I haven't been able to read all of them."

May's sympathetic tone melted all of Evelyn's frail defenses. She hadn't told May of her embarrassing incident with Porter, having been too mortified to admit the truth. But it had boiled up inside her for so long now that she simply had to tell her.

"Oh, May! I can't even tell you, it's all so embarrassing! It happened months ago, and it still feels so fresh."

"Then you must tell me," May said, rising from her desk chair and sitting in the chair across from Evelyn. "You may begin."

Evelyn forgot the tea while recounting the humiliating situation with Porter and the staff, ending with indignant tears and an emphatic promise—not for the first time—to never forgive Nell.

"She just sat there and let him berate me," Evelyn whispered. "Over a lazy servant who should have been doing her job. My life has been unbearable since then. I can't ask any of the servants for help because they just ignore me. I hear them gossiping when they think I'm not listening, and Nell! Nell doesn't trust me at all anymore."

"That is a tough situation, Evie," May said, finally pouring the tea herself. "But it was your fault."

Evelyn gave May a wounded look. "It's my fault that Nell sided with Porter?"

"You're twenty years old and still haven't gained control over your emotions," May said in a chiding way, adopting a firm maternal glare. "What have we talked about before?"

Evelyn studied the lace work around her wrist, not wanting to see the truth in May's daunting gaze. "The only way to win in a political game is subtlety," she said from memory, recalling many days of May's lectures in front of the attic fire.

"Indeed. Was it subtle to threaten to fire a servant when you didn't have the proper authorization?"

"No. But in my defense, I thought I had that power! I've never been denied anything at Chatham Castle before."

May ignored her outburst. "Do you see that it's your fault for acting on rash emotions?"

Evelyn's nostrils flared as she looked away, but her fury had no real strength. If May believed she'd been wrong, then that was simply the truth of it. She gave in with a resigned sigh. "Yes."

"Good. Then what can we improve in the future so our plans are not jeopardized?"

"I shall control my thoughts," Evelyn promised, contrite. "And my temper," she amended when May opened her mouth, finally earning the coveted nod of approval.

Nell's words that day had wounded Evelyn to the core. *I'm very disappointed in you. It seems to be a recurring theme lately.* Evelyn simply couldn't bear it if she disappointed May, whom she looked up to more than anyone. It seemed that whenever she acted in a way that pleased May, she disappointed Nell. If she pleased Nell, she would disappoint May. It gave her a headache, and she pressed a hand to her head.

All I want is for them to be proud of me. Why is that so hard?

May studied her for a minute. "Let me comfort you, Evelyn. In the end, this incident won't matter. You're going to take over the Network and turn things around. Once you've gained a bit more trust and written a Network law that runs according to wealth and education, none of this shall happen again. Let's think on this as a blessing."

"A blessing!" Evelyn cried. "How is my humiliation in front of the entire castle a blessing?"

May shook her head. "You are an emotional trap, aren't you? It's like you feel something and never let it go. This incident proved to me that our cause is justified. The servants in the castle have too much freedom. If we don't limit their liberties, they'll take over, and we shall lose even more innocent witches than we already have."

Evelyn thought it over. "Yes," she whispered, surprised to find some comfort. "Perhaps you're right."

If it must be so painful, at least her cause was just. They must work harder to make the Network a better place. To keep other witches from the same pain. To protect them from themselves.

"You've learned a great deal as well," May said. "We also know now that Porter will be an obstacle."

"He'll be the first to go," Evelyn muttered. "I'll not keep him a moment longer than I have to. Oh, I do hate him!"

"That's a good girl," May said, sitting back in her chair. "How is our plan coming along?"

Evelyn glanced up, pulled from her reveries of revenge. "Slow," she admitted with hesitation. "There's not much time outside of meetings and social events to plot the new law."

"Or have you been spending too much time with Council Member Grant?"

Evelyn blushed, unable to meet May's sharp gaze. "No! Well, I suppose I have spent a lot of time with him lately but in a professional regard."

May frowned. "Have you clearly established our goals?"

"Yes, of course," Evelyn said eagerly, grateful to have one right answer. "Together you and I shall establish me as Council Member and, finally, as High Priestess, where I shall remove education for the poor and increase funding to the struggling wealthy oppressed by the poor. Once Donovan dies, I shall destroy the Esmelda Scrolls and get rid of the current Network so I may institute our law."

May's arch look of disapproval stung. "Yes, but that's old news. Have you created an actual plan yet?"

Evelyn swallowed. "Not beyond that, no," she said, averting her eyes and fiddling with her tea cup, afraid to view May's frightening displeasure.

"I see," May murmured as she smoothed out a wrinkle in her organza dress. "Do I need to find someone more committed to improving our Network? I'm sure my granddaughter Mabel would love to—"

"No!" Evelyn cried. "No, please don't take this opportunity away from me! I-I just got busy and forgot how much it all means to me. I'll start writing up the plans immediately, I swear."

"Very well," May said with a low purr of her husky voice, like a contented cat. "I'll give you one more chance."

"How am I to start the plan?" Evelyn asked, swallowing. "I'm quite overwhelmed and—"

"I'll leave that to you to figure out," May said, as if they were discussing the weather. "But whatever you do, do it carefully. We don't want Nell or Donovan finding out about our plans, do we?"

Evelyn, emotionally exhausted from her vent, and now uncertain how to please her favored mentor, leaned back in her seat. May's demands never ended and often seemed unfair and heavy. But Evelyn didn't dare admit it, for May did not appreciate weakness.

And Evelyn would not be weak.

"I shall try."

"That's all I ask," May said, and they finished their tea in silence.

Weaknesses

2nd Month of Fall

May,

It's been weeks since we had tea, but there's still little change to report in regards to our plans. They move forward steadily and slowly, one day at a time. With the goals established, I'm continuing to develop the specifics and note the little details—such as how to reward our supporters—as you suggested.

Nell and I don't speak outside of business matters. I'm so hurt by her constant disapproval of my new political views that I can't even bear it. I fear our relationship will never be repaired. Perhaps I should talk with her about the Porter situation? What do you think I should do?

Continuing to find special favor with the Council Members and Coven Leaders, as you counseled me to do, seems to be working. I have a good idea who to recruit to our cause when the time comes. Council Member Grant and I continue to spend time together. He's apathetic about business concerns but likes to follow. As he rules over your Covens, I figured you'd know what a good addition he could be. I haven't yet invited him into our circle of confidence but feel that I shall eventually.

Please write. I know how busy you are, but I hear from you so rarely, and I write you so often, that it does cheer me when I receive a response.

Your adoring student,
Evelyn

3rd Month of Fall

Darling Evie,

Forgive my late reply. I've been on a business trip to the Southern Covens and just returned. I'm happy to hear that plans are moving forward and always glad to hear from you.

The incident with Porter taught you that you cannot trust Nell; that's why it hurts so much still. In your moment of need, she stepped aside and let Porter run all over you. Don't forget, dear girl, that the only witch you've ever been able to really trust is me. Am I not the one you turn to in need? The friend who comforts you? Nell hasn't been able to give you what you needed since you were a little girl. I must counsel you not to forget the pain she's caused. Reconciling with Nell will only bring you more heartbreak when she betrays you again, and I can't bear to see you in more pain. Please take my advice: Maintain a respectful professional relationship, but do not be influenced by her.

Grant shall make a trustworthy addition to our plans. What of Council Member Rand? I know he's very chummy with Donovan, but greedy. He seems like the sort that can be persuaded with promises of currency and power.

One thing I would advise you: Learn how to find their weaknesses. Then you shall know how you can exploit them, and that gives you a great deal of power. I want you to start with Nell and report back on what you find in your next letter.

I think you'll see it is very enlightening and will give you a great opportunity to gain more power in the political sphere.

Regards,
May

1st Month of Spring

Dear May,

I've been thinking about Nell's weaknesses for the past several months. Indeed, I can barely get it off my mind. I couldn't figure out at first why you wanted me to find Nell's soft spot, but I've done as you said. Now I think I understand.

I'm Nell's weakness, aren't I?

It bothers me, and thrills me, at the same time. I find myself struggling with guilt at night because I can't help but plan how to use this weakness against her. Every time I think of it, I remember the humiliation of meeting with Porter and find new determination to see our plans through. That is what you would want of me, isn't it?

Should I be ashamed of myself for wanting to go against someone who took me in as a child? She was there for me from the moment Mama and Papa died in the riots. It feels wrong to go against her in this way.

Your most devoted friend,
Evelyn

2nd Month of Summer

Evelyn,

Ashamed for working to achieve a greater end for the Network? Indeed, you shall not be ashamed. I'm very proud of you. Like Esmelda, you are paving a new path for a better Network. It will be difficult, yes. It may even be lonely. But won't it be worth it?

Yes, you are Nell's greatest weakness. The question we must ask ourselves now is this: In what way can you use this weakness to your advantage? It's likely that your withdrawal of love has steered her into her recent depressive episode. (Do not blame yourself,

Evie. For she was the one that turned against you and no longer deserves your love!)

Ask yourself: How can I use Nell's depression to further our cause?

Think on that. In the meantime, pay attention to those around you. Think even of Grant and his weaknesses, for you shall need to be thorough in order to be successful.

Don't forget to stop by for tea next month on your twenty-first birthday.

Regards,
May

3rd Month of Winter

May,

I took your advice to try being kind to Nell when I wanted something from her. When Nell was in her usual winter depression this month, I provided extra support. She fell into my hands like melted butter, giving me tasks that she would normally do herself. I had hoped that if I did it well, she'd let me continue to do things for her, but alas, it's not meant to be. She's pulled out of her depression again and has resumed all her previous duties. It didn't last long, but I learned a lot and worked myself into a few more social spheres that I hadn't been able to breach before.

This movement of ours will go forward, I'm determined, even if it takes time. Although, it does seem to be taking much longer than I ever imagined. Sometimes it feels as if I'll be waiting for my future forever.

All my love,
Your Evie

1st Month of Spring

Dear Mildred,

It's hard to believe that two years have passed and you are finished as High Witch of York and DuPont. Congratulations on your wonderful achievement! York and DuPont have even come to Porter's attention as the most industrious villages in the Network. It's all thanks to you, of course.

Irene and I had a conversation over lunch the other day that involved you. Suffice it to say, she and I have worked together for the past month and have found a wonderful surprise for you. You have a job at Chatham Castle! I know you always hated the idea of it, but you're going to be the new librarian. Living at Chatham will allow you to establish connections that you'll never make in York. I do hope you'll take the position.

Let's meet up for dinner again this weekend, and we'll chat over the details. Dale will be out on a mission, and I'll need some company. I do long to catch up with you. I haven't heard much from Evelyn in several weeks, so I can't promise she'll come. She seems to be quite busy lately, but with what I can't get her to say.

Things with Rand are going well. I zapped him with a hex the other day when he tried to get fresh, and he's left me alone ever since. Perhaps, now that it's been two years since I started working with him, he's finally realized that I won't tolerate his advances. One can only hope, right?

All my love,
Stella

The Librarian

"So many witches to quarantine," Porter muttered to himself, shaking his head. "And hardly any herbs coming from the Bickers Mill Coven."

Porter paced the length of his office while reviewing reports of the chimeral plague. The erratic warmth of spring had settled on the castle, so he left his windows open to the fresh air. He contemplated ignoring the knock on his door, but called out with a sigh, "Come in, come in."

A young witch with short burgundy hair and characteristic solemn gravity walked in. "Mildred Graeme," she said in a husky voice, arm extended. She moved with the stocky build of a rather short workhorse. A haughty glint gleamed in her small eyes. He couldn't help but feel amused.

What a peculiar witch.

"Council Member Porter," he said, hesitating for just a beat before taking her forearm in his hand. "What can I do for you?"

"I was the High Witch over York and DuPont. Irene arranged for me to take over as the new librarian for Chatham Castle."

Her tone suggested she was less than pleased with the appointment, but he couldn't be sure that it wasn't just her serious bearing. Mildred held out a letter with Irene's handwriting on the front. Porter brightened.

"Oh, yes. I hadn't expected you so soon."

Mildred adjusted her hold on a shabby brown valise. "I had nothing to delay me in York."

"How old are you anyway?" he asked, perusing her with a critical eye. She seemed very young to be a High Witch.

"I turned twenty-one in the fall."

"And you were a High Witch?"

"Yes."

"I suppose that qualifies you as a librarian," he said, handing the letter back without reading it. "Come. I'll take you there now."

"May I also request my name be placed on the Assistant waiting list?" she asked, pulling three scrolls from her pocket. "Here is all the required paperwork, as well as letters of recommendation and my graduation scroll."

"Let me guess," he said in a wry tone. "You want to be a Council Member and change the Network?"

Mildred met his gaze straight on. "Yes."

He paused, taken aback. "You're very forthright to admit your intentions so blatantly. You may want to refrain from it in the future, as some would say it makes you seem too eager."

"That seems backward to me." She frowned. "If there was a witch wanting a political position that affected my life, I'd want to know exactly what her intentions were."

"Suppose you never reach your goal?"

"I don't suppose anything."

Porter almost laughed but found he couldn't with her sober eyes drilling into him. He'd seen too many witches flounder in their own political aspirations for years, only to stop caring in the end. Arrogant confidence rolled off Mildred, making him more curious than skeptical.

"Becoming an Assistant is very competitive right now. The average wait time is eight years. Are you prepared to work as a librarian that long?"

He had the distinct impression that she refrained from rolling her eyes. "I understand," she said, which didn't answer his question at all.

Who is this strange witch?

Porter set her paperwork on the desk behind him, then motioned to the door with a swing of his arm. "Good. Let's take a look at the library. The good gods know you've got your work cut out for you."

They slipped through the cavernous dining hall, past the grand staircase with white marble veined in black, and stopped in front of two tall double doors on the left. A pair of stained glass windows depicted Letum Wood and a sapphire blue sky. Mildred followed Porter inside.

"Here we are," he said, sweeping his arms to the side. "The library. It's not in very good shape. It's going to need a lot of work, and you'll be the only librarian."

Dilapidated shelves lined the walls of the three-story room, half-filled with books and tattered scrolls. Mountainous piles of cheap novels and old tomes littered the floor. The rest of the library threatened to topple from overpacked shelves and disrepair. Mildred wasn't entirely sure she'd be willing to work here for eight years.

"Lovely," she muttered, stepping over shards of broken glass.

"Er, yes, well, she needs some work, but we're still proud of her." Porter adjusted his coat with a little cough. "Or what she used to be, anyway. I'm afraid to say she's been neglected for the past two years. Funds have been short, despite the tax increase last year."

"I can see that."

Porter continued into the room, blithely avoiding a teetering stack of scrolls. Mildred whispered an incantation under her breath as she strode past, and the scrolls built themselves into an organized pyramid.

A giant circular desk stood on a platform in the middle of the library, its cherry wood carved with images of forest nymphs. A crooked sign bearing the words, *Librarians Only*, dangled from one side. The interior molted paper. Books needing new bindings lay in one pile, and ripped maps clotted the floor. Mildred set her valise down.

"Your new throne, if you will," he said, grinning at his own joke.

"Where is the previous librarian?" she asked, running her eyes along the water-stained mural on the domed ceiling.

"Gone. We couldn't afford the staff. I can only pay you one sacran a week, on top of room and board, of course. It's a pittance." He scowled and kicked aside a torn lampshade. "But it will have to do. I'm paying you out of my own pocket. I can't bear to see the library in such a state any longer."

"I'll take it."

She would have worked for just room and board but didn't tell him. Porter pulled out a pocket watch.

"Glad to hear it. Let me know if you need anything. Do the best you can to clean this up and get it running. My Assistant will come by later tonight to show you your room. Questions?"

"No."

"Good luck, Mildred. You're going to need it."

The enticing smell of sautéed mushrooms greeted Mildred when she entered the kitchen that evening.

Exploring the halls of Chatham had been a nostalgic ramble through her past. She ran her fingertips along the cool walls and remembered being six again, hiding behind statues whenever someone passed, running at Evelyn's side after they stole eclairs from Mrs. F's fresh stash. It would be wonderful to be here with her friends again.

Nothing in the kitchens had changed since her last visit. She navigated her way through the maze of cupboards, bread racks, and ceiling-high sacks of flour. The smell of sugar and cream lingered in the air. An aging Mrs. F greeted her with a warm embrace. Flour dotted her bosom, covering a frilly blue apron.

"Oh, little Milly!" Mrs. F cried, hugging her so violently that white powder poofed into the air. "But I suppose you aren't little anymore, are you?" she said, pulling away. "Well, yes, you are still quite short. It's so good to see you again!"

Mildred smiled. The warm bustle of the kitchen had always been a safe place for her and her friends thanks to Mrs. F.

"Come," Mrs. F said, waving a plump hand, her cheeks ruddy from an oven belching waves of heat. "Your timing is perfect. I need help in the worst way!"

Mildred was forced to follow as Mrs. F navigated the kitchens, her feet pitter-pattering so fast Mildred could hardly keep up. They moved through the oven room and into a cooler area. Two young cooks were bent over a cake, piping an intricate design in swirls along the edges.

"I'm supposed to meet Stella and Evelyn down here for dinner," Mildred said. "I've just moved into the castle and—"

"I suppose I should put you back to work washing dishes, shouldn't I?" Mrs. F asked and winked over her shoulder as she toddled along. "I need some help frosting these small cakes. It's easy enough. You can do it while the three of you gab."

"We were going to—"

"Posh, posh," Mrs. F said with an impatient wave of her hand. "I need the help, and you have the time. I'll give you something to eat afterwards."

Knowing better than to argue, Mildred accepted a tray of small cakes and a spatula and watched as Mrs. F placed six vats of frosting in front of her.

"There are five hundred little cakes on the racks behind you, and they all have to be frosted by tonight. Use the spatulas and do the best you can. I'll fix any imperfections later. Let me know if you have questions!"

Mrs. F soared out of the kitchen before Mildred could get a word in edgewise. She stared at the cakes in disbelief, not entirely certain she knew *how* to frost them. Wasn't there an incantation for tasks such as this? Magic would frost them more perfectly, but Mildred wasn't versed in incantations for the kitchen. With a sigh, she dipped a spatula into the butter-yellow frosting and scraped it across the top of one cake.

Evelyn and Stella arrived ten minutes later. Mildred had only frosted two cakes, a yellow and a red, and started on her third. Although it had taken her a while, they were perfect.

"Oh!" Stella laughed, practically skipping to Mildred's side. "Look, she really did put Mildred to work! I can't wait to frost a couple."

"A couple?" Mildred retorted. "Try four hundred and ninety-seven."

"So much for dinner," Evelyn said, strolling in behind Stella with a lithe smile. Her hair sat in a shiny red bun at the base of her neck, accenting her thin curves beneath her peach crepe dress. "Perhaps we should just eat cakes instead of roast?"

"I certainly hope you plan on helping," Mildred said, glancing at the three cakes. "I won't even finish a tray at the rate I'm going."

"Milly can't finish a project unless her product is flawless," Stella said, grabbing an apron off a hook behind her and tying the sash. She sampled the bright orange frosting with the tip of her finger. "Oh, it's good to be together in the kitchens again. Just like old times, isn't it?"

Evelyn peered into a tub of crimson frosting, ignoring the apron Stella threw at her. She ran a finger along the edge of the bowl and popped it in her mouth. "Well, at least it tastes delicious, if we must be free slave labor again."

Mildred had just set down her third cake when Evelyn pulled up a stool and sat across from them. She propped her elbows on the table and said, "Tell me what you thought of the library this morning, Milly. It's an absolute disaster, isn't it?"

"Yes," Mildred said, reaching for another cake. Stella pulled the royal purple frosting closer and reached in with her spatula, sleeves rolled up to her elbows. "But I'll get it together."

"I'm sure you will," Evelyn said. "It's a good starting point, at any rate. At least it gets you into the castle, even if I doubt you'll take advantage of the social scene the way I do."

"No one is quite as social as you, Evie," she replied, and Evelyn perked up a bit at the praise.

"Evelyn, you've been busy lately," Stella said. "Anything fun?"

"Just the usual Assistant work," Evelyn said with a heavy sigh, drawing a circle in a blob of flour that had been left behind. "I suppose being Assistant to the High Priestess doesn't come without sacrifice of time and energy. Nell is always busy. Who are we kidding? Nell is doing most of Donovan's work on top of her own because his bad knee is acting up again. This Network would fall apart without her."

"Let's not talk business. We always talk business! Can I tell you my good news?" Stella asked, glancing from one friend to the other with a conspiratorial smile. Evelyn straightened with instant suspicion.

"What is it?" she asked. A slow, radiant smile crept across Stella's bright face.

"I'm getting married!"

"What?" Evelyn leapt to her feet. "What do you mean?"

"Dale?" Mildred asked. Stella pressed the backs of her hands to her flushed cheeks as if she needed something to keep her from flying.

"Yes!" she said in a breathy voice. "Oh, girls. It's so wonderful! *He's* wonderful! He's . . . he's just everything I have ever—"

She broke off with another delighted shake of her head, unable to finish. She gave no childish giggle the way girls had at school. She didn't ramble about all of Dale's good qualities or fall into twittering hysterics. She just shone with a bright light that made her glow from within.

Perhaps not all emotion associated with love is uncontrolled and controlling at the same time, Mildred thought in surprise. She'd always imagined that falling in love meant she'd have to give up parts of herself to the pandemonium and chaos of emotion. But Stella certainly didn't seem any different. *Perhaps love is a manageable thing. Perhaps it's something that doesn't take over one's sense of self.*

She pondered the fact that everything she had once assumed about love wasn't universal, for Stella was certainly no worse for loving Dale. Despite Mildred's apathy toward all things associated with such unpredictable emotions as love and lust, she experienced a pang of jealousy. Dale was a wonderful witch and a talented Guardian. He'd be a perfect husband, something she doubted she'd ever have herself.

And marriage? It seemed so . . . final. So *not* what Mildred had envisioned for the three of them. What about their dreams of life in the castle as politicians? Mildred had just arrived! They had so much work to do.

"What does this mean?" Evelyn finally asked, sitting so straight her spine looked like it might snap. The question encompassed so much, and yet not enough. Mildred knew what the flash of fear in Evelyn's eyes meant; she'd seen it before, on the day they found out Mildred would be moving. She felt it herself. Would all of their mutual dreams disappear? Would Stella leave the castle and not be part of their lives? They'd managed to keep the Witches' Oath, and their friendship, alive through the past years by sheer determination and sacrifice. But now they were adults and life had become much more complicated.

Stella's delicate eyebrows lifted her face into a demure smile. "You're asking me if I'd leave my career and everything I've worked for at Chatham Castle."

"Yes!" Evelyn cried in a passionate outburst. "Would you be happy as a housewife? Would you be happy without Milly and I? Screaming children and dirty diapers and—"

"I want to be a Council Member, one day, but I don't want to do it at the expense of living. I could never be High Priestess. Forbidden from marrying! What about children? What about family? No, I shall live my life and have a career," Stella said easily, with a confidence Mildred envied. "Look at Council Member Terry over the Western Covens. She has a husband and two children. I believe it makes her a better Council Member."

Since neither Evelyn nor Mildred knew what to say, and Evelyn made no attempt to hide her blatant disapproval, Mildred asked, "When is the hand fasting ceremony, Stella?"

"In a year. We'll be hand fasted the second month of next spring, back at home, when the cherry trees are blossoming. It will be lovely."

"No, Stella," Mildred said with a genuine smile and warm embrace, pushing aside all her logical fears and reservations so she could be happy for her friend. "It won't just be lovely. It will be perfect."

New Friends

The servants' dining hall lacked style. Tables cluttered every available space, packing Guardians, Assistants, maids, butlers, fireboys, and other workers right up to each wall. Wooden tables, chandeliers made of rusted wagon wheels, and a hearth big enough for ten people to stand in decorated the landscape. Yet it wasn't the sheer size of the room that cowed Mildred at first, but the number of witches filling it.

Not a chance, she thought, eyeing the teeming mass of voices and dirty plates. The quiet safety of the library beckoned her back, although it had begun to feel like a trap after she had worked in it without a break for five days.

"It's overwhelming at first," a male voice said from behind. "But not if you know where to hide. Would you like me to show you?"

She whirled around to find a Captain of the Guardians surveying the crowded prospect with a similar frown. He had no hair, warm hazel eyes, and lashes so long and dark they might have been tree branches.

"Yes," Mildred said, eager to get away from the echoing laughter. "I'd appreciate that very much."

"Excellent. Follow me."

They wove through the spaces between tables to the other side of the dining hall, and then around a corner on the far edge. The overwhelming noises muted to a manageable level. Smaller tables ran along a wall of windows that overlooked the east grounds of the castle. Only two other witches sat back amongst the fifteen or so tables.

"Lovely." Mildred set down her plate with a relieved sigh. "Thank you very much. What's your name?"

He smiled with a charming boyish quality that reminded her of Jorden. If Mildred sought attractive traits in others, which she rarely allowed herself to do, she would have considered him handsome. "My name is Marten. I always hide back here. Do you mind if I join you?"

"No. I owe you that much for showing me this spot."

"Would you like something to drink?"

Mildred settled in her chair with surprise. "Oh. That would be very kind, thank you. I'll have water."

He returned with a foaming mug of pale ipsum for himself and a frosty glass of water. "You're new, aren't you?" he asked as he sat down.

"Yes. This is my second day here. Do I seem so lost?"

"Not lost, just uncertain," he said with a wry grin. "What brings you to Chatham?"

"I'm the new librarian. My name is on the waiting list to become an Assistant."

He didn't roll his eyes or laugh at her the way Porter did. He accepted it with an easy nod, and she relaxed immediately. "Wonderful," he said. "The library needs some work."

"A lot of work. More than I can do myself, I'm afraid. I'll need to search out grimoires on home improvements. There's no budget to hire anyone to fix everything that's broken or peeling or splintered."

Marten's eyes narrowed in thought, but he shook away whatever idea captured his attention. Another spell of silence fell between them, to Mildred's relief. It gave her a second to compose her ruffled nerves. What was she supposed to say next? How did one start a conversation out of nothing with a total stranger? She avoided these awkward situations for a reason.

"You don't like small talk, do you?" he asked, studying her with twinkling eyes.

"No. I despise it."

"Then let's discuss something meaningful. Do you keep up with the *Chatterer* newsscroll? There are rumors circulating through the castle that the Almorran *Book of Spells* has been found. Again. A witch in the Southern Network keeps making a big fuss over someone stealing it from him. Something about finding it in an old farmhouse and then losing it-"

Mildred shot him a withering glare.

"That's your definition of meaningful discussion? Gossip about a book of dark magic that may or may not exist?"

He shrugged, but she saw a flash of amusement in his eyes. "Perhaps, to you, it may be. I don't know you yet. I have yet to learn what interests you, so I chose one extreme."

"You chose wrong."

"Then I'll have to find something on the other end." He chewed in thought. "All right, I think I've got one. How about the plight of our educational system? The lack of education for the poor has, in my opinion, doomed our Network to the fires of rioting and crime."

Mildred barely contained her surprise at his adept choice. There was nothing she'd rather talk about than education or the failings of their Network. "I agree," she said immediately. "The fastest route to disaster is bad education."

Marten quirked an eyebrow. "You do know about it then."

"Indeed," she said. "At least as it concerns Chatham City and her outer villages. Where are you from?"

"The Letum Wood Covens."

"Is education there as terrible as it is here?"

"Worse," he said with a shake of his head. "Far worse."

"Tell me."

"Gladly."

Mildred set down her utensils and focused her whole attention on him. By the time he finished, her food was cold.

"What a depressing discussion," she said, moving aside a pile of congealed gravy, her appetite gone. "We don't teach our poor, which means they will never advance their station in life. We've doomed them to life in the dust. Of course they react with violence! What else do they know? We haven't taught them any other way."

"It is depressing," he said, leaning back from his empty plate. He ate with speed and efficiency, like most Guardians. "But only if you plan on it continuing in that way."

Mildred stared at him in surprise for the second time.

"How would it change?"

Marten shrugged. "There are still witches in the Network that care, like Council Member Porter. The Head of Guardians, Dolph, is a good man." Marten motioned to her with a dip of his head. "You clearly care. As long as witches like us don't give in, we'll be able to fight back and create change."

"You're more optimistic than I. I tend not to think the best of witches in general."

Marten pushed his plate away and set his napkin on the table. "Sometimes an optimistic outlook is the only thing that stops witches from becoming too lazy to care. At any rate, I must be going. Thank you, Mildred, for the pleasure of this discussion. I look forward to more of them."

To her disappointment, he stood to leave. It had been a long time since she'd had such a well-founded chat with a witch besides Evelyn. A fresh buzz of life gave her renewed energy.

"I hope to see you again," she said. Marten smiled, gathered his empty plate, and disappeared around the corner.

Mildred's room was buried deep in the servants' quarters of the South Wing. She had a bed, a white dresser, a little stove for the cold winter nights, and a window not much larger than a book. Though close and tight, it sufficed, so Mildred hadn't given the utilitarian design a second thought.

Her candle floated next to her as she walked down a tight spiral staircase, belly full of warm food after dinner with Evelyn, who seemed distant and snappish. Mildred had been working at the library for two weeks now and had seen no further signs of Marten. She would have forgotten him completely if he hadn't been so blasted informed and intelligent.

She was so caught up in thinking that she didn't see a small maid sitting in the stairwell and nearly tripped over her. The thin girl pressed herself against the wall with a little shriek.

"What in the name of the good gods are you doing there?" Mildred snapped. The terrified maid dissolved into tears, her face hidden in a pair of reddened hands.

"I'm sorry!" she wailed. "I didn't see ya coming!"

"I suppose I should have been paying attention as well." Mildred's sharp tone faded. "I'm not sure how I didn't hear you in the first place, you're blubbering so loudly. What is wrong with you? Did someone die?"

The poor girl shook her head, unable to answer. She looked so pathetic and scared that Mildred's heart softened, despite her instinct to flee such an emotional creature.

"Do you have a name?" she asked.

"L-Lavinia."

"Lavinia," she said, her lips twisting. What an odd name for such a little thing. "I'm Mildred."

She stuck out her arm in greeting. Lavinia stared at her with watery, red-rimmed eyes. "What am I supposed ta do with that?" she asked, gesturing to Mildred's arm.

"You're supposed to grasp it. It's a way of introducing yourself."

Lavinia turned away with a hiccup. "I don't know social rules like ya do."

"Clearly, or you wouldn't be sobbing in a stairwell."

Lavinia curled into herself a little more, tucking her shoulders down. "Don't matter. No one cares about me! Just leave me be."

"Excellent. I'll be on my way."

"Wait!" Lavinia called as Mildred stepped down a stair. "Ya were supposed ta ask me ta tell ya again."

Mildred paused to find the logic in Lavinia's strange statement, but found none. "That doesn't make any sense. I already asked you what was wrong. Why didn't you just answer the first time?"

Lavinia shrugged. "It's what witches say."

"Well witches are idiots. Communicate exactly what you mean next time."

Lavinia nodded with large, solemn eyes.

"Now," Mildred drew in a fresh breath and began again. "What is bothering you?"

"M-my family sent me a letter," Lavinia whispered, holding up a soggy envelope. It looked like she'd used it to blow her nose.

"*That* is why you're crying?"

"Well, I can't read!" Lavinia wailed.

"Can't read? Don't they teach the servants anymore?"

Lavinia dragged the back of her arm under her nose. "Teach the servants? When did they do that?"

Mildred pulled out a handkerchief and handed it to her with a grimace.

"Try this," she said. "It's not very good manners to wipe your snot on your arm when you have to clean with it later. I certainly wouldn't want you anywhere near my room right now."

Lavinia blew her nose, mopped up her face, and extended the crumpled material back to Mildred. She waved it off and gestured to the letter. "Can't you get someone to read the letter for you?" she asked.

"Only one or two upper maids can read," she said with another hiccup. "They hate me because I used to steal their desserts, and Mrs. F is just too busy to read it for me. I miss my family so terribly and . . . and . . ."

Mildred reached over and plucked the paper from Lavinia's chapped hands, hoping to prevent another round of dramatic grief.

"Let me help," she muttered, unfurling the envelope. The handwriting, while not altogether unreadable, was difficult to make out. She read through it once to get the gist, twice to make sure she understood, then out loud the third time. Lavinia's tears changed into a wobbly smile.

"They're all right!" she cried, clapping. "My brother is back ta work after breaking his leg. I worried they wouldn't eat well with him unable to work. Thank ya for reading it. I needed ta hear from them. I feel loads better."

Mildred folded the envelope back up. Lavinia took it with a toothy smile and tucked it carefully into her pocket, as if it were a great treasure. Her outfit had erratic red stitching occasionally replaced with mismatched black and gold thread, as if completed by someone who had no idea how to use a needle. Mildred used silent magic to fix the puckered fabric, changing the thread to a uniform red and straightening the lopsided shoulders. Lavinia was too relieved about her family to notice the subtle changes.

"How long have you worked here, Lavinia?"

"Three years." Lavinia slumped back against the wall. "I started after I got in trouble stealing a pastry when I was ten."

"You're thirteen?"

"No, fourteen. I always got inta trouble stealing 'cause I was so hungry. My parents were going ta send me ta work anyway ta help pay the bills. My sister Leslee works with the High Priestess and got me the job. Sometimes I help her, but for now I just clean."

"So you never went to school?"

"School? No. I wish. But I can polish silver faster than any other maid!"

"Commendable," Mildred said in a dry tone, "but hardly progressive. Do you have any goals for your life?"

"Goals?"

"Yes. Don't you want to achieve something?"

"I want ta be the Head Housekeeper when I'm older," she said, watching Mildred's face for any sign of amusement. When none came, she continued. "The Head of Housekeeping knows just about everything that's going on, and I'd like that. Besides, I already know about secret stairwells and rooms that even she hasn't seen. I like to spy."

"You can't be Head of anything if you aren't able to read and write."

Her shoulders drooped. "I know."

"What would you say if I offered to teach you?" Mildred asked quickly, before Lavinia could cry again.

Lavinia gasped. "I want ta learn how ta read and write! I love stories so much."

Mildred knew she'd regret this—she didn't have the energy to deal with a volatile young girl—but she couldn't help herself. Lavinia needed education, and she could give it. No doubt education of servants had been cut since the Network couldn't even afford to keep most common schools open. Not to mention the state of the library. Her experience working in the castle so far painted a grim picture.

"Come to the library tomorrow on your lunch break, and I'll begin teaching you," Mildred said. "There's no reason you can't learn while you're here."

"You mean it? You'll really teach me?"

"Of course I do," Mildred retorted haughtily. "I always mean what I say."

"Thank ya!" Lavinia said, breathing rapidly. "I don't know what ta say. I-I can't pay ya—"

"It's fine." Mildred started down the stairs again. "Be on time or the lesson is canceled."

"Noon," Lavinia said, her delighted voice echoing down the hall after Mildred. "I'll be there at noon!"

Lavinia showed up at noon as promised, and brought ten other maids with her.

They filed around a heavy oak table at the back of the library and waited behind the chairs, fidgeting and nudging each other with their skinny elbows. Mildred stopped mid-step when she noticed them. Seeing the shocked look on her face, Lavinia broke away from the group and rushed forward.

"I only told one of my friends, I promise!" she said, wringing her hands together as if she'd brought a dirty dishrag from the kitchen. "But somehow word got out and . . . well . . . they all came. Aw, please don't be mad at me! Please? We all want ta learn so badly."

Lavinia bit her bottom lip, glanced at the girls, then back at Mildred. Mildred opened her mouth but closed it again. Despite the bubble of panic welling up from the bottom of her stomach, she didn't have the heart to vent her anger. Education didn't belong to one witch.

"It's fine." She hadn't mentally prepared for a crowd and had to do so rather promptly, something she wasn't inclined to do.

"So ya will still teach us?" Lavinia asked.

"Yes."

Lavinia whirled around, her arms spread. "She'll teach us!"

A mutual cry rose from the girls. Mildred, forgetting her anxiety, stepped forward. "Be quiet!" she snapped. "This is a library."

The maids fell silent. Lavinia gave a quick curtsy and hustled back to her seat, grinning. Mildred, seeing that she had control of the group, calmed.

"Very well," she said, her voice severe. "While I don't like surprises, I'm willing to make an exception. As long as everyone agrees to do what I say and takes learning seriously, I shall teach all of you."

Several heads bobbed in emphatic, silent enthusiasm. Mildred swallowed. They all *seemed* friendly enough.

"Let's begin your education," she said, warming to the idea of conducting her own small class. "You may be seated."

While magic hadn't ever been easy, Mildred had excelled in subjects like reading and writing, so starting the class felt natural. The maids remained silent during the duration of the lesson, responded as appropriate, and eventually left with murmured thanks and a promise to return the next day. Mildred let out a long breath, startled to find that she'd enjoyed the hour.

"Well," she said to herself, smoothing her dress. "That wasn't so bad. Far better than shelving books, anyway."

Moments after they departed, the boom of marching feet drew her attention to the hallway. The double doors of the library burst open and an entire contingent of Guardians trooped in. Their burly bodies took up all the space as they filtered around broken chairs in a half-formation. They bowed their heads, clasped their hands behind their backs, and stood straight as arrows.

"What is this?"

"We're here to help you restore the library," a voice said. Marten appeared from behind the wall of muscular bodies. "I apologize for the delay, but I had to take a contingent on a two-week detail. Hopefully we aren't too late to help."

"Oh, no. You're not too late." She gestured to the still-broken library walls. "Obviously."

Marten smiled. "Good."

He said something in the Guardian language, and the group dissolved into four clumps of four.

"These four will restore the ceiling, these four will clean, these four will fix the broken furniture, and I will take these four to fix the bookshelves," he said. "Between the seventeen of us, I think we should have it covered."

Mildred laughed in spite of herself. His thoroughness and organization made him quite attractive. "This sounds wonderful. I don't know how to thank you."

"Dinner tonight should do it." Marten winked at her. "I'll see you there. Fall out, boys! We've got work to do for the lady. Do good work, or she won't grant me another date!"

Before she could utter another syllable, sixteen Guardians and Marten split off to their duties. They cleaned with precision, banged wood against wood, shouted back and forth to each other, moved around like elephants, and, in time, restored the library to a fresh, pristine condition. The water marks on the ceiling faded, leaving vibrant paintings in their wake. They straightened shelves, collected books together, and polished wall sconces until they shone with new light.

"My goodness," Mildred whispered, whirling around only a few hours later. "It looks . . . well, it looks marvelous."

Marten came up to her, hands clasped behind his back. A twinkle of pride glinted from his soft eyes.

"They're good workers."

"I can't imagine why this hadn't been done before," she said, eyeing a statue that had been uncovered from a back room. "It didn't take too long."

"Not at all."

She turned to him. "Thank you, Marten. You've given me a great gift. I even feel as if I could stand working here for eight years if I have to."

His bald brow furrowed. "Eight years?"

She laughed it off. "Don't worry about it. Just accept my sincere appreciation."

"I'll see you tonight at dinner," he said, bowing. "It was my pleasure to earn the honor of your company, Miss Mildred."

"Tonight," she said, returning his smile. "I'll be there."

Marten and his contingent filtered out, leaving an impressed Mildred standing in the middle of the library floor. Left to herself, and reeling in the aftermath of Marten's warm smile, she sank to a chair.

"Maybe it won't be so bad working in a library," she concluded, thinking of her fledgling reading class and dinner with Marten. "It's not what I expected, but I may even enjoy my time here."

She let out a contented sigh and sank back into the soft cushions to enjoy the clean silence for the first time since her arrival weeks before.

Hand Fasted

Mildred's first year as librarian passed like a recurring dream. She shelved books, taught reading classes to the maids, helped Stella with hand fasting preparations, discussed political history with Evelyn over tea, and enjoyed the sweetness of living life with her best friends again. The harrowing memory of Mother's unexpected death faded, losing its grip on her heart. She thrived in the organized structure of the library, wrote Jorden weekly letters, and shared debates over dinner with Marten every night.

"Perfect," she said to herself one bright afternoon after winter had faded. "It's a perfect spring day."

She stopped walking in the middle of the James' dirt driveway and pulled in a long, sweet draught of cherry-blossom tinged air. The afternoon sun warmed her face, washing away the cold, drafty days of her first winter cooped up in the chilly stone halls of Chatham Castle. A soft spring breeze drifted by, releasing blooms from the trees in a waterfall of petals. It felt wonderful to step away from the library for a while.

"Isn't this a beautiful day for a hand fasting ceremony?" she asked Marten. He walked quietly at her side, as if they were taking their weekly stroll through the gardens at Chatham.

"Yes," he said, glancing at the pockets of white-blossomed cherry trees surrounding the James' imposing estate. "It feels wonderful to be in the sun again."

Mildred fell back into a comfortable silence, grateful that she could just *be* with Marten and not feel as if she had to entertain him with small talk.

They approached a red brick mansion ringed by cherry orchards on the left and apple orchards on the right. Trees surrounded the estate in an endless skirt of blossoms and perfume. Freshly scrubbed windows sparkled in the late sunshine, and tables laden with food stretched across the open lawn.

"I used to sleep over here in the summer when I had a break from Miss Jane's. It was a lovely time," Mildred said with a fond smile, waving to Agatha, Stella's plump, bright-eyed mother. "Thank you for coming with me, Marten. I loathe meeting new people. At least now I have someone with whom to sit and won't have to avoid small talk with strangers."

He laughed. "The more I learn about you, the more miraculous I consider our friendship to be. I love meeting new people."

She sent him a sidelong glance. "Very odd."

Marten laughed again. "Dale and I have known each other since he joined the Guardians, so it was my pleasure to come. Oh, how odd. I never expected to see him here."

Marten had paused mid-step, facing the opposite side of the yard. A tall pole pierced the sky, decorated on top with ribbons fluttering in a gentle breeze.

"Who?" Mildred asked, trying to follow his gaze.

"Council Member Grant is here. He's standing by Evelyn." Marten motioned toward them with a jerk of his head. "He doesn't seem as if he's enjoying himself, does he? Evelyn must have brought him. I can't imagine why else he'd be here."

"He's her beau of sorts," Mildred said. "Neither of them will admit it—I think because they both want to flirt with whomever they want—but Evie spends a lot of time with him."

"Grant, a beau?" Marten's face wrinkled. "I doubt it. I can't imagine he'd ever like anyone more than he liked himself."

"Sounds like he'd be perfect for Evelyn."

"Speaking of your friend, there she is now."

He gestured to a group of girls surrounding Evelyn's perfectly coiffed red hair. Her old school chums. Mildred recognized a few of the faces and felt no desire to interfere. She hadn't been overly fond of the girls from Miss Mabel's School for Girls whenever she had visited and veered away from them now, doubly grateful for Marten's company.

Grant stood a few steps away from Evelyn and her crowd. A cheroot dangled from his lips, which he removed only to take a sip of wine. The young women spoke in near shouts, each competing to be heard over the others as they debated the way the ribbons should weave around the pole.

"I haven't officially met Grant yet," Mildred admitted. "Evelyn doesn't really bring him around. It's like she wants to keep us separate from him or something. Nor do I see him around the castle because, well, I don't really get out much."

"You aren't missing anything," Marten said under his breath. "He's run the Bickers Mill Covens for a few years. He met Donovan while at the tailor's, and so enchanted the High Priest with his droll wit and penchant for expensive attire that Donovan hired him as Council Member the moment the next slot became available."

"You're joking, right?" Mildred asked, her tone dry, mouth curled in disgust. Marten shook his head, his lips pursed in a way that suggested he wished he was.

"Dolph and I have worked with Grant on a few issues in his Covens. He's amiable enough and certainly has the good looks to back up his sociability, but he cares nothing for business. He delegates most of his job to other witches."

A pasted smile slipped across Marten's face when Grant hailed him, striding over on long, sure legs. Grant appeared to be a brash, thirty-something witch who smelled of tobacco leaves. His chiseled, fresh-shaven jaw gave him a handsome, if sardonic, expression that left Mildred annoyed.

Yes, he'd be perfect for Evelyn.

"Grant," Marten said jovially, taking his forearm. Despite herself, Mildred was impressed with Marten's display; she could never act so pleased to see someone so unexpected. It took all her energy some days just to visit Stella and Evelyn. "It's good to see a fellow male witch here."

Grant laughed and dropped his cheroot to the grass, where he ground it in with his heel. "Yes. You and I will let all the ladies simper and giggle for a while so they can get it out of their systems. The good gods know Evelyn loves the attention. Enough about them! What do you think of this new jacket? Is it all right for a hand fasting ceremony?"

Marten's polite expression didn't change. "Looks very nice."

Grant adjusted the sleeves. "I found a witch in Ashleigh that charges exorbitant rates but makes me look like a god, so it's worth it."

A rustle in the grass just behind Mildred shifted her attention from Grant's less-than-fascinating conversation to the sensation that someone stood just behind her. No one could be seen.

"Milly," Stella's hushed voice implored softly in her left ear. "Come speak with me, won't you? Just on the side of the house? I'm so nervous . . . I don't want to face anyone else yet."

Marten's eyes flickered their direction as Mildred picked up her skirt, nodded to both him and Grant—who hadn't stopped talking about his new coat—and made her way to the side of the house. The sun sank closer to the spiny trees, casting long shadows on the grass. Once the sounds of the party were well behind them, Stella materialized next to Mildred.

"Oh, Stella," Mildred said, holding her at arm's distance. "You look truly stunning."

Stella beamed and took Mildred's hands.

"Do you like it?"

The gold stitching on Stella's layered ivory gown glimmered in the fading sunshine. Gently curling strands of light brown hair, streaked with a tawny tinge, fell onto her shoulders, every piece looking as purposeful and perfect as if it had been set there individually.

"Your eyes have never been so blue nor so happy. I'm very excited for you!"

"Oh, Mildred, I'm a jumble of nerves!" she said, laughing. "We almost didn't get the dress finished in time. Wouldn't that have been the worst?"

"What are you so nervous about?" Mildred asked. "It's only Dale and your best friends here. He already knows your faults."

"What if I say the wrong thing?" she cried, but giggled when Mildred rolled her eyes. "Or what if I trip and fall off the platform?"

"Dale will catch you," Mildred quipped. "He's still very young and spry."

"Were you and Marten able to move everything into our new apartment in downtown Chatham?"

"Yes. Evelyn and I moved all of your things. Marten and a few other Guardians moved Dale's. I swept it and cleaned it up a bit to make sure it was tidy when you came home. Evelyn was going to get you some groceries, but she forgot."

Stella smiled. "Sounds just like her. Thank you, Milly. It won't be so hard getting married and moving away from the castle again knowing I shall still see you whenever I want. And you can transport to my apartment any time you need it."

"Of course, Stella. This is good change, not bad change. None of us have any reason to fear."

"I knew you'd make me feel better. You always do. Oh, thank you for coming, Mildred. I couldn't have gone through it without you."

"Don't be daft," Mildred said, though she felt a pang of envy deep in her heart. "You would have done fine without anyone else here. You could have run off to Newberry with the rest of the heathens and been handfasted by a cheap High Witch that makes currency preying on amorous young couples like you and Dale."

Stella clutched her sides, in stitches. "Oh stop! You'll make me cry."

"Have you seen Dale?"

"No." Stella shook her head, then her eyes widened. "Have you? How does he look? Is he here on time? Were his parents here?"

"I haven't seen him. I only—"

A bell rang across the yard three times, stopping her response. Both girls paused, their ears turned to the front porch from whence the sound came.

"The hand fasting ceremony will begin in ten minutes," called the droll voice of the James' butler. "The bride asks that you all be in your seats five minutes before the ceremony begins."

Stella turned back to Mildred. "I suppose that includes the bride?"

"Only at some weddings," Mildred said with a wry smile. "Take your time, Stell. They certainly won't start without you."

Stella shimmered like the setting sun when she joined Dale on an elevated platform just outside the orchard. An arbor decorated with bouquets of cherry blossoms gave the bride and groom the appearance of floating through piles of cloud. Rays of sunlight twisted through the trees and flowers in strands of gold and crimson.

The officiating Coven Leader, a short, squat man with no neck and very large hands, called for the crowd to quiet.

"The hand fasting ceremony will now begin," he said, looking up at Stella, who shone with dappled shadows and light.

"Are you Stella?" he asked.

"I am."

"What is your desire?"

Stella smiled, tears of joy sparkling in her eyes. "To be made one with Dale."

"Are you Dale?"

Dale's deep response rang over the crowd. "I am."

"What is your desire?"

He couldn't contain his jaunty grin. "To be made one with Stella."

The chubby Coven Leader smiled on both of them. "Then let us begin the ceremony."

At Stella's insistence, the Coven Leader kept the ceremony brief and sweet. By the time he'd finished his remarks, sniffles punctuated the congregation, and Agatha wept at her husband's side.

"Stella, Dale." The Coven Leader brought their hands together and clasped them firmly before him. "You are now hand fasted together for as long as the love between you shall last. Be happy. So mote it be."

"So mote it be," Mildred murmured with the rest of the congregation. Stella and Dale embraced in a lovers' kiss underneath the blooming flowers, accompanied by a raucous, frenzied whoop from the crowd. Stella's words rang through Mildred's mind as she stood and applauded her friend who, at that moment, seemed far braver than she.

I want to be a Council Member one day, but I don't want to do it at the expense of living. I could never be High Priestess. Forbidden from marrying! What about children? What about family? No, I shall live my life and have a career.

"Make it a beautiful life, Stella," Mildred whispered, smiling at her best friend. "Live it for me."

A Wonderful Secret

"It was a lovely opera," Evelyn said with a sigh, stepping into the warm summer evening. "I do love a dramatic ending."

"An acceptable twenty-third birthday gift?" Grant enquired with a droll lift of his eyebrows. Making Evelyn happy was a challenge few dared to tackle. Fortunately, Grant was just bored enough with his job to care.

"Yes! The past few months have been unbearably boring. Stella is always with her new husband, and Mildred lives in her own little world in the library. I think she has something going on there, but I can't figure out what it is. Far too many servants loiter around her."

Grant rolled his eyes. "Let's not talk about them. Let's get some food."

"I think I'd love a good drink of tea to close out my birthday celebrations," she said, pointing across the street. "You can get some food there."

"Tea?" Grant cried, flicking the ashes off the end of his cheroot and grinding them with his foot. "Don't you mean ipsum? It's too hot out for tea. It's summertime!"

Her nose wrinkled. "It's my birthday, Grant. We're getting tea, and you'll like it. I told my friends I couldn't make our annual tea party because of this date, so I must have tea with you instead."

"Very well," Grant muttered. "As you wish." He draped her skinny arm through his, and together they stepped away from the stage house and onto the well-kept streets of downtown Ashleigh.

Unlike Chatham City, Ashleigh was clean and manicured and smelled like cinnamon-roasted almonds instead of sewer rats. Patrolling Guardians kept homeless vagrants away. Donovan considered Ashleigh the greatest city in the Network and spared more Guardians to protect the streets and maintain the law than he sent to patrol the Central Network's borders. Grant didn't really care, except Ashleigh had a more prestigious social scene and more tailors to suit his requirement for expert fashion.

Evelyn managed to tug him across the street and into a quaint little tea house. Wallpaper sprigged with tiny flowers decorated the walls and backed the shelves of china. Grant lit the end of a hand-rolled cheroot while Evelyn chose a pale pink tea set rimmed with gold, requested a raspberry leaf blend from the hostess, and settled in a cozy table near the front window.

"Really, Grant? A cheroot in here?"

"Ah, she doesn't mind," he said, gesturing with a careless hand to the bumbling old woman that owned the shop. "It's not a smelly mix, Evie. My gardeners gave me the finest, most expensive mix of herbs and tobacco. I'm Council Member over the best herb gardeners in all of Antebellum. It's one of the perks."

She rolled her eyes, then leaned forward and took his hand across the table. "I've got a wonderful secret I'd like to tell you, Grant. That's why I ditched my friends and wanted you to myself tonight."

"Are you sure it wasn't just for the free entertainment?" he asked wryly, smoke trailing between his lips.

"I'm serious. May I trust you?"

He snuffed out the cheroot in his palm with a wicked smile. Seeing Evelyn pretend to be serious about anything except her social life was always amusing. "You could trust me with anything, funny girl."

Evelyn glanced out of the corner of her eye to make sure the squat old lady wasn't eavesdropping. "I have a few ideas on how to pull the Network out of the trouble we're headed for, and I need your help doing it. What do you say?"

"Sure you do," he said, chuckling and reaching inside his pocket to find his watch. "You've always wanted to save the world."

She recoiled, tossing his hand away from her. His eyes jerked up to her in surprise. "What's wrong?" he asked, a bit of ash dribbling to the table from his cheroot.

Evelyn leaned back in the chair and folded her arms across her chest. "Mock me if you must. I'll not tell you a single secret ever again. You lost your chance and shall never regain it!"

Grant blinked several times, staring at his rejected hand. He couldn't imagine what had come over the fickle thing. "I had no idea you meant it so seriously, Evie. I understand now. Give me a second chance?"

"No," she said, turning her face to the window.

Grant took her hand, feeling a surge of hope when she didn't pull away. "Aw, don't be like that, darling. Please?"

She met his eyes briefly, hesitated, and softened. "Do you mean it, Grant? Will you support me?"

His eyes narrowed with a moment of uncertainty. "Is it dangerous?" he asked.

"Very."

His forehead furrowed into concerned lines. He simply didn't know how to respond. This was a new side to Evelyn that he hadn't anticipated, and he wasn't entirely certain he liked it. It was so . . . fastidious. "My goodness. I've never seen you this serious."

Evelyn leaned into the table again.

"I'm dedicating my life to this idea," she whispered. "I've been planning it for ages now. May is my mentor and helps me with the big things but trusts the details to me. I need to start finding witches with the same ideals." She reached up to trail the tip of her finger down his face with a hopeful smile. "I thought of you first, of course."

Grant couldn't help but feel skeptical because he didn't really have ideals. He'd often entertained Evelyn's impulsive ideas because she amused him and was an attractive enough distraction, but seeing the serious intent on her face set him back. He didn't like pleasure to get too mixed up with business. In fact, he really didn't like business at all, and this reeked of it.

"What exactly are you talking about doing?" he asked warily.

Evelyn lifted a shrewd eyebrow. "Do you swear to not speak of it to another living soul?"

He gave her a trying, half-hearted smile of amusement. "Of course." She stuck out her arm.

"Then make a vow with me."

"A vow?" he repeated, eyes widening. "Evelyn, what is this about?"

"I shan't tell you until I have complete confidence that you won't betray me."

Grant studied her eyes, which had darkened into disks of the deepest emerald. The owner of the shop bustled over and set down the teapot and two glasses. Evelyn didn't break eye contact, even while the woman placed a complimentary plate of scones between them and departed.

Grant glanced at Evelyn's hand, then her face, and finally grasped her forearm. "Very well," he said, already regretting it. Evelyn smiled and whispered the incantation so quietly he couldn't make it out. The magic of the vow started at her palm and transferred to his.

"I vow to tell you my secret if you vow on your life to never betray all that I am about to tell you."

"I accept."

The magic thrummed, spiraling through his arm in a bead of light until it slipped into his chest and disappeared, like someone pulling a string through his heart. Grant, suddenly weary from all this seriousness, sank back in his seat.

"Well?" he asked. Evelyn reached for the teapot and began to pour.

"I want to change the Network. I want to prevent violence and unnecessary death. The poor are beginning to take over under Donovan's reign, and I plan to see that they don't. I'm going to become the most powerful witch in the Central Network and clean up this mess." She slid a teacup across the table toward him with a bright smile. "Even if I have to get rid of some witches to do it."

His composure faltered. "The good gods," he choked out. "Evelyn, you could be speaking of treason!"

"Which is why you aren't going to tell anyone," she hissed. Her face melted into rapturous joy. "Oh, it's so exciting to think of having such power and making things work better, isn't it?"

Her eyes blazed with passion, so much so that Grant reared back to separate himself from her pocket of madness. If he began to care too much about anything, the way Evelyn did in fits and bursts, it would lead to more problems and less pleasure.

"This is quite serious, Evie."

"Yes, it is. Which is why you and May and I are the only witches that know about it for now. Not even Stella or Mildred know yet. Our main goal *must* be to get me into power as soon as possible, for I can't change anything as an Assistant."

Change what? He wanted to know, but the light in her eyes was such that he dared not ask and wondered, with some fear, what he should do. "This could be dangerous for me. Why should I support you in something that could lead to our deaths?"

A flash of anger rippled through her electric eyes but settled after a moment. "A fair question," she said. "Do you want to improve the Network?"

He shrugged. "I don't really care."

Her eyes narrowed in pinched thought. "Then what if I promised you more currency and power?"

"More currency?" He leaned forward. "What exactly do you mean?"

Evelyn smiled. "If you help me, I will give you power and wealth you've never dreamed of having. Help me reform the Central Network into a safer place, and we shall be powerful together. No more oppression from the poor. No more riots in the night."

He sucked in a sharp breath. Well, if currency were involved, that would be a different situation altogether. "It's a steep proposition. Sounds like a lot of work, really. You know how I feel about working too much."

"It will be a lot of work. The Network is a mess, but I'll do most of it. I'll just include you when I need you every now and then, that's all."

"And the reward will be the same?"

"The very same."

Grant forced himself back into his usual expression of indolent disregard lest Evelyn see his building excitement. Little work but more power and wealth? A perfect proposition. Besides, Evie had a wild look in her eye he didn't trust and certainly wouldn't fight.

Truth be told, if any witch could pull off such a wild plan, she could. The idea of power had a certain appeal. With enough currency he could pay a servant to remove the cheroot from his mouth if he wanted. He sighed. Becoming a Council Member had made his life decidedly more complicated.

But not always in the worst ways.

"All right, Evie, I shall support you. But don't rely on me too much, will you?"

"Of course not. It's a long way off, of course. As May says, we must be patient if we want to bring about change."

Grant thought of what he could do with more currency, then shrugged the whole uncomfortable mess off to think about later.

"Now, Evie. Let's talk about your plans for the rest of the night. I'm ravenous, and I don't mean for scones."

Interruptions

"I want all of you to make your own cards with each letter of the alphabet drawn on one side. Quiz yourself in preparation for the test next week. Are there any questions?"

Mildred's hawk-like eyes scanned the classroom, catching a movement in the corner near the door. Council Member Porter slipped into the room, eyebrows pulled low. Her heart skipped a beat. She hadn't exactly *asked* permission to hold classes again for the servants. Her evening reading class was so full it nearly burst out the window of her old classroom in the servants' quarters. It was a surly summer evening. So many witches had come that half of them had to stand in the sticky heat.

"Don't forget to bring a quill if you have one," she continued as if she hadn't noticed Porter lurking in the back. "I'll provide as many as I can, but if we're this full, I can't guarantee you'll have your own. Thank you for coming. You're dismissed."

The class hesitated.

"Well?" she cried. "What are you waiting for? Leave! I have another class in twenty minutes."

Porter pressed himself against the wall as witches filed by, greeting them by name. Mildred watched the servants carefully, noticing their easy smiles and warm affection toward the Council Member. The fact that a busy Council Member—a member of the upper class—would know the individual names of the workers eased her fears. She hadn't even told her friends about her push for servant education. Knowing

Evelyn's views on the poor, and uncertain that Stella could keep a secret from Evelyn's shrewd mind, Mildred had simply said nothing.

"We aren't doing anything wrong!" Lavinia squeaked when she passed Porter, her hair pasted to the sides of her neck from the damp heat. "We aren't breaking any rules, Council Member! Please don't get mad at Miss Mildred!"

He smiled to reassure her. "Of course not, Lavinia. Miss Mildred is not in trouble."

Though she wouldn't admit to uneasy discomfort in the first place, Mildred breathed a bit better after his promise. The eraser cleaned off the chalkboard in the meantime. Chairs and long tables slid back in order of their own accord. Textbooks flew over to her desk from the tables and stacked themselves in a neat pile. Mildred orchestrated the cleanup without much thought. Teaching had increased her own magical powers, as if sharing knowledge expanded her abilities. Being around so many witches didn't exhaust her the way it used to, either. Standing behind the desk put her in a different frame of mind, like a barrier preventing her hatred of social events from taking over. In fact, she looked forward to seeing her pupils.

"Do you mind if I talk with you a minute?" Porter asked once the last student had gone. He wore a freshly pressed white shirt that brought attention to the white hues of his gray hair.

"I have a few minutes to spare."

With the absence of bodies, the temperature of the room fell several degrees. Mildred motioned for him to take a seat, but he opted to lean against a table instead. She didn't know him well but doubted he would have been so genial if he'd come to shut the operation down.

"Is something wrong, Council Member?"

"No, nothing's wrong. I've been hearing rumors that education for the servants had started back up again and wanted to find out who was running it. How long has this been going on?"

"Since I started as librarian, really. It was smaller then but has grown."

"Over a year now?"

"Yes. I run classes every evening and during the day."

His eyes widened. "Really?"

"Yes."

"On top of your work in the library?"

"Yes."

"How many classes?"

"At least six per day."

"I had no idea you were educating so many. What subjects?"

"Many," she said. "Most of them need the basics since they can't read or write. Mrs. F asked me to teach some of the younger cooks incantations that will help them in the kitchen because she doesn't have the time to critique all of them."

"And you know all the kitchen spells?" he asked in surprise.

"I do now. Mrs. F taught them to me one night, and now I'm teaching the rest of the kitchen staff at a slower pace. It's helping efficiency, although many of them are still learning."

"Impressive," he murmured, glancing around.

"Do you have any objections?" she asked when the silence became unbearable.

"No," he said. "Quite the opposite, in fact. I can't offer to pay you more because of what you're doing—"

"I'm not doing it for the currency."

Porter smiled. "I never thought you were. Since I can't give you currency, please accept my appreciation. It's not every librarian that would set up something so expansive. I hated firing the teacher that taught the servants and their children. Resources have been very tight." His eyes grew distant. "They'll never really succeed in life without an education, and I would never willingly doom them to servitude for the rest of their lives. Do you mind if I ask . . . that is . . . why *are* you doing it? "

"Education doesn't belong to one witch."

He seemed to digest that for a moment, then smiled. "Well, Mildred. Carry on." He paused halfway to the door before spinning back around on his heel. "Let me know if you have any problems, will you? If anyone approaches you about it, send them to me. I'll take care of it."

The queer look in his eyes unsettled her, but he left the room before she could ask what he meant. *Problems? Who would approach me?*

Mildred stared at the door, then sat in the chair with a sigh. What a strange experience working as a librarian had become. She remained only a moment longer before gaining her feet and preparing for her next class, Beginning Potions.

"I have a new idea, Lavinia," Mildred said one morning during the second month of Fall, setting an old grimoire on the rough-hewn table top between them. "Look at what I've found."

Lavinia, who sat studiously straight and proper the way Mildred insisted, glanced up from a book of poetry. Her eyes skimmed over the page Mildred showed her, but she didn't seem to comprehend the tight writing and ancient words.

"What is it, Miss Mildred?"

"That," Mildred said, pointing to a collection of words in the middle of the page, "is a spell I think we can use to communicate with most of the students. They wouldn't have to worry about writing letters or sneaking to the library during work to ask me a question."

Lavinia's eyes widened. "Really?"

"Yes, really. You and I will be the first to try it. What do you think?"

"Of course!"

Mildred placed her hand, palm down, on the table by Lavinia and studied the book for several quiet moments.

"I think I've got it," she said. "Now pay attention and watch my middle finger. I'm not sure this will work on my first attempt, but let's try."

Mildred whispered the spell under her breath. A warm tingle started at the bottom of her palm, then radiated through her nerves and into the tips of her fingers. Within a flash, her hand felt hot. A thousand prickles developed under her skin in a swirl. As quickly as it came, the sensation disappeared, leaving a faint light around her middle finger between the second and third knuckle in the shape of a ring. Specks of light appeared above it, one at a time, until Lavinia had to glance away from the brightness. Once it faded, two light gray tattoos remained behind. A whirling ring around her finger sat below the head of a lioness and between the two knuckles closest to her palm.

"What is it?" Lavinia asked, breathless. Mildred opened and closed her hand in a fist. The tingling lingered like the discomfort of plunging a cold hand into very warm water.

"It's called a silenda," Mildred said, staring at it with a furrowed brow. She certainly hadn't intended to put a lioness on her hand. "It's a communication spell."

"What is the lioness?"

"My personal symbol, I suppose," she said, lifting her hand to inspect it. "The grimoire said that every witch's symbol would be different, based on their personality and magic. I suppose I'm a lioness. Now give me your hand."

Lavinia hesitated. "Does it hurt?"

"Felt like a very warm bee sting."

Lavinia rolled her eyes and dropped her hand in Mildred's. "Father used to take the belt to my back when I got in trouble stealing, so a bee sting's nothing."

Mildred skimmed the grimoire again, finding a different spell for extending the silenda to another witch. She pressed their palms together and entwined their fingers.

"I have to bind you to the magic of my silenda," she said, translating the directions. "Whenever you use this spell to communicate, it will draw from my power."

Lavinia recoiled in horror. "I can't take from your magic, Miss Mildred! What if I drain it all?"

"I doubt you could if you tried," Mildred said with a droll smile. "It doesn't sound like it requires much magic. I won't even notice it, I think. The grimoire says, if I'm reading it correctly, that it can be used with hundreds of witches depending on the power of the witch giving it."

Lavinia didn't say a word throughout the process; she just stared with intense concentration at the light swirling on her middle finger. When it finished, she pulled away and inspected her hand.

"My symbol is a quill!" Her face scrunched in confusion. "Why do you think it's a quill?"

"Perhaps it's something you have to learn about yourself."

Lavinia drifted into thought until Mildred brought her back to the present.

"Now I'll teach you how it works on a basic level, although it can be quite complicated if you want more organization," she said. "Don't worry about the deeper levels; that's something I'll figure out later when we have more students involved. This magic is really quite simple, which is why I chose it. You repeat the incantation and state whatever message you want to send. The shorter, the better. The silenda will transfer the message to my hand. Let me show you."

Mildred used silent magic for the incantation and sent a message. The quill on Lavinia's hand rearranged itself into the shape of Mildred's growling lioness, and the words, *Don't forget your homework,* appeared where the ring had once been. They faded after ten seconds, leaving the ring and Lavinia's quill behind. Lavinia cracked a wide grin.

"It worked!" she breathed. "Oh, Miss Mildred, this is simply wonderful! It will be so easy now."

Lavinia practiced the incantation, and a careful pronunciation of her words, until she was correct every time.

"Thank you, Miss Mildred!"

"I'll need to extend the silenda to the rest of the students," Mildred said, already mapping out a plan. "We'll do it during class, I suppose. That will be easiest. For those who can't read, I'll send a message through the silenda an hour before class starts as a reminder. They can at least recognize my picture. Or I'll send the homework assignment. There are many possibilities, and this will prevent the flood of letters and the streams of students leaving work to ask questions."

"Of course, Miss Mildred!" Lavinia said, beaming. "I'm honored that you would trust me to be the first to receive it."

The shuffle of approaching feet recalled Mildred to her feet and her job. No doubt there were annoyed library patrons trying to find her.

"Thank you, Lavinia," she said. "I shall see you later this weekend."

Mildred slipped between the bookshelves, disappearing into the bowels of the library without another word.

I'll Protect You

Evelyn shut the door to Nell's stuffy office with a sigh of relief. The chilly air of the hall revived her from her sleepy state. Sitting in a chair reviewing paperwork all day made her grouchy, tired, and hungry. She longed for the refreshing distraction of people and conversation.

"I hope Donovan's little dinner gathering isn't over," she muttered, pinning her wild red hair into a loose bun at her neck. "Or I'll be very upset."

The halls were unusually quiet; then again, she *had* been working very late for Nell on a special project. A recent snowstorm left delicate swirls of frost on the windowpanes when she walked past, her burgundy dress rustling as she shivered in the cold halls. An unfamiliar sound stopped her. She stood in the middle of the corridor until the noise came again from just around the corner to her left. A muted cry followed.

"No! Please, no!"

Evelyn slipped around the corner and halted. Donovan lay on the ground like a beached whale. A feminine pair of lace slippers stuck out from beneath his massive legs, where a hint of a dress lay on the floor.

"Oh, a jolly one!" Donovan said, his sausage-like fingers clamped over the mouth and nose of a young girl Evelyn had seen before. Tears streaked the poor girl's face as she thrashed back and forth, trying to scream. Perspiration wetted Donovan's hair while he struggled to subdue her with one hand and keep her silenced with the other. "I like them feisty!"

"Well, well," Evelyn murmured with a smile. "Merry meet, Donovan," she called, striding toward them. "Just what do you think you're doing?"

He tried to twist his head around, but she cast a paralyzing incantation. His moist face dropped, nearly smacking the girl on the nose. The rest of his body went limp.

"Help!" the young woman screamed, shaking Donovan's hand off her face and pulling in a deep breath. "Please, help!"

"There, there," Evelyn said, kneeling next to the girl and shoving Donovan's arm off her neck. "Be still. I'm here to help."

The girl panted, pinned beneath Donovan's vast girth, tears and snot streaked across her face. Evelyn used another incantation to roll Donovan off her, and the girl scrambled to freedom with a sob.

"Hush," Evelyn crooned. "Everything will be all right."

The girl had round cheeks and pale blonde eyelashes that matched her mussed hair. She couldn't have been older than fourteen. The sleeve of an elegant evening gown dangled from her left shoulder. Evelyn whispered a calming blessing. The girl's shuddering gasps slowed into ragged, deep pants.

"What's your name?" Evelyn asked.

"A-Aneeta," the girl whispered, wiping her face with the back of her arm. "My name's Aneeta."

"I'm Evelyn."

"I know who you are. Everyone knows who you are."

"Yes, they do, don't they? You seem familiar."

"My uncle works here."

"Who is your uncle?"

"Noah, the Head of Protectors," she said in a tremulous voice. Her bottom lip quivered. "I'm here visiting. Just for a day or two. My parents are on vacation. Please! Take me to him. I'm scared!"

Evelyn leaned back in surprise. Donovan had just attempted to rape the beloved niece of his Head of Protectors. Talented, dangerous Noah would kill Donovan before he could wake from his drunken stupor.

You make your own luck, sang May's voice in the back of her mind. *Just keep your eyes open, and you'll find chances to be great.*

Evelyn's heart hammered with a sudden rush of energy and giddiness. She'd just stumbled on the opportunity of a lifetime! With careful management, she could make things happen that even May would be proud of. The very idea made her buzz with renewed life.

Evelyn glanced over her shoulder at Donovan's prostrate body. The unshaven hairs of his pudgy chin held on to several crumbs from dinner. Wine stained the front of his shirt, blending with the sharp tang of ipsum. He stared blankly at the ceiling, unable to move on his own, although he could still hear and see.

She would have to play this very carefully.

"I'm sorry this happened, Aneeta," she said. "I'm so glad I stumbled down this way to save you. I'm going to move Donovan to his office. Can you walk with me?"

Aneeta snuck a glance at Donovan before nodding. Taking it as a good sign, Evelyn helped her stand. She trembled like an aspen leaf in the wind. Once straightened, her knees gave out. Evelyn caught her before she fell.

"Put your arm around me," Evelyn instructed. "We'll go together."

Aneeta hesitated, her dilated eyes darting everywhere at once.

"Donovan can't hurt you now. I'll make sure he never touches you again. Understand? As soon as we get him in his office, I'll take you right to your uncle. That's a good girl."

Evelyn cast another incantation on Donovan and started toward the High Priest's office down the hall to the left. His flaccid body trailed behind them.

"Just in here," Evelyn said, turning. "Have a seat."

Aneeta fell into a chair near the fire, her entire body shuddering. She folded her arms across her middle, her face pale and eyes wide, and stared at the floor.

"Now for you," Evelyn muttered, facing Donovan with a raised eyebrow. She lifted him with a magical spell onto an extra wide couch made for his expansive body. Once he lay there, she released the paralyzing incantation. Instead of leaping off the couch in a fury, as most witches would have done, Donovan didn't so much as twitch. Except for the grating sound of his deep snore, he didn't change at all. She pulled the key from his front pocket and tucked it into her own.

"I'll take that, thank you."

Evelyn carefully approached Aneeta, who was now in a deep daze.

"Aneeta, let's find your uncle," she whispered, brushing her shoulder with a gentle hand. Aneeta leapt off the chair, but relaxed when she saw Evelyn. Evelyn wrapped an arm around Aneeta's shaking shoulders again.

"That's a good girl," Evelyn murmured, guiding her into the hallway and locking the door behind them. "Pick up your feet. There we go. You're going to be just fine."

Noah had the shoulders of an ox and the sleuthing ability of a panther.

He'd started as one of the youngest Heads of Protectors in Network history. Instead of protecting the Central Network in an organized mass like the Guardians, the Protectors were a quiet Brotherhood of thirteen exceptionally skilled male witches who spied, crossed enemy lies, and performed any sneaky, dangerous magical work the Highest Witch or Head of Guardians needed done.

Noah had excelled his Guardian superiors in magical skill from the day he began as a young Guardian, thanks to years of experience living on the street. He seemed to have an eye for all things underhanded, which meant he breezed through the Guardian requirements so quickly he caught the eye of the Head of Protectors. With time, Noah made it through the wearisome selection process for Protectors and became, at eighteen years old, the youngest to join.

Now, at thirty, he worked as Head of Protectors with unusual daring. His success stroked his prodigious ego. Because of his roots in survival by thievery, he wasn't a perfectly moral witch by any account, something Donovan overlooked because of his undeniable skill.

Noah stood at his chamber window in tense, coiled anger. His jaw felt so tight it threatened to snap and spill teeth all over the floor. Evelyn stood several paces away in the quiet darkness of his personal quarters, illuminated only by the moonlight spilling in a long beam across her shoulders. Noah hadn't spoken since she'd shown up at his door with a sobbing Aneeta on her arm and a whispered explanation. Aneeta slept soundly on Noah's couch, thanks to a powerful blessing from Evelyn. Noah refused to take his eyes off her.

"I can't imagine what you must be feeling," Evelyn said. "But whatever it is, you can't let anger overtake you. I believe there's a chance we can make something good come of this."

Noah's nostrils flared, but he said nothing. Something good come of senseless violence to his innocent niece? As Head of Protectors, tradition dictated he was not allowed to marry or have children; Aneeta was the closest thing he'd ever have to a daughter. His fists clenched. Only a lifetime of schooling kept him from pounding Donovan's door down and—

"I'm sure giving Donovan his just due is at the forefront of your mind right now," Evelyn said, jerking him from his reveries of revenge. "It must be, because it's all I can think about on Aneeta's behalf, but I must implore you not to take any action against the High Priest and jeopardize your own life."

"And why not?"

"If you really want to get back at Donovan, I can help you." Her voice acquired an edge that piqued his attention. "Using methods far more comprehensive. Besides, you can't kill the High Priest without retribution crushing you and your family."

"I have my Brotherhood," he snapped. "They will help. The blame will not fall to me."

"They are loyal to the Network."

"They are loyal to me!" He thumped his chest with a fist. "No one is loyal to Donovan."

He looked like a madman, but Evelyn met his wild, red-hot stare without fear. His grudging surprise earned her one more minute of his time. If she didn't startle as easily as the rest, perhaps she had something to say.

"Trust me when I say you aren't alone," she said. "But let's look at this from a political standpoint, taking the view of the world Donovan lives in. Destroy Donovan's career. It's what he lives for, after all, isn't it? There are those of us that are . . . less than sympathetic to Donovan and his tempestuous reign as High Priest. We can and will help you destroy him."

He stared her down with narrowed eyes. Letting Donovan get away with his despicable actions was completely unacceptable. Then again, she had a point. He couldn't kill the High Priest without harm falling on his family, and by extension, the niece he would die to protect.

But if Evelyn had an alternative . . .

"We?" he asked.

Evelyn smiled. "Yes," she said. "I don't stand alone, though I won't tell you of any others just yet. You'll have to earn my trust."

"Who says I trust you?"

"You don't trust me yet, which is fine. But you will eventually because you know I am your best bet at revenge."

A pregnant pause filled the night air, broken only by the wispy breaths of Aneeta in her deep but troubled sleep. Noah could appreciate the power of confidence as well as anyone, but Evelyn appeared more than confident. If anything, she was certain. While it annoyed him, he couldn't help admit curiosity.

"Fine," he muttered. "I'll wait, but this better be worth it."

Evelyn grinned, and her teeth gleamed a bright white in the moonlight.

"I'll be in touch."

Evelyn strolled into Donovan's office the next morning with a fresh face and bright smile. At least, that's what he assumed, since he couldn't see much through his hazy double vision. Nor did he want to really see her. If he had to face anyone, he didn't want it to be Evelyn.

"Good morning, Donovan," she said, a chirp in her voice, throwing his heavy drapes wide open. Bright winter sunshine streamed into his opulent office, spilling light onto walls of cream and gold. An elk head hung over the fireplace, wide-eyed and still. He closed his eyes to block it all out.

Too much light.

"Go away," he moaned. He'd fallen on his face sometime in the night and hadn't the energy to move. How long had he been in his office? The last thing he remembered was Rand pouring him another drink of dark ipsum, then stumbling to relieve himself . . .

"You're a wallowing disaster, Donovan," Evelyn said, nudging his leg with a pointed shoe. "And you smell like urine. Get off the floor. We need to have a chat about last night before your Assistant pops in."

His forehead moved into three fat rolls as he tried to concentrate on what she meant, but everything moved in circles, so he stopped. His stomach roiled. He needed a drink to wake him up.

"Leave me or get me a drink," he said.

Evelyn stopped a hand's breadth from his face. He stared at her glaring red shoes in an unsuccessful attempt to bring them into focus. She held a glass of amber liquid in her right hand, just out of reach.

"Is this what you want?" she asked.

Motivated by the thought of getting the tart juice in his body, Donovan pushed off the floor, regretting it when he pitched forward again, landing back on the chilly stone floor with a slap. His head pounded; his vision grew blurry and then black. Evelyn's giggle penetrated the depths of his mental fog.

"You shouldn't drink so much, you know," she said, setting the glass on a table and sitting down, draping one long leg over the other. "Then you do naughty, naughty things."

Vague memories flipped through Donovan's bloated mind. Ripping fabric. The ceiling moving. Evelyn's voice. "What are you talking about?" he muttered, rubbing his face.

"You don't remember?" she asked. Even hungover, he could still hear the note of sarcasm in her tone. "Strange. I'd think attacking and attempting to rape Noah's niece in the middle of the night would be noteworthy, even if you were stone drunk."

The words took a moment to register. *Attempting to rape Noah's niece.* It took even longer for him to remember who Noah was, and when he did, all the blood left his face in a chilly rush of fear.

"What?" he whispered in panic. Evelyn leaned forward with a smile.

"You tried to rape a young girl last night, High Priest. Not just any girl, either. Sweet little Aneeta, the witch your Head of Protectors loves and treasures above all others. Are you frightened yet? Because he's ready to kill you."

Donovan stared at her for several minutes. Was it possible? Had he finally pushed his drinking too far? He knew this day would come but never dreamed he'd do something so stupid. Evelyn lounged back again, rolling her ankle in circles and drawing attention to her long, pale legs.

"He can't kill me," Donovan whispered.

"Oh?" Evelyn asked archly. "Are you sure about that?"

In his current state of half-panic, half-drunkenness, he wasn't sure at all. Surely there was some kind of protection in the law, something . . . no. Was there? He put a shaky hand to his aching head. Just one drink would clear this mental snowfall, give him the power to comprehend.

"Fortunately, I happened by and paralyzed you," Evelyn said. "You didn't complete the nasty deed. You didn't even make it that far, really."

Bits and pieces of Donovan's memory began to reassemble in a delirious mess. He blinked his hot eyes and realized that Evelyn was still talking.

"If it had been anyone but me—Council Member Porter, perhaps?—he might have called the Guardians. Porter is a pompous ass, but he's intelligent. He would have sent a letter to the *Chatterer* to spread the word, or maybe he'd just let Noah deal with you. Either way, Porter is just waiting for you to mess up big time so he can institute the old rules and vote you out. What Council Member would remain on your side after you tried to rape a teenager?"

"Blessed be," Donovan said. She was right. Evelyn Ringer had saved his career, if not his life, by intervening. The thought of being in her debt made him gag. If he'd had anything in his stomach, it would have come out.

Evelyn lounged back in the chair. "Don't fear. I'm here as your guardian of mercy to get you out of this stink. I convinced Noah to spare your life for one night, but it's going to cost you a lot more than that if you want me to allay him for good."

Donovan, taking every motion a breath at a time, sat up and pressed his back against the couch. His entire body ached, even the teeth in his cottony mouth. The glass of amber liquid sat just out of reach, beckoning him. His body needed it to get going. He was in far over his head and hardly able to think.

Just one drink.

"Give me that ipsum," he growled.

"Not until I've had my say," she said in a light little trill.

Donovan meant to moan, but it came out as more of a whimper. "Fine," he muttered. "I'll do whatever you say, now give me the ipsum!"

"Whatever I say?"

"Yes!"

Evelyn smiled and slid the tumbler across the table with a spell. Donovan grabbed it with both hands and drank as if it would be his last.

"That's what I thought," she said. "Now, I think it's time I became a Council Member, don't you? You owe me at least that much for saving your life and career."

Evelyn sat across from May's desk three days later, clenching a scroll in one hand and striving for a cool facade.

She'll surely approve, Evelyn thought with a thrill of joy she could hardly suppress. May's demands were not subtle, and they were not easy, which made it impossible to do things just right. Evelyn could understand why; taking over the Network and staging what would be an eventual overthrow was not for the weak of heart. All the same, she did wish that May wasn't so reticent with her praise.

But not anymore.

Evelyn had effectively pulled off one of the greatest tricks in political history. Donovan wasn't the first High Priest to be blackmailed, but he would be the last. When she was in power, she simply wouldn't stand for it. The Esmelda Scrolls prevented a High Priest or High

Priestess from taking the life of a Council Member as punishment unless certain criteria were met, which seemed silly nowadays. Esmelda
had written a good law for that time, but magic and the world of
Antebellum had evolved in the thousands of years that had passed. It
was time for a newer, more appropriate law.

I shall be in control one day and make the world a better place,
Evelyn thought, reassuring herself yet again. Some days it felt like she
was falling, slipping into something terribly frightening and dark. It
stole her breath when she thought about it, paralyzing her in fear in
the few moments when it gripped her. But it always passed, and she
let it go without much thought. Surely some anxiety was natural in
the pursuit of such a cause.

May entered the room by sound first. Evelyn heard the swish of
her dress over the floorboards. The gentle clutter of May's desk, the
tick of the clock, the vague scent of something musky all made Evelyn
feel as if she were a young teenager again. Her heart pounded in her
chest.

Please like what I've done, she begged silently, exhaling one final
calming breath. *Please don't give me that sour, disapproving face again.*

"What are you doing here so unexpectedly, Evelyn?" May asked.
The door clicked shut behind her. She walked into Evelyn's field of vision and stood just behind her desk. The sharp tone of voice and firm
stare didn't even concern Evelyn, not today.

"I had something very important to discuss with you," she said
with an impressive calm that made her feel more in control. May
studied her with her usual frank expression, and must have seen the
confidence flickering in Evelyn's eyes, for she sat down.

"Explain."

Evelyn sent May the scroll in her hand with an incantation. It
unfurled itself a comfortable distance from her face, hovering in the
air so that both could see the words. Evelyn refrained from shout-
ing an explanation before May finished; emotional stability was key.
But oh, how hard it was! All she wanted to do was sing from the
rooftops.

*I've done it! I've finally secured my future and shan't have to wait
much longer.*

When May finished reading the document, she looked at Evelyn. A bright sparkle lingered in her eyes. Evelyn held her breath. Dare she hope for approval? Was May actually . . . proud of her? Proud the way a mother would be? Just the thought sent Evelyn's throat into a thick mess. She swallowed past it and kept calm by sheer force.

"Suffice it to say," Evelyn heard herself say in a cool, measured tone, "that I stumbled on Donovan in a . . . troubling situation. Thanks to fast thinking and a little blackmail while he was hungover, I am now in possession of a binding signed by the High Priest that guarantees my ascent to power as Council Member within the next two weeks. Not only that, but he's agreed to never remove me as Council Member or speak of this to anyone. My job is secured."

May's eyes shone with a fantastic light that Evelyn recognized.

"I'm . . ." May paused, staring at her with her head tilted at an odd angle. Her eyes narrowed in delight, as if she were savoring a very rich treat. "I'm quite impressed, Evelyn. You have finally done well, my girl."

Evelyn's heart soared. She collected the words and wrapped them in a special place in her heart. She'd never forget this day. Never! May was pleased, Evelyn would be Council Member by the end of the month, and she felt as if nothing would ever stop her again.

"Thank you," she said, suppressing the need to weep. She found herself wishing some nights that it wasn't so necessary to distance herself from Nell. She longed for her maternal affection. But now May was giving it to her, and Evelyn would never need anything else.

"Do you know when he will appoint you?" May asked, her eyes flickering to a calendar on the wall.

"He insisted on time to figure out which Council Member he would remove, but I'm hoping it's Pamela so I can take over the Ashleigh Covens. In fact, I strongly suggested that course of action to him."

"That would remove another competitive figure for High Priestess later," May said, her hands steepled in front of her face.

"Yes," Evelyn said, "yes I suppose you're right. I hadn't thought of that."

May smiled and stood up from behind her desk. "That's why I'm here, to think of what you do not. Now, let me instruct you on a few key points."

She began to pace across the width of the room. Evelyn watched in fascination as May's lips moved wordlessly in a silent, subtle conversation. She'd scrunch her face, bite her lip, then shake her head and turn around again. Evelyn had just started to get nervous when May stopped and turned to face her.

"You becoming Council Member at twenty-three will stir up a lot of gossip. We can't avoid it, so we must deal with it the best we can. Our first plan after you take power will be to lay low."

"Lay low?"

"Yes, yes," May snapped. When Evelyn reared back in surprise, May's face softened again. She released a long breath. "You'll be drawing enough speculation by rising to Council Member unexpectedly. You don't want anything else to come up. No, that's best. This will take time."

She spoke quietly now, almost as if she were talking to herself.

"How long shall we lay low?" Evelyn asked.

"As long as it takes."

Evelyn fingered the edge of her sleeve. The reason she had truly come to speak with May in person lingered on the tip of her tongue.

"There's much to figure out," Evelyn said, feeling breathless and lightheaded and giddy all at the same time. "Like when we shall put other plans in motion, or who my Assistant shall be."

May stopped mid-pace. Her shoulders tensed ever so slightly.

"Yes," she said. "You'll have big decisions to make. We shall also need to start writing the law of the New Central Network so that we're prepared. You shan't take over as High Priestess for years, but we wouldn't want to miss the opportunity, would we?"

"Might I ask you a question, May?"

May's eyes snapped back to Evelyn. "Yes," she said, but she must have suspected something from the nervous tremor in Evelyn's tone because her voice had softened. "What is it, Evie?"

"Would you be my Assistant?"

A full smile wreathed May's face this time, one that Evelyn felt all the way to her bones. How wonderful to have made May so happy!

After all the time May had spent teaching and mentoring her, Evelyn felt that giving such a gift back meant everything.

"I should be very happy to be your Assistant, Council Member." May dipped her head, and Evelyn leapt to her feet, another thrill of delight running through her. She *was* going to be a Council Member soon, wasn't she?

"Oh, thank you, May! I won't be so scared of all these new responsibilities if I know that you'll be there to help me."

"Of course I will be." May's smile grew wide but still didn't quite extend to her eyes. "I'm always here to help you. Now let's talk about our plans, and I must insist you keep all of these details quiet, even from your friends. We don't want any bad publicity that we can avoid. Let's get started. I'll have Celia send up some fresh snacks."

Jorden's Graduation

3rd Month of Winter

Mildred,

I'm sorry I haven't written in several weeks. We've been on a training mission in the Borderlands, but I have received all your weekly letters. You're as dependable as the sun! I always look forward to the middle of the week when I hear from you.

I thought you'd like to know that I graduate from the Captain of the Guardians training this weekend. Can you be there?

Jorden

The morning of Jorden's graduation dawned with a cold winter sun.

The newly graduated Captains of the Guardians marched out in perfect formation, wearing dress uniforms of heavy crimson wool. Their polished swords glinted in the sunlight. Jorden stood in the back row, his gaze forward and eyebrows low. He'd matured into an attractive young man with a firm jaw and bright eyes.

"Witches," the Captain of New Recruits bellowed. "Please be seated."

"It shouldn't take long," Marten whispered to Mildred from where they stood in the back. "They have other ceremonies here after this."

Mildred smoothed her hair back even though it hadn't been in her way. "Good," she said. "I'm very excited to see him again."

"You look lovely today, by the way."

Marten cast her a glance from the corner of his eye. She wore a green velvet skirt that Evelyn had given her, a cream top, and a black cloak for warmth. She smiled and took his hand.

"Thank you."

Until she met Marten, she'd never been called lovely before. He complimented her in some small way almost daily, and it still didn't feel any less awkward to her. She wasn't beautiful in the same way Stella was, but Marten made it seem like that didn't matter.

"Guardians," the Captain said. "Begin!"

The brief ceremony concluded twenty minutes later. Jorden broke away from his new friends, rushed up to Mildred, lifted her off the ground, and spun her around.

"Put me down!" she said—although she didn't have the heart to be *truly* annoyed—then cried in delight. "Goodness, Jorden. You have grown! I hardly recognize you!"

"Merry meet, Mildred," he said, setting her back on her feet with a twinkle in his eye. "It's so good to see you."

His shoulders had broadened and his voice deepened. The boy was entirely gone from his face. His arms looked strong and sturdy, like cords of rope, and he wore his hair in a long ponytail, like the other Guardians.

"You look very handsome indeed. I'm so proud of you."

A blush rose on his cheeks.

"This is my friend Marten," she said. Marten stepped forward, and the two of them clasped forearms in a manly grip.

"Oh, we all know Marten," Jorden said with a droll grin. "It's good to finally meet you."

Marten laughed as if Jorden had told a joke.

"I don't understand," Mildred said, brow furrowed. "How do you know of Marten?"

"Marten is the Assistant to the Head of the Guardians. Didn't you know that, Milly?"

Mildred shot Marten an accusatory glare, feeling like a true dolt. Assistant to the Head of Guardians was an honorable position, difficult to attain. How had they been friends for so long, and she'd never discovered it? Was she so wrapped up in her lessons? Didn't he speak often of Dolph?

"No," she muttered. "He never mentioned it."

"It wasn't an important detail to our friendship," Marten replied easily. "Don't be mad, Mildred. It doesn't matter in the slightest. I often work with Guardians in the field and am not restricted to the office, which is why you didn't know."

"He's just humble, Milly."

"Come," she said, wanting to put the embarrassment behind her. "Let's get something to eat. I'm excited to hear about all your new experiences and plans."

"Agreed. I'm starving," Jorden said, pressing a hand to his stomach.

"The two of you go," Marten said, taking a step back. "I have business to attend to. Wonderful ceremony, Jorden, and good to meet you. Mildred, I'll see you at dinner, like always."

Marten drifted away, heading toward the group of Guardians in the middle of the Bailey. Jorden gave Mildred a sidelong glance and nudged her with his elbow when they started for the gigantic wooden doors leading to Chatham Road. "Are you getting chummy with my superior, Mildred? Eh?"

"Not in the slightest," she retorted. "He and I have dinner together every night because we happen to enjoy debate and intelligent conversation. That's all."

"Sure, sure. That's why you were holding his hand."

Her palm tingled a little. They held hands often now, though it didn't mean they were about to get married.

"It's nothing."

"Tell yourself that," Jorden said with a chuckle. "But I see it in your eyes."

"Let's not talk about me. Let's talk about your new job and all your experiences. Tell me everything. I want to hear all that you've done and learned about yourself the past couple of years. Your letters are short and lack detail. When I get them at all, that is."

Jorden told her everything while they strolled into Chatham City. Mildred laughed until she cried, gasped when she heard of his injuries, and rejoiced over his accomplishments.

"Let's stop here," she said, pointing to Stella's favorite bakery. The smell of hot gravy and buttery crusts floated toward them from inside. They bought a few pies for lunch, and settled onto a warm bench in the sunlight. A fountain in the shape of a wood nymph glistened with melting ice, but the water continued to run despite the chilly air.

"Are you already assigned somewhere?"

"Yes," he said, swallowing a meat pie in two bites. "I leave in the morning for the Borderlands. It's a routine assignment guarding the border, nothing too exciting."

The Borderlands were a tract of land between the Western and Central Networks. Only coyotes and rodents thrived in the sandy soil. If it weren't for the river that ran into the Central Network from the mountains of the North via the Borderlands, they would have been as desolate as the arid deserts of the West.

"I'm excited for you," she said, and meant it. "You always did need adventure, didn't you? Mother would be very proud."

"Do you still think about her?" he asked, squinting at a beam of sunlight that filtered through the clouds.

"Yes. Every day."

"Me too," he said, staring out at the bustling street. "I miss her sometimes, but it's not so bad now. It's been a busy four years."

"Yes," Mildred said, standing. "It doesn't hurt quite as much as it once did, though I think I'll always miss her. Now, tell me about what you'll be doing in the Borderlands while we walk back. I want to know what your life will be like there."

The streets of Chatham City boiled with midday traffic. Scrollboys paraded up and down the cobblestones, calling out headlines and waving the *Chatterer*. A few well-dressed female witches walked past with tilted smiles aimed at Jorden. They returned to the High Bailey in what felt like no time at all. A queue of new Captains had begun gathering again in the center, and they beckoned with a wave at Jorden.

"Good luck, brother," Mildred said with a warm smile. "The Borderlands will be lucky to have you. Please keep in touch. Even if you do write terrible letters."

Jorden grinned. Unlike Mildred, he had Father's wide, bright eyes.

"Of course. I'll write," he said, squeezing her hand. "Perhaps I'll even improve at it."

"I should like that, but I won't hold my breath." She laughed. "Make sure to tell me just what it's like there. I've never been to the Borderlands, so I want to know everything."

Jorden gathered her in a brotherly hug. "Merry part, Mildred. I love you."

"Keep yourself safe. I love you too."

A Rotten Old Witch

The library remained quiet the next morning, and Mildred enjoyed the lengthy stillness. Not a single patron had come through, and her early classes had been particularly attentive. Patterns of frost swirled in a delicate winter signature on the windows, hiding a windy storm outside. Every book sat in its proper place on the shelves and new chandeliers donated by a wealthy old witch seeking higher political placement cast a bright and cozy glow on the room. The sense of organization relaxed Mildred.

She was eyeing the list of late notices when a crotchety voice snapped at her from the other side of the circular desk.

"I need a book," the unknown witch demanded. "I want it on the historical impact of garden gnomes. I want it to be small, and I want it in the next five minutes."

Mildred looked up to find an elderly man standing in front of her. He wasn't very tall, more like a pocket than a man, and his bristling white mustache stood out like an uncomfortable pillow on his face. Deep creases around his eyes gave him a surly look. Council Member Stephan, the oldest member of the Council. But why hadn't his Assistant come for such a mundane task?

"The gardening books are over in that corner," she said, directing him to the far side of the room. "You may help yourself."

His wrinkled brow lowered over his eyes. "That's your job!"

"No. Finding a book just because you don't want to is not in my job description."

"I will not!"

"Then you will not read a book on garden gnomes today."

"Like hell I won't! You're just lazy and don't want to do your job."

He tried a propulsion curse that would have sent her flying across the room, but Mildred overpowered it with the counter-curse before she'd left the desk. She'd never countered a curse so fast in her life. The shock on his face was gratifying.

"The good gods!" she cried. "You're an impertinent old man."

He glared at her from under his eyebrows, and when he tried to move her again, she cast an immobility hex on him that only lasted a minute.

"My job is to keep the library organized, the shelves clean, and the books stocked." She gifted him with a withering glare of her own. "Your job is to find something to read, remain quiet, respect the books, and bring them back on time."

His eyes narrowed into slits as the hex faded. "Do you know who I am? I am not someone to be trifled with."

"I don't care who you might be. You're acting like a small child."

He jerked his shoulders back, puffed out his weak chest, and tilted his head to the side. "I am Council Member Stephan, and I demand an interesting book to take with me to my meeting."

Mildred rolled her eyes.

"I don't care if you're the High Priest. You can go get your own book."

"I'm going to report you to Porter!"

"Tell Porter whatever you want."

Stephan's cheeks reddened, and his head shook until Mildred thought he'd explode from the inside out. He whirled around and stormed out, tossing his wrinkled hands in the air and yelling as he went. Books soared off the shelves in his wake, but Mildred redirected them with a different spell, and they returned to their shelves before hitting the ground.

Lavinia, walking in for her daily solo magic lesson—having progressed with impressive speed for such an uneducated girl—ducked out of Stephan's way just in time.

"Blessed be," she said, setting a pile of books on the desk. "What was that about?"

"A rotten old witch wanted a book," Mildred replied. "Here is your assignment. Please get started, and I'll be over in a few minutes."

"He wasn't any old witch. That's Stephan! He's as mean as a snake. He cursed one of the fireboys last year, you know. Turned him into a toad. Porter had to force him to overturn it. Did he yell at ya? He always yells at me. He says I take up the whole hallway when I walk."

"Don't say 'ya,' Lavinia," Mildred said with a weary sigh. "It's *you*. We've discussed proper pronunciation a hundred times. Stephan is a grumpy old witch and that's all. You shouldn't be frightened by bullies."

"He'll have you fired!" Lavinia said, attending to her accent with particular attention. "Then who will teach us magic and mathematics?"

"Let him try," Mildred said. "If Porter is willing to fire me over Stephan's laziness, then I don't want to work for him anymore. Get started on your lesson."

Lavinia opened her mouth to say something, decided against it, and obediently headed to the back corner. Mildred glanced at the doors where Stephan had disappeared and bid him a secret good riddance.

What Have I Done?

Evelyn blazed into Nell's office one bitter winter evening wearing a strapless black gown and a glittering necklace of diamonds. Her wavy red hair fell on freckled shoulders in long, shiny waves.

"Are my diamond earrings in here?" she asked, heading straight for her desk. "I thought I took them off after lunch yesterday."

Nell had been sitting behind her own desk and slowly rose. "You didn't come to work today, Evelyn. Where were you?"

"Busy."

Evelyn yanked open a drawer and began rooting through it. A low fire crackled in the hearth, sending a spray of sparks into the air. Leslee bustled in the background, tidying the room before Nell settled into a quiet dinner.

"Where are you going?" Nell asked.

"The ball celebrating the opening of Donovan's Ashleigh House." Evelyn violently tugged open another drawer. "Where are my pearls?"

"Evelyn, I needed you this morning," Nell said, ignoring her question. "I'm far behind now. You can't just leave your responsibilities without explanation or—"

"Well, I can't go back and change the past."

Nell said nothing.

"Out of my way!" Evelyn snapped when Leslee nearly bumped into her.

"Evelyn!" Nell cried, aghast. "You apologize right now! You can't come in here and act so disrespectfully to my servants."

"No." Evelyn slammed the drawer shut. "I didn't do anything

wrong. Your precious Leslee, whom you obviously care more for than me, should know better than to get in the way. Then again, she is just a servant."

Nell's eyes widened. "I've never heard such disrespect from your lips! What has that awful May done to you?"

Evelyn whirled around, her green eyes blazing. "May has done nothing but love and support me when you wouldn't! She understands me, and you never will!"

Evelyn headed for a small silver box on the fireplace. Nell watched helplessly, completely taken aback by the rash display. Evelyn had always been passionate, but it seemed she had lost control over it lately, waving back and forth as violently as a nervous wind. When she wasn't oscillating between emotions, she was staring out the window, so lost in thought she appeared unable to work.

"What's happened?" Nell implored. "I feel like I don't even know you anymore. What have I done? What has May done?"

"You aren't asking the right question," Evelyn said, snatching the small silver case from the mantle. "You should be asking what you *didn't* do."

"Fine." Nell threw her hands in the air. "What didn't I do?"

"You didn't stand up for me!"

"What are you talking about?"

Evelyn let out a triumphant cry and extracted two earrings from the silver box. "Surely you remember our conversation with Porter?" she inquired coldly.

"Porter?" Nell asked, then her eyes widened in understanding. "Do you mean with the servants? Evelyn, that was so long ago."

"It was humiliating!" Evelyn cried, fumbling with the silver box until it dropped from her hands. A dozen jewels spilled across the floor in a glittering fan. "You just sat there while he tried to tell me that I wasn't good enough for the servants to help. They talked about it for weeks. The servants mocked me! *Me!*"

"I tried to help you," Nell said, stepping forward. "You were in the wrong, Evie. I can't protect you from your own mistakes forever. Perhaps I tried to do so for too long. Now look what's become of you! You're irresponsible and impertinent."

Evelyn flinched. "You didn't even speak up for me."

"I never meant to—"

"I don't have to explain myself to May. She understands."

Nell reared back, pale and wide-eyed. *May. May.* The infernal teacher that destroyed Evelyn! Nell couldn't bear hearing her name from Evie's lips. It was just too painful. "What more could I have done for you, Evie?" she whispered. "I gave you everything. What more do you want?"

A flash of something slipped into Evelyn's eyes. Longing, perhaps. Sadness. It disappeared as quickly as it came, and Evelyn turned away.

"I want you to leave me alone," she said, swallowing. "I'll make it easy on you. Donovan is announcing tonight that I'm taking over the Ashleigh Covens as Council Member, which means we won't have to face each other every day. Good night, High Priestess."

Evelyn whipped around and stalked from the room without another word, her hair flashing in the firelight as she slammed the door.

"Evie, please!" Nell called, "Let's talk about this!"

But there was no response. Nell fumbled for something to hold on to, wondering if she was caught in a bad dream. But no, she wasn't. The flash of hatred in Evelyn's eyes had been as real as the pain it sent through her heart.

"Sit down, High Priestess," Leslee said, rushing to Nell's side and putting an arm around her shoulders. "Oh, please sit down. You've lost all color!"

"What have I done, Leslee?" Nell asked in a gaunt whisper. "What have I done?"

"Please, Your Highness. Sit down."

Nell collapsed into a chair that Leslee brought over with a spell, her weak legs trembling. A long tear streaked her wrinkled face.

"What have I done?"

Evelyn stood in the hallway outside Nell's office, struggling to compose herself before Donovan's grand ball. She hadn't planned to part with Nell in such a violent manner. She'd planned to slip quietly away from Nell's life and leave her to her servants. Hadn't that been happening for months—years—now anyway?

Her eyes glittered with unshed tears. She swallowed them back again. She hadn't expected it to hurt so much.

"No tears. This is for the best," Evelyn whispered, picturing May's approving face to give herself strength. She could do anything if it would help her grow closer to May. May, who would approve of her decisions, who wouldn't call her impertinent. May, who guided her in the right path and, occasionally, loved her like a mother. "May said it long ago; I needed to cut ties with Nell. I needed to do it."

But still her heart cramped with painful clarity, just like the day her real Mama had died.

The poor people trampled your mother to death in the Tobacco Riots. We can't let the poor have that kind of power again, can we? They took everything from you, and they'll do the same to anyone. Nell and Donovan coddle the poor. We shall put the poor in their place and prevent another disaster like yours from happening again.

"I must do this." Evelyn balled her hand into a fist. "For Mama. For the Network."

Evelyn transported away in a whisper, leaving the faint sound of Nell's heart-rending cries to fade into the night.

Thorough Justice

Mildred squinted up at the heavy bank of snow clouds settling over Chatham City like a massive iron plug. Darkness came early with the storm, overshadowing the warm yellow glow of lanterns that bobbed up and down Chatham City's busiest streets. A breeze brushed leaves and a square of parchment down the cobblestones while hints of melted sugar teased the air. Stella and Evelyn flanked her, heads bent to the wind.

"What a horrid night," Mildred muttered, pulling her cloak more tightly around her shoulders when the breeze whipped it back.

"Don't worry!" Evelyn said, her voice high-pitched with squeaky excitement. "It's nice to get away, isn't it? Besides, Owen's has decent cinnamon pretzels. Since we're celebrating my ascension to Council Member today, I'm buying!"

They slipped inside a white brick building, heralded by a hanging sign marked by a giant bulldog and the words *Owen's Pub*. They headed for the last booth on the right, where cobwebs hung in the eaves, floating in the wind admitted by a whistling windowpane. Most of the tables were already packed with patrons who had ducked out of the impending early winter storm. The room smelled of yeast, cinnamon, and body odor.

"I knew ya'd come back!" a jolly voice said from the back wall, behind the bar. "It's been weeks now, Miss Evelyn. Why would ya make an old man wait so long?"

Evelyn slipped out of her cloak, tossed it on a small boy an arm's length away, and threw herself into the burly arms of a white-haired man standing behind a long counter. Mildred rolled her eyes and headed for a high-sided booth in the corner.

"You wouldn't believe how busy I am these days, Owen," Evelyn said, straightening her dress with a teasing smile. "I've only just escaped to see you."

With beefy shoulders, a wide face, and a tooth that jutted up from his bottom jaw, Owen needed only another set of legs to look just like the bulldog on his pub sign.

"Send the usual," Evelyn said, strolling to the table. "And a bottle of wine with two glasses, and a water for Mildred. See that we're not disturbed."

"Of course." Owen barked at the servant boy, who appeared at the table with a wicker basket of soft, folded pretzels rolled in cinnamon and sugar as if they'd been tossed in the sand. He slid two empty wine glasses onto the table and disappeared.

"Delicious!" Evelyn said, her eyes glowing as she picked up a pretzel and bit into it. Mildred and Stella followed suit, not speaking until after the boy brought Mildred's cold glass of water.

"Thank you, Evelyn. You always remember," Mildred said. The odor of ipsum saturated the air in the pub. She'd never cared for ipsum. The smell of it brought memories of her abusive father and the bruising she'd find around Mother's eyes. Not to mention that ipsum altered personality, which meant she couldn't keep herself under control *nor* remember what happened. An odd drink to like, in her opinion. Even wine had a taste she wasn't overly fond of, although she tolerated it when social functions dictated she drink it.

"I remember little things," Evelyn said, twiddling her fingers until the largest crumbs of sugar fell back into the basket. "I have an excellent memory."

"Tell us, Evelyn," Stella said, leaning forward. "How did it happen? How on earth did you become Council Member so young? Everyone is talking about it."

Evelyn preened like a bird trying to ruffle its feathers, her eyes shining with a bright zeal that Mildred couldn't help feeling a little jealous of. Evelyn had achieved so many of her goals so soon. Mildred, on the other hand, was still a librarian and an underground teacher.

"You don't think I earned the job on merit alone, Stella?" Evelyn feigned surprise. "Maybe it was just my good looks and charming personality."

"No," Mildred said. "It was something else."

Evelyn's eyes flashed, but it disappeared beneath something of a sheepish smile. "Well, I suppose you're right," she admitted while removing the cork from the wine bottle. "But I can't really tell you how I've done it."

Stella's eyebrows lifted. "Are you under a vow of secrecy?"

"Perhaps," Evelyn said with a coy smile.

Stella leaned back, blinking. "I don't understand," she said. "Why can't you tell us whatever it is you've done?"

"Because she's blackmailed the High Priest," Mildred said, gauging Evelyn's reaction. There was no sense of guilt or denial in Evelyn's inscrutable expression. In fact, she nodded.

Stella's eyes popped open. "Evelyn! How could you?"

Evelyn laughed, and the wine made a *glugging* sound as it poured out of the bottle and into the two crystal glasses. The scent—or maybe Evelyn's attitude—curled Mildred's stomach.

"Oh, Stella," Evelyn said, laughing. "Your naiveté is charming, you know. I'm sure if you had discovered the same situation I happened upon, you would have done the same thing."

A wave of disgust passed over Mildred. "Blackmail, Evie?" she asked, though she wasn't as surprised as Stella. Evelyn had always been doggedly determined to make something of herself. Once she set her mind on something, no one could stop her. What could Evelyn have found that would have frightened Donovan enough to give her a position as Council Member?

"You must have stumbled on something truly terrible," Stella said. "It was."

"Yet you found means for personal gain," said Mildred.

"Which is exactly why I shall continue to progress through the Network's political structure." Her tone conveyed a hint of ice that hadn't been there before. "Do you honestly think Rand is qualified to be a Council Member? Donovan gave him the job because they're friends from their Network school days. It's just how things are done.

I, on the other hand, am *very* qualified for the job. At least I ensured that a fitting replacement was put in, didn't I?"

Stella and Mildred fell quiet. Evelyn *was* qualified. She possessed great magical ability, knew everyone, and had worked for the High Priestess for over five years now. But most Assistants were in their jobs for upwards of ten years before they were given a Council Member position.

"And I'm taking over the Ashleigh Covens," Evelyn pointed out. "I love Ashleigh, and so does Grant. He was almost as delighted as I when I told him the news. Only no one was more excited than May."

"What of Pamela?" Stella asked. "Did Donovan fire her?"

Evelyn shrugged and took another sip of wine. "I don't know under what grounds he removed her as Council Member, and I'm not sure I really care. Pamela isn't my problem. I have bigger concerns."

Mildred and Stella exchanged a worried glance.

"Really, girls!" Evelyn said. Mildred's upper lip curled at the sudden condescension in her tone. "Don't you know how politics work? It's all about who and, more importantly, *what* you know. It has nothing to do with how long you've been doing it."

"That begs for a corrupted Network," Mildred said, furious. The two of them had never really seen eye-to-eye on politics, but never had the divide between them been so great. "No position should be determined by an ability to blackmail one's way into the game."

"Or perhaps it's a narrowing ground," Evelyn quipped, her back straightening. "Those who are the most able to survive such a hostile environment will. Besides, Mildred, it's not as if I'm not qualified. I've worked as an Assistant for years, lived at the castle nearly my whole life, and graduated with the highest honors. No one loves the wealth and prosperity of the Ashleigh Covens more than I."

While Evelyn's words had a sense of truth, Mildred couldn't get comfortable with the idea of blackmail. Why was Mildred working so hard if others would gain their positions by luck or social status? Perhaps education was a better fit for her; at least she felt useful there.

"Well I think it's wonderful that you're going to be a Council Member," Stella said, breaking the sudden strain. "I'm sure that whatever you did to bring it to pass was for the best. I'm excited for you!"

Evelyn smiled and pushed her hair away from her face, leaving a trail of sugar crystals in the long strands.

"Thank you," she said. "Working my way to the top has never been so thrilling."

"To the top?" Mildred asked, her surprise doubling. "I thought your goal was to make a difference."

Stella kicked Mildred under the table with the pointy tip of her boot, but Mildred ignored it. Evelyn paused, regarding Mildred with an odd mixture of pity and exasperation.

"I simply don't know how I *can* make a difference unless I get to the top," Evelyn said, smiling before biting into another cinnamon treat. Stella turned the conversation to Evelyn's schedule over the next month or two, and the tension blew away with a draft from the pub windows. Mildred hated herself for it, but a traitorous thought flickered through her mind.

What if Evelyn is right? What if the only way to make a difference is to get to a position of power, no matter what it takes?

She felt a long moment of self-doubt in her own convictions. Perhaps she was wasting her time in politics, grasping for an ideal that faded like a vapor as soon as she caught it. Unlike Evelyn, Mildred wouldn't play this game. But Evelyn would do whatever it took to accomplish her goals. Perhaps politicians had to. Did honor in politics exist? Could she give up on her ideals and adopt a new paradigm?

"Mildred," Stella asked, diverting her from the weight of her heavy thoughts. "What do you think of Evelyn's idea?"

"What?" she asked, shaking off the last of her reverie. "I'm sorry, I was thinking."

"You usually are," Evelyn said, teasing, her eyes bright as ever, as if the subtle uncertainty of their prior conversation hadn't occurred. "There are a few plays in Ashleigh tonight. Let's go catch one of them! I know one of the owners that will let us slip in the back. It would be the perfect way to celebrate my new appointment."

Mildred hesitated. A play in Ashleigh would eat up all her meager funds, but she'd stirred up enough waters between her friends tonight and didn't have the heart to refuse. Besides, it wasn't the worst idea. She'd rather sit in the audience of a dark stage than engage in small talk. All she wanted to do was find Marten and tell him about all she'd learned tonight. Marten would agree with her, even comfort her. He almost always did.

Almost.

"All right." Mildred pushed her philosophies into the back of her mind to analyze later. "Let's go."

Evelyn squealed with excitement and headed for the front door without another word, leaving the wine and pretzels behind. Stella followed, trying to stop Evelyn from leaving before she told them where to transport.

Mildred stood up and caught Owen's eye. She motioned to the empty booth. "Do we owe you any—"

He waved her off with a hairy hand.

"Can't charge a witch like Evelyn," he muttered, turning away. "Or else she'll suddenly own your entire life."

Porter hated waking up cold in the springtime.

It seemed like a cruel joke to see the sun, feel a warm breeze, but still feel chilled to his bones. Despite the inherent beauty and charm of Chatham Castle, the drafty stone walls never warmed up until summer descended, and then they held in the heat like a baking oven. He walked to his office instead of transporting, just to get his blood moving. His Assistant had already started a fire, but its heat hadn't permeated the room, so he stood by it, keeping his toes as close to the flame as he could tolerate. A gentle tap interrupted his solitude.

"Come in," he said, adding under his breath, "and why not? I never get a moment to myself."

Mildred entered Porter's office with what appeared to be stoic disregard of the cold. If the tip of her nose hadn't been bright red, or if a shawl wasn't draped around her shoulders, he would have questioned whether she felt anything at all. It was clear she had no idea why he'd called her in.

Porter let out a long breath, suddenly feeling ill prepared. There was a sternness about Mildred that commanded a certain level of respect, if not trepidation. Never mind he was old enough to be her father. He'd sensed a softening toward himself on her part ever since he'd approved her classes, but they hadn't spoken much since. In fact, she didn't seem to speak much at all, except with Marten, his old Assistant's daughter Stella, and, unfortunately, Evelyn. They were the strangest trio of friends that he'd ever seen.

"You sent for me, Council Member?"

Here goes nothing, he thought.

"Welcome, Mildred," he said, bringing two chairs close to the fire with an incantation. "Please have a seat. Thank you for coming on such short notice."

Mildred obliged without a word. She sat with her back straight, hands in her lap, and a humorless expression on her face. If he hadn't known better, he would have sworn that she was in her late thirties, not her early twenties. He'd been thinking over the proposal he was about to make for a long time, but now that Mildred sat in front of him, in person, he wondered if it was a bad idea.

Too late now.

"Er, yes. Well, shall we discuss why I've called you into my office?" he asked. The cold leather creaked when he sat against it, and he sucked in an uncomfortable breath.

"I would appreciate that."

"How do you like working in the library, Mildred?"

"I'm grateful to have employment." He was certain that a little glimmer of suspicion lurked in her gaze.

"Do you find it fulfilling?"

"No."

He chuckled. "No, I suppose it's not when you have your eyes set on something higher. Do you think you can endure many more years shelving books while your friends continue to advance their political careers?"

Her neck stiffened. "If I have to."

"You check the Assistant's list every week, don't you?"

"Yes."

"So you know it's longer than it's ever been."

Mildred hesitated. "Yes, I do realize that."

Porter leaned back in his chair. "The last Assistant chosen had been Assistant to a Coven Leader, and most of the Assistants before that had four marks under their belt. And of course they'd networked extensively. I was looking over your graduation records earlier and noticed that you tried for four marks but only received three. I never see you at social functions or—"

"Can we get to the point?" she asked, clipping each word. "Whatever you're trying to do here won't work. Either offer me the position you are hoping I'll take, or fire me."

Porter straightened. "How do you know that I want to offer you a position?" he asked.

"Why else would you be looking at my record or trying to make me afraid of my future? There's clearly something you want from this conversation or you wouldn't have said any of it."

Completely taken aback, Porter stared at her. "Very well," he finally managed to say. "Here it is. Mildred, I called you in here to see if you would be Assistant to Council Member Stephan."

Her usual emotional restraint impressed Porter, but his question caused her to lose it for a fleeting second. Her mouth dropped open. For a brief moment, she seemed like any other witch.

"What?"

Porter grinned, gratified to have delivered a shocking blow of his own. Feeling the sides more even, and a great deal more confident, Porter continued his explanation.

"Stephan's last Assistant quit after her first month. Her exact words were, I believe, *he's a miserable old cretin full of bitterness and meanness.* She swears she'll never return to the castle. She was his fifth Assistant in eighteen months. It's become quite clear that he can't have just anyone; he'll need someone as strong-willed as he. Someone that's a bit of a . . . lion, if you will."

Mildred had gone pale and clenched her right hand in a fist, but after a moment she regained most of her composure. He didn't blame her reaction. Stephan had been a role model for Porter ever since he started his career at Chatham Castle, but that didn't mean he wanted to sit in an office with him every day.

"What are the stipulations?"

"That's where it gets tricky," Porter said, bracing his elbows on his knees and leaning forward. "You see . . . Stephan doesn't know that I'm hiring you on his behalf."

"What?"

"Last time I suggested it, he hexed me with a boil curse. I had sores on my skin for days before I convinced him to remove it."

Mildred stared at him. For a moment, he wasn't sure she'd even heard him until she asked, "Then why are you doing it?"

"A couple of reasons. This business with Evelyn becoming Council Member three months ago has made me uneasy. And the Middle Covens need help. I think you're just the witch to pull them back together before they completely disintegrate."

Mildred's forehead furrowed into deep lines. "Wouldn't it be better for the Network if Stephan was replaced as Council Member?"

The idea sent a little shiver of worry through Porter. He bit his bottom lip, studying her with open regard. She met his gaze without fear. How blunt and honest could he be? He'd heard favorable reports about her from the servants but knew nothing concrete. Her willingness to teach so many students without pay said enough of her character.

"May I be blunt?" he asked.

"I'd prefer it."

"May I trust you?"

She seemed to sense the weight behind his words. She opened her mouth to reply, then stopped. After some thought, she finally concluded, "Yes. You may trust my discretion."

Porter let out a weary breath. "The Central Network is in a very tenuous place. Donovan is not a strong High Priest. Over the past decade, he's replaced most Council Members with friends, unqualified fools who don't even know how to balance a budget properly. Now we're beginning to feel the effects. The efforts of Nell, Terry, myself, and sometimes Stephan have been the only thing keeping the Network from utter ruin. I fear the day we lose Nell."

Mildred's annoyance seemed to fade into concern. When she offered no disagreement to his assessment, Porter continued.

"Unfortunately, Nell is getting older. Ever since she appointed Evelyn as her Assistant, Nell's depressions have been deeper and of greater duration. We will eventually face the day when Donovan will rule without her balancing power at his side. No doubt he'll institute one of his own cronies as High Priestess, and then we'll be in real trouble."

"You don't think the Esmelda Scrolls will protect the Network?" Mildred asked as soon as he paused.

"They protect our law, and they govern the actions of the Highest Witch, preventing tyranny, oppression, or open persecution. But the Esmelda Scrolls can't correct for laziness or gluttony or overtaxation. Unfortunately, not even magic can force witches to behave, nor would we want it to."

Her shoulders slumped a bit at this, as if he'd just kicked the last leg of her stool of hope out from underneath her. He sympathized. He'd felt the same way himself the past five years.

"At any rate, when the day comes that we lose Nell, I need as many trustworthy Council Members as possible." Porter's voice softened with affection. "Stephan was my mentor. I was his Assistant for ten years. He taught me to love the Central Network. Even though he doesn't do much anymore, he helps us keep Donovan's peers from overcoming the Council. Not only that, but he deserves better than to be turned away after devoting his entire life to serving us."

"He doesn't have to be turned away," Mildred pointed out diplomatically. "He could simply retire. Council Members are only required to serve five years once they take the oath, and then they may retire when they wish. I'm sure his family would love to see more of him in his twilight years."

Porter glanced down at his desk. "Stephan's story is not mine to tell," he said, after a hurried attempt to find the right words to air his thoughts. "Suffice it to say that he has no one. He lost everything in a tragic fire ten years ago. Wife, sons, daughters, grandchildren. All gone."

Mildred's eyebrows lifted. "Oh."

"I know what you must be thinking," Porter said quietly. "That compassion for a miserly old witch cannot take the place of justice in politics. Perhaps you're right. But, in this case, I ask you to look at it from the perspective of what you could accomplish."

Mildred stared at the fire, then turned to him. "Do you have a piece of parchment and a quill that I may borrow?"

Porter waved his favorite white quill, a jar of ink, and a square of blank parchment over without question. They settled onto a small desk that slid over next to her seat. She began writing without hesitation, and continued for the next ten minutes. The slow tock of the clock sounded in the background until she finished. When she set aside the quill, the parchment was divided into two sections on the front and back, with her small, precise handwriting filling up each column.

She nodded with resolution, as if she'd come to a decision, and looked up at him. Porter watched it all unfold with curiosity.

"From what I've seen and heard of Stephan, he's a pompous, impertinent witch," she said. "But I also stand to gain much from serving as his Assistant. And, considering that you and I agree as to the Central Network's current precarious position, I will be happy to help prevent further devastation in whatever way possible."

Relief swept through Porter with dizzying force. He didn't know if things would work with Mildred and Stephan; perhaps their strong personalities would clash until they destroyed one another, but she was truly his last hope for the old man. And, perhaps, for the Council.

"Thank you, Mildred," he said. "I cannot tell you what this means to all of us. You also have Nell and Terry's gratitude, as well as the thanks of the witches of the Middle Covens, though they may never know to whom they are indebted."

Mildred didn't appear so sure. "Is that all?" she asked.

"I have one last question. Will you maintain the education of the servants?"

She thought it over for a stretch of time before saying, "I don't know. But I'll try."

"See what you can do," he said. "I'll help if I can."

"Why are you so intent on maintaining the education of the servants?" she asked, eyes tapered in question. She thought she already knew the answer, but she wanted him to confess it.

"Because dark days are coming, and they will be even darker if the growing movement of Elitists in the upper class are able to oppress the poor by withholding education. Half of the common schools are closed already. It's only a matter of time before the rest fall as well."

She nodded. He set both hands on his knees.

"I'll draw up the contract for you to sign tonight, but for now, consider this our verbal agreement. Please let me know if you need help with anything."

She looked a bit pale. Perhaps dazed was the right word. Porter had just given her the future she'd long desired on a platter of thorns.

The New Assistant

"**R**otten brat!" Stephan screamed. "Get back here and build the fire!"

A young fireboy darted into the hallway from Stephan's office, eyes wide. He sprinted past Mildred, dropping an armful of logs in his haste. She gazed down at the strewn pieces of wood with a sigh.

"Wonderful," she muttered, collecting the firewood back together with an incantation. Telling Stephan she was his new Assistant would be downright dangerous.

"Where's my firewood?"

Mildred stepped into the doorway to find Stephan standing in the middle of his office. His shock-white hair stood up on end, and loose skin hung off his neck like a waddle. His sleeves were pushed up to his elbows, his jacket off, and shirt askew. A watch that clearly didn't work dangled from a chain out of an inner pocket.

"If you weren't such a terror, they wouldn't be afraid of you," Mildred said, sending the logs to the fireplace with a spell. Stephan regarded her with deep suspicion.

"You're that ornery librarian that won't work. I'm still going to file a complaint about you."

"I was that librarian."

"Was?" His voice piqued with hope. "Were you fired? You came to apologize?"

"I'm your new Assistant."

A current of air whistled past Mildred. The room blurred, and she found herself out in the hallway with the door slammed shut in her face.

"Shove me outside with magic, will you?" she muttered, pushing her sleeves up. "Two can play at that game."

Mildred transported back into the office with an invisible protection shield around her.

"I don't need an Assistant!" he bellowed. "Leave!"

"An attitude change is what you need," she said, breezing past him. He tried to send her outside again, but his incantation fizzled into sparks.

"You can cast all the incantations to get rid of me that you want," Mildred said, "but I don't intend on leaving just because you're childish. This is my only shot to get out of the library. And I'm going to make the best of it."

"Childish?" he yelled. "You're the child!"

She stepped over a pile of scattered books and an old dinner tray. The half-open window admitted message after message soaring at such frantic speeds that they looked like birds having seizures in flight.

"Your office is a disaster," she said, nose wrinkling when she pulled a sock off the back of his desk chair. She rolled her eyes, a headache already forming at the base of her neck. This would certainly prove to be the longest day of her life. "We have a few things to discuss before I sign a contract to work with you."

"Get out of here!"

"Be quiet," she said. "You may speak to me like an adult, but you may not yell at me."

Stephan's nostrils flared, but he calmed himself for the moment.

"Your career is about to be yanked out from under your feet if we don't do something about it," Mildred said. "Would you like to starve on the streets?"

"I've done nothing wrong," he shouted, balling his hands into fists. "Except serve an ungrateful Network that—"

She cast a silencing incantation for a moment of peace. His lips continued to move, but no sound came from his mouth.

"Yes," Mildred said, drawing herself to her full height, which really wasn't much taller than his. "I just set a silencing spell on you because of your disrespectful and, quite frankly, embarrassing mouth. Now, listen to me. I'm your last shot at an Assistant. If you don't shape up, Donovan will fire you, replace you with one of his nitwit friends, and you'll die alone. After an entire lifetime of hard work, is that how you want it all to end?"

He growled deep in his throat in response but averted his eyes. The moment of silence gave Mildred a chance to regain her scattered thoughts and compose herself.

"I'll remove the incantation if you promise not to yell. Do we have an agreement?"

Stephan shot her another murderous glare, waded to his chair through piles of papers, and fell into the fluffy cushions. In the wake of his tantrum, he looked very old. Mildred took it as a yes and whispered a spell reversal.

"I want breakfast," he said. Mildred blinked.

"Breakfast?"

"Yes!" he snapped. "Two eggs, a cup of coffee, and potatoes cut up into little squares. With tomatoes!"

"Well, I want to be the Assistant to a respectful Council Member. We can work something out if you calm that infernal temper and ask me politely."

"Order me breakfast."

"No."

After five minutes of repartee, during which neither would back down, Stephan mumbled something faintly resembling a *please*, although she distinctly heard the words *dotty bat* follow it. Ignoring his attitude, Mildred wrote a request on a scrap of messenger paper and sent it to the kitchen with a spell.

"I want it clear," Stephan said, pointing at her. "I don't like Assistants. Stopped trying to get a competent one years ago. You're not worth my time!"

"That's fine. I don't want to be your Assistant either. We'll both do something we don't want and hope that something good comes out of it. My first order of business will be to establish what you need done. Let's start with an organized list, then we can get to cleaning this place," she said, walking in a circle around his cluttered desk, waving a misplaced hanky out of her way with a flick of her wrist. It smacked him in the face. "I refuse to work in such a horrid environment."

"Don't touch my desk!"

"We can discuss my wages next week, once you've seen how I work." She extracted two books from a mound of papers and sent them to the bookshelves. "Please keep in mind that I'm your Assistant, not your nanny."

The room began showing signs of life for the first time in what had likely been months. The fire blazed a little higher, papers shuffled on the desk, sorting themselves into neat piles. Books continued to fly from the floor and onto the wall. He grabbed a novel as it sped past and opened it to the middle. Before he could properly start reading, the book snapped shut and flew to Mildred's waiting hand.

"You may read after we've discussed what needs to be done."

His squawks of protest fell on deaf ears. Mildred collected her supplies and a chair.

"I've already noted extensive housekeeping," she said, unfurling a blank scroll. Instead of answering, he turned away and stared at the fire with a glower. Mildred added *contact library students to notify of canceled classes for the next week* to the list. She'd need all the time she could get to figure out her new job. Surely they'd understand, and maybe even appreciate, a break.

Stephan still hadn't spoken a single word.

"If you don't tell me what you want done, I'll just do what I want," Mildred said, hoping he didn't see her heart slamming in her throat. If he knew how uncomfortable she was, she'd never gain the upper hand.

"Cookies," he said, turning to face her with his wild hair flying out in all directions. The loose skin under his jaw wobbled whenever he spoke.

"Excuse me?"

He tucked his wrinkled hands, speckled with liver spots, into the too-small pockets of his vest and puffed out his chest. "I want you to make sure I have a plate of cookies, a glass of cold milk, and plenty of firewood to keep me warm. Also, ensure that my laundry is completed every week."

"I'm not your wife."

"No, you're my Assistant and must do what I say."

"I must not."

"Then you're fired!"

"You can't fire me the first day," she said. "I'm guaranteed a trial period of one month."

"Don't get the wrong cookies," he mumbled with a scowl.

Mildred clenched her jaw at the idea of doting on him like a child. She hadn't survived years of learning magic, doing homework until all hours of the night, and working as a librarian to dote on a grumpy old man.

"I'll note *reviewing tax records*," she said, forcing a calm tone. "When did you last meet with your Coven Leaders?"

"I love gardening," he continued as if she hadn't spoken, "so you need to make sure that my pile of books on plants never falls below seven. I've read everything in the gardening section, so you'll have to find something else like it."

"You probably met with the Coven Leaders last year then. Lovely."

"And don't forget to order my hot chocolate in the morning!"

"I'll order your hot chocolate as soon as you tell me something worthwhile," Mildred countered testily, feeling the last remnants of her control fading. "I'm here to assist you in your business as a Council Member, not in your creature comforts. It's an insult to assume I want anything to do with your laundry."

His bushy eyebrows drooped until they nearly covered his dark eyes. "I won't help you unless I'm taken care of."

They stared at each other, mute with tension.

"Chocolate chip for the basic weekday," he said. "But every weekend I'll want snickerdoodles. Don't forget to request extra marshmallows in my hot chocolate, and have my slippers replaced by the end of the week."

Mildred itched to set a hex on him, and she refrained only because an envelope soared underneath the door and hovered between them. A wax seal in the shape of a dragon indicated the letter had come from the High Priest's office. Mildred plucked it from the air.

"It's a notice," she said, frowning. "The Esbat is tonight."

"The Esbat?"

"Yes."

"Ha!" he hooted, looking altogether like an owl with his erratic hair and excited eyes. "Good luck with it, you intolerable monster! You'll look like a fool tonight."

With that, he snapped his mouth shut, folded his arms, and refused to say another word.

Mildred walked into the Council Room behind Stephan that evening, her nerves as frayed as an old string. She would have happily throttled him and his stubborn attitude if the idea of failing on her first day of work wasn't so repulsive.

Her repeated pleas for help to Stella and Evelyn kept returning unanswered. Wherever they were, the letters weren't able to get through. She fudged her way through the entire day, trying to make sense of tax ledgers, boundary documents, and property disputes. Stephan adamantly refused to speak, so Mildred ignored him, organizing the office and making as much noise as possible whenever he tried to nap.

"Welcome," Porter said with a warm smile that was very nearly Mildred's undoing. He checked her wrist for the Esbat mark and was about to ask a question—no doubt to see how it was going—but stopped when he saw the murderous look on her face. Without saying a word, he patted her on the shoulder. "I'll try to speak with him. Don't worry, Mildred. Give it time."

He moved to check Stephan's wrist. She clutched a thick scroll to her chest and stepped to the wall where she could wait for her friends to arrive. Throughout the day she'd taken random notes from the papers she'd sorted, but the figures and conclusions meant next to nothing to her. All the same, it felt better to have something with her for the meeting.

Salvation soon sashayed into the Council Room. Stella, who walked just behind Rand so she could see where his hands were at all times, stopped once she saw Mildred.

"Milly?" she mouthed.

"Let's begin!" Donovan called, heaving his massive body onto his chair, a discernible redness in his eyes. "Seal the doors."

Mildred had been so distracted she hadn't even noticed how full the Council Room had become. Stella joined Mildred's side, grabbed her arm, and sat next to her.

"What's going on?" Stella whispered, glancing at Stephan over Mildred's shoulder. His eyes were closed and his mouth open in a dissonant snore.

"I was hired as Stephan's Assistant this morning," Mildred said, running a hand over her face. "Stella, it's been such a nightmare. He refuses to tell me anything and has tried to curse me at least ten times. What do I do? What does Donovan expect?"

Stella pressed her lips together. "You'll have to give the first report," she said, monitoring Donovan out of the corner of her eye. Council Member Terry stood for the invocation of blessings. Stella motioned for Mildred to be quiet, but reached for a nearby quill while Terry called down powers of wisdom and clarity. She took Mildred's hand and wrote on the back of it.

"Middle Covens!" Donovan said the moment Terry finished, glaring from underneath his fatty eyebrows. "Report!"

"My new Assistant would love to report," Stephan said with glee, then added under his breath, "See if you're so confident now, eh, Margaret?"

"This is what you'll need to go over," Stella whispered, shoving Mildred's hand back. "Make it up if you have to. Just stand up and get it over with. Try to appear confident."

Mildred's heart slammed in her chest. The pressure of sitting amongst so many influential witches left her nearly paralyzed. She didn't have the time or knowledge to prepare for such a meeting. She didn't even know the names of the Coven Leaders in the Middle Covens!

"Well?" Donovan snapped, his jowls wiggling. "What's your report?"

"Stand up," Stella whispered, pinching her elbow. "Hurry!"

Mildred rose to find her knees shaking. "I-I will report for the Middle Covens."

"W-will you?" Donovan asked. "W-what's your name then?"

The sheer injustice of his mocking, as well as the stifled titters coming from around the room, made Mildred white hot with anger. She was a professional! They weren't supposed to mock her like they were all still schoolchildren.

"My name is Mildred Graeme."

"What's your problem? Report already!"

"I just started as Stephan's Assistant this morning. To be honest, I—"

"I don't care if you started five years ago, just give your report and be done! I have a meeting after this," Donovan growled, but his eyes slipped to Rand, who grinned. She suspected that Donovan's *meeting* had nothing to do with business, and more to do with the popular pastime of boxing.

The words Stella had scribbled on her hand were of little help. The wet ink had begun to run, but she managed to make the words out.

Changes
Expenses
Needs

Mildred scanned the list and realized with another flutter of panic that she had no idea what their changes, expenses, or needs would be. She willed herself to ignore the gossipy murmurs in the room. She'd not lose her future because of a grumpy curmudgeon and a surly, immature High Priest who cared more about gambling than the state of the Covens. She set her fingertips on the table in front of her to gain some balance.

"I'll report what I know, Your Highness, which isn't much considering I just started this morning. The Middle Covens are an unmitigated disaster."

"Would you be quiet?" Stephan cried, whacking her with his cane. She caught it in her hand without looking and transformed it into a pencil, which she tucked behind her ear. Chortles filled the air, and Stephan's ears flushed bright red.

"Bravo," Stella whispered, laughing.

"What are you talking about?" Donovan snapped. "Everything was fine last month."

"Where would you like me to start?" Mildred asked with renewed confidence. If she could do nothing else, she would at least stand firm in the truth. "I believe crime is high because I found six letters from different Coven Leaders complaining about looting. Jobs seem to be scarce because half the people can't afford to pay their taxes. At least, that's what the ledgers from five years ago say. They've only been updated erratically, and by different witches, for the last eighteen months. That's just the beginning. I can go into greater detail if you'd like."

"No!" Donovan stopped her as she reached for her thick scroll. His uncomfortable glare suggested that he expected her to take responsibility for the Middle Coven's years of neglect, something she refused to do.

"What would you like me to report?" Mildred asked. "Do you want me to lie to you and tell you everything is fine when it clearly isn't?"

A flicker of movement off to the left caught her eye. Evelyn sent her a bolstering smile. Mildred's courage grew again. She wasn't alone, for her friends always stood behind her.

"I don't like you," Donovan said, regarding her with distrust. "Not at all. You're impertinent and lazy if you don't even know what's happening in your Covens. I can't imagine it would take more than an hour or two to figure out the highlights."

Mildred said nothing, shocked at his severe disconnection from reality. Did he really believe that she could understand Coven business in an hour? Or were the Middle Covens simply *that* disastrous? No wonder Porter worried about Donovan's reign without Nell.

Donovan huffed. "I'm done hearing from you. You've bothered me, and now I'm in a foul mood for the—for my meeting. Get it straightened out by next month. Rand, report."

Mildred slowly returned to her seat. She'd never really respected Donovan as High Priest, despite his reputed skill with intricate spells. He always seemed to find the easy way out of a situation, pawn responsibilities off on others, and rely too heavily on his old knee injury as a crutch instead of actually doing his job. But experiencing his laziness in person disappointed her so deeply that it felt like she'd woken from a dream and realized her ideals had never been real.

"Well done," Stephan hissed. "Now you've gotten us both in trouble."

Mildred ignored him, and he eventually fell back to sleep. Stella sent her an empathetic little smile, but Mildred didn't have the energy to return it.

Her goal of becoming an Assistant had finally been realized, only she'd made a fool of herself, aligned with a Council Member that hated her, and become an enemy of the Highest Witch before the end of the day.

"What a wonderful beginning," she muttered.

Leave Me Alone

"I didn't complete my Network school education so I could fluff your pillows," Mildred said two weeks later. She sat behind Stephan's desk, where the late evening light that slanted through his windows fell in warm rays. "I'm supposed to be conducting business, not taking off your shoes."

His dinner tray hovered in the air next to him, waiting to be eaten. "I can't eat like this!" he said. "I need to prop my feet up."

"There's an ottoman just across from you," she said primly, casting her eyes on the clock to find it was well past seven. "Use that."

"Position it for me."

"No."

"That's an order!"

"This is a refusal."

Mildred returned her attention back to the desk, which continued to be a destructive mess of paperwork and messages. She'd spent an hour organizing it that morning, only to return after her lunch with Marten to find it cluttered with new messages. The tips of her fingers kneaded her temples in a poor attempt to remove a lingering headache.

"My feet need a cushion!" Stephan insisted, rapping his side table with a fist. "Give me the ottoman!"

"No."

He growled. The ottoman rested no more than two arms' length from his feet. He could easily move it with a spell. She would put Stephan to sleep with a nap hex to get some peace and quiet again, as she'd done yesterday, but she needed him to answer a few questions so she could leave and go to bed.

"It's your job to make me comfortable!" he bellowed, turning red in the face like a toddler throwing a tantrum.

"It's my job to figure out this blasted mess. Who is the Coven Leader for Stilton? I've sent at least two messages and haven't heard back."

Stephan folded his arms across his chest. "I can't answer any questions when I'm this uncomfortable and hungry, you shrew. You're nothing like the rest of them, you know! *They* used to do everything I said."

Mildred narrowed her bloodshot eyes on him. "Yes, and you ran them out after a month or two. Now the Middle Covens are a disaster that won't be cleaned up by me taking care of you. You're perfectly capable of moving the ottoman."

"I'm an old man," he said with a pout in his lower lip. "I shouldn't have to work. You should!"

Mildred ignored him. In the end, however, she couldn't do anything more until she found out who ran Stilton Coven. She could find no correspondences or record of fully paid taxes. Not that there were good records of anything else. She gritted her teeth and prepared herself by taking five long, deep breaths. Not even an all-girls school had challenged her patience or pride on this level. She walked over to stand in front of him.

"Fine," she said through clenched teeth. "I'll move your ottoman if you tell me about the Coven Leader for Stilton."

Stephan's eyes lit up in a triumphant smile. "Get to work then!" he cried, flapping a hand. "If my dinner is cold, I'm sending for another tray and you'll regret it!"

Mildred pulled the ottoman closer with a spell, but it ran into Stephan's toes. "Lift my feet onto it," he said.

"Absolutely not. The deal was to bring the ottoman to you. I did that, now answer my question."

Stephan pressed his lips together and stared at her. She suppressed the urge to slap him, instead using a spell to jerk his legs into the air. They moved so quickly he nearly toppled backward. She shoved the ottoman underneath him with her foot, slammed his dinner tray onto his lap, and said, "Who is the Coven Leader for Stilton?"

Stephan glared at her, frozen with surprise, until he slowly regained his composure. He stared at her with a smug expression of distaste.

"I don't know who the Coven Leader is. Last I knew it was a male, but that may have changed."

Mildred nearly exploded. She turned her back to him with her fists clenched, feeling her rage bloom into her face until it nearly overcame her. All for nothing!

"The soup is cold!" he howled. "Send it back right now!"

She stalked to the door and slipped into the empty hall, her composure shattered. Once in the cool, dark hall, illuminated by the occasional torch, she leaned back against the wall and released a deep breath.

The injustice of her situation burned white hot. How had she ended up with the most difficult witch on the Council? Rand might be a lech, but at least he set expectations. She certainly wasn't wrong to deny Stephan so many ridiculous tasks; when it came to morals, she was rarely wrong about anything. Her Network education had nothing to do with nannying a tetchy old man.

Her hand warmed when a new message came through the silenda. It had been so long since she'd used it that the feeling startled her out of her irate depression.

A moment to meet with you? the message inquired, showing Lavinia's quill between her knuckles. Just seeing Lavinia's symbol brought a fresh wave of guilt and panic.

"Classes," Mildred whispered, closing her eyes. "I've forgotten about classes." She used silent magic to send a message back to Lavinia.

Yes. Come to Stephan's office.
On my way.

Mildred remained in the hall, listening to the distant sound of Stephan's demands for more soup until she could tolerate it no more and set a silencing incantation on the doorway. Lavinia rushed down the hall at a run five minutes later, her thin cheeks flushed.

"I'm sorry for the unexpected request, Miss Mildred," she said, panting, "but I just . . . had to come see you."

"What's wrong?"

Lavinia's breathing calmed. She hesitated for just long enough that Mildred snapped at her. "What? I'm very busy!"

"Have you forgotten us?" Lavinia asked, looking like a cast-aside puppy. Mildred paused with a flash of shame and embarrassment.

"Of course not," she said. The lie burned on her tongue. "I've been very busy."

"Yes, of course," Lavinia said, fidgeting with the bottom of her sleeves. "And I understand. But . . . it's just that . . . are you going to stop classes? I only ask because we don't want to keep our hopes up that you'll come back if you aren't going to."

"I'm not sure."

Lavinia's shoulders slumped in avid dejection. "I haven't learned to transport yet," she mumbled, her eyes on the floor as she scuffed the toe of her boot back and forth. "Or cleaning spells."

Mildred stared at her with a shrewd eye. Either Lavinia was trying to guilt her into coming back, or she truly felt this worried.

"If I say no, would you continue to learn on your own?"

"A few things," Lavinia said. "I've already been doing that. But I can't learn to transport on my own."

"True."

In the time that Mildred had been teaching, at least half of the servants learned to read and passably wrote letters or copied poems. It didn't seem unreasonable that they could continue learning on their own or teaching each other.

No, Mildred thought. *They wouldn't teach it correctly. They need me to guide them.*

The thought rose so suddenly that she stopped to analyze it. *Did* the students need her—as opposed to any other teacher—or did she simply want to teach them? There was no doubt she longed for the easy days of the classroom compared to the hell of her current life.

"We miss you, Miss Mildred, not just the classes. We miss learning," Lavinia said, tucking her hands behind her.

And I miss teaching.

She actually missed her students, the dusty smell of chalk in the classroom, and the expressions of joy on the faces of those reading for the first time. Teaching had given her a sense of fulfillment and progression that she imagined working as Assistant to Stephan could never give her.

Not so long as she was pushing ottomans around, anyway.

"Blessed be," she muttered under her breath. "Lavinia, I appreciate you taking the time to communicate how you feel."

"Does that mean you'll teach us again?" Lavinia asked, breathless. "Will you come back? We want you back so badly! I have so many questions!"

Mildred's mind spun with the same question. But when could she fit classes in? Would she have the energy to teach after dealing with Stephan all day? She brushed that aside to ask the most pressing question.

"If all of the students have been so worried about learning, why haven't you contacted me through the silenda?"

"I have," Lavinia said quietly. "But you never responded until tonight. That's why I ran all the way here."

"You have?"

"Many times, Miss Mildred."

"When?" Mildred demanded, annoyed that she could be at fault in anything. She recalled ignoring one or two messages on the silenda while dealing with the Middle Covens, but had she ignored so many?

"Almost every day around lunch. I have questions about what I'm learning. The rest of the students won't contact you because they think you've moved on like the rest of them."

"The rest of them?"

Lavinia shrugged. Mildred schooled her face into a neutral expression. If she looked too stern, Lavinia would give up; the girl worried about Mildred's disapproval above all else. Mildred had felt the same way about her mother. It had been a wonderful motivator, so for Lavinia's sake she sought to never over-approve.

"The rest of the witches that work at the castle don't think about the servants," Lavinia said. "To some of them, like Miss Evelyn and

Council Member Rand, we're hardly human. A lot of them say we shouldn't be educated."

"Really?" Mildred murmured in surprise, recalling Porter's worry about the rise of Elitism in the Council. "Who?"

"Rand said it to one of the fireboys when he caught him reading a newsscroll. Evelyn makes remarks all the time about maids not needing to know how to read in order to do their jobs."

A worried stir moved through Mildred's chest at the thought of Evelyn. Refraining from educating the lower class was the highest form of Elitism. Did her friend even realize the wave she was caught up in, or was she simply riding the popular opinions of the day? Evelyn must not know—she couldn't. Evelyn was motivated . . . but tyrannical? No. Mildred refused to believe it, and wondered where the Elitism had begun.

"Lavinia, I must be honest with you. I simply cannot teach right now."

"Oh."

"I refuse to set up unrealistic expectations," Mildred said, folding her hands in front of her. "I don't have time. But I shall teach again, within the next few months, when I figure out my job."

"All right."

Lavinia's voice had shrunk, as if it had curled away into a small place inside of her. Mildred felt a stab of guilt, and then annoyance. She simply *couldn't* take on teaching, not even if she missed it.

"I shall contact you as soon as I'm able," Mildred said, hardening her heart against Lavinia's despondent face.

"Thank you, Assistant Mildred," Lavinia said, her pointy chin drawn up. She avoided meeting Mildred's eyes. "I appreciate your time."

Resisting Lavinia's wretched expression and the subtle accusation laced in the word *Assistant* wasn't as easy as Mildred hoped.

The Elitists are now making it known that they don't want education for the lower classes, she thought with a grim shudder as Lavinia departed without another word. *If they keep growing they will eventually divide the Council.*

The incantation around Stephan's office should have faded, so when no sounds came from within, she cracked open the door to find him asleep in his chair, soup dribbling down his chin and onto his shirt. The bowl was empty. With a sigh of relief, she closed the door and transported to her room.

Let him wake up in the middle of the night and go to bed himself, she thought, settling on the side of her bed. Removing her tight boots felt wonderful, and she massaged the sore muscles of her feet. Her conversation with Lavinia floated hazily through her mind.

I have questions about learning.

A lot of them say we shouldn't be educated.

The thought of Elitism amongst the Council made her sick. Open sentiments against education? It was nothing but passive oppression based on financial status. She stopped rubbing her foot to stare at a spot on the floor.

"They must be stopped," Mildred whispered with the burn of a small, righteous spark within. "Or at the very least, subverted. I can teach, at least."

With a sigh, Mildred sent a message to Lavinia through the silenda.

Meet me before breakfast. I have decided to resume classes immediately.

The jostling motion of the carriage—and the privacy it afforded—soothed Mildred's frazzled nerves. Because she'd never been to the Middle Covens, she couldn't safely transport to meet the Coven Leaders. So for a few hours while she rode alone down the Central Highway in a carriage, she closed her eyes, let her mind go blank, and enjoyed thinking of nothing.

Her first month as Assistant had passed in a blur of paperwork, boundary lines, and classes. Evelyn came and went, kept busy by her new life as Council Member, leaving Stella as Mildred's main crutch to lean on. Dinner with Marten remained her only anchor of normalcy. No one else could draw her into a meaningful discussion about her day, and she looked forward to sharing her thoughts with him. His gentle ways and dark eyes had a calming effect on her.

Stephan, little more than a thunderous gray cloud sitting near the fire, emitted occasional rumblings while Mildred worked frantically. They existed in a mostly tolerant silence, ignoring each other except for when she insisted he answer her questions. When Stephan became stubborn, Porter attempted to help.

Fed up with not knowing the identities of the Coven Leaders were, or even the locations of Coven boundaries, she packed her valise and declared, "I'll be visiting the Covens for the next couple of days, Stephan. Try not to kill anyone with your apathy while I'm gone."

He grunted and turned a page in his book.

A small Coven at the border of the Ashleigh Covens and the Middle Covens was Mildred's first stop. For all the prosperity at the heart of Ashleigh City, rampant poverty ran through the rest of her vineyards, spilling south into the farming lands of the Middle Covens.

"Stop here," Mildred called to the driver when a worn shack appeared off to the left. Smoke billowed from a rickety brick chimney, matching the fog that crept along the forest floor. Letum Wood had nearly engulfed the dilapidated structure in boughs and deadwood.

"Here?" the driver asked. "You can't be serious."

"I'm always serious."

"I'll wait right here," he said with a note of warning in his tone, keeping his wary gaze on the dead scrub oak. Mildred rolled her eyes and opened the door. If there was any danger, it certainly wouldn't lurk in the trees. It would come from the frightening hut she was about to approach. Setting aside her fears, she strode up to the shanty and rapped on the door. Several loud thumps came from inside just before the door opened a crack.

"What do you want?" a deep voice growled.

"I want to speak to the Coven Leader."

An awkward pause preceded his response. "Well? Go ahead."

"I won't speak to someone I can't see," she said. "I'd like to know who you are."

"Then we won't speak."

He made a movement to shut the door, but she jammed the toe of her boot in the gap before he could. It slammed against her foot, and she winced. "I'm on orders from Council Member Stephan."

"So?"

Of course Stephan's name wouldn't invoke any kind of respect. She couldn't stand him either. She hesitated before trying a different approach. "I'm just here to help. I know the leadership hasn't been what it should, and I want to change that."

"Help what? Help us pay taxes we can't afford while letting us wallow in poverty with bad roads?"

"What does this Coven need?"

His suspicious eyes stared at her for several seconds longer, then the door opened to reveal a man whose broad chest was matted with tight black curls. Dried mud and soot coated a sad pair of breeches with holes in both knees. The smell of body odor drifted into the chilly air. Mildred took a steadying breath through her mouth. Good heavens. He smelled—and looked—as if he'd died and clawed his way back out of the grave.

"My name is Mildred. I'm the new Assistant to Council Member Stephan."

"Congratulations. I don't have any problems except for you. Now leave."

"I didn't ask about you," she snapped, irritated to find her patience wearing thin so early in the day. "I asked about your Coven. You are the Coven Leader, aren't you?"

He shrugged his meaty shoulders. "Sure."

"You don't know if you're the Coven Leader or not?"

"There's no one else out here." He gestured around with a paw-like hand. The icy branches of Letum Wood spiraled out in gnarled fingers, creating an intricate gray web and not much else. A haunting stillness emanated from the quiet forest. Mildred wished she could bottle it up and take it back with her to the noisy castle.

"Are there no other witches in your Coven?" she asked.

"No."

"And what's your name?"

"Bart."

"This, by all accounts, should be the Northeast Middle Coven," she said, motioning behind her. "It's the smallest Coven in the middle Covens. Does that sound familiar?"

"Sure."

Mildred pushed aside her frustration. What had she expected? No one knew her. She hadn't earned their trust, which meant she'd just have to take whatever they were willing to give.

"Can I do something to help you, Bart? Is there something the Network could help you with? Provide something that you're not getting now?"

His heavy brow furrowed. "You can leave me alone."

"That I can do. I'll return in six weeks. Please send me a notice if you need any—"

The door slammed in her face before she finished. Mildred lifted an eyebrow, studied the slats, and returned to the carriage, unaware that Bart watched from the belly of his house as she climbed into the carriage and continued down the dirt road.

Mildred rode through five villages, some small, some sprawling into towns, all while meeting the same distrust she'd seen in Bart. It wasn't until she passed a dead, bloated body on the side of the road and saw two young children with swollen bellies playing in a muddy ditch that she realized the extent of the poverty she dealt with.

Most witches stared at her when she introduced herself. Some pointed her to broken-down buildings, where she'd find other witches that were no more helpful. She wrote copious notes and spoke with every witch that didn't run from her, but she found no real starting point. There weren't many Coven Leaders willing to step forward, and most villages or towns didn't want one.

How can I show them that change can be a good thing? she thought as they passed a shack with chickens running out the front door. She turned to her scroll and started her twenty-fourth list while they rode to Stilton Coven.

By the time they arrived at Stilton, the most prosperous city in the Middle Covens, Mildred's bones ached, her hands were stiff with cold, and the tip of her nose shone as jolly red as a cranberry. The driver stopped at a two-story house that had been converted into the Stilton Coven office, and Mildred climbed free of the carriage. She had to knock twice before the office door opened enough for a small face to peer out at her.

"The Coven Leader is busy," a squeaky voice said. "Come back next week."

Mildred shoved her boot in the path of a closing door for the second time that day. "Tell him to clear his schedule," she demanded. "I have business with him."

The small face turned out to be a young boy, no doubt hired to send people away. Mildred pressed into the office, recoiling the moment she entered. Thick, choking smoke filled the room, washing over her with a sulfuric smell that left a metallic taste in her mouth.

"Blessed be," she cried, waving a hand in front of her face. "What is that stench?"

"Medicine," the boy said, woozy and wide-eyed. Mildred stepped through the fog, using silent magic to open a nearby window. It groaned in protest but moved upward.

"Where is the Coven Leader?" she asked.

"Where he always is." The little boy motioned to the back of the room. Mildred marched forward, using magic to open every window as she went. The offensive odor poured outside, and the haze began to clear.

"Excuse me?" she called. "Excuse me?"

A witch with a paunchy belly, an overgrown beard, and a vapid, detached expression appeared from the mist. He lounged back on a chair and stared into moving shadows that only he could see.

"What's his name?" Mildred asked the boy, who stumbled along next to her. She put a hand on his shoulder to keep him from falling.

"Carthage," the boy mumbled. "You won't fire me, will you?"

"No." She grabbed a scroll and whacked the lumpy, insentient man on the arm. "Carthage, I command you to wake up."

He remained entrenched in his stupor. His muscles displayed no form of life. If he hadn't been puffing weakly on his pipe, which spewed an obnoxious blue smoke, she would have thought him dead.

"How long has he been like this?"

"He's always like this."

Mildred snatched the pipe from Carthage's cracked lips and chucked it out the window. He gave an annoyed little stir and his forehead puckered, but then he slipped back into vague dreams.

"Fool." She burst into a coughing fit. The three letters she'd sent sat on top of a pile of unopened envelopes. A roll of blankets lay across the floor. Hardened crusts of bread littered the pillow, and a few candle stubs sat on the desk. The rest of the two-story office was a mass of dust.

"It's my guess he doesn't conduct much business?"

The little boy shook his head, nearly falling from the effort. A flare of rage bloomed in her chest. A leader in such a deplorable condition! How could *any* witch figure out how to run a Coven with such imbeciles in positions of power?

"Very well," she said, brushing off her hands. "I'll take care of this."

She returned to the wide porch of the office to find a small queue of curious witches on the lawn. Everyone seemed to hold their breath as soon as she appeared. Behind her, the house leaked putrid smoke like water through a thimble.

"Is there anyone here who works with the Coven Leader or has in the past?" she asked. Witches stepped out of the businesses lining the street to listen, but no one spoke up.

"Well?" she called. "Anyone?"

A man with unassuming brown eyes, a gentle face, and a groomed beard came forward from the apothecary shop across the street.

"I've worked with Carthage before," he said. Although quiet, his voice carried over the crowd. "I'm the Assistant Apothecary."

"What's your name?" Mildred asked, taking a mental checklist of him. He stood tall and straight. He appeared clean. Three things she'd seen little enough of in the past few hours.

"William."

"Very well, William. What can you tell me about Carthage?"

He glanced behind him as a striking woman with gray eyes and black hair stepped out of the apothecary.

"We hardly see him," William said. "Trying to get an appointment is impossible. Every now and then he'll leave to get a few supplies, but he often just ends up at the tavern or—" He motioned helplessly to the blue smoke spewing from the office.

"And who are you?" someone asked from the anonymity of the gathering crowd.

"My name is Mildred. I'm the new Assistant for Council Member Stephan. I've come to introduce myself and discuss the needs of your Coven."

"We need food!" a woman cried.

"And jobs."

"And our common schools back!"

A clamor of voices assaulted her.

"Silence!" she called. "All of you. I'll take care of everything as best I can. In the meantime, I need a Coven Leader. William, how do you feel about taking over for Carthage?"

His light brown eyes grew wide. "Take over?"

The black-haired woman stepped to his side and put a hand on his shoulder. William calmed, as if her simple touch gave him physical strength. "It would be an honor to serve our Coven," she said.

William looked to the woman with a questioning gaze. She smiled. He responded with one of his own, then turned to Mildred with a nod.

"Yes," he said. "My wife, Lily, and I will help in any way that we can."

"Thank you," Mildred said. "Let's start with clearing that office out. You, and you." She pointed to two swarthy men standing nearby. "I'd appreciate you bringing Carthage out."

They stared at her, and she felt a momentary shock of fear. What if they didn't listen? What if they didn't respect her authority?

No, she thought. *I will* NOT *fail. I've failed at enough already.* "Well? Get to it. We have a lot to do and not enough time."

They hesitated a heartbeat longer, then started to the office together. She barely came to their shoulders when they slipped past her and disappeared inside.

"You, and you," she said, pointing to a woman and a girl who appeared to be her daughter. "Do you have current employment?"

"No, Miss Mildred," the mother said.

"Does someone clean this office?"

"No."

"You're hired. Please start immediately. Record how many hours it takes you until it's spotless, and I'll personally pay your wages. Leave all the paperwork and business to William and his wife."

The two men struggled out of the house, holding Carthage by his chubby ankles and sweat-lined shoulders. His pinpoint eyes stared out at the crowd without comprehension.

"Take him to the inn to let him sleep it off," she said, gaining confidence with every passing moment. All it took was a show of authority. "The rest of you, go home. I will return in one week to take your complaints and questions. Spread the word to your neighbors."

The stunned faces gradually fell away, but not for some time after she strode back inside the office and began to throw things out the window. The mother and daughter tasked with cleaning reappeared. William, who wouldn't let his wife inside a building with such foul air, joined Mildred, his shirt over his nose.

"Thank you for accepting," she said, straightening. "Let's get right to business."

As Stephan maintained no requirements of his Coven Leaders or High Witches, Mildred devised her own to guide him.

"I want a report every two weeks on the state of the Coven and current problems," she said while she paced back and forth across the front porch. He wrote her expectations down for the next half-hour. "And you shall be in charge of managing and communicating with the tax collectors . . ."

By the time they left the office, which still reeked of stale eggs and tobacco, night had long since descended. Mildred's feet ached, her tired back felt cramped, and a dull headache throbbed at the base of her skull. They stood on the porch for a moment.

"Thank you for your help," she said. William locked the door behind him but left some of the windows open to the chilly night so the building could breathe.

"Do you need a place to stay?" he asked. "Your driver is at the inn, I believe."

"I'll transport back to the castle," she said. "Please tell him to return to Chatham in the morning. I shall be in touch within the next couple of days."

Without a farewell or word of explanation, Mildred transported back to her bedroom. She heated a small cauldron of water, peeled off her stinking clothes, scrubbed her skin and hair, and collapsed into bed to stare at the ceiling.

It's done, she thought. The first challenge had passed, and she'd handled it tolerably well. She reviewed each part of the day in methodical, precise detail, noting further additions to her mental list of ways to improve. At the very least, she'd reached out, met the residents, seen the poverty, and removed a corrupt leader. For the first time in over a month as Assistant, she felt like she might, with dedicated hard work, tolerate the job.

Fortunately, she wasn't afraid of working.

She fell into a deep sleep while thinking that life was never as straightforward as her plans and wondering what Marten would have to say about that at dinner the next day.

Bad News

"I have some bad news to report, Council Member."
May stood in front of Evelyn's desk, an envelope in hand and an unusually severe expression on her face. Evelyn glanced up, surprised that the buzz she felt when addressed as *Council Member* still hadn't faded after six months.

Paperwork and correspondences surrounded her in an ocean of parchment and scroll. Four separate quills kept active by complex magical incantations worked around her desk; one hovered in the air for lack of space. Ink dripped onto the floor, but she'd have the servants clean it up later. The beginnings of summer filled the room with stuffy warmth.

"What happened this time?" she asked, biting back another sigh. Where had all of these disasters come from? Evelyn couldn't recall this many problems when she'd served as the High Priestess's Assistant. Then again, Nell dealt with a broader spectrum of issues, not these ridiculous tiffs between Coven Leaders and tax collectors. At this rate, it would take her three years to be efficient, or at least sleep a full night.

The thought that perhaps she wasn't as ready to be Council Member as she'd believed filtered through her mind, but she pushed it away. Improving the Network came at a definable cost; one she would pay.

"A report from the vineyards just came from Milton DeAngelo." May handed an opened letter to her. "He owns the most profitable vineyard in Ashleigh and says there are rumors of riots breaking out amongst his workers."

"Riots?" Evelyn asked with a scowl, eyes still on a letter from Norbert, the Head of Finances, asking why they'd underpaid last month. The last thing she needed was a riot *and* underpaid taxes, so she would send the requested thirty pentacles to prevent Norbert from telling Donovan. Once she was in power she'd get rid of corrupt witches like Norbert. In the meantime, she'd just have to tolerate him. "What are they rioting about now?"

"The vineyards are only producing at fifty percent for the third year in a row. Milton cut their wages so he didn't have to close the vineyard, and they're throwing a fit. A violent fit, of course."

Evelyn plucked the letter from May's hand and perused it. The handwriting was so sloppy she could barely make out the words.

"Building discontent," she murmured, only able to read in bits and snatches. "Low wages . . . workers angry . . . waiting outside main gates. Requesting your presence."

The last line was clear enough.

"I think you should go," May said, folding her hands in front of her. She wore a dark gray dress with long, fitted sleeves and a slight puff in the shoulder. The color drew attention to her blue eyes. "You know how the poor are, Evie. One irrational fear will escalate into a bloodbath. A threatened riot is as good as a violent one."

"Yes," Evelyn said, pushing her hair out of her face at the grim thought. "To protect the innocents, we must get on top of the riots before they turn deadly."

"Exactly. I'm glad to hear such sense spoken from one in power. You prove your worthiness to hold your position time and time again. In six months, you still haven't lost your edge or forgotten your ideals."

The warmth of the compliment tingled through Evelyn's body. She stood, shucking off the papers in her way.

"Well, May, let's go to the vineyards, shall we?"

Milton DeAngelo was a short, fat man with a gray goatee that nearly reached the top button of his overcoat. He always wore a hat, and as far as Evelyn could ascertain, had never once touched a grapevine.

"I bought the place ten years ago," he said, standing in the parlor of his estate. "The foreman Elijah runs the day-to-day work. Good with plants, you know. Grew up around grapevines. He's usually the go-between for me and the workers. Speaks their language, you know."

Evelyn murmured her agreement. May shot her a quiet, knowing look that Evelyn understood at once. *Milton could be a supporter.* She filed his name in the back of her mind. Milton DeAngelo was just the kind of wealthy witch that Evelyn would need to back her righteous cause. Wasn't he living the beginning of her nightmares? The rise of the poor against the educated upper class that ran the Network and supplied it with ability and talent? All the more reason to subdue this ridiculous discontent.

Not to mention the consequences of everyone finding out one of my Covens rioted within my first six months, she thought, suppressing the need to fidget. She'd look incompetent if she couldn't keep things running smoothly her first year, and she was determined to prove her capability.

DeAngelo's four-story mansion sat behind endless fields of gnarled plants stretching in lines until they met Letum Wood in the distance. Evelyn sipped her tea, impressed by the interior decor of the parlor. Porcelain figurines of young women graced the shelves on the wooden walls, the air smelled like musty potpourri, and an elaborate rug from the mills of the Middle Covens covered the floor.

"Tell me, Milton," Evelyn said, carefully setting her teacup on the saucer and facing him with a warm smile. "Your vineyards have fallen on hard times, have they not?"

His wrinkled old face fell. "Indeed, Council Member," he said with a quiet duck of his head, as if they had just spoken of someone who had recently died. "A disease moved through my fields, and the foreman had to burn over half of the plants. I thought we'd recover this spring, only . . ." He trailed off, head shaking. "It wasn't meant to be."

Milton reached for a pastry on the platter in the middle of the table with his chubby pincer fingers. Evelyn spotted the sparkle of a cufflink with a cluster of purple diamond grapes and wondered if Grant would like it.

"I understand your frustration," she said. "And now all your workers are threatening to riot?"

"I can't pay them the same I used to," he said, sounding desperate. "How could I? We've only half the revenue coming in. I must save for the future or else the vineyard will go under completely, so I fired some and cut the pay of the rest. They don't understand that I had to do it to keep running. It's a game of numbers, plain and simple. I simply *can't* afford to pay them more currency when I have none to give. If I were to keep operations running as they were before the blight, all of it would close, and everyone would lose their jobs."

"And you've explained it to them?"

"Of course," he huffed. "A lot of good it did. Well, I suppose *I* didn't explain it, but Elijah said he'd talk to them. They just yelled at him about decreasing wages and feeding their children. I understand they're scared. I daresay I would be as well, but the numbers don't lie."

"No," Evelyn said, "the poor rarely do understand the economics of business. You can't be held responsible for the individual life of every worker."

"Exactly," he said in relief. "Though they expect me to, you know."

"Bearing the responsibility of leadership is difficult: to lead those that don't want to be led, to make them understand things outside their control. It's a terrible burden. What can I do to support you?"

Milton's gaze had traveled outside and locked onto something across the way. He stood, finger pointing. "There!" he cried. "You see? They're gathering in groups outside my house! I want them gone! I shan't pay them at all if they keep forming posses and riots. I'll fire them all and hire witches from the Southern Covens."

A queue of ten witches had walked up to the wrought iron gate that separated Milton's yard from the rest of the vineyards. Evelyn's forehead ruffled. They were a ragtag group, with dirty pants, old caps, and skin that looked as if it hadn't been washed in ages. Although they never touched the gate, and made no move to do so, their very presence outside Milton's house was unsettling.

I must protect him and his life's work, Evelyn thought, rallying her courage. *I must guard the DeAngelos from harm.*

"I see exactly what you mean," Evelyn said.

"Elijah says they want their jobs back, but I say that's madness. He proposed a tax break, but that's even more ridiculous! They still live on the land and use the roads," Milton said. "Just because they make a sacran or two less doesn't mean they shouldn't have to pay for the same privileges I pay for, does it?"

"No. I agree with you, Milton."

His chest huffed with a sigh of relief. "Good," he said, and his voice softened to the weary tone of a grandfather. "I don't want to lose my vineyard because they demand I pay them currency I don't have."

"Don't fear," Evelyn said, standing. She moved closer to the window, but remained off to the side to stay out of sight. "The Network shall protect you, your family, and your interests. May, send a request for half a contingent of Guardians to stand guard for the next three weeks."

The shuffle of May rooting through her bag and the sudden appearance of a quill in her hand sounded in the quiet room while Evelyn paused, mapping out a plan.

"Specify that any witch participating in a riot or protest will be sent to the dungeons for a one-year sentence."

"Forgive my impertinence, Council Member," May murmured, "but do you feel that is steep enough?"

"Get them off my land if they're going to hurt me!" Milton called, shaking a fist at the window. "I don't want them coming after my wife when I'm at the club, you know. What's one year? Look at them! They're trying to memorize the layout of my house so they can break in!"

It was quite odd that they should just stand outside. There could be no innocent intent behind such a gesture. Swift, sure justice would be best.

Evelyn sucked in a breath. "You're right," she said. "A life sentence."

May nodded as Evelyn continued her instruction. "Tell the Guardians that they are to patrol the estate, break up any pockets of witches greater than two, and report back to me if there are any problems."

Milton DeAngelo swallowed another pastry. "Thank you, Council Member," he said in relief, lifting a teacup from a silver platter.

"Let us just hope that the presence of the Guardians will show them how serious we are. They'll move on, I hope."

Milton agreed with a nod. "You've saved my family, my home, and my vineyard today. I shall forever be in your debt."

Evelyn smiled. It felt wonderful to finally make a difference.

Once Evelyn returned to Chatham Castle, an array of garden parties and late night social events captured her attention. She gratefully put Milton DeAngelo's vineyards out of her mind—feeling good about her decision to imprison the rioters—and didn't think of them again for three weeks.

"It's quite hot today," May said from her desk, where she lounged against her seat. A fan hovered in the air, waving back and forth, cooling her flushed cheeks.

Evelyn set aside a stack of paperwork and straightened herself. Her back ached from slouching over her desk. She drank a sip of cool water, though the ice shipped all the way from the Southern Covens had already melted, leaving the glass sweating and wet.

"Blasted summer," she muttered, lifting the hair off the nape of her neck. A wave of brutal heat moved into her office when the door to the hall opened and closed, momentarily overriding the spell that Evelyn had used to cool the room.

"Council Member?"

A tall, strapping young man with brown hair and eyes set in a tanned face stepped into the room. Something vaguely familiar lingered in his solemn expression and brisk, militaristic manner, though she couldn't place it exactly. The insignia on his chest indicated he was a Captain of the Guards. The initials J. G. sat beneath the insignia.

"Yes?" she asked. May peered over the rim of her glasses with disinterest before turning back to her paperwork.

"Three weeks ago my contingent was assigned to protect Milton DeAngelo's vineyard in the Ashleigh Covens. I've come to report."

She brightened. "Of course. How many people did you imprison?"

"Three."

Her eyebrows rose in surprise. "Why so few?"

"We observed no problems during our three week stay," he said, instead of answering her question directly. He paused, and his lips moved as if he'd just run a tongue over the front of his teeth.

"There must have been or you wouldn't have arrested three. What did they do?"

A definitive uneasiness lingered in his steely gaze. "Those we apprehended were drunk and didn't even know where they were. They didn't deserve imprisonment for being drunk, but we followed your orders."

"At least they are put away for life so Milton can sleep easier. And how is the DeAngelo family and estate?"

"Safe. Two Guardians will remain for the next week to ensure his safety. Milton was smoking a cigar on his porch and eating eclairs when I left, Council Member."

"How many riots?"

"None."

"None?"

He nodded to affirm it, his hands folded behind his back. "There were no rumors of riots either."

She looked back on her original meeting with Milton with regret. The presence of the Guardians had scared the poor away. They'd apprehended none of the rioters, which meant they were still free to make trouble. She should have had those hooligans outside the estate arrested while she was there. Next time she'd act much more decisively.

Goodness, she thought. *The strange lessons I must learn.*

"What of that Elijah?" she snapped. "He's their leader, isn't he? Milton seems to trust him, but I don't."

"I met and spoke with Elijah at length during my time there. He's a good witch," the Captain said, chin tilted high. "He cares for the workers that he takes responsibility for, and fears for their future. He also cares about his own job and would never defy his boss."

She would have protested, but found his follow-up sufficient and was too hot to address his unsolicited opinion. "I see," she said. "Well, that's very disappointing."

"Disappointing?"

"I was hoping you would make the Ashleigh Covens safer for those of us under attack," she said in a cutting tone. A vision of Mama's red hair flashed through her mind. She felt a distinct sense of failure; she hadn't really protected Milton and his family, had she? She'd simply scared away a mob for now; no doubt they'd react violently once the Guardians were gone.

Next time I'll let them riot, and we'll round them up for good. Wipe out their chances of getting away.

"Forgive me for saying so, Council Member, but the DeAngelo vineyards have nothing to fear from the workers. Milton may have perceived a threat that wasn't—"

"Do not presume to tell me where the threats are or are not. Your job is to do as I say. You've completed the mission, though not to my liking, and I shall report it to Dolph. Hopefully this will help you improve in the future."

The Captain drew himself taller with an indifferent gaze. He paused, mouth open, then, deciding not to voice his thoughts, said, "Understood, Council Member."

"You're dismissed."

He gave a slight bow and departed without another word. Whatever he left unsaid lingered, nudging at Evelyn. She *should* be satisfied that violence had been prevented—and she was—so why did she feel a sense of letdown that someone hadn't been brought to justice?

"You scared the rioters," May said as soon as the door closed behind him. "But they'll be back once the Guardians are gone. Mark my words. Don't let your defenses down."

Evelyn clenched her jaw. This was one fight she wouldn't lose.

"I agree. Will you please send a message to Grant? I'd like to have lunch with him today. He's been avoiding me, and I want to find out why."

You're Fired!

D espite the sticky humidity in the Council Room, Stephan fell asleep shortly after he sat down. Mildred fanned herself with an old piece of parchment, her cheeks bright red. Even with a dozen active incantations quelling the heat, it still felt miserable. Since there seemed to be no way to rid the room of the hot summer air, they all suffered in painful silence.

"I hope this goes quickly," Mildred said under her breath. Stella, who sat at her left as always, agreed with a low murmur. The previous Esbat had lasted an interminable three hours, and now they'd advanced into the second month of summer.

"Middle Covens," Donovan called from the wide chair tailored for his expansive bottom. Sweat streaked the sides of his face. "The Head of Finances reports that you underpaid Network taxes by 23,000 pentacles last month. Explain yourself."

An unsuccessfully stifled yawn distorted his voice.

"We apologize, Your Highness," Mildred said, having braced for his accusation. The Head of Finances sent her a message earlier that week warning her that he'd tell Donovan about their tax deficiency unless she paid him thirty pentacles. She'd burned the letter and prepared herself for the worst, refusing to give in to corruption. "We only collected enough to pay 7,000 pentacles."

"That's not even half!"

"Yes," she said, nostrils flaring as she suppressed a snide comment on his ability to do math. "Their crops are still growing and not yet ready to sell."

She'd been Stephan's Assistant for eight months now—and a more tempestuous eight months had never been experienced—which meant she'd faced Donovan in the Esbat eight times, and she still couldn't stand him. Every month brought a new struggle between them. She'd finally accepted that they would never like each other.

"Taxes in the farming Covens are one pentacle per family member per month," he cried. "It's not that much to ask!"

"Most witches only make one sacran for a full day's work," Mildred replied in frustration. "With five sacrans to a pentacle, an entire week of work goes to taxes for each person in a family. The cotton farmers with more than two or three children barely make enough to eat, even with both parents working."

"That's not Donovan's fault," Council Member Eddy piped up. "If they can't afford to feed their children, they shouldn't have them."

"Miserable wretches make excuses for everything," Rand muttered. "The poor breed like lice, don't they? Then they expect the rest of us to take care of them."

Mildred's sensitive temper flared when Evelyn smiled slyly at Eddy and Rand, as if they shared a secret. Their growing Elitist attitudes frightened Mildred far more than facing Donovan without enough currency, and she wondered if Eddy was the originator of the movement.

"Yes," Donovan said, brightening at the small group of supporters rallying around him. "Witches do make excuses, don't they? The Middle Covens has 30,000 residents. 30,000 pentacles is a fair tax. How am I supposed to run the Network with so little currency coming in?"

You could start by closing Ashleigh House, your personal retreat built by the exploitation of the poor, Mildred thought, but she schooled her emotions into apathy.

"7,000 is twice what we were able to get last month, which means we are slowly improving. We've had to replace and train Coven Leaders and tax collectors."

Donovan's eyes bulged. "You only posted 3,500 pentacles last month?"

Mildred's heart nearly stopped. What a foolish mistake! Of course

Donovan hadn't looked back to previous months. She'd errone-
ously assumed the Head of Finances would have told him all their
indiscretions.

Too late, she thought, forcing a fearless facade by squaring her
shoulders and meeting his irate gaze.

"Yes."

Stephan hadn't moved an inch at her side, but regarded her with
the same open astonishment as everyone else. She could almost feel
him yelling at her in his head. *Why didn't you just pay off the Head of
Finances like everyone else?* As of eight months ago, the Middle Covens
had fallen under her leadership. Though she wasn't Council Member
on paper, she'd answer for every failure of the Covens.

"Yes?" Donovan bellowed. "That's it? You aren't going to give me
an explanation?"

"I tried. But you ignored it."

Donovan flipped a hand at her. "Get out of here! You're fired! You
can't even get taxes paid."

Mildred's breath stopped in her throat. Stella made a noise of
shocked protest but remained in her seat.

"You're firing me for telling the truth?" Mildred asked, unable to
stop herself. Donovan's eyes narrowed again. Evelyn shook her head
frantically back and forth, while Stella pinched her leg under the table.

"Mildred!" she hissed from behind her hand. "Are you crazy? You
can't speak to the High Priest like that!"

"I'm firing you because you're a failure!" Donovan yelled, mop-
ping his sweaty forehead with a sleeve. "And impertinent at that.
Leave immediately."

Mildred opened her mouth to speak, but Stella grabbed her elbow
and jerked her down into her chair. To her great surprise, Stephan
slammed his hands on the table.

"No!" he yelled. "No!"

He used the table to brace himself, slowly standing on knobby,
trembling knees. "You can't fire my Assistant," he cried, bushy eyebrows knitted together. "She works for me, not you."

"I'm the High Priest! I can do whatever I please."

"No you can't!" Stephan said. "I'm tired of teaching Assistants how to do their job, and I refuse to get another one. Of course she didn't get all the taxes. Do you want to know why? Because I keep losing Assistants!"

He rapped the table with his large knuckles.

"You take responsibility for her?" Donovan asked, mirroring Mildred's shock. Stella's grip had loosened, and even Evelyn and Grant were listening with rapt interest. Stephan hadn't taken responsibility for anything in years.

"No!" Stephan yelled. "I don't like her either, but she's the only one that's collected even a quarter of the required taxes. Maybe you weren't paying attention, but we haven't paid 7,000 pentacles in taxes for almost two years. Why? Because all the Assistants left it a mess! Jikes, Donovan! When you took over the Southern Covens, you underpaid taxes for the first year. You even borrowed from the Network to pay your workers. The Middle Covens didn't even ask for currency!"

Donovan sank into a distant memory for nearly a minute while an uneasy silence reigned. Stella's head whipped back and forth between them so fast she nearly hit Mildred with flying locks of hair.

"Er, yes. Perhaps." Donovan wriggled in his chair and swiped sweat from his eyes. Beneath the tense exchange, the room felt even more like a baking oven.

"If you fire her, she's under no obligation to remain behind and explain what she's done for the Middle Covens, and my memory is terrible." Stephan wagged a long finger. "I can guarantee you won't get taxes for the next six months if either of us go."

"I hadn't thought of that."

"Do it! Fire us!" Stephan said. "I dare you! The Middle Covens will really fall apart, you'll not get taxes, the textiles won't get made, and then you won't be able to get any clothes or cotton."

Mildred held her breath while Donovan glared down at them. "Fine," he shouted. "Assistant Margaret—"

"Mildred," she retorted.

"Whatever! You may stay, but only because it would be less convenient to fire you. I better have the full tax by the end of the year. You hear? The end of the year! Letum Wood Covens, report!"

Stephan collapsed into the chair with a growl. Mildred sat back, dazed and a bit shaky. Had Stephan, of all witches, just saved her job? She thought of thanking him, but stopped. He'd insulted her, too. He only wanted to keep her so he wouldn't have to work.

Mildred pulled out a fresh scroll and a quill and redirected her attention to taking notes as if nothing unusual had happened. Stephan leaned back, folded his hands across his middle, and promptly fell back to sleep in the miserable heat.

After the Esbat, Mildred set her bag on the far edge of Stephan's desk and leaned against it with a deep sigh. Her dress clung to her sweaty body when she waved the window open with a spell, but it did little to relieve the heat. Mildred spoke a wind incantation, and the slight breeze cooled her skin a bit. Stephan hobbled to his chair, muttering under his breath as he moved.

"Thank you," Mildred said, breaking a stretch of stillness. He glanced at her from the corners of his eyes, made a *hurmph* sound, and propped his cheek on his hand to stare at the empty fireplace.

"How did you know what to say to Donovan?" Mildred asked.

"I know Donovan," Stephan retorted with annoyance that filtered away as he spoke. "I've worked with him for years. He's lazy now. He wasn't always, but he injured that damn knee. Sometimes, in politics, you have to turn what you know against people. You learn where they're weak, and you use it."

Mildred sat on the chair across from him. "Sounds barbaric," she said with a frown. "Deliberately seeking out a weakness to exploit later."

"It's politics. You think I became Council Member by sitting around and letting Assistants do all the work? I used to be busy. I used to take care of things."

His words echoed through the empty air. *Used to. Used to.*

"I suppose you've taught me something tonight," she admitted grudgingly. As far-fetched as it sounded, Stephan had helped her career for once, instead of hindering it.

"Politics aren't logical," he said. "That's your problem. You're trying to put it in a box that you can mold, but you can't! When you work in politics, you work with witches, and witches aren't predictable. Half of them are crazy anyway. You can't control them, so stop trying."

Present company included, she wanted to add.

"I'll remember that," she said after thinking over his conclusion. The logic made sense. While she didn't like to think of a chaotic world that didn't involve the safety of rationality, and she was uncomfortable with the idea of exploiting another witch for gain, she couldn't deny the truth of his words. Perhaps there was a grain of truth beneath the way Evelyn worked, too. Once again Mildred found herself questioning what she believed. How was one supposed to navigate such an uncertain and tempestuous sea?

Stephan glowered from beneath his bushy white eyebrows. "Just get the taxes straightened out before the end of the year."

She'd have four months to pull 30,000 pentacles out of the starving, work-weary Middle Covens. It had taken her eight months just to get 7,000 steady pentacles. She was tempted to ask Stephan how they'd managed before she came, but she held back. Likely it had something to do with bribes, corruption, and chosen blindness. It didn't matter now. They would move forward.

The taste of her swallowed pride thickened her throat. "I can't do it alone," she said, folding her hands on her lap. "I need your help. Perhaps we can break our impasse tonight and agree to work together more amicably."

"Obviously you can't do it yourself." He rolled his eyes. "Or else I wouldn't have had to bail you out."

"Are you going to help me or not? You know the Middle Covens better than anyone."

"Knew," he said with a hint of regret. Stephan closed his eyes. "I don't know anything anymore, and I haven't cared since she die—"

He stopped, and his entire body went rigid, though his eyes still flickered with pain. The portrait of his dead wife that hung above the fire drew both their gazes. Stephan hadn't once mentioned his family in the time she had worked with him. She realized with a start that his gritty personality hid nothing but a lonely, frightened old man.

"I'll get started on the taxes in the morning, I suppose," Mildred said, arms folded tightly across her chest. But how? The new, trustworthy Coven Leaders would help, but she still had to train half of them. Then came the not-so-simple matter of collecting crime reports, answering pleas from Head Witches, dealing with failed crops, and increasing the output of the mills. Three piles of tottering envelopes awaited her attention.

And that didn't even include planning her lessons for the staff three times a week.

I've failed to do this job well so far, she thought. *That's the simple matter of it. While Evelyn and Stella press forward with confidence in their careers, I'm still floundering to figure out how to be an Assistant after eight months. I can't even get my Council Member to help.*

"One hour," Stephan said, startling her from her thoughts. "I'll give you an hour of my time after breakfast, before my nap."

"And one hour after lunch," she said.

"Ungrateful witch," he muttered. "Fine, I'll give you an hour after lunch as well. But you have to make sure my meals arrive on time. Buy me a new pair of slippers to wear around the office. I get chilly in here. Make sure I have a fresh pile of books, too, and cookies on the plate at all times."

Relief rippled through Mildred's chest, although it felt more like desperation. She'd forget her pride and pamper him the way he wanted—perhaps he missed the way his wife had taken care of him—if he helped her. She'd stuff his face full of chocolates if they could meet Donovan's 30,000 pentacle requirement.

"Agreed."

He made another sound in the back of his throat, closed his eyes, and promptly fell asleep while Mildred transported to the library, seeking a fresh stack of gardening books and a recommendation on where to buy slippers.

This Is Wonderful

The comfort of a predictable schedule—and figuring out how to do her job, thanks to Stephan's new involvement in Coven business—felt like loosening a corset; Mildred took her first real breath in years. Forward movement in her life had never felt so wonderful, even if it rolled on the wheels of meetings, paperwork, and caring for Stephan while also doing most of his job.

"I'm leaving early today," Mildred announced on the warm summer evening of her twenty-fifth birthday. She set a vase of fresh flowers from the gardens on the windowsill, rearranged them so two of the same color weren't side by side, and stepped back to survey her work with a satisfied nod. A beautiful birthday gift from Marten. "The reports from all Coven Leaders were in on time this month, which means I'm giving them a luncheon in Hampstead as a thank you."

She knew he didn't really care, but saying it out loud helped her feel accomplished. Stephan waved her out from behind his book and grunted.

"Your dinner is ordered and will arrive at promptly six," she said, tucking the blanket in around his legs despite the uncomfortable warmth in the room. "I ordered the steak with extra gravy, just the way you like it, and a separate container of salt so you can season your own potatoes."

His cup of milk remained full, kept cold by a spell from a grimoire Mildred found in the library a few weeks before. If it warmed at all, he would send her a message demanding she return and bring him a new glass. A stack of scrolls on the best method of growing annuals waited at his fingertips, and a plate of cookies rested within reach. He reached for one and left a trail of crumbs on the pages of his current read, *Growing Grass in the Southern Covens*. It held his rapt attention. Mildred had gone all the way to a library in the Eastern Covens to find a book he hadn't read yet.

With one last glance to make certain he had enough firewood for the evening, Mildred grabbed her bag and slipped into the hallway without a word. After being cooped up inside all day, she'd left enough time in her schedule to walk to the tea house for their annual birthday tradition. Stretching her legs and inhaling the crisp tint in the air that signaled the impending autumn felt like the most glorious birthday present of all. She arrived on the exact minute she'd planned.

"Happy birthday to me," she murmured with a pleased smile. Nothing felt as satisfactory as arriving on time.

A little bell on the door chimed when she stepped inside, welcoming her to the quaint shop that still smelled faintly of glue. Charles and his wife waved from behind the counter.

"It's all yours, Miss Mildred," he said, hailing her with an uplifted hand. "Cake is just about ready, and you're the first one here. A bit early, aren't you?"

"Yes, I have some letters to read before Stella and Evelyn arrive. Thank you, Charles."

She started up a narrow set of stairs in the back corner. The square table by the window of the second floor awaited her with a pot of iced tea, three cups, a bottle of wine for Evelyn, and small plates for the cake. The window had just been cleaned, giving her a pristine view of the sunset and the bustle of Chatham City below. Mildred sat down, let out a contented sigh, and pulled out Jorden's latest letter.

Dearest Mildred,

I received your letter and apologize for not returning it sooner. I'm a lax brother. My latest assignment in Ashleigh has kept me busy, but—no. That's not entirely true. Are you ready to hear the truth? Of course you are. You're always prepared for anything.

Mildred read the words with a rueful chuckle. Jorden always had a great deal more faith in her than she had in herself.

This is the truth, sister: I'm madly in love. I met a girl named Imogen while on patrol last fall, and I can't tear myself away from her. She's poor, and has worked the vineyards her whole life. Her father is a man named Elijah and runs the DeAngelo vineyards. I love her. Luckily, I should be stationed in Ashleigh for the next six months, so she and I can spend all the time together we want. I plan on teaching her to transport, as she doesn't know how, to make it easier for us to be together when I do leave. She's wonderful, Mildred. Quiet, but incredibly smart and learns fast. I know you'll like her.

I plan on marrying her. I'll send you notice of when, for you must be there. I could never marry without you at my side.

Your brother,
Jorden

PS- Happy 25th birthday, dear sister.

Mildred read it twice before folding the letter together in relief. Knowing that Jorden had someone to love released a burden of worry she felt for him. Whether the girl was rich or not didn't matter a bit, so long as she would be good to him.

I want to be a Council Member one day, but I don't want to do it at the expense of living. Stella's voice called from the depths of her memory. *I could never be High Priestess. Forbidden from marrying! What about children? What about family? No, I shall live my life* AND *have a career.*

First Stella, now Jorden would settled into a family life, something Mildred still had difficulty comprehending. Was there something wrong with her? She couldn't help but wonder if the assumptions she'd carried around about careers and marriage were wrong. Could she be brave like Stella and Jorden and give herself permission to love? The very idea tightened her chest.

But then Marten's warm hazel eyes and thick eyelashes swam

through her mind. She associated no panic or fear with him. Just calm strength.

Hadn't she already fallen in love?

Emotions don't always have the rampant grip over rationality I imagined.

She lost herself in a rare moment of daydreaming, imagining herself in a quiet little cottage with Marten at her side. Jorden would visit whenever he wanted, and she could pursue teaching. She felt more alive when she taught. No busy castle. No messages awaiting her immediate attention. No meetings or taxes or forced social interaction. For the first time in her life, she wondered if the path of Council Member on which she'd adamantly decided as a little girl wasn't actually the best path after all.

Being with Marten and teaching does sound wonderful, she thought ruefully. *But to change? To alter every expectation?* She was good at running the Middle Covens. She knew, without a shred of arrogance, that she was skilled at leadership, but she didn't love it—wasn't passionate for it. Paperwork and messages and meetings didn't give her the same buzz of life that teaching did.

"Milly?" She caught a glimpse of Stella's baby blue eyes in her peripheral vision. Stella's forehead furrowed in concern. "Oh, I'm sorry! Have I interrupted your private time?"

"No," Mildred said, grateful for a distraction from her unexpected thoughts. "You're fine. Please have a seat."

Stella sat across from her with a weak smile. "Evelyn should be here soon. I sent her a message this morning but haven't heard back."

"The Ashleigh Covens are keeping her quite busy. I received a letter from her yesterday when she canceled our lunch meeting."

Stella didn't respond, staring at the cup and saucer in front of her without making a move to pour. Mildred set her cup down and waited. When a span of silence stretched for several minutes, she asked, "Is something bothering you, Stella?"

Stella lifted her luminous eyes to Mildred. "Can I tell you a secret?" she implored, wrapping her hands around each other and setting her elbows on the tabletop. "I have something on my mind, and it's . . . it's heavy."

"You may."

"I'm pregnant."

Mildred's heart stuttered.

"Oh, I'm so confused," Stella cried, putting her face in her hands. "I'm so excited and so happy and so scared and so sad that I don't even know what to think. I don't even know what I feel!"

Mildred searched for an appropriate reply, but her brain seized. She'd never known how to say the right thing at the right time, and she'd rarely felt the burden of comforting more strongly than right then.

"Stella . . . this is wonderful."

"Yes, it is," she said from the muffled cave of her hands. "But it's also frightening. What if I'm not good at it? What if I'm not happy being a mother? What about my career? I don't . . . I don't even know what to think anymore."

"Then don't think," Mildred replied, although she would never have taken her own advice. "Just go from here, and do what you can."

"I *have* to think about it. I can't stop thinking about it. Oh, Mildred. How complicated life gets!" Stella pulled away from her hands and stared out the window. Tears clung to her eyelashes

"Have you told Dale?"

"No," Stella whispered, her eyes welling up again. "Not yet. He's on a month-long mission and returns in a week. I wanted some time to think everything over, but . . . perhaps you're right. Maybe I am thinking too much. Rand is going to fire me; I just know it. All my hard work will be for nothing!"

"Your five-year contract is up in the spring," Mildred said, grateful to switch to something concrete and less emotion-laden. "You must be due around then anyway, right?"

Stella perked up a bit. "Yes," she said, wiping at her eyes. "Yes, I am. I believe I'm due the third month of winter, and my contract is up the first month of spring."

"Rand doesn't have to know yet," Mildred said, relieved to find a vein of logic to travel. "Talk to Dale about what he thinks, and see how you feel. Maybe you can work up until you deliver and fulfill the contract instead of leaving early. Fulfilling the contract will certainly look better on your resume. Of course, leaving Chatham Castle may mean you never get back in."

The cold, hard truth, while unsympathetic, had the intended effect. Stella's labile emotions ebbed, at least for the moment. Her crumpled face straightened.

"You're right, Mildred. You always are, aren't you?"

"I like to think so."

"I could cry all day," Stella said, the tears returning. Her voice hardened, becoming resolute. "But I won't, I can't."

"You're having a baby," Mildred said in a dry tone. "You're not dying."

Uncertain of what to do, and knowing there was nothing she could say that would change the situation, Mildred reached out and put her hand on top of Stella's. Stella swallowed and gave her a teary smile.

"It's going to be okay, Stella."

"Thank you."

A message fluttered between them, appearing with little more than a *pop* to announce it. Mildred's forehead scrunched, recognizing Evelyn's handwriting. She tore it open and read aloud.

Very busy today. The Ashleigh Covens just can't function without my leadership, you know. These poor people are overrunning my vineyards. Save me a slice of cake. The part with the number.

—E

Stella's eyes widened. "She's rarely too busy to come for our birthday tradition!"

"Except for when she went to the opera with Grant instead," Mildred said with a roll of her eyes. "I'm not quite sure what to make of Evie anymore."

Evelyn's absence wasn't what bothered Mildred the most. Truth be told, Mildred wasn't in the mood to deal with Evelyn's mercurial emotions and strong opinions. But the line, *these poor people are overrunning my vineyards,* made her uneasy. She read it twice, then set the message to fire with an incantation. The paper disappeared in a puff of smoke.

"Well," Mildred said, picking up her fork and setting her troubled thoughts of Evelyn aside. "I believe we have our twenty-fifth birthdays to celebrate tonight, don't we? Let's have Charles bring up the cake and change the frosting to yellow. Evelyn isn't here to demand it be purple, so let's take advantage of it."

The Yule Ball

The pandemonium of the Ashleigh Covens seemed to settle down after the summer, as if escape from the roasting heat reminded witches of their patience and humanity. Evelyn let out a deep breath of relief when the threats of riots ebbed into rumors, and then mere whispers that she imagined remained but couldn't confirm. By the time a cool stream of winter winds and snow settled into Chatham Castle, she'd turned most of her focus back to social events, and left May to deal with the business side of the Ashleigh Covens.

"Blasted thing," Evelyn said, annoyed by the scratchy feel of pine needles on her skin. She shook the green pointers free from the matching velvet of her sleeve and straightened her white fur collar. All the glimmering gold buttons up the middle of her dress remained aligned despite her struggle with the evergreen bough.

"Perfect," she murmured with a smile. "I look perfect. The decorations look perfect. This whole Yule Ball is perfect, thanks to me."

A pair of hands wrapped around her waist and whirled her around. Grant stood there, the first dance of the Yule Ball whirling in dizzying array behind him. A string quartet sang in the background, guiding the dancers in a beautiful rhythm. Candles and torches lit the room in a warm yellow light, but their wax wouldn't drip on the guests thanks to a complicated spell that Donovan had just taught Evelyn that night. She executed it flawlessly, of course. Few magical spells stumped her natural talent.

Grant smiled, and his perfectly white teeth gleamed. "You look ravishing tonight, Evelyn."

"Yes, I know."

"Why haven't you answered any of my messages? I come by your office every night, but you never answer."

"I'm very busy, Grant."

His lips pouted like a little boy. "Too busy for entertaining me now, I suppose. I don't like you so business-oriented. I want to have fun adventures in Ashleigh City again. I miss your opinionated, impulsive self."

"I would miss me as well, but don't worry, I'm as opinionated as ever. Here's an opinion for you, in fact. You're looking quite handsome tonight, Grant."

He wore a black pair of pants, perfectly tailored to his slim waist, with a green velvet vest that matched her own dress to a suspicious degree. No doubt he bribed her seamstress to tell him what fabric she'd used, the silly witch. He was always trying to impress her.

"We are perfect together," he said, reaching into an inner pocket of his jacket for another cheroot. Evelyn scowled and pushed him away. Grant was handsome to a fault, but he inevitably annoyed her after only a few minutes.

"You would look much more attractive if you didn't smoke so many cheroots, you know. It makes you smell like weeds."

He laughed, and it rang out as clear and defining as a bell. "Really, Evie. It's my one vice. Without it, I'd have to live amongst the gods instead of mere witches."

"Why aren't you mingling?" she asked, inspecting the room over his shoulder. "I need this to be the most successful ball of the year. Donovan entrusted it to me because Nell is in the midst of another depressive episode and couldn't organize anything."

"You are so beautiful tonight I simply couldn't help myself." He moved in closer, clearly intent on nuzzling her neck, but she sidestepped him.

"Not here, Grant!" she hissed, with just a hint of playful enjoyment beneath it, lest he take her too seriously. He might have annoyed her, but she couldn't lose his support. "Honestly. Would you ruin my flawless reputation?"

"Flawless, is it?" he inquired in a sultry, low murmur that send a shiver up her spine. He attempted one last play at flirtation, but she ducked beneath his arm with a wicked smile.

"Later," she said in a low voice of promise. "For now, I must make a grand impression."

He let out a long sigh. "Oh, Evie. You already have a wonderful reputation."

"But there's always room for improvement."

"Must it *always* be about work?"

"Yes. It must. Now, go mingle, just like May. Try to find others that might join us in our righteous cause against Donovan. I've already secured the loyalties of Rand, Eddy, Gloria, and Milton DeAngelo, amongst a few others. Wayne, over the Northern Covens, is my next conquest. Butter him up somehow."

Grant straightened his perfect bow tie. "Anything for you, Evie," he replied drily, though she sensed an undercurrent of impatience in his tone. She brushed it aside. He'd endure. He always did, for she was worth the wait.

Evelyn moved to the top of the ballroom to survey her work. Boughs of evergreen hung at even intervals along the walls, joined by looping ribbons of red velvet tied in a bow at the bottom of each wreath. Freshly washed crystal sparkled across the tables.

"Wonderful," she sighed in relief. Even May had approved. It was exactly as beautiful as she had imagined it. "Nothing feels so good as having everything work just right."

If there was one thing Evelyn did right, it was parties.

"It's lovely, Evelyn!" Stella declared, walking up with a wide smile and bright eyes. A round bump stuck out from underneath her silk dress laced with deep red ribbons. Dale, wearing his Guardian uniform, hovered at Stella's side, admonishing her at every other step to *be careful. Don't jostle the baby. Watch that rug.*

"You look wonderful, Stella." Evelyn kissed her cheek. "Even with that baby sucking the life out of you, and Dale dictating your every move."

Stella smiled, and Dale blushed. "Thanks, Evie," Stella said, laughing. "He's just concerned for me."

Despite her pregnant radiance, a definable fatigue showed in the bags under her eyes. Evelyn felt a flash of worry for her friend.

"Are you all right though, Stell? You seem so tired."

Stella rested a hand on her belly. "I am tired, but doing well. Only a few more months until the baby is out of here."

"Please take care of yourself," Evelyn said. "I simply couldn't live without my two best friends. Can you imagine Mildred and me trying to manage without you? We'd pull each other's hair out without you there to mediate our arguments."

Stella laughed. "Speaking of Mildred, where is she?"

"The Yule Ball isn't mandatory, so she won't be attending." Evelyn rolled her eyes. "I've never seen a witch so odd in all my life."

"But we love her for it."

"Try to eat more, Stell. You look gaunt," Evelyn said, patting Stella's belly and turning her most radiant hostess smile on Dale. "Thanks for coming, Dale. You make the ball look even more regal with your Guardian uniform."

Evelyn chatted with them for a few minutes more. When Stella and Dale drifted to the refreshments table to appease her pregnant appetite, Evelyn wandered through the crowd, merrily greeting and laughing with all she found. The luxurious dinner of such delicacies as roasted lamb, stuffed pheasant, and frozen custard made of the finest cream drew praise from all corners of the room.

While the mingling crowd chattered quietly—only a few of them able to continue dancing after such an elegant meal—Evelyn worked her way over to May on the far side of the ball.

"You've really pulled together a true Central Network Yule Ball," May said, sipping a flute of champagne. "Donovan certainly seems to be enjoying himself."

Donovan sat at the high table with Rand, laughing so hard his face turned a dark shade of purple around the edges. His usual decanter of dark ipsum wasn't far from reach, nor was his Assistant, Harold, who stood back in the shadows and waited to be beckoned. Evelyn sipped at a glass of mellow red wine. The overwhelming, heady smell of cinnamon from the scented pinecones had given her a headache.

"Well, it's all thanks to you running the Ashleigh Covens and doing business in my name."

May smiled. "It's my pleasure to share power with you. Just look what you've done here! You'll make a fabulous High Priestess."

While May's praise usually made Evelyn giddy enough to float in the clouds, tonight it rang empty and verbose. High Priestess? She was barely getting a good grip on Council Member. Remembering how overwhelmed she'd felt adjusting to her last promotion made her a bit shy of rising too quickly. That wasn't the only problem, of course.

Evelyn's stomach trembled when she looked at Nell's empty place at the high table. For Evelyn to become High Priestess, Nell could no longer exist. She still couldn't quite convince herself that was okay, no matter what May said.

"Thank you," Evelyn finally murmured, realizing May was waiting for a retort. She ignored May's studious gaze, not wanting to explain her sudden melancholy.

The massive Yule log, the biggest the castle had ever seen, still burned bright in the expansive fireplace that kept the room warm. Just a few more hours before it would peter out. They would gather the ash into small parcels and distribute them to the attendees for good luck. Evelyn wondered idly if she'd take one. She didn't believe in luck. She believed in influence.

"It's almost time to extinguish the candles and gather around the fireplace," Evelyn said after her thoughts ran their course. "I'll be happy when this is over and I can get back to handling normal business in the Covens."

May smiled. "I didn't mind running the Covens for a while, Evie. We're partners, after all, aren't we?"

"Yes," Evelyn said with a smile, though she felt uneasy at May's willingness to include herself in everything she did. "Modern-day Esmeldas, really. Thank you for coming, and for your support. I shall go inform the butler he should begin the final ceremonies of the ball. I'd say it's been a rousing success that Donovan won't be able to ignore."

I Want More

M ildred received an urgent message on the silenda during a snowy evening in the second month of winter. Since she was involved in her Intermediate Potion Making class, she ignored it at first, but her finger heated so quickly and with such intensity that she finally glanced down at her hand.

"Excuse me," she said, touching the silenda so that the message faded. "I must leave. Lavinia will duplicate my lecture notes and pass them out to you." She glanced at the corner of the classroom, and Lavinia nodded. "Please accept my apologies."

She transported away, leaving a confused classroom of fifteen without any further explanation. She arrived in Stella's apartment, right outside her bedroom door, rapped on it, pushed it open to admit herself, and found an astonishing, unexpected sight.

A cauldron of boiling water bubbled in a bright fireplace. Dark shadows danced on the wall. A woman as short as Mildred but twice as wide bustled around Stella's bed, adjusting the pillows, checking Stella's pulse, and humming under her breath. Rather than a calamity of screams of pain and blood dripping on the floor—which Mildred expected when a witch went into labor—the scene was so calm that if Stella hadn't looked miserable and flushed Mildred would have asked for tea.

"Oh!" Stella cried, reaching a hand out to her. "Oh, Mildred! I'm so glad you're here. The contractions started this morning, but I didn't want to alarm anyone."

"It's too early, isn't it?" Mildred asked.

"Yes!" Stella said. "By at least a month, but the midwife thinks it might be all right."

Mildred grasped Stella's sweaty hand. "How is it going?"

"Dale—"

Stella stopped, clenched Mildred's hand, held her breath, and moaned. Mildred knelt down at her side until the contraction passed.

"That was two minutes, Stella," the midwife said, pushing Mildred aside to wipe Stella's face with a cool washcloth. "It's getting closer."

"No!" Stella gasped. "Dale isn't here!"

"Did you send for him?" Mildred asked, and the midwife nodded.

"I sent Marten after Dale," Stella said, her bottom lip trembling, "but he just wrote to say they can't find him yet. I won't do it without him, Mildred. I won't!"

"I'm sure Marten will find him."

"What if he doesn't? I won't have this child without Dale. I'll cross my legs!"

"You may have to do this without him, Stella."

"I can't!"

"You don't have a choice."

Stella pressed her free hand to her eyes and sobbed. "I don't want to! Can't I wait another day or two?"

"No. Where's your mother?"

"She just transported home for a minute to eat a quick dinner. She's been at my side all day and said she'd be right back, but I just . . . oh!"

Stella squeezed Mildred's hand in an impressive death grip, her face turning red as she endured another contraction. The midwife smiled as she trundled past, a pile of towels in her arms.

"Why hasn't my mother returned?" Stella cried. "It's been ten minutes already. I won't have this baby, Mildred. I refuse. It hurts too much already!"

"Too bad," Mildred said. "You must have this baby tonight. You cannot wait another day or two. You can do it, Stella, whether you believe me or not."

Stella, still teary, fell back against the pillows to rest until the next round. Her mother, Agatha, arrived moments later, and the final minutes of Stella's labor progressed in what felt like seconds. Suddenly the midwife shoved Mildred out of the way, handed Agatha several clean towels, and barked orders to Stella like a Captain of the Guards.

"Get the scissors," she bellowed to a red-faced Assistant that had transported in. "She's ready to go."

Mildred paced back and forth at the end of Stella's bed, giving the frightened, panting mother-to-be firm glances meant to impart strength. She'd never felt more stressed in her life. How could she support a woman in the middle of labor? What if something happened to Stella? The thought of anything bad happening to either of her friends rarely crossed Mildred's mind, and the idea terrified her now.

"Okay, Stella. Push when I say," the midwife yelled, and Mildred expected her to hold a flag in the air at any moment and declare war. "Let's bring this baby into the world!"

The door to the bedroom slammed open.

"Stella!" Dale rushed across the room and dropped to his knees at her side. Dirt streaked his broad face, and his eyes were drawn with fatigue and worry, but he stared at Stella as if nothing in the world could have stopped him from coming. "I'm so sorry!"

"I knew you would make it!" Stella cried through a moan. "I knew it!"

Stella grabbed his hand, clutching her swollen belly with her free hand. Mildred shrank back. With Dale and her mother there, Stella didn't need Mildred. She *should* leave but couldn't tear herself away. Stella, gritting her teeth together and gazing deep into Dale's eyes, nodded once.

"Okay," she said, panting and crying and laughing at the same time. "Let's have our baby."

"Now!" the midwife cried. "Give a good push now!"

Mildred retreated farther into the shadows but didn't leave until she heard a weak, wonderful cry and saw a slippery baby placed in Stella's arms. In between Stella's laughter and Dale's cry of, "It's a boy!" Mildred opened the door and slipped into the hall. Once in the cool air and dark safety of Stella's apartment, she pressed her back to the wall, let out a sigh, and closed her misty eyes.

"Are you all right, my dear Milly?" Marten asked. He was leaning against the wall, arms folded across his chest, gazing on her with a worried expression. He must have transported back with Dale.

"Oh Marten," she whispered, her voice tremulous. "How absolutely marvelous for Stella. She can live her life in ways I never will."

Marten stepped forward and enveloped her in his strong arms. Mildred folded against him, sobbing.

"You can live your life however you want, Mildred. It's yours to decide."

"I can't give my career up. I'm not strong like Stella."

"You, silly witch, are a lioness. Don't you know that you can do anything you want?" Marten's chest rumbled with a low, affectionate chuckle. "Are you happy as an Assistant?"

"Yes, but . . . no," she whispered, forehead pressed against his chest. He stroked her hair and held her close. "I'm happy when I see the Covens improve. I'm happy when I do something difficult. But I'm not . . . passionate about it."

"You're a wonderful leader for the Middle Covens. You'd make the best Council Member of the lot, since that's basically what you're already doing. But is that enough for you?"

Is that enough for you?

Mildred thought through his question for so long, and her thoughts trailed so far away, that she nearly forgot to answer.

"It's not enough," she said, still clinging to him. "I think . . . I think that I want more, but I know I won't take it."

Mildred rarely thought of the future outside of her Covens or her classes, but now, in the aftermath of a miracle so pure, she couldn't help but feel terribly heartbroken. Would she always be helping other people live but never live herself? Would she look back on her years and see only paperwork, messages, and meetings?

Was working to become a Council Member enough?

The painful clarity of her logical soul spoke the truth: *It alone is not enough.* Mildred cried into Marten's warm embrace, unable to bear the changed whisperings of her heart that she knew she'd force herself to forget. She'd continue to work, for she needed to change the world. She wanted to give it all up in one selfish move and live in the cottage with Marten, teaching, forgetting the Middle Covens and all the struggling poor, but she wouldn't.

She knew she wouldn't, but it didn't quiet the cry of her soul.

I want more.

The New Law

2nd Month of Winter

Dearest May,

Porter's become a real nuisance lately. Have you noticed? I feel as if I see him everywhere, which severely limits my interactions with our supporters. As I don't trust the servants (he probably hires them as spies), I don't feel safe discussing our plans at the castle.

For the past year, I've been intently studying the law as written by Esmelda. I didn't realize how detailed and extensive her law was. Nevertheless, I press forward for the good of all those who shall benefit from our hard work.

I've already begun a first draft to send for your approval. It should be finished by the first month of spring.

Your friend,
Evelyn

3rd Month of Summer

Evelyn,

I read over the second draft of the law you've written and saw many glaring mistakes, some of which you didn't fix from the first draft. I attribute this to how busy and inexperienced you are. Do you see now why it's so important that I know all the decisions you plan to make regarding the New CN? Without someone to check you, you're prone to make mistakes in your excitement. You are still so very inclined to flights of emotion. Together we will build a great Network.

Let's chat over my suggestions during your 26th birthday tea next month. We'll start with the most obvious problem: your desire to keep the Covens. That is a horrid idea. Splitting up the Central Network into semi-private sections of land that we'll distribute amongst our supporters is the best choice. For now, let's call the supporters Rulers. Dividing the Central Network into parcels of land will allow you to collect the greatest tax flow from the Rulers. It will be easier for them to control the poor as well. I'm thinking that the Rulers will pay fifty percent taxes to the Highest Witch (which will first be you, my darling), the actual owner of the land (as written in the new law). They can then do whatever they like with the other fifty percent. Of course, the Network won't have to worry about things like highways. The Rulers will deal with that on their own land.

As I said, let us discuss this more in greater confidence later.

Yours,
May

2nd Month of Winter

Dearest May,

I've revised the written law twice, as you instructed in your last letter. The current scroll I'm enclosing for your approval is the fourth draft. I know you are right: We must divide the poor and the wealthy, for the two cannot coexist happily. Such is obvious from the state of the Network now. My newfound knowledge of law and what goes into the creation of it only cements what I've always known: We need justice and order before mercy.

Nell has taken to another depression. I'm both saddened and exhilarated at the same time. Although Nell and I haven't really spoken in years, she did raise me, and I'll always hold some kind of odd, misplaced affection for her. But, at the same time, knowing she'll pass within the next couple of years means I shall have my opportunity to really improve the Network at last. You know how I hate waiting, and while I feel some trepidation at the thought of becoming High Priestess, I also feel confident I'll figure it out.

As you mentioned at tea last month when we decided land laws at your school, between my social status, the complete trust Donovan's shown in me, allowing me to run all of the social events at Chatham Castle, and my youth and exuberance, how could I not be chosen as the next High Priestess?

It is delightful to write that in words.

Sincerely Yours,
Evie

1st Month of Summer

Dear Evelyn,

The sixth draft of the new law is the best so far; I believe this is what I was wanting for the Network, although I do feel we need to look more into water distribution. Start researching how it's been done historically, and I shall check the imports and exports we shall expect from each parcel of land. Are you still coming by this weekend to work on a final layout of the land distributions? I think we should have twenty total. It's a round number and easy to remember. Not to mention that it gives you room for twenty Rulers to whom you can promise wealth and prosperity in exchange for their support for our plan.

I'll be late to work Monday morning. I need to stop by Milton DeAngelo's vineyards in Ashleigh again. He's decided to close the vineyards for good due to a lack of currency and a fresh round of disease. The poor are about to revolt with violence, so I may imprison many in your name.

We'll need to discuss the process for finding a replacement Highest Witch in the new law. Let's plan on it in two months, when you come for your twenty-seventh birthday tea at the school.

Your Assistant,
May

3rd Month of Fall

Dearest May,

Can you believe it? I think the day has finally come. The ninth and final version of the Law of the New Central Network is enclosed for your perusal and approval.

I never dreamed it would take so long to address the little details. Surely, after so much work, there are no witches more fit than us to bring the Central Network out of widespread violence and into a better place.

I'm going to take a nice long break now while you critique it. At least a month. As it's the final edition, handwritten by me, I believe you'll find everything in order. My brain is so fried, I can barely stand it. I'm off to have dinner with my friends. Stella is coming into Chatham City with her son, and Mildred and I are meeting her for dinner. I haven't seen them in months because I've been too busy working with you on the new leadership structure for the Guardians. I do miss them, actually.

I've been thinking about your request to separate myself from Stella and Mildred, but I'm not sure I can. Why must I? They are my biggest supports. Mildred and I argue about our differing opinions, of course, but I argue with anyone that isn't you or Stella. They've stuck by me through so much.

Always,
Evelyn

Katie Cross

3rd Month of Winter

Evelyn,

I'm concerned about your continued uneasiness in distancing yourself from your friends. Why do you cling to them? Stella has no influence whatsoever now that she gave up her career to be a mother, and Mildred . . . well, let's face it. Mildred is arrogant, severe, and aloof. Don't you remember the rumors that she used to advocate for teaching the servants? I hardly think we'll find an ally in her.

Your unwillingness to do everything you can to turn this Network around, even at personal sacrifice, has me worried.

May

1st Month of Spring

Dearest May,

What if I can prove to you that my friends would be loyal to me? Would that allay your fears?

Stella will be easy enough, as you said. But I think you're too hard on Mildred. She'll see my side now that she's worked in the Covens with ignorant witches who don't want to better their lives. All her high-handed opinions before were based on ignorance, I'm confident.

Mildred and Stella are my best friends. They shall support me when the time comes. I will prove it to you. If they do not, I will make a vow next time we meet to ban them from my life.

Always,
Evelyn

1st Month of Spring

Evelyn,

I shall hold you to that vow.

May

2nd Month of Summer

Evelyn,

I dare not address this out loud at the castle, though I desperately wish I could. How I look forward to the day when you and I don't have such secrecy!

I've just heard that the High Priestess has fallen ill in her latest depressive episode. I believe that it shall only be a few more weeks before she passes.

Although I trust that you're doing all you can, I must beg that you speak with your supporters to establish a plan. Donovan must choose you as High Priestess. You've already chosen the twenty Rulers for the New Central Network. Now is their time to earn that right.

Though we won't be able to institute the New Central Network until Donovan dies and you're made Highest Witch by the appearance of the Esmelda Scrolls, we must have it ready. You cannot work on the new law under Donovan's nose; you may well be caught.

Brace yourself, Evie. Your time as High Priestess is coming—I suspect before your twenty-eighth birthday.

Your Assistant,
May

Elitism on the Rise

"**M**y teaching schedule for the next month will be quite tight," Mildred announced to her evening class. "If any of you have questions, a copy of it will be on the board."

A piece of chalk drew out a large square and split it into the rows of a calendar on the chalkboard behind her. The quiet shuffle of movement and paper accompanied the occasional screech of the chalk as it dictated the schedule of education for the second month of summer.

"Due to the number of witches requesting classes, I've asked three other students to teach reading, writing, and mathematics. Lavinia will teach literature this month while I teach Magical Potions and Cures."

She looked out on a sea of thirty anxious faces. Commissioning other teachers from amongst the servants who had demonstrated impressive skill in the classes had been one of Mildred's greatest ideas, but her greatest idea by far had been to appoint Lavinia as her Assistant. The girl ruled the organization of the class schedule with an iron thumb, freeing up more time for Mildred to answer questions and help students with incantation pronunciation.

"They don't dare antagonize me now that I'm one of your Assistants, Miss Mildred!" Lavinia had said one evening, jamming a fist into her open palm. "They know I answer right to you, and you scare all of them."

The chalk had continued to fill in the blanks on the calendar while Mildred eyed the syllabus for the evening. The rise of a hand on the front row stopped her.

"Miss Mildred," squeaked Alice, an upper-floor maid with shiny hair and a smudge of freckles. "May we ask you a question?"

"Of course."

Alice hesitated, and the maid next to her nudged her in the ribs.

"It's about this," she said, lifting a clipping from a newsscroll. Mildred stared at it in surprise. If a witch cut apart a newsscroll, she would save the article, but the scroll couldn't be used again. For a poor maid like Alice, a newsscroll was a rare luxury.

"I read this article in the *Chatham Chatterer* yesterday," Alice said when Mildred took the article from her. "I almost didn't see it because it was at the end of the scroll. We—all of us—read it out loud before class and wondered if you could help us understand what it meant."

ELITISM ON THE RISE

It may not be news to anyone in the political ring at Chatham Castle, but it's come to the attention of many business witches in the Network that Elitism—a political belief that the division of classes is essential to the proper functioning of a society—is on the rise.

"My High Witch said I was in the lower class," reports a grocer from Mirphy. "He wouldn't invite me to his house because I wasn't part of the 'upper class.' Said it wouldn't be right."

Unfortunately, this isn't the only example of Elitism to be found in the Network. The closure of half the common schools years ago (a move reported to be driven by necessary budget cuts) sounded the first alarm for Jarrod in the Middle Covens.

"Closing the common schools was just the beginning," he said. "They're trying to dumb us down so they can take over, that's all. Just you wait. They'll close them all eventually."

While there's no definitive leader of the Elitist movement so far, it's hard to deny that recent actions—such as Council Member Evelyn's use of Guardians to subdue non-violent protests—have come under close scrutiny lately. Evelyn is not alone, however; similar tactics have been employed by both Council Member Gloria and Council Member Grant.

Is the gap between the rich and the poor widening? Is Elitism spreading through the Council? Or are we looking at circumstantial occurrences with no root in certainty?

Mildred folded the article in half with a cold feeling in the pit of her stomach. Alfred Quinten, the editor of the *Chatterer*, usually extrapolated for pages. The brevity of the article likely meant he was too nervous to say more. If witches outside Chatham Castle had begun to notice Elitist attitudes, going so far as to write about it in the newsscroll . . . it signaled a frightening reality.

"What are your questions, Alice?" Mildred asked, buying time to organize her thoughts so she didn't feed her students' fear.

Alice's front teeth bit into her bottom lip. "What does it mean?"

"Elitism is a belief system that assumes wealth breeds an ability to rule what some might call the lower class, or the workers. In a pure Elitist system, the workers would spend most of their time honing a single talent, such as blacksmithing, instead of pursuing an overall education. I believe some of you have heard the claims of Elitists here in the castle that maids don't need to know how to read to do their jobs. They believe that education, the economy, and government should be left to the upper class."

"It's bullocks!" someone shouted in the back.

"Indeed," she said with a grim nod. "They hold that educating the upper class to regulate the business side of things will keep a Network running smoothly. That it gives the lower class a chance to build their skills in a single area and work according to their talents and abilities. Those are the basic premises, anyway."

"We're just as smart!"

"They wouldn't know how to work if it hit them in the face!"

"Who says they're born smarter just because they eat with silver spoons?"

"Movements such as these rarely advance this far," Mildred said, waving the newsscroll clipping. "Several factors must align. First, they need diffuse support throughout the upper class. Second, they need an unstable Network structure, and third . . . " She paused for a moment. "They rely on the workers, or the 'lower class' as they put it, not to fight back."

A deafening silence permeated the room. A burly kitchen worker named Todd stood against the back wall and spoke in a deep voice that reverberated through the room.

"How do we fight back?"

Mildred motioned around them. "Just like this. You educate yourself. You don't give in to their demands. You form a group and stand up as one power. You show them that we are every bit as strong and intelligent as they are."

"If the Elitists take over the Council, will you lead us against them, Miss Mildred?" Todd asked.

Mildred chortled. "It won't happen."

"But if it does?"

She halted, mouth open. All of them stared back at her in quiet expectation. "That's an awfully big promise to make."

"You said it won't happen, though, so you shouldn't be frightened to make it," Todd said. "I know it would help me sleep better at night if I knew we had someone on our side that was one of us, and also one of them."

Am I one of them? she wondered.

"Me too," Alice said, and a small chorus of similar replies echoed in the room. Mildred drew in a deep breath of surprise. Although she wouldn't admit it, making such a promise terrified her. The Elitists already showed far more progress than she'd expected, and there were so few on the Council that would support her in an effort against the majority that she wasn't even sure a resistance would work.

Not to mention the ugly business of Evelyn's role in this ungainly group. Mildred intimately knew Evelyn's quick mind and powerful magic, and she wasn't the only strong, talented witch on the Council. Mildred wasn't sure she could fight her best friend in such a way.

"Miss Mildred would never leave us without a fight," Lavinia said from where she sat in the front corner. "She'll help us."

The entire classroom stared at her with the same round, hopeful eyes.

There's nothing to be done, she thought with regret. *I couldn't just leave them to the wolves, could I? Perhaps they see something in me that I don't.*

"If the Elitists take over, then yes, I'll help. But don't fear. This article doesn't mean they've permeated the Council with enough strength to gain traction. It's not a good sign," she said. "But it's not the end either."

"How does something like this happen?" Alice asked.

"Slowly," Mildred said, thinking of her first conversation with Marten. "And due to the apathy of those who could stop it but don't."

"That won't happen though, will it Miss Mildred?" Todd asked. "Because you've already promised us you'd help us stop it, and you've already been resisting the Elitists by teaching us all along. They don't even know how smart we are."

A chorus of agreement rippled through the room, taking Mildred by surprise. She schooled her expression into one of placid disinterest, though her heart hammered in her chest. They were right, of course.

"Yes, but I can't do anything if I have a bunch of ignorant students to work with. Crack open your books; we still have much to learn today."

A Pile of Ash

On the afternoon of her twenty-eighth birthday, a letter floated to Evelyn's desk with the slow drift of a falling feather.

She glanced at the unfamiliar handwriting and thought about disregarding it like she'd ignored the hundreds of envelopes now cluttering the floor around her. Likely another birthday message, or a plea from Mildred to join her and Stella for their birthday tea.

No time, Milly, she'd already written, but Mildred was stubborn and insisted on the holiness of tradition. Evelyn had started ignoring most of her correspondences.

Thinking of her friends left Evelyn feeling her office was as lonely as a tomb. May was off in Ashleigh, taking care of . . . something. Evelyn worked fanatically to catch up with the work she'd fallen behind on while finishing the new law. Like bribing Norbert, the Head of Finances, with fifty pentacles again.

"He has a real racket going, the miserable cretin. He'll be one of the first I fire when I take over," she muttered. "Right after Porter."

The envelope fluttered in front of her. Evelyn snatched it from the air and tore through the button-sized wax seal, glad for a momentary distraction. The letter practically unfolded itself, revealing two lines.

Nell is dying and requests one last visit from you. If you are so inclined, come immediately.

The hand was neat and proper, which meant it was unlikely that it was from a servant. She promptly burned it, watching it curl at the edges, turning from white to yellow to brown, and then disintegrating into deep black ash that tumbled to the floor. The words *Nell is dying* hadn't surprised Evelyn; everyone knew she wouldn't live much longer. But Evelyn's body felt cold, starting in her core and spreading out to her fingertips.

"Let her die alone." She folded her arms across her chest. "The way she left me when Porter attacked my honor."

A little voice in the back of her mind nagged her incessantly until she gave in and pushed away from her messy desk, littered with an empty tea tray and unanswered letters.

Evelyn stood outside Nell's personal quarters for nearly ten minutes, her sweaty hands clenched at her side. She remembered arguing with Mama about meeting the old High Priestess, and the numb pain deep in her stomach when Nell told her that her Mama was dead.

Am I losing my mind?

She thought often of Mama but never relived the old days with such detail. The memories of her lost parents flashed by in a blur of indistinct colors and emotions. She reviewed them with a disconnected air, as if they were scenes in the life of a stranger. After a few moments of seeing Nell's affectionate gaze again and again, remembering tea and cookies and dancing and laughter, Evelyn forced the memories away. They cramped her heart. Some days, losing Mama and Papa still felt as fresh as the whisper living in her ear.

Avenge us, Evelyn. Don't let this happen again.

Only, the voice sounded like May instead of Mama. No matter how hard she tried, Evelyn couldn't remember Mama's voice anymore. It seemed May had taken over everything, even her memories. Like Grant, May had slowly been losing her appeal. She seemed to dominate even the smallest decisions.

I shan't think of any of this, Evelyn thought, blinking away tears. *Not now. It will just weaken me. I'll start a New Central Network, one that I want. Not what May wants. That's what I must focus on, for I've given up far too much to back away now.*

Life would go on without Nell. She'd eventually forget Nell's chalky scent and the lackluster eyes that waned from depression. Just like she had been forgetting Mama. It hurt, but it was necessary.

We must make personal sacrifices to bring about a better Central Network, the way Esmelda did, May reminded her constantly. Evelyn wondered if Esmelda ever suffered pain in this way.

When Evelyn stepped into Nell's room unannounced, the smells of death swamped her: mentholatum, peppermint, and something stale, like wood that had been sitting in the sun for too long.

"Her Highness isn't well," Leslee said, stepping in Evelyn's path with her two buck teeth and overly large eyes. Evelyn stopped. Leslee stuck her bottom jaw up and out in determination, as if that would frighten Evelyn off. "I invited you because she keeps repeating your name, but the moment you upset her, I'll turn you out."

So the letter *had* been from a servant. Odd. The writing had looked unusually neat. Evelyn knew Leslee; she'd worked with Nell for several years, and she didn't recall her having been educated.

"Nell's dying, isn't she?" Evelyn asked carelessly, her eyes moving to the lumpy figure in bed. "My presence won't make it happen faster."

"Unless you break her heart again," Leslee replied with impressive resolution. "Like you've done so often in the past. Ten minutes. Then you'll have to go."

Evelyn headed for the bed, ignoring the pompous maid but secretly grateful to have an excuse not to linger. She couldn't even say why she'd come, as it would surely mean another harrowing trip down the dark highways of her past.

Nell's hair lay fluffy and white now, like strings of curling snowflakes. Her breath rose and fell with erratic sighs. The long-buried emotions of comfort and love Evelyn attached to Nell burrowed up through the iron layers of her heart.

What am I doing? she thought, even as her feet propelled her toward the bed. *Nell hasn't been part of my life since she betrayed me . . . so long ago I can hardly remember when.*

Not remembering the very day and moment of Nell's deep betrayal felt strange. Evelyn had held onto it for years, trapping it inside her the way she'd boxed up so many other things. Perhaps the bitterness toward Nell had finally just consumed her, integrating itself into the fabric of her soul. She couldn't even look at Nell without both disgust and longing.

Nell is weak, May's voice said. *She can't help us.*

Evelyn shoved the voice away, wishing it would stop cropping up all the time. Leslee bustled around the High Priestess's bedroom, keeping a sharp eye on Evelyn. Nell was fading, as fragile as a gust of wind.

"I don't know what to say to you," Evelyn murmured under her breath, staring at Nell's still form. A dizzy wave passed over her, and she forced herself to pull in a deep breath instead of holding it. She didn't like this situation at all.

"You look terrible," Evelyn said stiffly, standing just out of reach. Nell stirred but didn't rouse. "I've come . . . actually, I'm not sure why. Probably because I never had a chance to say goodbye to Mama or Papa."

"Find Evie," Nell mumbled, her eyelids fluttering open and closed. "Please get Evie. Don't want . . . don't want to die . . . without her."

To Evelyn's great surprise, Nell's eyes opened and latched onto her, sending a cold chill straight into her spine. It spread to the rest of her body, paralyzing her.

"Where's Evie?" Nell asked. "I miss her."

"She's not here," Evelyn replied, not knowing what else to say. She licked her lips, finding it difficult to speak. "She's quite busy."

Nell's eyes closed again. "Yes," she whispered. "So busy now."

Leslee had moved to the corner of the room. Grasping her only moment of privacy, Evelyn stepped to the edge of the bed, hovering so close to Nell she could smell the powder on her papery skin.

"Nell," she whispered so eagerly she didn't even recognize the sound of her own voice. "It's Evie. I'm here to see you."

Nell's eyes fluttered open. "Evie?" she asked, lifting her head up to glance around. "Where is she?"

"Right here, Nell. I'm Evie." Evelyn reached forward to touch Nell's hand, but stopped. Her sudden childish fervor settled. Touch Nell? She nearly gagged at the repulsive idea. She pressed a hand to her own head instead, feeling another headache begin. How could she shuttle through so many emotions? She felt as if she had no control.

A flicker of recognition spun through the depths of Nell's aged eyes but disappeared into the vague shadows of her withering life.

"I miss my Evie," Nell murmured, leaning back against the pillow. "I miss her."

Nell didn't even recognize her in death, and it hurt. Evelyn winced, hating herself for caring so much.

Evelyn glanced up to see Leslee standing in the middle of the room, hands on her hips and eyes narrowed with intense distrust. Evelyn ignored her but backed a step away from Nell's bedside anyway. Nell fidgeted with the top of her sheet, blinking as she stared into the distance of the room, no doubt viewing images of her past instead of the lavish four-poster bed and crackling fire. Despite a pile of blankets to keep her warm, Nell looked cold, like she rapped on death's door that very moment.

"Evie," Nell whispered, slipping into sleep. "She was . . . all that mattered. I . . . loved her."

"Time's up," Leslee announced, but stepped back when Evelyn moved, as if she feared being struck. Evelyn scowled. Oh, what did it matter? Nell had no real comprehension anymore. This had all been for nothing! She whirled around and stalked to the door, feeling like a fool. A fool that cared. A fool that tried. A fool that still hung on to ghosts of the past.

"She may not live through the night," Leslee called, stopping Evelyn just as she put her hand on the doorknob. "I thought you'd like to know."

"I know what death looks like," Evelyn snapped.

"Do you?" Leslee asked. "Then you understand that the real Nell died years ago, when you broke her heart."

Evelyn's nostrils flared. She yanked the door open and slammed it behind her as loudly as she could, hoping that the explosive noise would overpower the painful thrum of her heart. Nell's weak body and diminishing voice felt as final as death had ever been. Perhaps even as final as Mama's and Papa's.

"She's gone," Evelyn said, pacing back and forth across the privacy of her personal chambers with feverish tenacity. "She's gone, she's gone, she's gone. The role of High Priestess is mine. It's everything I wanted. Everything. My plan is finally falling into place."

She raked a hand through her hair, but she didn't feel giddy. Instead, she heard only the wails of a frightened little girl in her head.

Mildred walked through Chatham City without breaking stride, headed for Miss Holly's Candy Shop before Stephan awoke and required his breakfast. Witches scuttled back and forth, wagons rolled through puddles in the cobblestones, and scrollboys called out from the sidewalks.

"New toll on the Central Highway! All witches must pay to use it."

They sounded like they were announcing doomsday. A new toll? What could Donovan possibly need the currency for now? If he added another wing to his mansion in Ashleigh, she'd move to the Northern Network. Her mind strayed to the Middle Covens. How would her witches react to the toll? Many of them used the Central Highway to transport their cotton to the mills. She made a mental note to contact her Coven Leaders with a warning regarding possible discontent.

Mildred dodged a mangy cat and crossed the street, following the smell of sugar and melted butter wafting from Miss Holly's Candy Shop.

Wide glass windows displayed hundreds of confections stacked in tiers, lining wooden shelves. A gaggle of children ran past, lollipops and brown bags clenched in their grubby fists. Mildred strode by them and stepped into the house of sours and sprinkles. It felt strange to enter such a frivolous shop so early in the morning.

Her middle finger tingled. She glanced down to see Lavinia's quill but didn't read the message yet, too distracted by the cacophony of colors and smells assaulting her. It would stay on her hand until she acknowledged it.

"Be right with you!" a voice called from the back, and, seconds later, a striking woman with dirty blonde hair, bright blue eyes, and a plethora of necklaces and bracelets popped into view. Not unlike the candies in her store, she was a veritable display of color. "How can I help you?"

"I want to buy some candy," Mildred said, running her eyes over a shelf of hard sweets that ran the length of the back wall.

"Well you came to the right place!" the woman said, spreading her arms. She wore a turquoise apron with ruffles that matched her bright eyes. "This is my candy shop. I'm Miss Holly. It's good to meet you. Who are you buying for? I just created new caramels that promise to be fabulous if I can stop my three daughters from eating them. Do you like caramels?"

"No. I mean, yes." Mildred struggled to reply, unable to take her eyes off the sparkling dragonfly adornment in Holly's hair. "Perhaps."

"Well you'd love these caramels. I'm going to offer them in vanilla, too. Is there something on my neck, or do you just like my necklaces?"

Embarrassed to be caught openly staring, Mildred glanced away from a wide blue amulet nestled in Miss Holly's bosom. "They're very nice."

"Oh, don't be embarrassed. Everyone stares at my bits and bobbles. I can't get enough of them, truly. I'm like a busy biddy drowning in my jewelry."

"Indeed," Mildred drawled with one last awkward glance. "I'm buying candy for a class I teach. They all passed their exam on basic household incantations, and I promised them a reward. Do you have anything that I can buy in bulk?"

Holly pressed a finger to her red lips and perused the barrels of gumdrops, flavored fizzy packets, pretzels dipped in chocolate and coated with sprinkles, and swirled peppermints. A blackboard above each barrel identified the candy in red chalk.

"I know it!" Miss Holly declared, beckoning with a wave of her hand that jangled her bracelets. "I've got some sweet little treats that fizzle in the mouth. Everybody loves them! Think they'd like a caramel?"

Mildred purchased a large brown bag of the wafer-sized candies and stepped out of the saccharine-coated air. She'd gone no further than five steps into the warm summer sunshine when a gathering crowd in the middle of Market Street caught her attention.

"It's true!" a young voice yelled. "I heard it with my own ears, I tell ya! They sent me with this message for the editor at the *Chatterer!*"

"Give it here," an older witch demanded. Mildred walked up in time to see a skinny young boy dive out of the way when several witches reached for a rolled-up piece of parchment in his hand.

"No!" he cried. "I'll only give it ta the editor!"

"The High Priestess isn't dead, you little liar!" the old witch yelled. "You're just trying to get attention, that's all."

"I'm telling' ya! The High Priestess is dead! Ya will see soon enough."

Mildred stopped walking. The words hit her like a punch to the stomach.

The High Priestess is dead.

In an effort to get away from the ornery old witch that kept swatting at him, the young boy, whom Mildred recognized as a fireboy from the castle, nearly backed into her. She grabbed his shoulder, and he whirled around with a yelp.

"Whoa!" He threw his hands over his head. "Not ya! I swear, Assistant Mildred, I didn't do anything wrong! Don't glare me ta ashes!"

"Glare you to ashes?" she asked incredulously. "What are you talking about?"

The boy peered through his skinny arms.

"They say that ya glare will turn a witch ta ashes," he whispered, gulping. "I didn't tell lies, I promise! I don't want ta be a pile of ash!"

"Calm down," she said, grabbing the sleeve of his coat before he could squirm away. "I want to know what you're making such a big fuss about. What is this about the High Priestess dying?"

He hesitated. "Ya won't turn me to ash?"

"Not if you cooperate."

"They sent me ta the *Chatterer* with a message," he said, tightening his puny fist around the flattened scroll. "The High Priestess just died. They're going ta announce it with bells any moment now."

"Why are you telling people on the street?" she asked. He hesitated, glancing around.

"Musta slipped out," he said, shrugging with a feigned innocence. She rolled her eyes. "I can't help my mouth. Mother says it's gonna get me in all kinds of trouble someday—"

"Go right to the *Chatterer*," she said, releasing his coat. "Don't stray again, and don't speak a word. Do you understand?"

"Y-yes, Assistant."

The growing crowd hummed with whispered questions. The old witch, his steel gray mustache bristling, held his hat in his hands and asked Mildred in a quiet voice, "Is sweet Nell dead then?"

Mildred met his eyes, hesitated, and looked at the young fireboy's back as he wound through the busy, store-lined street. Lavinia sent a second message to her silenda.

Nell is gone.

"It would appear so," Mildred said, then transported away.

Good Show

Council Member Eddy of the Western Covens listened to Evelyn for one reason: her intoxicating promise of land, power, and wealth.

If any other witch had requested such a bold favor from him, Eddy would have laughed. Evelyn, however, possessed social position, experience, and above all, a willingness to share a little power.

"Why are you doing this?" he'd asked when she'd approached him in a pastry shop far from the castle. She'd leaned closer to him, her red hair spilling over her shoulders like strands of fire. The scent of cinnamon wafted from her body.

"Because we have to make our own luck, don't we?"

Which was precisely why Eddy wanted to help Evelyn achieve her goal in whatever way he could. In a roundabout way, making Evelyn High Priestess would funnel more currency and influence to himself, and nothing appealed to him more. So he'd signed her binding to help Grant convince the High Priest that Evelyn should be empowered as High Priestess in Nell's wake.

Eddy strode down the hall toward Donovan's office, sandwiched between Grant and Evelyn, ready to earn his place in what she called the New Central Network. It was a budding idea of course, kept under wraps in the strictest confidence. New laws. New taxes. New leadership. The Central Network could certainly use an overhaul—Eddy wouldn't deny that.

The maids had opened the windows, allowing the warm air of summer to blow through Chatham's dank corridors and bring new life in the bitter wake of Nell's death the day before. Grant kept glancing at Evelyn, but she didn't seem to notice his fervent attention—captured in a swirl of thoughts and plans no doubt—and it was altogether quite awkward for Eddy.

"Do either of you have questions?" she asked, lifting an eyebrow. "I need both of you to convince Donovan without being obvious. The opinions of his friends always sway him more than his own instincts."

"Understood," Eddy said. Grant nodded and dug around in his pockets for his tin of tobacco, a slip of white paper ready in his free hand.

Evelyn stopped to straighten her dress, check her hair in a mirror, and let out a long breath. Grant adjusted his necktie, patted back his hair, winked at his reflection, and fidgeted again with his tie.

"Hurry!" Evelyn ordered, already on the move. "We haven't time for you to preen all day in front of the mirror."

"There's always time to look presentable," Grant said with mild insolence. "Calm down, Evie. We have this under control."

Evelyn didn't say another word as they approached Donovan's door, but her eyes twinkled with a mischievous excitement when Grant rapped on the door.

"Don't disappoint me," she mouthed, tucking out of sight. Grant and Eddy stepped into Donovan's office with a chorus of friendly greetings.

"She's a bit mad, isn't she?" Grant muttered when the door had closed. He turned all his attention to Donovan, who waved them over to his desk with a sweep of his arm. Eddy squirmed, having no idea what to say. Luckily, Donovan was in a bright enough mood already, which Eddy took full advantage of.

"You're looking good today, High Priest," he called jovially, sitting in a plush velvet chair just across from Donovan's desk. "Have you found a new tailor?"

"Scoundrel!" Grant said. "He'd better not have! I've sent him to the best already. He's just lost a few pounds is all. Are you on a diet, High Priest?"

A plate of bread and luxury cheese from the dairies of the Western Covens sat on the desk at Donovan's fingertips.

"Er . . . yes," he mumbled through a mouthful of crumbling cheese. "A diet."

Eddy leaned back, hiding his grin by rubbing his upper lip as if it itched.

"We've come to discuss some business with you, old boy," Grant said as Donovan's Assistant Harold passed around a decanter of dark ipsum. Eddy and Grant both accepted a full glass, while Donovan took the bottle and set it next to the glass at his fingertips.

"Business?" He scowled at them. "It's too early for business."

Eddy's eyes strayed to the clock. Just past two in the afternoon. He remembered Donovan as a shrewd witch, not this fat, crumb-strewn buffoon reading scrolls on hunting supplies. Donovan hadn't become High Priest by accident. He used to play the political game well, using his vast knowledge of intricate magic to set himself apart from the rest of the Council. The best Eddy could figure was that years of dark ipsum and a debilitating knee injury had taken their toll.

"It's business that will only take a second," Grant said, reassuring him with a wry smile. He clapped Eddy on the back of his shoulder. "Eddy here wants to know where to find the best hunting ground, as he takes the sport very seriously."

Donovan's scowled dropped, replaced by a wide grin.

"That's the kind of business I like!" he cried. Eddy grinned and lifted his glass of ipsum in salute. Donovan roared with laughter, downed his own glass, and gestured for Harold to refill it. "And here I thought you were serious about work! I get so tired of doing Network business, you know. Especially with the sad case of Nell dying. Seems like it's all just piling up now."

Grant sobered. "Of course. That must be putting a great strain on you. How are you holding up, Your Highness?"

"Terrible," Donovan said, reaching for another slice of cheese. "I can't decide who to put in as High Priestess. It's not an easy decision, you know. And the Council Members are down there talking and gossiping and—"

"Don't worry!" Grant said, gesturing to himself and Eddy, who had fallen silent in surprise. "We're here to take some of the burden off your tired, capable shoulders and help you out. Who are you considering? Sometimes an outside opinion helps shed more light."

Donovan perked up. "Good idea," he said. "A good idea indeed."

Eddy made a silent note to watch himself. Donovan had just played right into Grant's capable hands without Grant once mentioning the position of High Priestess. Eddy felt suffocated by the abilities of these masters of subterfuge. No telling what they could, or would, do.

Grant leaned back, lighting the lazy cheroot that dangled between his soft, full lips. "Tell us your thoughts," he said. "Then you can decide, and we can get back to important matters, such as sport and manliness."

"It's simple," Donovan said. "There are three female Council Members that I could appoint. Gloria, Terry and—" He stopped when Grant ruffled his nose and puckered his lips as if he'd eaten something sour. "What? Why did you make such a face?"

Grant hesitated, glancing at Eddy, and finally said after long deliberation. "I do *hate* to be this kind of witch, but Gloria? Is she truly in the running?"

He looked to Eddy for backup. Eddy licked his lips and hoped he could measure up to such superb acting.

"Glora is . . . well . . ." Eddy let out a heavy sigh. "She's not very attractive, is she? An ugly High Priestess wouldn't be popular. She could turn public sentiment away from the Network leadership, which would be a shame, especially since you're so handsome yourself."

"Nell was a lovely woman," Grant pointed out. "Have you seen how the Network is mourning her? Gloria's looks impress no one. It seems like a risk."

"Not to mention," Eddy said, "that Gloria has a bit of a problem." His eyes widened, and he mimicked her drinking a flask. Donovan recoiled.

"No! Does she really?"

Eddy nodded, his lips pressed together, relieved to find his act had passed.

Grant shrugged. "Seems risky to institute Gloria," he said.

"You're right," Donovan said. "Can't have a Council Member with a drinking problem. No honor in that. How about Terry then?"

He gazed at them in studious concern.

"Terry?" Eddy repeated, searching madly for an excuse against her. In truth, she'd make a wonderful High Priestess. Steady and dependable, she'd pulled the Eastern Covens out of a lumber crisis ten years earlier. But she wouldn't guarantee Eddy power.

"She's old," Grant said. "At least in her sixties."

"So?" Donovan retorted sharply, as if he were personally insulted. "What's wrong with a little age in a leader?"

Grant smiled. "Absolutely nothing, except it means she'll die sooner. It's hard on a Network to lose leaders so fast."

"You'll want younger blood," Eddy said.

"Someone who can stay in the role for a long time and keep the Network steady. The good gods know it hasn't been easy for you."

Donovan relaxed, sinking back in his chair in thought. "Suppose you're right."

"Pamela would have been a wonderful High Priestess," Grant said. "But you replaced her a few years back with someone else. Who was that again?"

Donovan's eyes flashed with something akin to panic.

"Evelyn Ringer," Eddy said. "And a good choice it was. Why, look at how she's turned the Ashleigh Covens around!"

The High Priest's sudden anxiety faded.

"Evelyn Ringer," Grant murmured, rolling the name around. "Evelyn Ringer. Now there's a candidate for High Priestess if I've ever met one. Attractive, young, capable. Knows everyone there is to know."

"Best socialite I've ever met."

"She can throw a party too. Remember the Yule Ball Donovan put her in charge of a few years ago, when Nell started feeling really ill?" Grant asked.

"With the ice sculptures? Who doesn't? Magnificent pieces. The swan was my personal favorite."

Donovan said nothing but seemed to sink deeper in thought. Eddy and Grant didn't interrupt, letting Donovan's thoughts flow for a few minutes. "She's very young," Donovan said with hesitation, showing a spark of intelligence in his fatty face. "A lot of witches would oppose it."

"More will object if you put in Gloria."

"Definitely," Eddy said, keeping Terry's name out of it. No reason to bring her back up if Donovan was hesitating. "Gloria is a mess."

Donovan hemmed and hawed, stuffing cracker after cracker into his mouth, his gaze focused elsewhere.

"Porter would have something to say about Evelyn getting the position," Donovan said, spewing crumbs on the rest of the tray.

"But Porter isn't the Highest Witch, is he?" Grant gave a droll smile. "Don't be afraid of your power, old chum. Embrace it! Instituting Evelyn isn't against the Esmelda Scrolls, is it?"

"No," Donovan said, brightening. "Not at all."

"Well there you go. You would do nothing wrong by putting Evelyn in as High Priestess. What does Porter know anyway?"

"I'm simply instituting the best replacement for Nell," Donovan agreed with a murmur. "Evelyn's a bit bossy, though."

Eddy didn't dare respond because he agreed. Apparently Grant felt the same way, for he paused before replying.

"You'll need a woman with a firm hand to take over when your knee is acting up, won't you? She may be bossy, but she gets work done."

"True," Donovan said. "Bad knee and all."

"What does your gut tell you to do?" Eddy asked, fascinated by the stages of rationalization Donovan moved through so quickly and with such ease. "You tend to make the best decisions."

"Donovan always does. Why else would he be the High Priest?"

"Right," Donovan said, wrapping his hands around his girth and clearing his throat. "Feels good. Let's do it. Make it happen, Harold. Call Evelyn in for a meeting this evening."

"Of course, Your Highness," Harold said from the other side of the room.

"Good show of leadership," Eddy said with quiet applause. "You've made the right decision."

"A drink to celebrate, I think?" Grant asked, waving a decanter of dark ipsum from where he stood at the far wall.

"Always!" Donovan cried. "To the Network! Now, let's talk about hunting locations."

We Will Be Strong!

The succulent smell of spit-roasted quail, duck, and chicken drifted over the buzzing crowd of witches in the high and low baileys. Clusters of apples, pears, and plums nestled in the branches of small evergreen trees decorating the tables. Food lined the buffet tables set up along the four-story wall that surrounded both baileys.

Evelyn observed the crowd below her with a sharp, assessing eye, pleased with the growing numbers.

"Here you are, High Priestess," May said, approaching with a sheer black overlay. Evelyn slipped her arms into the silky fabric, allowing May to cinch it at her waist. An emerald silk gown rustled below the overlay. She'd ordered it at great expense since the Middle Covens hadn't produced as much cotton or silk this year, but she knew that every piece would be worth it.

I'm a High Priestess now, she thought. *I will dress and act like it.*

May finished setting the overlay, inspected it, and nodded once with unusual warmth. "It looks beautiful, High Priestess. Just beautiful. You picked the perfect dress for your ascension to power."

May and Evelyn shared a rare smile. Ever since Evelyn had officially secured her position as High Priestess during the Empowerment ceremony, May had glowed with praise and adoration, as delighted as if she herself had achieved the position. Evelyn allowed the praise but kept careful note of it. Today was *her* big day after all, and she wouldn't allow May to take it over the way she did most things.

I've finally done it! Evelyn thought, giddy with relief and excitement. All her years of work had finally paid off. The grief that accompanied Nell's death faded in the afterglow of Evelyn's bright new future. A heavy bracelet dangled from her right hand. Its silver face was etched with ancient words established by Esmelda.

SAC ERO DOS SUM MUS

She reached for the bracelet with her left hand, and her brow furrowed. The Empowerment ceremony had brutalized her. "The weight of the world sits on your shoulders for a short time," Donovan had said. "So miserable you can't breathe. Then it fades. It won't actually kill you, but it will feel like it's going to."

And so it had. Evelyn was glad it had passed, for she didn't want to relive it again.

"Where's Donovan?" Evelyn asked, glancing at a clock on the wall. "He was supposed to be here over fifteen minutes ago."

"He's on his way," May said, consulting the schedule book she kept with her at all times. "There was a delay in fitting his clothes. He's gained a little more weight, and the tailors had to use a few incantations to fix his robes."

"Let him gain all he wants," Evelyn said, tossing her hair and pushing all heavy thoughts from her mind. "He'll drown in his own fat, and I can finally save the Network."

May's eyes flashed with what appeared to be surprise, though she said nothing. Evelyn never took all the credit for changing the Network, but now that she was High Priestess, *she* would make the decisions, not May.

It felt wonderful to liberate herself for a moment.

When another five minutes passed with no sign of Donovan, Evelyn paced the room, her fists clenched. All her motions were off-kilter since Nell died. She didn't just *feel* anymore, she personified. If she felt angry, she trembled. Her occasional depressions seemed to swallow her in blankets of heaviest, blackest despair. Even the strength of her elation left her frightened. Always her thoughts returned to Nell, and always she tucked them away.

I did what I needed to do for the good of the Network.

She just wished it hadn't hurt so much.

Donovan struggled through the doorway five minutes later,

dressed in formal robes of crimson with gold stitching. The fat folds of his face wagged around his neck like melting wax.

"Let's get this done," he said, scratching at arms already bright red from previous irritation. "I need a drink, Harold. It's miserable, itching all the time. I don't have the energy for speeches."

"Later, Your Highness," Harold said, placing a gentle hand on Donovan's shoulder. "At the celebratory dinner. You need to address the Network now. They are all waiting."

"Merry meet, Donovan," Evelyn called with a wooden smile he'd be too distracted to read into. "It's good to see you."

He waved, then waddled past her and onto the balcony. Several Protectors wandered through the crowds, disappearing and reappearing at will. Guardians lined the wall and the baileys, actively watching the contentious hoard. Witches from all over the Network—only the well-to-do, of course—streamed in from Chatham Road. Under Evelyn's strict orders, no one without political office had been allowed in.

Donovan fell onto the chair awaiting him at the edge of the balcony. Most of the crowd wouldn't even be able to see his squat frame from where he sat, but Evelyn had never known him to care about those little details. In the direct sunlight his skin glowed with an unbecoming yellow tint, making him appear sicklier than ever. Melodic chimes from the bell tower silenced the waiting congregation.

"Witches of the Central Network," Donovan called, his voice projected over the bailey by an incantation. "Today we gather for a very special event."

Evelyn stepped into the shadows behind him, remaining just out of sight but able to survey the crowd below. Hundreds of witches waited. Her supporters infused the crowd; many had promised they'd bring supportive witches with them. A first impression would be crucial to win over those undecided about whether or not she deserved the position.

After all, she was *quite* young to be High Priestess.

Donovan caught his breath and wiped at his sweaty forehead with the back of his hand. "And so today, I want to introduce your new High Priestess: Evelyn Ringer!"

Her stomach leapt.

"Here I go," she whispered. "I shall save the world."

"Go, Evelyn," May whispered from behind her. "You shall do great things!"

Evelyn stepped forward with a beaming smile, waving as she glided into position next to Donovan. The ravenous applause, although expected, still surprised her. Once she stepped to the edge of the balcony, the true size of the crowd overwhelmed her. Witches filled both baileys and the road to Chatham City. She allowed the applause to continue for as long as it would, which felt like hours.

"I am honored to be your leader," she said the moment the clapping faded enough for the magic to carry her voice to every ear.

Council Member Gloria let out a piercing whistle, surrounded by faithful Coven Leaders, who began another round of applause. Grant lounged against the wall, arms tucked under his armpits, a lazy cheroot dangling from his lips as he tracked a hawk flying far above the castle.

Evelyn held up her hands and received an instant quiet from her obedient crowd.

How lovely, she thought. *They all obey.*

"First of all, let me thank you for the honor of serving you as High Priestess. To know that all of you love and trust me, as you have since I was a lost orphan wandering these halls, means a great deal." She forced her voice to falter. "I know Nell would be proud to see me here today to take her place. So mote it be."

A respectful silence followed.

"As High Priestess," she continued, "I make you a solid promise: I will help you bring about a better Central Network! I guarantee to aid Network school education with increased funding. I shall stop the madness: no more violent riots, no more fires. We will be safe! We will be strong!"

She let the newest round of applause rage, floating in its power like in a sweeping ocean current. Before it showed signs of fading, she called with a passionate cry, "I will do what is best for all of the Central Network. Do you trust me?"

Another cheer boiled through the crowd for almost five minutes.

Evelyn let it go, allowing it to infuse her blood and body until it faded, leaving behind a light patter of applause.

"In honor of this great occasion," she said. "I have graciously supplied a bounteous luncheon. Let us start our friendship by feasting together!"

With a grand flourish, Evelyn bowed and backed away from the balcony. Once out of sight, she whirled around and slipped inside the castle. Donovan followed close on her heels, barking at Harold for a glass of ipsum.

"You've worked hard, Your Highness," May said.

Evelyn walked past her without acknowledgement, turning suddenly to address Donovan. "Let me handle the ball at Ashleigh House tonight. You just rest, and I will take care of everything. Don't worry. The Network lies in good hands."

Donovan's personal retreat, Ashleigh House, was grand by any standard, but Mildred still didn't care for it.

The interior shone in tones of white and cream, highlighting its smooth tiles and sculpted pillars. Perhaps because of her roots in poverty and dirt floors, the sheer amount of marble—though aesthetically pleasing and minimalistic—made her want to roll her eyes. She snorted at the existence of such a lavish *personal retreat* for the High Priest. *What a waste of currency,* she thought, trailing her eyes along the engraved marble pillars near the staircase.

Donovan sat off to the side of the main doors in a striped jacket that matched a bluish bruise on the back of his hand. He greeted each witch as they moved inside. Harold was tucked back into a little alcove, holding Donovan's usual decanter and glass.

Her silenda warmed her hand, and while waiting in line, she answered three questions about homework, rearranged a class schedule for the next week, and planned a new curriculum in her head. The Middle Covens had settled down, which meant she would introduce one more class to her secret education initiative: *Magic for Gardeners.*

She'd been teaching herself the incantations and consulting Stephan for weeks now; he'd been only too happy to discuss herbology with her over lunch instead of Coven business.

"Might as well put the useless knowledge on shrubbery to use," she said, earning a cursory glance of disapproval from a nearby witch. The line shuffled forward, and Mildred found herself next to greet the High Priest.

"Merry meet, Your Highness." She nodded, curtsied, and moved on before he offered his hand to her, as he had to all the others. He blinked as she passed, clearly taken aback by the quick departure, but she didn't care.

Mildred followed the movement of the crowd into the ballroom, wishing Stella walked at her side. She missed her comforting presence more than ever. Marten was on a mission and hadn't been around for over a month. With Evelyn's ascent to the role of High Priestess, Mildred spent much of her time alone. She'd enjoyed the solitude until now, when she was forced to attend a social function.

All the more reason to leave early, Mildred thought to console herself. *No one here to stay for once I speak with Evie. She'll be busy.*

An army of witches paraded around Evelyn's celebratory ball in a great maw of silk, chiffon, and tulle. Butlers drifted by with silver platters of champagne, their steps so measured that the liquid didn't even shift. Three sprawling crystal chandeliers hung from the ceiling, throwing light in prisms on the walls. Shrubs sculpted into hearts and decorated with pale pink summer flowers littered the room. Mildred smirked. She knew the incantation that had made those shrubs.

"Goodness," she said, standing near the entrance, which was lined with gold filigree. Likely she could have paid three months of Coven taxes with the cost of this ball alone. Oh, the difference she could make in the Middle Covens with this kind of currency!

"Maybe that's just what our taxes went to," she murmured, staring at an ice sculpture on the other side of the room. A swan with a delicate, arched neck poised mid-flight, wings spread, water rushing up to meet its departing feet. The statue gleamed with frosty blue, silver, and white. It was the most beautiful thing she'd ever seen, but no doubt cost as much as most witches made in their lifetimes.

"Isn't it wonderful?" a passing witch asked, fanning herself. "A new High Priestess, and one so young!"

Then again, Mildred reasoned, they *were* celebrating a new High Priestess—her best friend. The rarity of the occasion meant Evelyn would have demanded it be all the grander.

An open window admitted a breeze that stirred the hot summer air. Mildred placed herself in front of it to keep from sweating. Her plain, buttery yellow dress almost looked severe in comparison when she stood near other Assistants, like Jayne. Mildred brushed the thought aside. At least it was comfortable, and that counted for far more than fashion.

A familiar head of red hair, pulled into an elegant updo, appeared with a bright, though perhaps somewhat forced, smile.

"Here you are, Mildred," Evelyn said. "I'm glad you showed up. I didn't think you'd come."

"Not come? You really think I'd miss your celebration tonight?"

Evelyn shrugged with false modesty.

"One can never tell."

Mildred studied her oddly subdued friend with tapered eyes. Evelyn seemed so distant. Why had she called her Mildred? Evelyn always called her Milly. Mildred wondered if Evelyn felt embarrassed to be seen talking to a lowly Assistant.

Despite the detailed tatting and full skirt of her emerald gown, Evelyn wasn't strikingly beautiful like Stella. Her passion and social grace gave her a dangerous, quick kind of attraction, like looking at something sparkly. When one glanced at it too often or for too long, the luster faded. Even as High Priestess, Evelyn seemed no different.

"Congratulations, Evie," Mildred managed to say. "Your speech impressed us all. You did beautifully, just as I knew you would."

"Yes," Evelyn said, waving to another witch over Mildred's head. "It was a perfect speech, wasn't it? May wanted to write it for me, but I wouldn't let her near it. I think I did just fine without her, don't you?"

Both their gazes drifted to the other side of the ballroom, where May spoke with Council Member Grant. She wore a plumed black dress that matched her hair, and a striking red sash looped around her slender waist.

"I think you did very well without her."

Evelyn's glittering eyes seemed to laugh. "I did."

Mildred had never understood May, nor Evelyn's rampant devotion to her. Stella had once admitted that she thought May brilliantly smart but a bit frightening. The rest of the Network, however, regarded May as an oddity, with her pale skin, jet-black hair, and aloof gaze. Rumors swirled that May had kicked her daughter, Angelina, out of her house when she came home pregnant. No one could confirm it, and May never spoke of it. When anyone tried to ask, she placed a hex on the witch who broached the subject. It rarely came up twice. Mildred brushed the thoughts aside. She had more important things to think about than a strange Assistant with sharp eyes in a pretty face.

"You presented your message very well," Mildred said, tearing her eyes away from Evelyn's mentor. "May can't take credit for that."

"No," Evelyn agreed. "I suppose not. Don't you just love these decorations? They cost quite a bit, but I just couldn't help myself. I deserve to be celebrated after attaining High Priestess at such a young age. Wouldn't you agree?"

Her eyes bore through Mildred with a sudden intensity that nearly took Mildred's breath away.

"Yes, I suppose so," Mildred said, and Evelyn relaxed.

"I do deserve to be celebrated," she murmured before taking a sip of champagne. "For I've given up much to earn this position. *I* have sacrificed, not May."

Mildred formed no reply, not understanding the sudden current of tension in Evelyn's voice, but her friend continued speaking without interruption, not having expected a response in the first place.

"I invited all the Coven Leaders from the Ashleigh Covens, Chatham City, and a few of the other influential witches," Evelyn said, setting her empty flute on the tray of a passing butler. To Mildred's relief, she didn't take another. Evelyn wasn't drunk yet, but it wouldn't be long at this rate.

"Why not invite all the Coven Leaders?" Mildred asked, glancing around with new eyes. It would have been nice to see people *she* knew, though she couldn't picture half of her Coven Leaders in so lavish an environment.

"Not all of them would know proper etiquette," Evelyn said, regarding Mildred with disbelief. "You're serious, aren't you? But how can you be? Mildred, think of it. Can you imagine some of your Coven Leaders at a gala such as this? They'd make fools of themselves!"

Mildred didn't respond, but not for lack of an opinion. She *wanted* to say plenty about Evelyn's Elitist attitudes and questionable friends, but she bit her tongue. Evelyn certainly had a point, loathe as Mildred was to admit it. She tried picturing Bart—a great oaf of a witch with holey clothes and matted hair—at the ball. She just couldn't see it ending well.

"It's just as May says," Evelyn continued. "Better to spare the poor the cost and embarrassment of such an extravagant party. I'll send them all gift baskets or something. Besides, this is a ball. A ball has standards that I must ensure are met. I am High Priestess now."

"Standards . . . right."

"That's why I didn't invite Stella, you know," Evelyn said as an afterthought, plucking a fresh glass of champagne off the tray of a passing waiter. Her voice held a hint of wistfulness.

Mildred reared back. "What?"

"Standards, Mildred," Evelyn repeated, as if she were teaching a belligerent child. "She's not part of the political world anymore, is she? She's wiping snot and changing diapers at home. How could I justify bringing her here when she has no place in the political world?"

Mildred's heart beat painfully in her throat. Stella had no place? Did Evelyn even realize what she was saying?

"Stella is your best friend," Mildred hissed. "Doesn't that count?"

Evelyn smiled, appearing unruffled by Mildred's scowl, but her green eyes cooled. "This is politics, Mildred. It's not personal. You of all witches must understand that."

"Even politicians have friends, Evie. You have them in loads. They're all dreadful, arrogant Elitists."

"Yes, but they're from the same caste as me, the same mold. All of my friends exert political influence. All except for Stella. She chose her path and is now nothing more than a mother and a Guardian's wife. When I want to go to tea and giggle about the past with a friend, of course I'll choose Stella. But I couldn't bring her here with these witches."

She gestured to the ballroom, and Mildred saw only a collection of Elitists that shared the same philosophy: *The only place for the poor was right under their heel.*

"Friends indeed," Mildred retorted, feeling sick to her stomach. She'd prepared herself for gloating and Evelyn's usual high-handed remarks, but she hadn't anticipated Evelyn turning her Elitist back on Stella. "They'd hang you and take your spot the first moment they had the chance, Evie. Stella and I are your true friends. We're the ones that really care and always have."

"I know," Evelyn admitted with a smile that reminded Mildred of her six-year-old friend. "It's true. You are still my best friend. But I can't make an exception for Stella in this sphere, can I? I'm allowing you to call me by my first name because we're as close to political equals as we'll ever be, since you'll never attain more than I while I'm alive. Stella, on the other hand, must call me High Priestess. Justice cannot be superseded by childhood friendship. I'm simply doing what's best for the Network."

"You're wrong," Mildred said. "Stella can be your friend no matter what influence she does or does not have. You're the High Priestess now, Evie. You're in the business of witches, not standards and tradition."

"Mercy and witches can't outweigh justice and tradition, or all would be chaos. I'm here to bring justice to a Network that lacks it. Why else are we falling apart?"

Mildred hesitated, with no way to get out the words in her throat. She felt shaken and startled and even a little frightened. She didn't know this Evelyn.

"I feel like your new power is going to your head," she concluded with chilling disapproval.

"Is it?" Evelyn asked archly. "Or are you jealous of my success as High Priestess?"

"Evelyn!"

"Well? What else am I to think? You're acting like a child. May warned me this would happen, you know. She told me years ago that you, of all the witches here, would get jealous."

Mildred's mind locked up. She couldn't think of anything beyond the sudden fear that Evelyn was right. What if she *was* jealous? Had Mildred let her emotions get away from her? She took a deep breath and forced herself to think logically; her mind retreated from its panic.

She wasn't feeling jealousy, she knew that right away. No, Mildred didn't want to be High Priestess. Not anymore. All she wanted was a small cottage and a life with Marten.

But she did feel fear. Fear for her best friend, for her Network. Fear that one day soon she'd have to fulfill her promise to her students and support them against a rising Elitist doctrine.

Against her best friend.

Mildred folded her hands in front of her, grateful that the ball moved on around them, oblivious to the sudden rift that stood between them like a chasm.

"I'm not jealous, Evie," she said. "While it's no secret that you and I don't agree on much, what I'm feeling is concern for you, that's all. The position of High Priestess came unexpectedly to a witch so young."

Evelyn's neck loosened, then her shoulders, her face, and finally the tight rage in her eyes. It flickered into something that looked like guilt, then longing, and settled into a distant indifference.

"I can handle it."

"I know," Mildred said, hoping to reach the six-year-old Evelyn buried somewhere in all the layers of pain and sadness. "That's why I tell you how I really feel. You're one of the strongest witches I know."

Despite her reservations, Mildred felt a wild sense of pride for Evelyn. She'd done what Mildred couldn't have—become High Priestess.

"Thank you, Milly." Evelyn's eyes clung to Mildred for just long enough to seem hopelessly lost, perhaps a bit frightened. When she looked away, tears lingered in her emerald eyes.

Mildred swallowed. "Enjoy your party," she said, clearing her gravelly voice. "Everyone is here to celebrate you, High Priestess, as they should. You've accomplished something grand."

Evelyn nodded, and all traces of previous vulnerability faded. "Merry part, Assistant Mildred."

Mildred watched her go, uncertain why she felt like mourning and not sure she wanted to know what it meant.

Riot

A volley of letters flew at Mildred like a cloud of darts the moment she entered Stephan's office a week later, nearly knocking her on her backside. She paralyzed them in mid-air.

"Goodness, what was that for?" she asked. Stephan stood near the fire in his usual disarray, one hand in his pocket, the tails of his shirt untucked and one suspender dangling by his elbow. His wrinkled brow fell low over his eyes like sagging snow clouds.

"Where have you been?" he snapped. "I've been waiting all afternoon! Letters are pouring in like birds, and I can't get a moment's rest. Get rid of them! I haven't even taken my afternoon tea yet."

Mildred's eyes flickered to the clock. So many letters at such a quiet hour of the day meant something sour was afoot.

"Did you eat, Stephan?" she asked, plucking the envelopes from the air one by one and sending him a reproachful look. "You always become surly when you're hungry."

"No," he said. "It's none of your business if I've eaten or not. Now do your job!"

Mildred studied him with shrewd eyes but said nothing. He rarely acted on his anger with such strength anymore. Striving for extra patience, she sent an order to the kitchens for his dinner, set his book by the footrest, and placed a blanket within reach. He continued to glower at the flames, lost in thought.

The first message undid itself the moment she touched the seal.

We need you in Stilton Coven immediately.
William

She opened several of the others. Most were from High Witches in Stilton, though one came from Hampstead and another from Tilton. Mildred stood, wearing a fresh coat of stress, and shoved all the letters into her bag.

"I'm going to Stilton Coven," she declared, transporting away without another word.

"What is it, William?" Mildred asked the moment she appeared in his office amid a cacophony of screams and guttural bellows from outside. She whipped around to find a window, and saw a sea of witches on the lawn. "Blessed be."

William stopped pacing in front of the fire and followed her gaze. Sweat beaded on his hairline, despite the threat of rain from low hanging clouds.

"They've been out there an hour. Several tried to break in with torches and oil, but two Guardians, who are here visiting family, came to help. They've kept the mob out so far."

"I see," Mildred said, her lips pressed into a thin line. One Guardian stood in front of the main door to the office while another protected the back. When a witch tried to elbow his way through the crowd and onto the porch, he hit a protective wall and flew backward. Torches littered the ring of people, who all wanted a chance to destroy the office.

"Have the Guardians sent for reinforcements?" she asked.

"Twice, but no word."

Mildred used the silenda to send a message to Marten, grateful that she'd welcomed him into the silenda months before when he started teaching a course on Defensive Magic to a few Guardian hopefuls amongst the servants. He'd respond immediately, no doubt.

"They're angry about the new toll on the Central Highway," William said. "A mob attacked two of the tax collectors early this morning when they tried to enforce the toll. Stilton residents can't pay their normal taxes because it all goes into the transportation of goods now. They simply don't have the currency. Lily is upstairs taking care of the tax collectors, but it doesn't look good for either. She expects both to die."

"Is your daughter Hazel safe?"

William hesitated with an expression on his face that clearly said, *Is anyone safe?* then nodded. "She's helping her mother."

An ear-splitting boom broke the air, rattling the cups on the table. The windows shuddered. The Guardians' shield held but wouldn't last forever. Mildred strengthened it with a spell of her own, and the yells from outside seemed to quiet a degree.

"Where is the majority of the violence?" she asked.

William gestured to a yellowing map on the desk. "The dots reflect areas with reports of discontent."

Mildred studied the collection of dots on the map to find that the violence wasn't focused in a single area but spread out through Stilton Coven. She'd been naive not to give more attention to the Covens after the announcement of the new toll, but in the pandemonium after Nell's death, she hadn't found time. A traitorous flicker of doubt flashed through her mind in Evelyn's voice.

The poor want to be led. Nay, they need to be led. The riots in Newberry are evidence enough of that. When they don't understand or get what they want, they turn to fire and violence.

Surely *all* of these witches couldn't be naturally violent. Scared, perhaps. But not violent. Mildred focused on the gnawing sense in her belly that told her the root of this problem lay in ignorance and fear, not bloodlust.

"How much tax for this month have you collected?" she asked.

"Less than half of what's due."

It felt like an icicle driving into her ribs. If the other Covens had amassed similar levels of currency, which she imagined was likely, she wouldn't even pull in half. Mildred ran her thoughts through a sieve, trying to catch what little tidbits of logic she could. Sliding back into not paying a full tax would shatter her pride, not to mention anger Donovan, and maybe even Evelyn. A full-blown riot would only cement Evelyn's horrid opinions.

"Well, that won't work at all," she said, pushing aside all feelings of panic to focus on the next step.

"Do you have any ideas?" William asked.

Dolph, the Head of Guardians, appeared a few paces away with a quiet whisper.

"Marten sent me," he said. Dolph, a wiry, thin witch with unassuming hazel eyes, stood just a little taller than Mildred. One could be sure, just by looking at him, that he understood whatever moved around him. He looked out the front and back windows, and over to Mildred. "A riot?"

"Almost. They've nearly killed two tax collectors, and we only have two Guardians keeping them from setting us on fire."

Dolph nodded once to William and marched to the back door, disappearing outside without another word.

"We must do something," William said.

Mildred met his gaze. "I'm going to talk to them."

"Talk to them?" His eyes bugged out. "They'll kill you the—"

"I won't give them the chance. In the meantime, I have a task for you."

He paused, disoriented by her fast switch of topics. "What?"

"Go to the kitchens in Chatham Castle and tell the head cook, Mrs. F, that I want as much food as she'll part with. Scraps, even." She pulled a velvet bag drawn shut by strings from her pocket and set it in his palm. "Tell her I'll pay from my own personal currency if she wishes, although I don't think she will. I want to feed this mob."

"Now?" he asked in disbelief. She nodded.

"Now."

"But—"

"Do it."

He tried to argue, but she ignored him. Once he left, she took advantage of the silence to reorganize her thoughts. One thing she knew for certain: Stilton Coven could not riot. If they lost control of their strongest Coven, the others would fail too, taking her, and the entire Middle Covens, down with them.

Dolph strode back into the room. "What's your plan?" he asked.

"I want to talk to them," she said, meeting his gaze. "Think you can make that happen without them killing me?"

"I can put a bubble around you. It'll lift you over them and protect you from projectiles," he said.

Mildred shook her head. "I want them to see me, but I don't want to stand high above them as if I'm better than them. I'll talk with them, one-on-one, the way a leader should. If my assumption is right, they're frightened and want answers."

Dolph studied her for a long pause. "Are you sure? It'll be dangerous."

"Not as dangerous as a full riot."

"Do what you need to, and I'll make sure no harm comes to you," he said. "A contingent of Guardians wearing civilian clothes over their armor is transporting here. They have orders to quietly infiltrate the mob. I'll give you three minutes to calm the crowd. If not, my Guardians act."

"Ten," she said. "I think I can reach them."

"Five." He glanced outside, then back at her. "They're ready to kill, Mildred. I won't give them the opportunity."

"Agreed," Mildred said, pulling in a deep breath. "Five minutes."

Mildred stepped onto the porch with only one thought on her mind: *I must not fail this time.*

The moment she appeared, the jeers of the crowd grew hysterical. She let them scream and chant, their faces disfigured by rage and desperation. The fear in their eyes reminded her of the dire poverty she'd experienced growing up.

They're frightened, that's all.

One witch threw a tomato, but Dolph deflected it with an incantation, and it flew over the rooftop. Another threw a heavy brick, but it crumbled into sand. Mildred used a spell to extinguish their torches, which only doubled the fervor. She transformed the buckets of oil into water just in case.

She stood in the same spot for a full three minutes, Dolph at her side, waiting for them to vent their aggression. Remembering from her first visit to Stilton that the people recognized her authority when she believed she had it, she squared her shoulders and drew in a deep breath.

"Silence!" she commanded, projecting her voice with an incantation.

The crowd raged on, lobbing bricks, nails, balls of mud, and whatever else they could get their hands on. All of the projectiles splattered against Dolph's invisible wall and disintegrated.

"One minute," Dolph muttered under his breath.

Mildred's nostrils flared. She wasn't sure she had the power to use a silencing incantation on such a massive crowd, but she had to try. Using silent magic to cast the spell, she wobbled on her feet. The spell required so much magic that, for a moment, she felt dizzy.

Seconds later, the frantic screams fell to whispers. Witches grabbed their throats, looking at each other and speaking in hushed conversation. It should have silenced them completely, but she took the whispers as success.

"Better," she said, her voice rising. "If you want to speak, you'll have to earn the privilege. I will not tolerate such blatant insubordination and violence. You have concerns. I understand. But you shall not act like children if you want me to help you."

Several witches still tried to scream, but she felt gratified that most of them had settled, their narrow, suspicious eyes focused on her.

I shall not fail.

"Most of you already know that my name is Mildred," she said. "I'm the Assistant to Council Member Stephan. I'm here to listen to your concerns. Before we begin, I want to make one thing clear: If you continue to use violence, I will take appropriate action. A contingent of Guardians awaits my command. Should you choose to act in a civilized manner, we will proceed to hear you out. If not, the Guardians will take control, and all of you will find yourselves in the dungeons at Chatham Castle."

A new layer of stillness settled over the crowd. Hopefully she had reached them before their collective fervor reached the frenzied height that prevented rational thought.

"I'll remove the silencing incantation from each individual witch who raises a hand to voice their concerns with me in a civilized manner. You may begin."

A wall of silence hung around them for a full minute before one hand rose in the back. Mildred motioned to it with a nod and issued a single-person spell reversal. Such intricate, complicated incantations would drain most of her energy if this continued for long.

"I have no currency left for taxes!" a scruffy male called, his voice cracking. "The cotton crop was poor this summer, which means we have hardly enough to pay the new tolls."

"Raise your hands if you're here about the same thing," Mildred called, feeling a quiver in her belly when every arm rose. She loosened the incantation from a witch near the edge of the crowd.

"We can't afford to feed our children under these taxes," he called in a thick brogue. "We can't even bring food from the Northern Covens' orchards because of the fallen bridge."

"How long has it been down?" she asked, her forehead furrowing into deep lines. "No one reported a fallen bridge to me."

"Two months. The Network hasn't sent their crews yet. It's in the Ashleigh Covens, though barely. The new Council Member for Ashleigh hasn't done anything about it."

Mildred summoned a quill and scroll from the office. They zipped through the open window, settling next to her to record every complaint. To her surprise, the silencing spell continued at full strength, without falter. Her powers must have strengthened more than she knew.

"I've noted that the bridge needs repair," Mildred said, ensuring the quill noted her thoughts appropriately. "What else?"

So it went for the next thirty minutes. Mildred heard every witch that wanted to speak, despite the similarity of the complaints, which centered on taxes, a fear for winter, and an inability to pay the toll on the Central Highway. A collective lull eventually settled over the group.

"Is that all?" she asked.

When no hand rose, Mildred let out a sigh of relief. Her scroll had unravelled in a mass of ink and paper. The quill moved at a frantic speed. William had appeared in the back, surrounded by a slew of servants from the castle bearing armfuls of food. They set it all out on a table, transporting in and out at random. Mrs. F had come through for her.

"Very well," Mildred said, gratified to still feel strength despite the toll the silencing spell had taken on her. "I hear you. All of you. You have legitimate worries for your families and your future. I also understand how high the taxes are. If you do not have the means to pay in currency, I am willing to negotiate."

If possible, their suspicions only deepened. Mildred didn't blame them. For the first time in her life, she spoke without a plan. How could she negotiate? She didn't have the authority to tell them they didn't have to pay taxes! Donovan would put her head on a platter.

"Then how will you collect your precious currency?" a woman hissed, clutching her child to her chest.

"I am meeting with all the Coven Leaders early in the morning to work out a solution. I will send that plan out to the Middle Covens through the tax collectors tomorrow evening. Guardians will accompany them. If you attempt to harm any of them, you will be placed in the dungeons, where I will personally visit you once a year for the rest of your life."

"And the bridge?"

"It will also be taken care of. Tomorrow evening, if you can handle congregating in a non-violent fashion, you may come back to the Coven office, and I'll explain my new plan. In the meantime, I have provided a meal for you before you go home. You will find food sufficient for your needs on the tables behind you. If there are leftovers, take them home. Go well."

She removed the spell suppressing their voices, spun around, and strode inside the office without another word. Dolph stepped to the middle of the porch, his eyes scanning the crowd. Several Guardians transported next to him and near to the table where William oversaw the distribution of food.

Once inside, Mildred leaned back against the door and closed her eyes.

It's over.

She'd done what she needed to do and curbed a full riot.

"You did wonderfully, Miss Mildred," Lily said from where she sat on the staircase, her pale face drawn with fatigue. Her daughter Hazel, a wide-eyed, black-haired young woman—a near replica of her mother—sat at her side. "Truly."

"Are the tax collectors going to make it?" Mildred asked. Lily shook her head.

"No," she whispered. "One just died."

"This is far from over," Mildred said. "They won't be the first to die if we don't get it under control somehow."

"They seem calm now, at least," Lily said, glancing out at the chattering crowd. Guardians stood at intervals along the edges, their swords glimmering in the torchlight.

"For tonight," Mildred replied. "Tell William I'll return early in the morning with the other Coven Leaders. We'll meet all day."

She transported back to her bedroom, falling into an exhausted heap on her bed. She composed a hasty letter to the Coven Leaders and sent a message of thanks to Marten through the silenda, promising to see him the next day, then peeled off her clothes, scrubbed her body, and fell into bed.

By the time the sun rose, Mildred had already awoken, eaten a small breakfast packed by Mrs. F, spoken with Marten, transported to Stilton, and begun dealing with the list of issues. Stephan showed up around lunch and, after being doted on by Lily and Hazel, decided to stay for the duration of the meeting.

Mildred conducted the six-hour meeting with the supreme efficiency of a trained Captain of the Guards. By late afternoon, she sent an announcement with each Coven Leader—signed by Stephan, no less—to duplicate and spread to every village and town.

"Do you think it'll work?" Mildred asked William, staring out the window at the slow bustle of downtown Stilton. Several witches had gathered to hear her plan already. He suppressed a yawn.

"It has to," he said.

"Donovan would be furious if he found out I'm allowing witches to rebuild the bridge and perform other jobs for the Coven in lieu of paying taxes," she said, speaking more to herself than to him. "Although I doubt he *will* find out, as he doesn't pay much attention to anything besides hunting. We'll save some currency by not paying for repairs, and the wealthier witches will still pay their pentacles, or pay in food, which we'll put in the storehouses for desperate moments during the winter, but I still don't know that we'll pull in enough currency to keep me in this job. He's already tried to fire me once."

"If you dip below 30,000 pentacles once or twice, Donovan won't fire you right away," Stephan said from where he sat at the fire, plucking dried grapes off a tray Hazel brought him. His aged forehead crinkled. "At least, I don't think he will. If you'd just pay Norbert off, Donovan wouldn't even know that you're low."

"I won't pay into corruption," she said, folding her arms across her chest with a sigh and hoping that Stephan was right.

In Charge

May looked lovely when the dappled light of early fall sifted through the silky strands of her ebony hair. The scent of honeysuckle drifted by, stirring the explosive red and orange leaves cluttering the ground. Evelyn inhaled the scent and thought of Nell.

One leaf in particular dangled from its high perch, threatening to fall as it fluttered back and forth. Evelyn eyed the struggling frond, feeling an odd connection to it. She felt ready to give in most days, clinging to her perch as High Priestess, waving back and forth on winds she couldn't control.

"Do you remember the advice I gave when you became Council Member?" May asked, plucking a leaf of Letum Ivy from a nearby vine and ripping it into small pieces that fell like confetti to the ground.

"You gave me a lot of advice."

Evelyn stood beneath a towering tree deep in Letum Wood, free from the prying eyes and ears of the castle servants and May's students. The distant chatter of teenage girls in the yard of Miss Mabel's School for Girls swept in now and then with the breeze.

"True," May said. "But you needed a lot of advice. You need less now, I think, but still are far from ready to be on your own."

A swell of fire rose in Evelyn's chest. *I'm not an incompetent child,* she thought. Though she clenched her fists, she stayed silent.

"Despite your successful ascension to High Priestess six weeks ago, I still believe that you need to lay low again."

Evelyn opened her mouth to reply, but May stopped her with a firm shake of her head.

"Listen to me," she said. "We must be twice as careful now as we were when you were just a Council Member. I believe we should wait for Donovan to die on his own, although I'd much rather kill him and be done with the whole mess. It's really too bad the Esmelda Scrolls prevent the successor from killing the Highest Witch."

Evelyn's eyebrows shot up. "You would kill the Highest Witch?" she asked, though she wasn't that surprised. May's brutal ruthlessness used to frighten Evelyn, when she was younger and without so much power. Before she'd become High Priestess.

May's eyes flickered. "If it meant achieving a greater end for our struggling Network, then yes. But it doesn't matter because we can't. Donovan's already sick, isn't he?"

"A liver issue," Evelyn said, her forehead furrowed. "I spoke with his apothecary just two days ago. If he stops drinking ipsum, he'll buy himself some time. If not, it could be just a matter of months before he dies a drunk."

"Then he'll go soon enough," May concluded, trailing the tips of her fingers along the twisting vine that swept down beside her face. "We need only to continue encouraging his bad habits. Despite how anxious both of us are to see you use your new power and influence, we don't want him to die *too* soon." May's tone dropped into the analytical cadence of one who studied every word she said. "You need time to build yourself up as a dutiful High Priestess and worthy companion. When you become Highest Witch, the Network will already trust you to use your power to make things right."

"I know you want me to lay low, but I think there's an opportunity to act here," Evelyn said quickly, lest May cut her off again. "Donovan could be convinced to go to Ashleigh House on a break to recover. If he spends three months alone at Ashleigh House with his ipsum and nothing else to do, he'll drink himself to death. Then I can take over as Highest Witch in his absence and implement my plan."

May arched a disapproving eyebrow and folded her arms across her chest. "What did you have in mind to execute *your* plan?"

"Rioters set fire to Newberry again," Evelyn said. "Two members of the upper class died when the poor stormed their house and set it on fire. Council Member Wayne can't get the lower class under control, not that I think he's tried that hard, so a firm hand must intervene. I'll suppress the riots, get rid of the leaders, and provide our supporters there more safety. We'll send the Guardians."

May seemed to think it over. "That would be for the best," she said, "but not coming from you. Many will be upset when the Guardians are used against them again, and we can't afford that backlash. But if you convince Donovan to authorize it, the bad publicity will fall on him."

Evelyn shrank back with annoyance. May was right, as usual. Would there ever come a day when she thought of the best course of action without May whispering it in her ear?

"Yes," she admitted, unable to keep bitterness from her voice. "That is a better plan." She turned her gaze to the variegated carpet of leaves on the floor of Letum Wood. Bulbous mushrooms sprang up from the ground in browns and grays.

"They broke up a major highway in the Eastern Covens, and the Ashleigh Covens continue to be tempestuous," May said, ticking the issues off one finger at a time. "The dungeons will be full soon. Donovan will have to execute prisoners if they don't die of disease first."

May flicked the words off her tongue as if annoyed, but Evelyn ignored her, having had enough of May's arrogant certainty. She'd never felt so restless in her life. All her power and influence as High Priestess, and May still wanted her to wait to use it. Magic coiled in her chest, and her body tensed.

May met Evelyn's gaze straight on. "I think it's too soon to send Donovan to Ashleigh House. You need to give it time."

Evelyn inwardly winced but showed no sign of it. Why did this take so much *time*? It seemed her whole life she'd lived at the edge, waiting for the right moment to go to work. She'd never expected that change required so much patience.

"The Network needs currency," Evelyn said, pulling herself from her heavy thoughts into the comforting rhythm of business. "I've been thinking of closing all the common schools and infusing that currency into the fund for Network education or the Guardians. Both are dwindling, as you know."

"Yes," May said with a grimace. "I *do* know. We weren't able to buy new schoolbooks this year."

"A perfect example. It's more important that we educate the witches that will succeed in life," Evelyn said. "Attendance at the common schools isn't even at one hundred percent. At least, I don't think it is. We may as well educate those who have proven they're born to lead by making it into the Network school system."

A breeze whispered by, sending a flutter of leaves into the air. They swirled in a funnel around them. Evelyn glanced up to find the stubborn leaf still holding on.

"I'd suggest more stringent requirements for children attending the Network school system," May suggested, plucking another leaf to tear into pieces, her upper lip curled with disdain. "Isadora isn't going to see our side of things, and we'd be better off getting rid of her. Witches with foresight make me nervous."

Evelyn stared at May. Why fear a witch with foresight? Isadora could prove helpful to the cause of the New Central Network. She opened her mouth to agree, so used as she was to May's authority, but stopped herself.

I'm the High Priestess. Not May.

"Isadora chooses based on merit," Evelyn said, lifting her chin. "A girl may be rich and stupid. I don't want to waste time educating them. Isadora stays."

May's eyes narrowed an infinitesimal degree. "Poor witches slip into the Network school system now," she said. "Your friend Mildred did."

Evelyn's spine stiffened. *Mildred.* The sorest spot—of many—that existed between her and May. Despite Evelyn's position as High Priestess, May still didn't feel the need to keep any of her opinions to herself.

"I won't speak about Mildred with you," she said through clenched teeth. "I've already told you that."

May pressed her lips together in a firm line. "I've said it once before, Evie, and I'm sure that I'll have to say it again: You must break off your friendship with Mildred. I don't like it. She gives me a bad feeling."

"But—"

"I know, I know. You say that Mildred will support you. You say that she'll come through. But you don't know that's true because you haven't tested her."

"That is my business, not yours."

"No!" May yelled so sharply that Evelyn reared back. "You have no idea what you're talking about, and you never have! You must listen to *me*! This *is* my business."

A flock of birds rose from the trees and scattered with grating squawks. Evelyn and May stared at each other in festering, shocked silence. She hadn't spoken with such maternal authority since Evelyn was a student.

But I'm not a student anymore, Evelyn thought, irate. *I'm the High Priestess. I don't answer to my Assistant.*

Perhaps I never should have.

"You forget yourself, Assistant," Evelyn hissed, fists clenched at her side. "We may be business partners, but I am still your High Priestess."

May's bright blue eyes widened in shock, closed into livid slits, and finally relaxed. She curtsied, though her back and shoulders remained as stiff as a sheet of metal. Her countenance hid the ice beneath her cool gaze.

"Of course, Your Highness."

For the first time since meeting May at tea at age fourteen, Evelyn felt like an adult in her presence. A rush of freedom and power nearly overwhelmed her, and she felt dizzy in a moment of breathless excitement.

"We shall not speak of Mildred again," Evelyn said. "I will press forward according to my own time schedule. If you ever indicate disapproval of my course of action again, I'll fire you on the spot. Am I understood?"

"Let me just say that—"

"No!" Evelyn roared. "You shall not give another unsolicited opinion. *I* am the High Priestess. *I* have sacrificed everything, and done all the work, and endured all the years of messages and meetings to get to where I am now. You depend on me. It's not the other way around."

May's face had gone as white as a sheet. Her nostrils flared and fists clenched, but Evelyn didn't care. It didn't matter anymore.

She was in charge.

"Do you understand me?" Evelyn asked in a low tone.

May acknowledged the question with an uneasy nod, her eyes averted. The rage boiling in Evelyn's chest subsided, leaving behind a new, intoxicating sense of power and control. No more living for May's approval. No more relying on others to decide the best course of action. Evelyn had freed herself.

"Good. I'll see you at work tomorrow. Enjoy the rest of your weekend."

She transported away without another word, finally leaving the conversation right where she wanted. May could stew on that for the rest of the day.

Now, it was time for Evelyn to lead the Central Network.

Good for You

"Stephan, why don't you let me find you a nice, comfortable house to retire in?" Mildred asked on his eightieth birthday. She used a spell to tack a *Happy Birthday* sign high on the wall above the fireplace, where several of his ivy plants had started to climb. "I'm sure we could find—"

He stopped her with a weak wave of his hand. "No," he said wearily. "I've spent my life at Chatham Castle. I shan't leave it to die somewhere by myself. I'll die working, the way I always planned."

Council Members weren't required to stay in their position until death, but they were allowed to, provided that business continued as usual. Mildred's nose wrinkled. Once, dying at her desk seemed the most likely, and even welcome, outcome of her life. But five years of working as his Assistant had changed those ideas. She'd die on her own terms, thank you very much.

"All right," Mildred said with a heavy sigh. "Let me cover you with this blanket. Don't you want your lunch?"

"No," he said, closing his eyes. His face looked unusually pale, though he hadn't had real color for some time. "Just a nap, like always."

Mildred removed the tray, draped a second blanket over him, waved a few more logs onto the fire, and headed to the door. She cast one last glance back, saw him staring at the portrait of his wife on the wall, and slipped out of the room, the tray following her. Marten waited outside.

"Sorry to keep you waiting," she said, smiling and taking his hand.

Stephan's full lunch tray drifted down the hall on its own, moving to the kitchen.

"Not at all," he replied, returning her warm smile. "It wasn't long."

They strolled hand in hand down the hallway until Mildred broke the silence. "I'm worried about Stephan."

"You've been worried about Stephan since you first met him," Marten quipped with a laugh.

"Well, yes, that's true, strictly speaking. But I'm worried in a different way. After working as his Assistant for so long, I've learned his ways. He's so calm right now. So . . . boring. He answers all my questions without a fight, and didn't even argue with me when I brought him a gardening book he'd already read. He just stares at the fire. He hasn't eaten a cookie in almost a week."

Marten caught on to the concern in her voice and met her troubled eyes. "What are you worried it means?"

"It can't be long until he dies, the poor man. Perhaps just weeks at the most. He is eighty, after all. Normally he demands a chocolate cake with white frosting, a new plant, a pair of slippers, and his dinner served on the finest bone china in the castle, but he hasn't spoken a word about his birthday today."

"Is that what's really bothering you? Stephan dying?"

Mildred had to pause to analyze her feelings about the inevitable loss of her mentor. *Yes,* she thought in surprise. *He is my mentor.* Somehow, over the years, she'd developed an unlikely friendship with Stephan. The end of their time together held a definite note of sadness, but one couldn't fight with nature. Death was no more under her control than the seasons.

"I'm quite sad about losing him, I suppose. I will miss the cantankerous old fart . . . sometimes. But there are more selfish reasons too. When he dies, I shall be out of a job."

"Someone else could choose you as Assistant," Marten pointed out. Mildred rolled her eyes.

"No one on *this* Council would have me—except maybe Porter, and he has no reason to give up his Assistant—nor would I work with anyone but him. That's just it, Marten. I wouldn't take it even if they did offer. I'm going to leave Chatham when Stephan dies. I decided it last week when he fell asleep in the middle of a sentence."

Marten stopped walking to stare at her. "Leave?"

"I don't want to be a Council Member."

"You spoke of something like this when Stella gave birth to Daniel, but you haven't mentioned it since. I figured you were happy once you made peace with Stephan."

"Well, I suppose I was," she said, tilting her head from side to side. She couldn't sort through her emotions in any organized manner. "But the only thing that makes me really happy, besides being with you and Jorden, is teaching."

"Who would you teach?"

Mildred lifted her shoulders in a shrug. "I'm not sure, but I thought of writing to Miss Jane. She may have a position available for me, and with all the experience I've gained teaching the servants these past years, I know I'd be a good fit in a Network school. Maybe even a common school, as I'm more used to working with new students."

Marten's mouth bobbed open and closed before he finally said, "Would this make you happy? Leaving politics to teach, I mean."

She thought the question over with a brutal thoroughness. The thought of leaving the Middle Covens to the care of another witch wasn't comfortable. "Partially happy, I suppose."

"Then what else is there?"

She stopped and met his eyes with a very matter-of-fact gaze. "Being with you. Avoiding messages and meetings. Transporting to Jorden and Imogen's cottage whenever the mood strikes me, not just on stolen weekends like I do now. Living away from the cold halls of Chatham Castle. I rather like the idea of finding a small cottage to live in with you. After we're hand fasted, of course."

"I'd like that very much," Marten said with a smile, trailing the back of his hand along her cheek, but his voice elongated. "But what of your goal to make a difference in the world? Can you give it up so easily?"

She shifted. "The Central Network is a disaster that's too big for me to fix, even as a Council Member. The Elitists have nearly taken over. Porter, Terry, and Stephan aside, of course. I feel my greatest contribution can be teaching."

"The Middle Covens will fend for themselves under a leader of Donovan's choosing."

"I know," she whispered. "But I can't fix it. Donovan would no sooner appoint me their Council Member than give up his ipsum."

Marten let out a sigh. "It feels wrong to leave the Middle Covens without a fight. Even I have come to love them."

"What more could we do than we've already done?"

"A resistance."

She paused, thinking back to the promise that she'd made to her students. It hadn't seemed real at the time, but now that Marten mentioned it, she couldn't help but wonder if all these events were funneling them to that one outcome.

"Perhaps," she said, gazing away, not ready for it to come to that.

"Let's just have a nice lunch," Marten suggested, running a hand over the top of his smooth head. "This is the first we've seen of each other since your twenty-eighth birthday. You've been working in the Covens without break."

"Nothing new about that," she said, and they walked to the dining hall in silence.

Mildred returned from their tense lunch feeling uneasy. She opened her mouth to greet Stephan, and stopped. He sat in his chair as usual, slumped to the side, a slight smile on his lifeless face.

"Oh," Mildred murmured weakly. She glanced up at the portrait of Stephan's wife and back at him again. For a moment, she worried she had brought his death upon him by speaking of it so frankly with Marten, but she dismissed the thought.

"Absurd," she whispered. "He was on his way out already."

The kind eyes of Stephan's wife smiled down from her spot above the fireplace. Mildred sank onto a chair.

Katie Cross

"Good for you, my old friend," she said with a sigh. "Go see your family again."

Evelyn prepared herself for her three o'clock appointment by staring out the window and collecting her thoughts. May wouldn't approve of what she was about to do, which made her want to do it even more. No matter May's opinion, Evelyn would give Mildred one chance to do the right thing before she let her go forever. She owed her at least that much. Evelyn's hand tingled when she remembered the vow she'd made.

If my friends Mildred Graeme and Stella James Rowe do not support my decisions as High Priestess, I shall release them from my life with no further attempts to continue the friendship.

"She'll be loyal to me," Evelyn said in a low murmur. "Mildred is always steadfast."

Things had been unusually tense and polite between Evelyn and May since their conversation in Letum Wood two weeks before. May did her job, remained quiet, and made no ripples in the water of Evelyn's budding career. Evelyn felt like a butterfly coming out of her cocoon, and the feeling sparked magic between her fingers.

"When Mildred arrives, I won't need you in the meeting, May," Evelyn said, breaking the monotony of silence. "I'll handle her appointment on my own."

May nodded, impassive.

"Yes, Your Highness."

Mildred entered her office at exactly three, just as Evelyn expected. May stood from behind her desk and moved into the hall. Once Evelyn sealed the door with a silencing incantation to thwart spying ears, she turned to Mildred with a cool smile.

"Merry meet, old friend. We haven't spoken much since I became High Priestess three months ago."

"We haven't. You didn't come to the birthday party this year either. Again."

"Yes, well, I'm sure you understand how busy I've been lately."

Mildred nodded, but her narrow eyes flickered. Evelyn didn't feel the need to explain why she hadn't gone but wondered if Mildred had already guessed. Taking tea with a young mother, a screaming child, and a Council Member's Assistant wasn't exactly in line with what was expected of a High Priestess. No matter how good of friends they were, Evelyn maintained standards. Even Mildred had to appreciate that. Besides, Nell had never taken tea outside the political sphere.

I must sacrifice for the greater good of the Network, Evelyn reminded herself with a resolute breath.

"I'm sure there can be no question as to why I've asked you here today," Evelyn said, eager to get the appointment over with now that Mildred stood before her.

"I don't know what you're speaking of, High Priestess."

"The Middle Covens need a new Council Member now that Stephan has passed. Since you've been taking care of them for so long—everyone knows you did Stephan's job for him—and as you are a close personal friend who I trust to follow my counsel, I've concluded that appointing you as Council Member will ensure the smoothest transition."

Mildred paused, her eyes as wide as if Evelyn had struck her face. "You want me to take Stephan's place?"

"Are you surprised?"

"Yes. I hadn't been expecting an offer of employment."

"Really? You've worked with Stephan for five and a half years now. It's not uncommon for an Assistant, especially one that's worked as hard as you, to take over when a Council Member dies or retires."

"I suppose I thought Donovan would assign the role," she admitted.

"Ah, that. I volunteered to take some of the work off his plate, and he allowed me to extend this to you on his behalf. He is in full agreement with the decision. What do you say? Will you take it?"

She'd almost called her *Milly,* but pulled it back at the last moment. Evelyn's left hand sat on her lap, clenched in a fist that Mildred couldn't see. If Mildred refused, all would be over between them.

Please do the right thing, Mildred. Please don't make me sacrifice you as well.

Mildred released a sharp, punctuated breath and opened a palm. "May I have a quill and a piece of parchment?"

"Make as many lists as you want."

Evelyn waved the supplies to her and sat back down. Mildred lowered herself into a nearby chair and wrote in silence for the next fifteen minutes. Once she finished scribbling, she stared at her notes for another ten minutes. Evelyn didn't dare say a word, not even when Mildred stood and set the quill back on her desk.

"I have no desire to give my life to the Network the way I once did," Mildred said, "but I won't leave the Middle Covens right now. Serving as Council Member is not my passion anymore. I'd grow old and bitter and disillusioned the way Stephan did, and I refuse to do that. For you, and the Middle Covens, I will take the position for the required five years. No more."

Evelyn's jaw dropped. "What?"

"It's complicated," Mildred said. "But suffice it to say that I don't want to remain in politics forever. I will stay for the Middle Covens."

Evelyn leaned back in her chair.

"When did this great change of heart occur?" she asked, secretly wounded that Mildred hadn't betrayed these thoughts to her before. Then again, when would they have talked? Their communication had eroded since Stella left.

"Recently," Mildred replied, clearing her throat. "Not too long ago."

Evelyn swallowed, and the chasm that formed between them seemed unsurpassable. She felt as if she spoke with a total stranger, not one of her best childhood friends.

"What would you do if not politics?"

"Leave this bloody madhouse. Visit my brother. Marry Marten. Work at a school of sorts. I don't really know yet. I'll deal with that once I fulfill my five years as Council Member. I know that by then you will have turned the Network around from Donovan's lazy rule, and I can move on with my life."

Mildred held Evelyn's gaze with stern expectation. Evelyn felt the weight all the way into her bones. She pressed her lips together until they blanched. A well of panic bloomed in her chest. The crushing grief from when Nell died returned with unrelenting strength, seizing her heart in a tight fist.

I don't even know my best friends anymore. I'm already losing everyone.

Mildred glanced over her shoulder when a plume of sparks erupted from the fireplace. By sheer willpower, Evelyn forced the boiling magic in her chest to calm; it felt as if it would consume her with sticky, black panic. Mildred wanted to leave. Stella was already gone. Despite all her efforts, they were slipping away, just like Mama and Papa.

I don't want to cut you loose the way I did Nell. I can't stand it again.

"I see," Evelyn whispered. "Well, I'm glad you're willing to take it. I'm surprised that you've lost your motivation for the political game, of course. You've pursued this dream for years."

"Things change," Mildred said, and Evelyn thought she heard something more behind the words.

"I'm glad to have you remain at the castle. I . . . I need my friends."

Mildred's chuckle came out as a bark. "You need us, Evelyn? Have you gone mad? You've never needed us! You've made that very clear lately. You never respond to my letters, you don't write Stella, and you stand me up for dinners every week."

Evelyn stared at her, hearing the wails of a little girl rise to a keening pitch inside her. Why couldn't she control these horrid emotions? Her body tingled; her chest burned. So much magic built inside her she thought she'd explode if she didn't use it. Her tone dropped into a low, desperate plea.

"Being High Priestess isn't what I thought it would be. It's . . . it's been difficult."

"That's something you should have thought of before you accepted."

Evelyn scoffed bitterly. "You never were one to give comfort, were you?"

"Do you want comfort?"

Evelyn met her small, beady eyes. "Yes," she whispered. "I want the comfort of knowing that my best friend is at my side, supporting me. Even if I haven't been a very good friend, I admit." She swallowed past the lump of pride that blocked her throat. "I . . . I have big plans, Mildred, and I need your help to execute them. They'll be life-changing. May is a competent Assistant, of course, but—"

But she's not a friend.

Mildred's eyes had narrowed, though her usual inscrutable expression remained.

"Thank you." Evelyn stood. "It will be a truly wonderful experience. I'll have my legalwitch draw up the contract tonight. You'll of course be afforded the usual two-year trial period during which you cannot be removed as Council Member unless you bring harm to the Covens or to other leaders. As you know, you'll serve a five-year minimum, according to the Esmelda Scrolls. I must admit, I hope five years as Council Member will change your mind, and that you'll stay."

Mildred held out her arm. Evelyn grasped it firmly.

"Thank you, Mildred. I know you won't regret it."

Unusual Confidence

After dinner with Marten to tell him the news—about which he was more excited than she—Mildred slept in her old room, finding comfort in the close walls and chilly air that smelled of fresh linen.

She woke to the sun streaming through her window, the covers warm. *I need to get a head start on taxes. Stephan will want an early breakfast this morning. He's been getting up so much earlier lately. Is his best suit laundered?* With a stretch, she rubbed her sleep-crusted eyes and swung her short legs out of bed. The cold stone floor met her feet with a hearty dose of reality. Her eyes popped open, and she dropped firmly in the lap of her new life.

Council Member. Evelyn.

Her life had tilted again. "Right," she muttered, squaring her shoulders. "Time to organize things."

Mildred scrubbed her face with a bit of rose petal soap, cleaned up with a short bath, dressed herself in a soft gown the color of mustard, grabbed her bag, and left the room.

"Council Member!"

Lavinia approached from the end of the hall, waving. She had matured into a striking young woman in her early twenties. Her hair was swept into an elegant bun on top of her head, which made the sharp angles of her face seem older and more prismatic. Instead of lugging around a mop and broom, she wore the more fashionably tailored black uniform with red ribbon trim that signified an experienced maid responsible for the upper floors.

"I heard the news this morning," Lavinia said with a smile. "Congratulations. If you'll follow me, Council Member, I'll take you to your new chambers upstairs."

Mildred's neck tightened imperceptibly. *Council Member.* How odd and distant it sounded coming from one of her students.

"Thank you, Lavinia."

Lavinia stopped in the hallway. "Will this change anything?" she asked with imploring eyes, and Mildred understood right away. Classes. She smiled.

"No, it won't."

"Thank you," she whispered with a grin, and continued walking. They came to an apartment on the fifth floor several minutes later. Mildred puffed her way up the stairs and stopped just behind Lavinia, breathless and wondering if she should exercise more.

"This is one of my favorite rooms," Lavinia said, opening it with an aged skeleton key. "I had the mirror brought in here because it suits you so much."

When she stepped into the apartment, Mildred first noticed an elegant mirror lined with ancient iron. The regal face of a lion sat on top of the mirror, and its mane traveled down the sides in curling locks.

To the right, she saw a small, windowless room with a wooden desk, several golden candle sconces, and a cupboard of thin slates meant to hold scrolls. She thought it looked like a miniature library swathed in shadows. Across from the entryway lay a small tea room with four cream chairs surrounding a tea table. A dark walnut four-poster bed dominated the sprawling bedroom, which was larger than her old family cottage. Carved, twisted rails spiraled into tree branches at the top. Velvety sapphire curtains hung from the sides, contrasting with a matching sky-blue divan next to the bed.

"Do you like it?" Lavinia asked. Mildred squirmed. She felt out of place.

"It's beautiful, Lavinia," Mildred said. "But I don't really want it. Perhaps I could work out an arrangement with the Head of Housekeeping to stay down in the servants' quarters?"

Lavinia cocked an eyebrow. "You can't be serious, Council Member."

"Quite serious."

Lavinia glanced around the elegant room. "You don't want to live here?"

"It's nothing personal, of course. I just prefer my own room."

"I-I suppose it wouldn't be a big deal . . . but what will witches say?"

Mildred shrugged. "Who cares?"

"You should! You're a Council Member now."

"Well, I don't. It's a matter of comfort, Lavinia, that's all, and I'd be more comfortable in my old room. They can say whatever they like. If you wouldn't mind speaking with the Head of Housekeeping, I'd be very obliged. Tell her to stop by my office if she has any questions. I'll see you in class tonight. I believe we'll be discussing protective shields lasting longer than one minute."

Lavinia's mouth bobbed open and closed.

"Can I at least bring the mirror to your bedroom?"

Mildred glanced at it over her shoulder. "Yes, you may. I think I should like that very much."

Letters

2nd Month of Spring

Mildred,

How I miss you lately. Daniel is doing well. We are staying with my parents while Dale embarks on a four-month mission to the Southern Covens. Little Daniel remains as rambunctious and stubborn as any three-year-old could be. He certainly keeps me on my toes.

I'll admit that my life has gone stagnant without Chatham Castle. I do miss it, although nothing makes me as happy as seeing my son's handsome face every morning. I often remember laughing at your stern expressions when someone said something you disagreed with at a meeting.

Oh, and congratulations, Council Member! I'm very excited for you, and not at all surprised. Of course you took Stephan's spot. Who else? You're keeping Evie in line, aren't you? I still don't hear from her, though I still write. I think you're correct. We are losing her, aren't we? I weep over it at night but feel there's nothing I can do. I just wish she'd answer my letters. I stopped by her office one day just to see how she was, but May turned me away and said she was too busy.

Please write soon. I look forward to having you for dinner one night when you aren't so busy. I hope everything is going well.

Your friend,
Stella

3rd Month of Summer

Mildred,

Happy 29th birthday, sister!

Imogen and I are excited to see you again. We're doing well, and so is little Markus. The birth went beautifully. He's shown a demanding temperament, just like Mother's, when he's hungry. We received your packages and hardly have room for all of the gifts. Thank you. It will help us more than you know.

Please tell me how things are really going at the castle. It can't be good. Evelyn's wavering popularity amongst the poor keeps the Guardians busy here in the Ashleigh Covens. She's given orders to imprison any witch with an opinion contrary to current Network practices. Is it written in the Esmelda Scrolls that we can't have our own opinions?

I hate arresting these witches, but if we don't, we would be arrested. We can often find a way to let them out of it, or help them escape, but not for all of them. These witches are desperate, and it's pushed them to violence. The rich continue to seem oblivious to the suffering of the witches that work for them—or used to work for them. I fear that the Guardian force may soon revolt against the Network if something isn't done.

Be safe, sister. I have a feeling that you are in far greater danger than I.

Your brother,
Jorden

1st Month of Fall

Dear Miss Mildred,

I'm enclosing the updated schedule for classes this month. The evening Protective Magic class is in such high demand that I found a larger room close to the dungeons. With additional space, we can admit more students. Would you be okay with that change? If so, I'll distribute directions through the silenda tonight.

I've also included a list of the servants who requested to take the vow of silence and join the silenda Network. Pending your approval, they will attend class this evening. There are ten this week. Including them, we now have over three hundred active students. I've spoken with the two maids you asked to teach the Incantations for Housekeeping class that has ten students on the wait list, and they've agreed to team teach.

I do hope the silenda is not draining your power with so many witches using it, Council Member. Thank you again for the honor of being your Assistant in this work. You know that it makes me very happy.

Yours,
Miss L

2nd Month of Fall

Dear Council Member,

It is with great regret that I write this letter to inform you of my one-week notice. Working as your Assistant for the last nine months has been a priceless experience, but I hate castle life. I cannot sleep at night, I don't enjoy meetings with so hostile a Council, and after all I've seen of politics and how hard you have to work to refrain from corruption, I find I don't desire to work for the Network anymore.

I plan to return to my home in the Western Covens as soon as this week is up, and I hope you can find a replacement soon. Thank you for all you've taught me, and thank you for not being one of them.

Sincerely,
Barnaby Taylor

2nd Month of Fall

Dearest Mildred,

Our dear grandson, Daniel, passed away from pneumonia last night. Stella has asked for your 'steadying presence' to help her pull through. We beg your help, in whatever form you can give it.

Sincerely,
Warren and Agatha James

You Always Will

Mildred transported to the outskirts of Newberry in the early morning hours.

A thick layer of mist curled away from the cobblestone roads, leaving weak lamplight to guide her up the long dirt driveway of the James' estate. The sun couldn't pierce the heavy mat of clouds threatening rain, as if even the skies mourned little Daniel.

Hundreds of apple trees shrouded the house in a close embrace of spiny branches and brittle leaves. An apricot tree in the middle of the yard caught Mildred's eye. Beneath the sprawling branches sat a headstone, alongside a witch sitting in the soggy grass. They'd already buried him.

Mildred altered her course and crossed the spongy lawn with quiet steps. She settled a bouquet of white irises on top of the grave and knelt next to Stella. Mildred had never seen her friend's face look so pale or her cheeks so gaunt. The slushy grass soaked through Mildred's dress, sending a chill up her arms.

"Can you speak comfort to me, Mildred?" Stella asked after a long silence, tears rimming her dim, bloodshot eyes. "Can you use your infallible logic to tell me why this happened?"

"No," Mildred whispered. "Sometimes not even logic can explain the greatest tragedies."

A tear trembled on Stella's lashes. "I want him back," she cried, doubling over with a guttural wail. "I want him back in my arms. That's where he belongs!"

"I know you do."

Stella swallowed. "But I can't have him. He'll never come back to me, will he?"

She finally looked at Mildred. Her hair lay flat on her head, limp from the rain, highlighting the sunken appearance of her once bright eyes. Mildred swallowed the lump of emotion rising in her throat. Hadn't Daniel come into the world with rampant emotions and tears of pain? How appropriate—bittersweet—that he left the same way.

"Not in this life, Stella, no," she said quietly. "But it doesn't end here, does it? There's more beyond this, that we can't see."

"Do you believe there's more? Does my son live on?"

"Yes," Mildred whispered, feeling her heart shudder as she thought of Mother's face. "I do. I don't believe our loved ones are that far gone from us."

Stella's bottom lip wobbled. "Then do you think Daniel is frightened?" she asked, another tear cascading down her cheek. "Do you think he's afraid, without me there to help him and keep him safe?"

Mildred shook her head. "No," she said, holding Stella's guileless gaze. "No, I think he's not frightened at all. In fact, I think he's going to stay quite close to you for a while, though you may not see him."

Stella gazed down at the headstone for a long time in silence. "He was too young to die. I love him more than anything in the world. More than Dale, more than myself. More than anything I'll ever have again."

"You always will, Stella."

Stella dropped her head into her hands with a tormented sob. Mildred put her arms around her friend and pulled her into a warm embrace.

"I'm so sorry," Mildred whispered, a tear dropping from her eye and landing on top of Stella's trembling head. "I'm so very, very sorry."

Stella cried for nearly half an hour in Mildred's arms, then pulled away with a shiver and wiped the excess tears from her cheek.

"Thank you," she said, fumbling with a lace handkerchief. "I knew your solid strength would help me. I feel that I'll go mad here, stuck amongst all the memories."

"Will you come back to the castle with me as my Assistant?" Mildred asked, lifting Stella's chin. "I happen to be in the market for one. My first one just quit because he hates politics as much as I do. It will give you something to do, and you can take any time off whenever you need it. You don't have to come right away, either."

Stella glanced up with a flicker of hope. "Do you mean it?"

"Absolutely," Mildred said. "You're my best friend, and I'd like nothing more than to have you at my side."

Evelyn's emerald silk dress swished around her legs as she moved down the hall, eyes fixed on her goal in the distance. Her time as High Priestess—had it already been a year?—had been good to her; working as Nell's Assistant had served her well. Although loathe to admit that May was right, Evelyn had played it carefully, but now she was done *laying low*. When this kind of opportunity fell into her lap, she'd not shun it, no matter how disapproving May had become.

Just be kind and supportive, she reminded herself. *If Donovan thinks it was his idea, he'll be likely to listen.*

May moved down the hallway just behind Evelyn, schedule scroll under her left arm, not saying a word. Her long black hair sat in a thick bun, shining every time they passed a sun-filled window. A few open windows admitted a mid-fall breeze, and Evelyn soaked in the tangy scent of crisp leaves.

May cleared her throat. "May I ask the purpose of your meeting with the High Priest? I didn't have it on the schedule for today and will need to rearrange a meeting with the Head of Highways."

Evelyn nodded to a passing Coven Leader from Bickers Mill and turned down a hallway to the right.

"Donovan continues to deteriorate," she replied. "His apothecary sent me a concerned letter today regarding his poor health. We both agree that he should spend some time at Ashleigh House to recover. I must convince him that it will be best for the Network."

"He's been ill for years," May said. "A break at Ashleigh House isn't going to heal him."

"Let's hope it will help." Evelyn forced a smile for a passing Coven

Leader. "We wouldn't want anything to happen to our dear High Priest now, would we?"

May stiffened with a sharp intake of breath. "This wouldn't have anything to do with an idea of yours—"

"Yes," Evelyn said crisply, head held high. "It absolutely does."

May remained quiet, but only for a moment. "I know you aren't seeking my opinion, High Priestess, but I must say that you've only been in power a year and—"

"You *must* not say anything. *Must* implies you have no choice, but you do. I decide my own life and make my own decisions, especially those required of me as High Priestess."

May continued at her side, but her voice became inflexible and her muscles tight. "I understand, High Priestess, but allow me to implore you to approach this carefully. If you push things too fast, the Network will—"

Evelyn came to a fast stop in front of Donovan's office, interrupting May's comment with a sharp rap on the door with her knuckles.

"The Network will do as I say, because I shall give it what it needs: a firm hand." She turned to smile at her old mentor, ignoring the flare in May's nostrils. "Trust me, May. I know what I'm doing."

"Yes, High Priestess."

The double doors into Donovan's office swung open, admitting Evelyn to the lavish room adorned with the preserved heads of animals he'd shot in his glory days. Evelyn ignored their glassy eyes as she approached his desk, unnerved by the idea of preserving death to look on every day.

"Merry meet, Evelyn," he muttered, running the tips of his nails along the red-hot skin of his forearms. The eerie yellow glow he'd been living with for over a year still emanated from his face, accenting the red lines along his chin where he'd been scratching. "What do you need?"

May loitered near the closed doors, hands folded in front of her and facial expression rigid.

Evelyn smiled. "Merry meet, High Priest. Do you mind sparing me a few minutes of your busy time?"

He glanced up from beneath his fatty eyebrows, setting down a merchandise scroll. "Er, yes," he said, sliding a paper over it. "What can I do for you?"

"I need your opinion on a matter that's come to my attention by letter."

"Of course," he said, straightening. "Always glad to give my expert advice. Being Highest Witch and all that."

Evelyn smiled, stopping just short of his desk. The rays of sun streaming through the window illuminated her hair, which had darkened through the years, simmering into a rich, deep auburn.

"The last year as High Priestess has opened my eyes to what you've gone through as High Priest all these years. Especially considering how sick Nell had been before she passed."

"Oh." He regarded her through narrowed eyes. "What brings this about?"

She pulled a long, slender envelope from her pocket. "I've noticed your ill health myself for a while, but I didn't realize how advanced the problem had become until this letter came from the apothecary today. He sent it to me, I think, hoping that I could convince you that what it says is very important."

Donovan sighed. "He's always bothering me. I'm fine! I don't need to stop drinking!"

Evelyn extended the letter to him. "Begging your pardon, Your Highness, but he would disagree with that. In very strong terms."

Donovan waved the letter away. "I don't want to read it. Just tell me what it says."

"Of course," she said, unfolding the thick paper. "It's a two-page letter, so I'll summarize. In short, the apothecary is concerned about your liver. He says it doesn't seem to be improving, despite the potions he's given you to combat the issue, and your, ahem, abstinence from ipsum."

Donovan cleared his throat and loosened the collar around his neck waddle. "Er, yes. Abstinence."

"As your body is already under stress, he feels that a break from work is justified to reset your health." She sent a meaningful glance at his raw arms. "I believe that it may even alleviate your constant itching."

One of Donovan's thin eyebrows lifted. He straightened. "Oh? The infernal itching could pass?"

"Yes," she murmured, perusing the letter. "He says here that a three, possibly four, month break should do it. What do you think, Your Highness? Of course, I defer to your judgment in matters such as these, but I can't help but agree with him."

Donovan leaned back in his chair. "That's a long time to sit around the castle not doing anything," he said, nose ruffling. "I'd go bloody mad."

"Here?" Evelyn asked in surprise. "Why would you stay here, Your Highness? We'd send you to Ashleigh House, of course. I would take care of everything here while you healed in the comfort of your own personal home."

And keep you nice and isolated in the meantime.

"Just to be thorough," she said, pulling another scroll from her pocket, "I checked the law and found a clause that gives the Highest Witch permission to take a break for medical purposes, provided there is a High Priest or High Priestess in place to take over the position as Highest Witch for a designated period of time."

"Indeed," he said. "Very interesting. Can't say that I knew . . ."

Evelyn folded the letter together again and tucked it back in her pocket. The scroll floated to his desk where it unfurled in front of him. Donovan skimmed the words, humming and murmuring unintelligibly under his breath.

"Can't ask you to do it, Evelyn," he said, pulling the edges of his vest around his vast girth. "Nope. Too much, I think."

"Oh, Your Highness, please don't worry about me," she said with a laugh, brushing a long wave of hair over her shoulder. "I've been High Priestess for over a year now. I can handle anything you throw at me."

Donovan said nothing, but regarded her from the corner of his eyes. "I'd feel like I was abandoning the Network," he said with a martyric sadness. Evelyn recognized the facade and nearly clapped. *I've got him.* He didn't really care, of course, but he had to act like it. It would be poor form to jump at the opportunity too quickly.

"Well, of course, if you're sure you want to go against what your apothecary feels is best—"

"No!" he cried, reaching out a hand. "No, of course not. If the apothecary thinks it would be for the best, perhaps I should at least think about it. Can't deny that it would be nice to have a break."

Evelyn smiled demurely. "I'm sure that Grant and Rand would visit you often to keep you entertained."

His eyes went distant. He shook his head, coming back to the present.

"Yes, yes, of course. Plenty of social events. Recover at home. I'll get back to you tomorrow. It's not a decision I'd make lightly."

"Of course," she agreed with a bow and a smile. "Thank you for your time, Your Highness. I know how busy you are, and I appreciate it."

Donovan waved it off, but his eyes glinted in calculation when she left, and Evelyn smiled in triumph when the door closed behind her. May followed without a word.

He's putty in my hands, Evelyn thought with a wicked smile.

On a bitter cold morning during the first month of winter, when flecks of ice decorated the window panes and the wind howled in a blizzard outside, Mildred stood at the front of her classroom with bleary eyes. To accommodate the number of students who wanted to learn, she'd started a Protective Incantations class in the early morning before the servants' work responsibilities began. Ten other classes, taught by previous students, dotted the servants' quarters every morning as well.

Twenty-five witches were waiting for her to launch into a lecture on shield spells when the door slammed open and hit the wall, admitting a familiar head of mousy blonde hair.

"Blessed be," she said. "What is wrong, Lavinia?"

"I'm so sorry, Council Member," Lavinia gasped, face pale as she plowed into the room and shoved a newsscroll into Mildred's hands. "But I just came across this in the *Chatterer* and thought I shouldn't wait to show it to you. It's the first article."

COMMON SCHOOLS CLOSING

High Priestess Evelyn Ringer released an announcement to all Council Members, Coven Leaders, and High Witches this morning to notify them of a change in policy. All common schools funded by Network currency are now closing.

"An investigation into attendance in the common school system shows it at an all-time low," the High Priestess reports in the letter. "To maximize use of Network currency, the common schools will close for the foreseeable future. The Network school system will benefit from the extra income to prepare the future leaders of this Network."

Mildred released the scroll. It whirred and then snapped shut. "That doesn't bode well," she murmured.

"What's happened?" someone asked.

"It must be bad. She's gone pale," another responded.

"Did Donovan die?"

Lavinia waited for Mildred to answer the questions, but when no explanation came, she said, "They've closed the common schools. They're giving the currency to the Network school system instead."

A mutual cry of confusion and outrage rose from the room, growing in size until Mildred quieted it with a silencing incantation that muted every student.

"Silence," she said. "I cannot think when you're squawking like a flock of birds. None of you will say a word unless you raise your hand and I give you permission to do so; is that understood?"

A haphazard array of bobbing heads responded, and she removed the spell. Lavinia shrank back a step.

"This means a variety of things," Mildred said, still perusing the article, as if new information would pop up and answer the most desperate question of all. *Why?* "It seems that the only education offered by the Network will be for those who can afford private tutors or are educated sufficiently at home that they'll be ready for acceptance into the Network school system."

"It also means that our High Priestess has violated everyone's right to receive a fair education," Lavinia piped up, directing her gaze to the ground when Mildred sent her a warning glare.

Katie Cross

A hand shot up in the back. "Yes, Charles?"

"It's the Elitists, doing it, isn't it? If we stop learning, the upper class wins."

Mildred drew in a deep breath, surprised by the ache in her chest. It wasn't just the Elitists; her best friend passed this law. Had Eddy or Rand gotten to Evelyn, or did she just not want to see the truth?

Would Evelyn truly lead the Network to a better place?

Oh, Evelyn. What have you done?

"Yes, Charles. I believe you're right. Removing education from the poor is a tenet of the Elitist party, which is exactly what we're seeing from our High Priestess now."

Another hand rose, and Mildred acknowledged it with a nod.

"It won't be a big deal, right?" a small maid from the kitchen asked. "We're learning here. W-we don't need the common schools, do we?"

"It may not seem like a big deal because you weren't attending the common schools," Mildred said, her jaw tight. "But this is all the more frightening because it's a sign the Elitists exert great power in the Network."

They soberly mimicked her deep concern. A helpless rage bubbled up from the depths of Mildred's heart. How had she been so foolish? All this time she'd simply assumed Evelyn took part in the Elitist movement because it was popular and catered to the rich. But something as drastic as the closure of all the common schools had to come from the High Priest or High Priestess. All this time, Evelyn had likely been the *leader* of the Elitists.

The shame of her own foolishness stabbed her like a knife.

"If the Elitists have taken over," Todd said from the back of the classroom, "that means it's time to fight. And you promised us that if we had to fight them, you'd help us."

Mildred recalled the day with pristine clarity. *I must make this right,* she thought. *I must do something about this.*

The bitter, ugly reality of the situation struck her. If she didn't try to stop Evelyn, if she didn't stand up for the lower class, who would? Facing Evelyn in any sort of battle of wills was a repulsive idea. But to make a stand against her friend's entire political career? It would mean a war Mildred didn't know she could win.

"Yes, Todd," she said. "I do remember that."

"So?" he asked. "Will you do it?"

"Of course."

A ripple of relief moved through the students, but Mildred ignored it. If the news caused this much concern here, her Covens would be in greater need.

"Forgive me, but I must visit a friend about this. Lavinia will discuss the importance of protection spells today. If you have any questions, please message me on the silenda later. Thank you."

Mildred grabbed her bag and the newsscroll, leaving the chattering class behind her.

"Silence!" Lavinia commanded, her voice fading as Mildred moved down the hall. "I'm in charge here."

You Broke Us

Mildred left the servants' quarters and went straight to the upper floors, two thoughts looping through her mind as she walked off the worst of her fury. To arrive at Evelyn's office out of control and fuzzy-minded would cripple her chances of surviving what would certainly be a ghastly confrontation.

Despite her best attempts at calming, she stormed into Evelyn's office with unusual fury, barreling through the door without a thought of knocking. May looked up from her desk in the corner but didn't move, quill frozen mid-stroke. Evelyn, who sat at her desk surrounded by countless envelopes, glanced up with calm indifference.

"Merry meet, Mildred."

"I knew you believed some Elitist doctrine, but this makes me sick," Mildred cried, throwing the newsscroll onto Evelyn's desk. "You're closing the common schools?"

Evelyn flicked the newsscroll away with an annoyed motion of her finger. "Yes, I am, and I don't appreciate your rude entrance to my private office. If you have something to discuss with me in a civilized manner, you can make an appointment with May and return at a later time. I'm busy."

"Evelyn, what are you thinking? You can't end education for the poor. It's . . . it's the move of a tyrant."

Evelyn's eyes narrowed on her with the focused intensity of a coiled snake. "Don't forget your place, *Council Member*. I am the High Priestess and your superior in every single way."

"Superior?" Mildred spat. "In what? Degenerate ideology? We're supposed to be friends!"

"There's no room for friendship in politics. I'm conducting business, and you're taking it personally."

"You're going to destroy the Network."

Evelyn slammed her hands on her desk. "You *will* address me according to my title, or I'll have you thrown in the dungeons for the night to remind you of your place."

"What are you doing? Why have you closed the common schools?"

"The funding is needed elsewhere."

"Where?"

Evelyn's eyes flashed with indignation. She stood, seeming to tower over Mildred from a new, powerful height. "I don't owe an explanation to a Council Member that only has her job because I gave it to her. You're speaking against the Elitist agenda? That agenda put you in power."

"You owe me an explanation because I am a member of the Central Network over which you preside."

"Really, Mildred. Are you that blind?" Evelyn asked with cool hauteur. "Or do you just want to avoid reality forever?"

"You're not just one of the Elitists. You're their leader, aren't you? And you have been this whole time."

"Yes, of course. Are you just realizing it?"

A pain deep in Mildred's chest pounded with every beat. "Perhaps I believed my best friend would do the right thing in the end, no matter what wave of political nonsense had caught her up."

"This is the right thing!" The fire ballooned, enveloping Mildred in a wave of heat. "You just refuse to see it! The poor want to be led. Nay, they need to be led."

The rampant poverty, the hooded gazes, and distrustful stares of the witches in her Covens created a seedling of doubt in Mildred's mind. Hadn't she been surprised at how closed off the witches had been to change? Evelyn smiled triumphantly.

"You've seen it too," she said. "You know what I'm talking about."

"Does Donovan know about this, or are you doing it behind his back?"

Evelyn rolled her eyes. "What Donovan doesn't know about, he doesn't care about. He's holed up in his mansion eating and drinking to his heart's delight while the Network moves on. He won't even know until it's all done, and by then it won't matter, will it? Because he'll see the wisdom behind it once he sees that nothing changed."

"You're wrong," Mildred said. "You're going to fail. Cease this madness. Elitism won't work. Not only will it collapse in on itself—it's economically inconsistent—but the poor will rise up against you. You may have more education, but the upper class will never beat them in numbers."

Evelyn's eyes shone with deadly calm. "Then we'll just have to keep them under a tight magical hand, won't we? I shall rule with an iron fist in ways Donovan never had the courage to."

"And what if some Covens pay for common schools from Coven funds?"

Evelyn's laugh held a discernible edge of challenge. "I'd love to see you try."

"You'd better believe I'll do it."

"You think you can resist my order?" Evelyn asked, leaning over her desk. Another wave of heat overcame Mildred, burning the backs of her arms.

She's starting to lose control, she thought. Evelyn had always been emotional but never so dangerously volatile. Mildred's eyes fell to the bracelet on Evelyn's arm. And never so endowed with power.

"I dare you to oppose me. I already have eyes on every one of your Covens. The moment the schools open back up, I'll set them on fire and nail you with misuse of Coven currency. You'll spend the rest of your two-year trial in the dungeons, and the Middle Covens will fall into pandemonium. Most prisoners are dying of disease these days, so you may not even live long enough for me to remove you from the Council."

"You would oppress anyone who holds an opinion contrary to yours?"

"I'm the High Priestess," Evelyn cried. "I know the law far better than you could ever hope to know it. I will make a firm impression. If you oppose me, I'll make an example of you. Don't press me to prove it!"

Mildred's nostrils flared. "You send out your spies, Evelyn," she muttered. "That doesn't frighten me into apathy, like it has everyone else. We were friends once, do you remember? I know you're capable of better."

"You'll never understand."

"No," Mildred said. "I will never understand what happened to you. I'll never understand how you've been blinded by your own lust for power. You aren't the Evelyn I bound myself to for a lifetime of friendship when I was six."

Evelyn's face hardened into rigid lines. "I hardly give credit to anything said by a witch from the slums that couldn't even do magic."

"You were from the streets as well! Or have you forgotten? Your father hit you, too. Both of us lived in poverty until the High Priestess took you in when your parents died. Nell ruined you by giving you everything you wanted."

"I was not poor!" Evelyn said in a shrill scream. Her face flushed a beet red, and the fire sizzled. "My father was a Guardian, and we lived in a comfortable house. I've never been part of the lower class. Never! They're desperate, murderous fiends that kill innocent witches when they don't get what they want. They must be stopped!"

"And your mother was a maid," Mildred snapped. "You were just as poor as I was, only you've let yourself believe that you weren't. You're the biggest hypocrite that I've ever met in my life. Do the Elitists know that you come from the very people you're trying to stand on?"

A hot rush of magic slammed into Mildred's chest, carrying her across the room and throwing her into the wall. Her right shoulder collided with a wall sconce and burned with pain. She countered the magic by instinct, sending the first spell that came to mind. Evelyn toppled to the floor like a rag doll. A paralyzing incantation. Evelyn shot back to her feet, having overpowered the spell in a matter of seconds, and pinned Mildred to the wall. May shrank behind a bookshelf, only one side of her face visible as she peered out.

"Is this what its come to?" Mildred asked, her voice low and tremulous. "We're fighting with each other now?"

Evelyn glanced away. "I had it all worked out, all planned out, for you, me, and Stella. Now you've ruined it. Get out of my sight. You've made it very clear that you'll never support me. You've ruined everything, Mildred," she whispered, her jaw tight.

The magic released Mildred from the wall, and she caught herself before she fell. She swallowed and squared her shoulders.

"So have you," Mildred answered, transporting away before Evelyn could really hurt her.

Evelyn's shoulders heaved with rage the moment Mildred left. She threw a book off her desk. It flew across the room and exploded in the fireplace. She grabbed a vial of ink, hurling it against the wall. It shattered in a spray of black that dripped down the stones.

"Damn you, Mildred! You broke us!"

A sob threatened to tear out of her throat, but she kept it locked inside with the rest of her anger. She'd destroy Mildred to save the Network. She'd give up everything, and no one would even appreciate it.

May stepped away from her hiding spot along the wall, her lips pinched and head held high. Evelyn didn't want to face her. Didn't want to admit that May had been right about Mildred all along.

I was wrong. I've lost everyone. I'm not strong enough to do this. This is too much. May's asking too much.

"Are you all right, High Priestess?"

"Leave me."

"Evelyn, I—"

"*Leave me!*" Evelyn screamed, and the fire bloomed out of the fireplace in a ball of flame and heat. A globe caught fire, crackling into an acrid black smoke. May recoiled with wide, frightened eyes.

"Yes, High Priestess," she said, and slipped out the door without another word. Evelyn waited until the door closed to cover her face with her hands, sink to the floor, and release the sobs pent up in her hot, hot chest.

Mildred found herself standing in the Forgotten Gardens, fists clenched, breathing fast and heavy.

"It's a betrayal, Stella. Evelyn is turning her back on everyone that isn't wealthy, including you and me. Only she turned her back on us a long time ago, didn't she? I shouldn't even be surprised that she would lead such a horrid movement."

Stella drew in a deep breath as if she were about to speak, but looked away at the ragged appearance of the garden instead. Vines grew in haphazard disarray over broken trellises, winding through brick and over a sculpture of a woman carrying a bucket.

"You angered her," Stella said with a sigh. "You backed her into a corner. Of course she reacted strongly. You know that Evelyn always fights her way out of everything."

"I don't regret what I said," Mildred snapped. "I only regret that I didn't stop her earlier."

"I never said you were wrong," Stella said. "Just that the circumstances built up to their inevitable conclusion."

The crack of a stick halted their conversation, and they both looked up as Marten stepped into their secluded hideaway at the edge of the castle grounds.

"Mildred, are you all right?" he asked. "I just received your message on the silenda."

Mildred tried to rally together, but failed. "Evelyn and I fought," she said stiffly, folding her arms across her chest. Marten looked to Stella in question, but she shook her head.

"Do you want to tell me what happened?" he asked.

Mildred relayed the argument verbatim with little inflection and less energy. Marten listened without saying a word until she finished, then ran a hand over his freshly shaven head.

"Oh."

"Evelyn and her Elitist party are making a move," Mildred said.

Katie Cross

"That's what this means. It doesn't matter whether or not attendance in the common schools was low."

"Do you think she'd actually do it?" Marten asked. "For the Elitists to truly take over, they'd have to destroy the Esmelda Scrolls and institute their own law."

Mildred paused to think it over, recalling the feel of her back slamming into the wall, the rage in Evelyn's eyes.

"Yes," Stella said, taking them both by surprise. "Evelyn seems to believe that she's doing the right thing. She hasn't spoken to me since I returned to the castle two months ago, but I don't really believe she'd do this unless she thought it was for the good of the Network."

Mildred wasn't so sure, but for Stella's sake didn't voice her thoughts aloud.

I've never been part of the lower class. Never! Evelyn's voice roared through her mind. *They're desperate, murderous fiends that kill innocent witches when they don't get what they want. They must be stopped!*

"She's blaming all poor people for the deaths of her parents. To make matters worse, her powers have grown." Mildred rubbed her right shoulder with a grimace. "She's more powerful and unpredictable than ever."

"We can't let her get away with it," Marten said.

"No," Mildred said. "And we won't."

Stella blanched. "She's our friend, Milly. We can't just get rid of her."

"She *was* our friend."

"The only way to stop her and save the Network is a Magia. Are you prepared to destroy her in a Magia?" Stella asked.

Mildred hesitated. If she killed Evelyn in a Magia—a dangerous and uncontrolled method of fighting without spells or defined magical intent—Evelyn's power and position would transfer to her. In a Magia, raw magic went against raw magic, often destroying both witches using it. Harnessing magic in such a state was difficult enough; surviving it was even harder. Some witches died just from releasing their power, for once it was released, it could not be called back.

Could she do that to Evelyn?

"I don't know," Mildred said. "Maybe it won't come to that."

"If it does?" Stella demanded. "Are you going to kill her?"

"Yes."

Stella's nostrils flared. She pursed her lips together and turned away, arms folded protectively in front of her. Marten cast a look of question at Mildred, but she shook her head.

"You already have a plan," Marten said.

"Of course I do!" Mildred snapped. "We need to fight back. I made a promise to my students that I would lead them if it ever came to this. Closing the common schools is only the first step. We need to press forward on the assumption that Evelyn will destroy the Esmelda Scrolls as soon as they appear to her after Donovan's death. She's only Highest Witch by proxy now, which means we have a little time to gather together and fight."

"How will you fight?" he asked. "The Elitist party likely influences more witches than you think."

"But they don't influence the poor or the servants, and they're not expecting us to resist. They're more educated, but we have the advantage of surprise and numbers. Anyway, I'll keep it simple. I'm going to teach them."

"Them?"

"My students," Mildred said, warming to the idea. "Between the servants in the castle and those taught in the Covens, we can muster nearly four hundred witches. I already sent Lavinia instructions to gather any students that want to fight back. We'll meet tomorrow evening."

Marten's eyebrow rose, wrinkling his forehead. "Evelyn already threatened you. She'll have you murdered if you're caught teaching servants."

"Yes, but Evelyn won't find out, will she?"

The Education Resistance

The students volunteered to fight against the Elitists with such gusto that, in lieu of holding classes, Lavinia split the meetings into five separate events starting early the next morning. Mildred's eyes shot around the bleak stone room packed to the brim with bodies, taking in the weak torchlight that cast shadows on all their determined faces.

"I found this room while exploring the other day," Lavinia said, craning her head back to peer into the dark eaves swabbed with cobwebs. Her nose wrinkled. "It's not the cleanest place, but it will hold many more witches than a single classroom will."

Nearly a hundred witches waited for the meeting to start with the collective murmur of anticipation that came with a crowd. Todd stood by the front doors, flanked by several other kitchen workers and Marten, who spoke with them in quiet conversation. Mildred studied all the familiar faces in the crowd with worry. She knew all of these witches like family. If they meant to carry this Resistance out underneath Evelyn's nose, they'd have to act with caution. She wouldn't stand for any loss of life, and she wasn't confident that Evelyn would refrain from murder.

"This will be a perfect meeting place, Lavinia," Mildred said, forcing her grim thoughts away. "Thank you for finding it."

Lavinia beamed. "Anything for you, Council Member. We'd follow you anywhere."

"Let's get started. I don't like congregating in a big group like this at the castle. I don't want any risk taken that doesn't have to be."

"Marten pulled the Head of Guardians into our plan, didn't he?" Lavinia asked, wringing her hands. "Won't Dolph help protect the hallways?"

"Yes." Mildred squirmed all the same, recalling the feel of Evelyn's power slamming her into the wall. "But it still makes me nervous."

Mildred signaled for Marten to close and seal the door, transformed a discarded piece of wood into a sturdy box to stand on, and climbed on top.

"Quiet! Attention, please. Thank you for coming," Mildred called above the din, waving her arms to catch their gaze. "Let's begin."

Accustomed to Mildred's strict discipline in class, the crowd fell into a respectful silence.

"We know why we're here, so I won't go into the messy details of the closure of the common schools yesterday and the reign of the Elitists. But we need to talk about what we're going to do about it."

A chorus of supportive whistles pealed through the air, easing Mildred's anxiety. She didn't know if she had what it took to lead them to victory, but at least they showed heart.

"We've already built up a family of witches that have proven the Elitists wrong," she said. "And they don't even know that we exist, which is just the way we want it for now. All of you are just as smart and capable as the Elitists are. We know that. Now let's show them."

Mildred held up her hands for silence when applause rippled through the room.

"Marten, Dolph, Stella, and I met last night to discuss the matter, and we believe that Evelyn intends to overthrow the Network when Donovan dies and establish a law of her own. If that's the case, we only have as long as Donovan has life left. We must get to work immediately."

"What do we do?" a voice cried from the back.

"Marten, Dolph, and I will be working out a definite plan tonight. Lavinia and I will also put together an education schedule to teach Protective and Defensive Magic classes. We'll meet together like this once a week to keep you informed and check on your progress. You must learn how to fight and defend yourselves. Do all you can to streamline this process. Learn the lessons we teach. Educate your friends and family. Do for them what the Network won't do for you."

"If you agree to this and we are caught, you could be charged with establishing an opposition against the Network," Marten said. "Which is why everyone will take a vow of silence before they leave."

Mildred unleashed her sternest glare on the room. "Our lives depend on secrecy. We'll be operating under Evelyn's very nose. I trust our Resistance's four hundred and twenty-six members implicitly."

"What if Evelyn has already destroyed the Esmelda Scrolls and instituted her own law?" Alice asked from the very front. "What if it's too late?"

"The Esmelda Scrolls will appear to Evelyn as soon as Donovan dies and she becomes Highest Witch. Under Esmelda's law, a High Priest or Priestess cannot kill their co-ruler, which means Evelyn can't act on her own. Once Donovan dies, the scrolls will be in her care. Until then, even though she's taken over Donovan's position as Highest Witch, she does not have access to them. Are there any more questions?"

No hands rose. Mildred paused, uncertain of how to proceed. They wouldn't expect any kind of emotional, rousing speech from her, but she should encourage them.

"Then let me just say that it is an honor and a privilege to stand before you as your friend, teacher, and mentor. All of you make me proud and are worth ten times any Elitist that stands in power today."

The raucous cheer that followed her words nearly shook the ground. She silenced it with an incantation, but their mouths remained opened in silent screams, and smattering bursts of applause echoed through the cavernous room. Despite her fear they'd be caught, Mildred couldn't help the welling up of pride in her chest. Once they calmed down, she removed the incantation, and the room filled with excited murmurs.

"What are we calling this?" Todd asked above the din. "Every good movement needs a name. You know, for the history books."

Mildred looked at Stella and Marten. "We'll call it what it is," she said, running her eyes over the congregation. "The Education Resistance."

"No!" Lavinia countered, her shrill voice rising above the rest. "This is Mildred's Resistance!"

"How are you doing?" Stella asked two days later, sending Mildred a sharp, appraising look over her desk.

"Fine. Why?"

"You swore almost fifty of your students' family members into the Resistance last night, which means nearly five hundred witches draw from your magic when they use the silenda. Are you feeling the strain at all?"

Mildred frowned and looked at her hand. The silenda network had grown so slowly the past several years that she hadn't noticed any drain. If anything had changed, she felt more powerful. She may have been a bit more tired than usual, but she had stayed up until three in the morning organizing new class schedules and curriculum.

"I didn't even think about it," she said, running the pad of her thumb over the lioness. "So I suppose my answer would be no. I'm not feeling any strain."

"Perhaps your powers have increased after all these years that you've given your magic to others for such a selfless purpose."

"Maybe," Mildred said. "Have you heard from Lavinia? She's supposed to bring the roster for tonight's meeting."

Stella had just shaken her head when an enveloped popped into the air in front of Mildred. Her stomach clenched when she recognized Evelyn's handwriting.

Dear Council Member,

Due to a recent change in leadership, I've decided to assign your office to Council Member Grant, who has demonstrated sufficient need for it. You will be relocated to one of the offices on the lower floors of the West Wing.

Katie Cross

Vacate your office by this evening at six.

Sincerely,
High Priestess Evelyn Ringer

Mildred read the note, then glanced at the clock with a roll of her eyes. Four o'clock. "Childish, Evelyn. So very childish."

Stella glanced up at the sound of Evelyn's name. "What is it?" she asked. "You heard from Evelyn?"

The sudden spark of hope in her eyes broke Mildred's heart. Poor Stella still couldn't accept what had happened to Evelyn, and always looked for a glimmer of goodness in her. Mildred sent the message to Stella with a spell.

"Yes. It only took her two days to kick us out."

Stella read it with a heavy, exasperated sigh and fell back under the melancholy that had surrounded her since Daniel's death. "Oh, Evie," she whispered, shaking her head, tears in her eyes. "What happened to you?"

Mildred sent Stella a sharp gaze. "Are you going to be able to come to terms with what we have to do?" she asked. "Evelyn is destroying herself and will ruin the Network if we don't stop her."

"I know," Stella said. "I just . . . I just need time. I don't know how you're able to face the fact that we may have to kill our best friend."

I'm not facing it. I'm thoroughly avoiding it.

Mildred said nothing more, but sent a message to Lavinia through the silenda to request her help.

After Mildred, Lavinia, and Stella had packed away all the belongings that Mildred wished to take, which only filled three wooden boxes, Lavinia led the way to the new office with the crates trailing behind them. They descended to a lower wing of the castle that Mildred had never seen. No one passed them in the halls, which held a few torches that sprang to life when they drew near. Their shoes left imprints in the layer of dust coating the floor.

"She didn't assign you a specific room, so I found the one that looked the best. Here it is," Lavinia said, gesturing to a door on the left carved with deep grooves. "Your new office. The Head of Housekeeping doesn't send maids to clean this low. It's just storage."

Mildred liked the idea of being so far away that no one would bother her. She would accomplish so much more in the gloomy quiet. And since Evelyn would have a harder time tracking her appointments here, she felt this might have been the best thing to happen to her yet.

"This is it?" Mildred asked, glancing into a depressing gray room of grime and shadow. Lavinia bit her peeling bottom lip and nodded, batting away a cobweb that danced in the doorframe.

"I must apologize for the lack of . . . cleanliness, Council Member."

"It's not your fault, Lavinia," Mildred said as she stepped inside. "You aren't in charge yet."

Mildred ran the tip of her finger along the edge of a sturdy desk, gathering a small pile of dust. She flicked it off her fingers and stared at a row of open slots, already mentally organizing the scrolls she'd place there.

"It will clean up just fine," she declared. Three long, skinny windows leaked sunlight around a pair of heavy drapes. She grasped the nearest and jerked it to the side. Dust bloomed in the air, but Mildred didn't even flinch. She opened the other two sets of drapes at once.

"Jikes," Stella whispered. "It looks worse in the sunlight."

It did look worse—*much* worse. Now, the few stray sun rays that made it through the windows, which were set halfway beneath the ground, highlighted its imperfections. When Mildred looked up, she couldn't see anything but dirt from the window well. Turning away, she found a leather armchair with stuffing puffed out of the rips in the seat like fat from a flesh wound. She looked forward to filling the empty bookshelves above the small fireplace. The whole office was barely a fifth of the size of Stephan's, and would be cramped with her and Stella.

"This will make it easier to run the Resistance, I think. We'll continue sorting through messages and paperwork in the hallway while you find a few maids to clean it for me, Lavinia."

"Yes," Lavinia said, brushing off soot that had smeared her cheek during a brief inspection of the inside of the fireplace. "That's a good idea. We can do this in a short time with many hands. I'll go immediately."

"Thank you."

Once Lavinia transported away, Mildred folded her arms and surveyed the room again.

"It could use a tapestry or two to cheer it up," she said, turning to the hall. "But it doesn't feel like a dungeon. In the meantime, let's get to work. We need to finish the tax forms for the month so we can grade homework tonight."

I Will Reign

HIGH PRIEST DYING. NEW NETWORK TAKEOVER?

No one realized the extent of our High Priest's illness until he shuffled his responsibilities as Highest Witch to High Priestess Evelyn to take a four-month break from Chatham Castle. News from Ashleigh House?

Nothing.

It's not unusual for a Highest Witch to take a break. Historically, High Priestess Merisa deferred her position as Highest Witch to High Priest James while undergoing a complicated recovery for heart issues. Six months of recuperation later, she returned to rule without another problem. Seems simple enough, right?

But James didn't show signs of aligning himself with a new political movement. Namely, the Elitists.

Evelyn's recent closure of the common schools, taken with her history of subduing peaceful protests with Guardian forces, imprisoning witches for dissenting opinions, and spouting ideologies about the separation of classes, lead to a dangerous arithmetic. Is our Highest-Witch-in-proxy trying to take over the Network while our true Highest Witch recovers from illness? Or is the plan to just get Donovan out of the way?

Despite the High Priestess's reports of low attendance in the common schools, protests of discontent have popped up all over the Network. A crowd of one hundred witches in the Letum Wood Covens gathered around a Coven Leader's office the day of the closure, showing no signs of violence. The Coven Leader summoned a contingent of Guardians, who dismissed the crowd—under the High Priestess's orders—by cursing everyone present. Two children were left blind, and the originator of the curses cannot be identified to remove them.

Is this what we are to expect from our new Highest Witch?

And, more importantly, are we going to allow it?

Evelyn fumed like a low-burning bed of coals.

She strode across her office in her deep sapphire gown, fists clenched around the newsscroll. Her thick hair kept falling from the silver combs holding it away from her face. May watched Evelyn warily, her lips pursed in blatant annoyance. Grant glanced up with a bored roll of his eyes when Evelyn whirled around and stalked toward him, embarking on another round of pacing.

"Alfred is starting a resistance, isn't he?" she asked. "He's trying to turn the Network against me when he doesn't know anything about what I've prevented. Those riots were about to turn violent. I saved witches, that's what I did! I stopped them from doing something they'd regret. Something terrible that could destroy the lives of those left behind forever!"

She put a hand to her forehead when her powers flared, spreading through her body until her skin tingled.

"You saved them by stuffing them in the dungeons to die of disease?" Grant asked with an acerbic grin. "Well done, Evie."

"That's not how it was supposed to be," she snapped. "They perpetrated the violence, not me! I'm just giving the Network what it needs: discipline! Where's Noah? I want him here now."

"I've already sent for him, High Priestess," May said. "I'm sure he'll be here as soon as he can."

"I'll exile Alfred for treason against the High Priestess. That's what I'll do."

"Evie, darling, let's go to the opera," Grant said, but Evelyn shot him a scorching look. He held up his hands in surrender and leaned back, filling the room with the smoke of his smelly cheroot. May had asked him to come reason with Evelyn as a desperate effort to calm her, but it wouldn't work. Short of getting rid of Alfred, nothing would calm her down. If anything, Grant's vapid expression and the scent of smoke deepened her annoyance. She twiddled her fingers, fighting off the urge to slap him.

"High Priestess, would you like a drink to calm down?" May asked, shooting her a less-than-subtle look that doubled Evelyn's rage. "A calming potion, perhaps. I have some here that the apothecary sent."

"I don't need your help calming down," Evelyn hissed, turning her back on both of them to focus on something else. She sucked in a deep breath. She wasn't a tyrant the way Alfred made her sound. She was a fixer, repairing the Network. They didn't realize how much they owed her. Evelyn closed her eyes, unable to quiet the screaming little girl in her head.

If I could just quiet this power. These emotions . . .

Images spun through her mind like a hurricane. Nell's face. Mama's smile. Papa screaming. Crashing glass. Mama's headstone. Evelyn pressed her fingertips into her forehead until her knuckles ached.

"High Priestess?"

May cleared her throat, calling to Evelyn from the safety of the other side of the room. Evelyn whipped around to find Noah standing in the doorway, hands behind his back.

"You summoned, High Priestess," he said, bowing.

"Yes," she said with a sigh of relief. "Thank you for coming. I want you to find and arrest Alfred Quinten for treason. Force him to redact his article in the Chatterer before you lock him up. I'll deal with him tonight before he can damage the Network any further."

Noah's eyes narrowed slightly. "What act of treason did he commit?"

"He's trying to raise a resistance against me," she snapped. "And he's published false, unsupported information to turn the populace. Imprison him so that I may talk to him."

May said, "She's worried that the article has ruined her image while Donovan is—"

"Silence!" Evelyn commanded. "You don't speak for me, or have you forgotten? Noah, I've given you an order I expect you to fulfill."

"Yes, High Priestess," Noah replied. "But if I may offer some—"

The windows burst open in a gust of wind so strong that May stumbled, a chair fell over, and papers blew into the air in a fluttering hysteria of white. Noah shielded his face with an arm.

"I'm trying to build a better Network! Now do as I say or your promised inheritance as Ruler will be revoked, and you'll find yourself in the same cell as Alfred. Do you understand?"

"Yes, Your Highness," Noah said. "It shall be done immediately."

Noah transported away, leaving Evelyn to stare at May and Grant through a cloud of slowly settling paperwork. May said nothing, her hair askew, her eyes as pinched as her pencil-thin lips.

"Let me guess," Evelyn whispered. "You disapprove? You think I'm doing the wrong thing?" Her voice crescendoed. "Well, wasn't it *you* who taught me to rule with strict discipline? Wasn't it you who told me I needed to bring change to the Network?"

May hesitated. "Yes, Your Highness. I did teach you that the Network needs a firmer hand, but—"

"But now you take it back? Just like Mildred? You withdraw your support like the worst kind of hypocrite, don't you?"

"We never planned to act with such speed," May said with quiet certainty. "I suggested a more subtle approach. You're throwing everything at them, Evelyn, and it's—"

"I am the High Priestess!" Evelyn thundered. "You will address me as such. I've earned it. I've done what you told me I needed to do, including giving up my life. I let go of Nell, Stella, and now Mildred. You told me it had to be that way. Well now it is! You can't take it back now!"

May nodded, eyes averted. "Yes, Your Highness, forgive me."

Evelyn turned away, her head pounding. "I've given it all up," she said. "Now I'll get back what I deserve no matter what it takes. This

Network will succeed under my reign. And I will command the fear and respect that Donovan didn't."

"You can hardly be surprised, High Priestess, that they've gathered like this."

Evelyn stood on the rounded balcony of her chamber the next day, looking down on the growing mass of witches at the gate leading into Chatham Castle.

"It's at least a hundred strong," Noah said. He stood next to her, hidden with an invisibility incantation.

"And growing," she replied.

"That's Alfred's wife," May murmured from Evelyn's other side, gesturing to a female witch that stood on a platform above the rest. "She and Council Member Terry organized this rally." May looked at Evelyn. "They're protesting Alfred's execution for treason."

Evelyn let out a long, weary breath.

"Let them protest," she said. "It's too late to do anything about it; he's dead. His widow can't face the truth of the allegations, so she's blaming me. It won't matter. He's taken care of, and a trustworthy editor writes in his place."

Evelyn had done her duty, no matter how much controversy it stirred up. She'd never expected the decisions required of her as High Priestess to be easy, but they'd turned out to be a great deal more murky and gray than she'd wanted. Had Alfred needed to die? She shook the thought away. No use questioning it now.

"Look at the road," Noah said. "More witches are pouring in from Chatham City every moment. If action isn't taken . . ."

A string of witches shuffled their way up Chatham Road, headed for the amassing crowd at the front gate. They would walk, of course, as few of the lower class could even transport. All the better for when she implemented the new law; subduing the poor would eat up fewer resources if they couldn't move great distances at will.

"This crowd, though peaceful now, has all the makings of

Newberry," May said demurely, and a flash of panic lit up Evelyn's chest. The poor in Newberry continued attacking the rich with fire, burning property and businesses. If she lost control of Chatham City, they'd overrun the place, and everything would burn.

"They aren't violent yet," Noah said, "but I'm worried they will be."

"And Terry is speaking against your decision, High Priestess," May said. "If you use an incantation, you'll hear exactly what she's saying. Not something I'd let slide if I were you. At least not at the beginning of your reign, since you keep insisting a bold front is essential."

Evelyn gritted her teeth together. She *had* been listening and already knew that Terry had called her inexperienced, irresponsible, and power-hungry. Of course May would assume she hadn't paid attention.

"She wouldn't be the first Council Member to speak against a Highest Witch," Evelyn replied, though she couldn't deny a desire to silence Terry. What could a Council Member know about these delicate matters? She didn't have a full view of the situation, and likely wasn't considering the frenzied mentality of the poor when they banded together in groups. Terry sided with Porter, who opposed anything that didn't involve saving the poor at the expense of the wealthy. Such policies spoke disaster for the Network.

"No," Noah said. "But she could be the first Council Member to stir up a rebellion against you because she doesn't like a decision you made."

A hoard of angry witches, a well-trained leader like Terry, and an unstable Network structure from years of Donovan's laziness. It was the beginning of a perfect storm—one that she had the power to dispel.

Evelyn paused to think it over, and sensed May retreat a few steps away to answer a knock at the door. She let out a breath, grateful for the distance between them.

"What can you do to prevent a catastrophe?" she asked Noah.

"We can disperse them."

Evelyn thought it over. "Can you arrest Terry?"

"I can do whatever you need me to do, High Priestess."

The chants from below rose through the sky, haunting her.

We want justice. We want justice. We want justice.

She stood far above them in education and understanding and judgment. Didn't they know she'd given them justice, and here they were getting upset over it? They'd never understand, so she must make them understand.

"Disperse them," she said. "And make sure they'll never want to regather. Kill them if you have to."

Evelyn heard the words come from her own lips and knew there was something wrong. If she looked deep enough, she'd find it. But she didn't want to know, not really. Deciding not to dwell on it, knowing that stopping the violence before it occurred would be for the best, Evelyn turned away from the window, her chest tight.

I must do what is best for the Network. I know what is best.

"Do what you must, Noah, and you'll be rewarded," she said, easing into the roiling darkness inside of her. "Let's make it clear that my reign as High Priestess won't lack discipline."

The long train of her dress trailed out behind her. She paused halfway to the door. The fervor of the chants turned hysterical the moment she disappeared from their view.

We want justice! We want justice! We want justice!

"Oh, and I don't want to see Terry at the meeting tomorrow morning. Make sure she doesn't survive."

Allegiance

"**N**o matter how we look at it, Mildred, we don't have enough Resistance members."

Stella delivered the news from her desk with a frustrated huff. Envelopes marked *urgent* soared around her head in mindless circles, enchanted to stay in flight until opened. With nearly every correspondence marked urgent these days, none of them received real priority. Papers scattered her desk in a mind-numbing array that Mildred couldn't even look at without wanting to drop everything and organize.

"Why not?" she asked, without looking up.

"We need Resistors watching the private houses of each Council Member, Guardians manning the dungeons and the cities in case of riots, and the entire maid staff taking charge of the secret passages. And, of course, the fireboys must transform into statues and watch every hallway to ensure that an Elitist doesn't get away. Jorden and Imogen's family will take care of Ashleigh City, but they'll need at least one hundred witches as reinforcements. We simply must find more."

Stella had dragged a hand through her hair so many times that the once-proud bun now lay in tatters around her neck. The clock ticked away, announcing six thirty in the evening. They hadn't eaten since breakfast.

"What specific jobs do we need more witches for?" Mildred asked. "If we have an idea in mind, it may be easier to recruit candidates."

"We need Resistors in Chatham City and Ashleigh City. Elitists lurk everywhere in both, and panic may spread there as soon as they hear what's happening."

"I don't know who else we can trust to bring in," Mildred admitted, chewing her bottom lip. "I have a few witches in my Covens—"

"You're using them to watch the Middle Covens, remember?"

"Oh, you're right. Yes." Mildred pressed a palm to her forehead. Her mind had been fuzzier than usual lately. Whether it resulted from the intensity of planning the Resistance under total secrecy or the drain on her powers from such heavy use of the silenda now that all the members of the Resistance communicated so often through it, she didn't know. "I forgot."

Stella shoved the papers aside and dropped her forehead onto the desk with a careless *thunk*.

"Stella, you need a break. We've been doing this since early this morning and haven't eaten. Why don't you go get dinner and clear your mind? We'll work something out, I promise."

She didn't respond right away, but eventually lifted her head. "Yes," she said. "You're right. I do need something to eat. Dale's transporting in at eight tonight for a short visit. He'll have to go right back, of course, but at least I'll get to see him for an hour. Wait, no. We have the Council Meeting."

Mildred rolled her eyes. "Nothing is ever said there that hasn't been said at the Esbat. I'll handle it on my own."

Stella sighed in relief. "Thank you, Mildred. The break would be nice."

Her quick agreement lifted some of Mildred's concern. Stella had shown little life ever since Daniel died, even in the frantic work of organizing the Resistance. Adding the loss of Evelyn as their friend didn't help her fragile state. "How are things in Newberry?" Mildred asked. "Does Dale report the same violence?"

"Yes. The poor are still rioting and setting fires. Evelyn just sent orders to the Guardians to kill anyone found rioting. She's cursing everyone else."

"I wish we could convince the rioters that their violence is worsening the situation," Mildred murmured. "Jorden transported north and tried on my behalf, but they're so desperate and angry they won't listen."

Stella rubbed a hand over her tired, sunken eyes. "Has Jorden had any luck figuring out a definite plan for the Resistance in Ashleigh City? We'll need him to arrest at least thirty High Witches that night."

Mildred opened her mouth to reply, but a loud groan from behind her prevented it. She turned around in surprise.

"Council Member, I have bad news," called a familiar, shrill voice.

Lavinia popped through the wall behind a tapestry, dirt smudged across her cheek. She'd discovered the secret entrance into Mildred's office while mapping each passage out and had been delighted at their good luck. Mildred, however, wasn't so sure. The young maid appeared at all hours now, though her face rarely looked so grim as it did now.

"What's wrong, Lavinia?"

"I've come from the upper floors," she said, panting. Lavinia was inspecting and committing every hidden passageway to memory in preparation for the final fight, so cobwebs clung to her dress. "We just had orders to clean out Council Member Terry's office. A Coven Leader from Ashleigh is moving in."

"What?" Stella asked, standing. "What's happened?"

Lavinia swallowed. "After we received the order, a servant came to me with the news." Her voice trembled. "I-it's terrible."

"What is it?" Mildred demanded.

"Terry and Mrs. Quinten staged a peaceful protest outside the castle gate, and Evelyn set the Guardians on them."

Stella let out a breath. "Don't say it," she whispered, a hand pressed to her face.

"Twenty are dead," Lavinia cried. "Including Terry and Mrs. Quinten. Their children are orphans now!"

Mildred leaned against her desk. "My goodness."

"Guardians can't use lethal force like that without permission, right?" Lavinia asked, her fists clenched and nostrils flaring. "They can't just attack us without . . . without . . ."

"Evelyn's command," Mildred said. "No, they couldn't have."

"Oh, Evie, what have you done?" Stella whispered, tears in her eyes when she looked at Mildred. "She's losing her mind, isn't she? To kill so many innocent witches in cold blood."

"I think it may already be gone," Mildred replied. "Thank you,

Lavinia. Let me know if you hear any more news. I have to attend the Council Meeting in twenty minutes. Perhaps I'll hear more there, since Evelyn doesn't attend. Be as careful as you can. Clearly none of us are safe anymore."

Grant lounged back in his seat at the head of the Council Room, a cheroot dangling from his lips. He propped his legs on the table-top and crossed his ankles, betraying a brand new pair of silk socks. He didn't particularly like the feel of the material on his feet, but it represented a higher style of living that was far more important than comfort.

"You leading tonight, Grant?" Rand asked, slapping him on the shoulder.

"It would appear so," he said, blowing a smoke circle. "Porter has taken a different seat now."

The two shared a knowing smirk, and Rand moved away.

Porter sat across the room now, instead of in the seat of power Grant currently filled. Despite Porter's seniority as Council Member—which meant that he led any Council Meetings that didn't involve the High Priest or Priestess—Evelyn didn't like Porter. At all. She'd demoted him to regular Council Member the very evening Donovan left. Whether she *could* do that was up for debate. Regardless, Porter allowed it to happen with only minimal protest, which left Grant to ease into the position with the prosperity and attractiveness it deserved.

And attractive he was.

He tugged at his jacket, straightened his collar—though neither needed the work—and realized that he hadn't prepared for the meeting. The Council Members spoke idly amongst themselves, except for Mildred and Porter, who sat in their respective seats and didn't look at anyone. Despite feeling too apathetic to separate the hum of voices and determine what they were talking about, the way Evelyn had commanded, he recognized a definite hum of excitement in the air.

Of course they were excited. This was an exciting time! For those on the right side, anyway.

"Call it to order," commanded a quiet voice behind his shoulder. "Everyone is here. Keep an eye on Porter. I'll watch Mildred. I don't trust them. We'll see just where their loyalties lie tonight."

He rolled his eyes, but only because Evelyn couldn't see him do it. If she had, she'd demote him to Porter's chair in a flash and place Rand in his spot. Power was a fickle thing to have when Evelyn was near. Or to not have, really, considering she wouldn't delegate this to him and was instead hiding with an invisibility incantation. He had tried to reassure her that her paranoia was misplaced, but it didn't matter. Evelyn didn't trust anybody and wanted to know what the Council said in her absence.

Grant took his time obeying her order, resenting the fact that he wanted so badly the currency and land she offered him, or else he wouldn't do so much work at her beck and call.

"Remember," she said, "only address the Terry situation in depth if they bring it up."

"Yes, all right," he called to the room, setting his feet on the floor. He rang a small desk bell with an incantation, and the tinkling sound drew the room to attention. They shuffled into their respective seats and sat down. "Let's get started, shall we? First order of business: Let's welcome our new Council Member. Darby Willshire will oversee the Western Covens in place of Terry."

A low murmur of welcome moved through the room.

Grant's eyes flickered over to Porter, who scowled. He looked at Mildred next, but her face hadn't changed expression. A hard cat to read, that one. He didn't like her a bit. Any witch that wore such out-dated dresses couldn't be trusted. Not to mention her razor-sharp eyes and severe hairstyle. He leaned back in his chair, gratified when all eyes remained on him. He could get used to all this attention.

"Keep going," Evelyn hissed.

"Oh, right. Must keep going, eh?" he asked, chuckling at his own faux pas. Reveling in his new popularity wouldn't get the work done. Not that he really cared whether the work finished, anyway.

"The Highest Witch Evelyn would like me to make an announcement: To quell the recent uprisings, not to mention the fact that we've run out of room in the dungeons and those miserable criminals just aren't dying of disease fast enough, our Highness has decided to institute another form of Network punishment, namely curses."

Porter's head lifted in shock. Rand snorted, then motioned for his Assistant to bring him a refill of dark ipsum. Gloria yawned.

"What do you mean by curses?" Wayne asked, his long fingers fiddling with a pocket watch. Grant rolled his eyes. Wayne's anxiety manifested about everything. No wonder the Northern Covens were constantly on fire.

"It's quite simple, Wayne" Grant said with a long-suffering sigh. "Should we suspect anyone of opposition to our sweet High Priestess, they'll be cursed for the rest of their lives. If not killed first, of course. It's much more effective than the dungeons."

No one responded, though no one seemed surprised.

"Tell them the curse options," Evelyn muttered. Grant leaned forward.

"There will be two options, of course: an Inheritance curse or any other debilitating curse. The point is to make the witches suffer forever so they don't *want* to revolt against us. Sure, she's willing to use death. But we'll need workers, won't we?"

A low chuckle rose at this, and Grant lifted his wine glass to the room in tribute.

"And the Network schools," Evelyn prompted with a quiet hiss. He could just picture her teeth clenched in frustration, and the thought gave him enough satisfaction to keep going.

"The Network Schools will adopt the same strategy. If any student is found not supporting our High Priest or High Priestess, or a teacher suspects disloyalty, they shall be struck with an Inheritance curse. Should the problem persist, they'll be thrown in the dungeons."

"Wouldn't look right to kill the young ones until after they graduate," Rand agreed, earning a chortle from a few others. Grant lifted an eyebrow in wry agreement.

"At any rate," Grant continued in a bored droll, "like I said, due to full dungeons, we've started putting two or three witches to a cell.

Who am I kidding? More like six or seven. If it gets much worse, Evelyn will start holding executions for the space."

"They live like that at home in their dirt hovels," said the newest addition, Darby, in a bitter voice. "Might as well give them the same treatment here."

"Indeed," Grant said. "If you have any solutions, well, it doesn't matter, quite frankly, as the Highest Witch has it under control. As there's no other real pressing business to attend to then we can—"

"Grant!" Evelyn muttered.

"Except for one more thing," he said, lifting a finger with a sheepish smile. "I've just now recalled it. Her Highness Evelyn has instituted a mandatory requirement, effective immediately. Every Council Member must sign a binding of fidelity and allegiance to the current administration as a sign of continued goodwill. She'll be asking for official signatures in the morning."

Porter's hand rose. Grant acknowledged it with a lazy nod.

"And if we don't sign?" Porter asked. Grant smiled.

"Why wouldn't you, old friend?"

Porter didn't respond. Grant could feel Evelyn's tension growing.

"You'll lose your life," Grant concluded with a shrug. "What traitor amongst us wouldn't swear his allegiance to the Highest Witch?"

The room burst into a chorus of murmurs. Grant kept a careful eye on Mildred, but her inscrutable expression remained. She stared at the tabletop, an occasional blink the only sign of life from her. Did she understand what this meant? Surely she must . . . although she didn't really appear to.

"That's all," Grant cried, rapping his open palm on the table. "You're all dismissed. Now, someone get me a glass of wine!"

I'll Destroy You

Mildred stood in front of Evelyn's desk early the next morning, hands resting at her sides. Her palms felt clammy, and her heart raced, but she maintained a cool expression. She'd been the first summoned to swear her fealty to Evelyn and didn't doubt Porter would be next. Evelyn wanted to get rid of them.

"Well, Mildred," Evelyn drawled from where she waited behind her desk. A fan of ebony feathers sprouted around her head in a halo from a chignon at the back of her neck. "Have you come to pledge your allegiance to the Network?"

A quill lifted into the air, hovering between them. Below it lay a piece of parchment with the words *Network Binding* scrawled across the top. A blob of ink fell onto the paper. Allegiance to the Network, indeed. No doubt it clarified allegiance to *Evelyn* somewhere in all that small writing.

It required all Mildred's effort to keep her emotions controlled while facing her best friend, allowing the vein of logic in her head to exert control. A wretched sense of disbelief had overtaken her. Despite having had so long to come to terms with her fight against Evelyn, she could still hardly reconcile the truth. Was Evelyn really her enemy? Or was Mildred just upset that it seemed believable?

"I think we both already know that I'm not going to sign that, Evelyn."

"But it's required. You know that."

Mildred had known she'd lose her job as Council Member and be kicked out of Chatham Castle the moment she heard Grant's announcement the night before. That's why she, Stella, and Lavinia had stayed up until nearly dawn packing, organizing, and moving the Resistance information to a safer location. Losing the Middle Covens wasn't what she wanted, but it didn't matter anymore. The Resistance moved forward of its own power, and she would march with it to the very end, Council Member or not. That meant the ugliest task remained: facing Evelyn one last time.

"I know. But I will not sign it."

Evelyn's brow arched. "Oh, really?"

"How is Donovan these days?" Mildred asked, eyes narrowing. "Ever since you murdered Alfred, his wife, and Terry, we've had no updates on the health of the High Priest. Is his break benefitting him? Or is he simply getting worse?"

Evelyn laughed, her bright red lips spreading in a cold smile.

"Donovan is as sick as ever. You know how he hangs on to ipsum like a mother's teat."

Mildred steadied her voice. "I'm sure his solitude, surrounded by crates of ipsum, hasn't helped. I'm also sure you're reassuring him that all goes well in the Network, even though it's burning to the ground. Since you control the *Chatterer* now, no one knows what's really happening."

"Well, well, Milly," Evelyn said, flicking the words off her tongue one at a time. "You don't sound loyal at all, do you? Do I have a little traitor on my hands? You won't sign an agreement of loyalty—though I should hardly be surprised, as you seem devoted to nothing but your own ideals—and now you're speculating that I have an agenda."

Mildred motioned to the binding awaiting her signature on the top of the desk.

"I'm not going to sign it, Evelyn," she said again, meeting her friend's chilly gaze. "If you hadn't already expected that, you're a bigger fool than I thought."

Evelyn's eyes flickered with something close to pain, or surprise, but she quickly hid it. The fire crackled with a sudden surge of heat.

"You won't support me? Fine. Then you'll lose everything!" Evelyn cried, her bright eyes flaring like flames. "I'll throw you in the dungeons for the rest of your life."

"No," Mildred retorted, "you won't. I'm not the little girl struggling with magic that I used to be, Evelyn. I have power. More power than you know. And I'm willing to fight to put a better leader into place. You may think you're giving justice to the Network, but you're only oppressing it."

"You're one to talk about justice!"

"Controlling the poor won't bring your parents back. It won't reverse the Tobacco Riots that killed them."

"I'll never let you free!" Evelyn screeched, panting. "You'll never be stronger than me!"

"And if I try to stop you?" Mildred asked, her stomach cold and heavy. She already knew what Evelyn was going to say. She saw it in the glittering depths of her darkening eyes. Evelyn lifted her chin.

"I'll destroy you."

Mildred let out a pained breath. Anticipating Evelyn's betrayal could never have prepared her for the blow. She'd known all along that it could come to this, but a part of her had hoped that Evelyn could be persuaded away from it. The single band around Mildred's pinky finger, where the Witches' Oath lay, began to burn. It disintegrated, fading into the wrinkles in her skin.

"So mote it be," Mildred whispered, transporting away before Evelyn could draw another breath.

Later that night, Jorden set a plate of food in front of Mildred and settled into a chair across from her. A pile of boiled potatoes waited, reminding her so much of her childhood that the mealy, bland texture looked appetizing. It just needed salt.

"Eat up," he said, pushing the salt container toward her with a knowing wink.

Jorden's wife Imogen, a petite, slender thing with thick blonde hair and a quiet smile, moved softly in the background of their little cottage in the countryside of the Ashleigh Covens. Their sweet little boy, a child with a glare as powerful as Mother's, slept in a crib near the fireplace, his golden curls reflecting the simmering light.

"He's a wonderful boy, Jorden," Mildred said, eyeing her nephew fondly. "He looks just like you."

He rubbed his jaw and smiled. "He *acts* like Mother."

Mildred smiled, and so did he. The warmth of the fire made the room cozy in a way that Chatham Castle could never be. Books stood on top of the mantle, and Imogen hummed whenever she moved. The quaint scene was so perfect for Jorden that it didn't matter they were as poor as Mildred had been growing up. Dirt floors were as good as marble. A pang of envy stabbed her aching heart. What she'd give for close wooden walls and the quiet movement of life!

"Thank you for letting me come," Mildred said, cutting a potato with a prong of her fork. "I won't stay the night, but I wanted to see how you were doing."

"Where are you going to sleep?"

"Marten and I worked out a few safe spots that I'll rotate through," she said, waving her hand. She caught the determined look in his eye and shook her head. "I won't tell you where, Jorden, so you can ban the idea from your head. I'm not telling anyone, not even Stella, who is also in hiding, so only contact her through the silenda. I won't put anyone in more danger than absolutely necessary."

His protest faltered. "Fine," he muttered. "It's not worth fighting with you over it. You're so stubborn; you always win."

Gratified, she returned her focus to the red potatoes. Imogen refilled Mildred's cup with cold water from a well, smiled, and moved away again. Jorden's face sobered when he leaned his elbows onto the table.

"Stella told me you've been running around the Network all day, talking to Resistance members and your Coven Leaders. I hope you were careful. Evelyn put a notice out for your arrest with a one hundred pentacle reward this morning, just after you left her office. Desperate witches might turn you in for far less."

Mildred snorted. "Evelyn doesn't frighten me. She couldn't even find me after I left. She tried to track my magic, but I transported from place to place too quickly, and she lost the impression. I'm stronger than she's giving me credit for."

"She should scare you," he said. "She proved today that she's willing to do anything to get what she wants."

A chilling note in his voice set her on edge. She glanced up. "What do you mean?"

"She killed Porter," he whispered. Mildred froze, fork hovering in mid-air above her steaming potatoes.

"What?"

"He wouldn't sign, so she killed him. He tried to leave, but she'd learned from your escape."

"There's been nothing about it in the *Chatterer*—" The response died on Mildred's lips. No, of course there wouldn't be an announcement. Evelyn controlled the newsscroll. She could have Porter killed, institute her own Council Member over Chatham City and Chatham Castle, and gain total control of the Council without anyone knowing.

"Dolph saw Porter's body," he said. "Told Marten that he recognized it as a rare death caused by an old spell, which means it's likely Noah killed him under Evelyn's orders."

Mildred set her fork down, too astonished to eat. Porter gone? She'd expected imprisonment—if he didn't break away as an outlaw the way she had—not secret murder. Why hadn't she warned him?

"Evelyn controls all of Chatham City and Castle now," she said.

"Which means the Resistance needs more witches to fight in Chatham City. Stella thinks it's not safe to continue with the current plan if we don't drum up more support."

A wave of dizziness passed over Mildred, clouding the edges of her vision. Her silenda warmed, and a queue of four messages came at the same time. She ignored them and sat without moving while the lightheaded moment passed, striving to look deep in thought instead of teetering on the verge of consciousness. The last thing she needed was to provoke Jorden's suspicion that she'd taken on too much.

"Stella's right," she admitted. "It's not safe. But then, this plan has never been guaranteed, has it? There's so much to worry about, really. I worry about all of it. The Resistors. Marten. Dolph. What if they're caught? What about Stella? What about you, Imogen, and the baby?"

Jorden folded his hands in front of him.

"Mother would tell you to focus on one problem at a time and then move on," he said with a wry smile. Mildred couldn't help but laugh. "No doubt Evelyn most influences Ashleigh City and Chatham City," he continued. "Imogen and I know a number of trustworthy witches in Ashleigh City. All fifty swore a vow of silence and allegiance to the Resistance, as you specified. But we still don't have enough to stop the Elitists from taking over Ashleigh City when they hear what's happening at the castle. The Elitists in Ashleigh City could provide a safe haven for other fleeing Elitists and fight back."

"My power is limited now," she said, holding out her palms as if to show him they were bare. "I can't return to the castle until I fight Evelyn. We don't have time to recruit and train more witches, nor would I trust that they weren't her spies. According to my Resistors at Ashleigh House, Donovan is sicker than ever before. He could die within weeks."

Her thoughts trailed away.

"Can I propose something?" Jorden asked, and Mildred glanced up at him in surprise. The firelight flickered across his face, and he looked mature in a way she'd never imagined her brother to be. Wouldn't they always be little kids, crouching in a closet, hiding from the wrath of their father? Or had their bullies simply taken on a different form now, and instead of cowering, they stood together?

"Of course," Mildred said, patting her lips and setting her napkin on her empty plate. "I'll take any help at this point."

"You aren't looking everywhere. Maybe there *is* a way to get a group of trustworthy witches on your side that you don't need to train in defensive magic. Or in any magic that Evelyn would anticipate."

"Just what do you suggest?" she asked.

He grinned. "Have you thought of the gypsies?"

We Fight

Two days passed before a response to Mildred's message came from the gypsy elder. She'd watched for it every day, sorting through each envelope in hope. The gypsies were a vast community of witches practicing a rarely understood magic. Vast, and angry. Their support could change the tide for the Resistance at this late stage, and she felt a twinge of pride that Jorden had thought of it.

The day the response arrived, Mildred was holed up in a temporary lodging in Bart's little hovel on the edge of his Coven where no one—not even her Coven Leaders—would look for her. Posters with her portrait and a reward listed for her capture littered every village and city in the Middle Covens. She ignored them. Most of her witches removed the fliers when the Guardians that patrolled the streets weren't watching, or transformed the pictures into a likeness of Evelyn with two buck teeth.

Bart's cottage smelled like rotten cheese. Lavinia had been updating her on happenings at the castle through the silenda, and she'd been responding to questions from Resistance team leaders, when a message slid underneath the door and stopped in front of her face. She tore into it immediately, recognizing the rough paper as a gypsy letter. They had finally responded.

Miss M.

Please meet at Merisa Street and Market Street, on da corner. I will find you there immediately.

Ann

Mildred read it twice. "Bart," she said, standing. "I'm leaving for a while. I'll be back later with some food. And for heavens sake, air this place out. It smells like you died five years ago."

Only minutes later she stood in the middle of a crowded intersection in downtown Chatham City, surrounded by scrollboys, carriages, and flower girls. She avoided a questionable puddle, dodged a stray elbow, and tried to forget the smell of rotting garbage that reminded her of Bart. While she normally loathed crowds, today she felt gratitude for the cover provided by so many witches. She'd seen a poster bearing her face, tacked up on buildings here and there. Coming into public without transforming her appearance was a mighty risk, but pressing forward without the gypsies would be more dangerous.

"Miss Mildred?"

She whirled around to find a female witch in a bright blue sash standing just behind her. Her ebony eyes smiled out of an attractive face. Thick strands of the blackest hair peeked out from beneath an exotic yellow shawl over her head. Her skin was the color of caramel, and her eyelashes thick and long.

"Ann, I presume," Mildred said, sticking out her arm. Ann glanced at it, but made no move to take it.

"Merry meet," she said with a wide, pearly smile. "It's good to meet da bravest woman in da Network. I thought you'd be taller. Come. I show you a safe place."

Instead of leading her north and taking her further into the city as Mildred had expected, Ann hastened in the other direction. The hectic streets faded into calm neighborhoods, and finally they arrived at the outskirts of Letum Wood. Ann ducked into the trees along a vague path, and they plunged into the forest together.

"Is this where you live?" Mildred asked, puffing from the effort of trying to keep up with Ann's long, graceful strides. The silky fabric of her sash waved with every movement while Mildred's short legs stumbled over roots and rocks. "In the midst of Letum Wood? It's not safe out here."

"We live here for now," Ann said. "We make it safe."

Ann didn't say another word, and Mildred didn't have breath to spare, so another ten minutes of walking passed before they stopped at the edge of a camp. The luminous colors of gypsy attire were absent; their tents, constructed of rough linen Mildred had never seen, blended in with the dark forest floor. Green vines draped over their homes for natural camouflage. If Ann hadn't stopped, Mildred might have walked right past it.

"This is home," Ann said, spreading her hands. Two young faces peeked out around a tent off to the right, then giggled and disappeared inside. Bodies seemed to melt from the trees, becoming arms, legs, and finally suspicious eyes. "We stay, but we want more. That's why we bring you."

Mildred's chest eased. Business, yes. Safe ground. "And you're willing to fight for more, I'm presuming?" she asked.

Ann met her eyes and nodded. "Yes." She motioned to an older man with white curls and a deep face standing between two trees. "This is our elder. He wishes to speak with you."

He regarded Mildred through narrowed, black-as-night eyes. "You fight," he said. "You fight da evil one."

"Yes."

He pointed to Ann, then himself, and made a circle motion in front of him.

"We fight."

"For what?"

He smiled with a toothy grin similar to Ann's.

"Home."

"Some want to stay in Chatham City," Ann said. "Da rest go back north. Will you allow us to stay?"

Mildred hesitated, glancing between them. The war between the gypsies and the Network was rooted more in stubbornness than true grievance. At least until recently. The gypsies were a strange breed of witch, with nomadic roots and odd magic. Most witches feared them and complained with such loud, united voices that Donovan had banned them from Chatham City without much investigation into the matter.

"Donovan is not our friend," Ann said, her eyes on the gypsy elder, who wore a necklace of strange bark chips that clinked together in the slight, honeysuckle-laden breeze. "Will you be?"

Katie Cross

Mildred held no paper, no scroll, no quill with which to sit down and make a list. She turned to her intuition instead of the comfort of logic. Promising the gypsies a place in Chatham City was a risk—a big one—and certain to be an unpopular decision in what could prove a hostile, frightened city after her takeover. She never strove for the approval of the masses, of course, but she didn't want to antagonize them either.

"I have rules," Mildred said. "You can't just do whatever you want in Chatham City. That's not my agreement."

"Of course."

"You must abide by the Esmelda Law."

Ann's wide eyes didn't falter. "We never broke it."

Mildred considered, startled to find that Ann was right. She could recall no instance in which the gypsies had broken the law, which made their exile all the more ironic and Donovan's lazy rule more pathetic.

"How many witches will fight with you?" Mildred asked, glancing around. The thick trail of a fire curled through the trees, smelling sickly sweet, like burning maple syrup.

"Two hundred. Maybe two-fifty." Ann shrugged. "We don't need that many, not with our magic, but we use them."

Mildred's heart beat so fast it nearly pounded out of her chest. She didn't understand gypsy magic, the odd chants and wails, nor did she want to. But a promise of those numbers represented all the reassurance she needed.

"Yes," Mildred said, sticking out her arm. "I'll allow you in Chatham City if I win, and if you fight for me. Do as I say, and we'll have an agreement."

Ann blinked several times. She exchanged an astonished glance with the elder. "That's it?" she whispered. "You agree?"

"Yes."

The elder turned to Ann in question, and an unfamiliar flow of clicking, foreign words spewed from their lips so quickly it sounded more like a stuttering hum than a language to Mildred. The elder's brow relaxed, and he nodded.

"Good," he said, but he held out a hand and shook his head. "No teach. We have magic. We use ours."

Mildred hesitated. "Is it safe?"

"To us, yes. To those against us, no."

Mildred laughed, unable to fault the logic of his statement. Her relief left her weak. She pressed her lips together in a small smile and dropped her hand back to her side, supposing it wasn't the gypsy way to seal an agreement with an arm clasp.

"We have an accord," she said. "I have instructions for your part in the plan. Do you want them?"

The elder nodded solemnly. "Not now. We gather all da gypsies tonight and wait for da brave one to return."

It took her a moment to realize he meant her, and she nodded awkwardly. "Tonight," she said. "I'll return to speak with all of you, and I'll bring my brother. He'll be the witch you speak with the most."

Attack

Mildred stifled a yawn and stretched her arms above her head a week later. An old farmer and his wife moved around upstairs, walking on creaky floors as they went about their daily business, pretending Mildred wasn't hiding in their cellar. She blinked several times to clear her blurry vision. Sleep had eluded her ever since she left Chatham Castle, hiding in cellars, attics, and basements to avoid the pair of Protectors hunting her. A flashing headline in the *Chatterer* blinked obnoxiously on the corner of the crate she used as a desk.

TWO HUNDRED PENTACLE REWARD FOR MILDRED GRAEME.

The whoosh of a transportation spell startled her heavy thoughts, and she glanced up just as a witch crumpled to the floor near a bucket of barley.

"Who are you?" Mildred demanded, shooting to her feet. "How did you know I was here—"

She stopped short, unable to believe her eyes. A mane of blonde hair flipped to the side, revealing a young female witch with attractive features and bright green eyes. The girl made a strange hiccuping sound deep in her chest, like she couldn't get a breath of air, and her small frame bucked up and down.

"Blessed be," Mildred said, dropping to her knees next to her. The girl's soundless lips had taken on a blue tinge. "You're cursed."

A quick repetition of every counter-curse for breathing Mildred could think of did nothing.

"They aren't working!" Mildred took the girl by the shoulders. Frantic, she tried to overpower the spell with another, but it didn't work. She caught the girl's flailing hand just as her blue eyes fluttered shut. Her body went limp.

"No!" Mildred cried in horror. "No!"

But it was too late. The muscles in the young woman's face relaxed, her neck slackened, and her head lolled to the side in death. Mildred glanced down at her own hand, which prickled with garbled messages she could barely decipher.

Stilton Coven attacked.
Need help immediately.
Unable to find Team Leader James.

Mildred reached over, closed the witch's eyes, and stood. "What have you done, Evelyn?"

Mildred landed in the attic of the Stilton Coven office and whispered an invisibility incantation. A cacophany of wails, shrieks, and screams rose from outside. She rushed to the window to find Guardians standing in the road, cursing witches.

"So this is what it's come to?" she muttered, casting a powerful paralyzing spell that would reach through the protective shields the Guardians hid behind. The two in the middle of the street dropped. Mildred rushed down the stairs to find Resistors barricading themselves inside. Bloody bodies lay prostrate on the ground, arms flung wide, legs splayed in unnatural, kinked positions. Two witches huddled together on a couch, weeping into blood-covered hands, clinging to each other.

"Block the back door!" Talbot, a High Witch from Stilton Coven, shouted. He hobbled across the room, blood dribbling down the side of his face. "Block it before they make it in and kill all of us!"

Mildred removed her invisibility spell and cast a protective incantation over the doorways. She swept the room with her gaze, finding

Katie Cross

frightened faces decorated with sprays of blood. Shards of glass littered the floor.

"Resistors," she said. "Be calm."

All of them whirled around to face her at the same time. The curtains over the windows drew closed, and the insistent banging of Guardians on the other side of the door seemed to grow muffled under her spells.

"Mildred!"

"Explained what happened," she ordered Talbot. "You have thirty seconds."

Talbot stumbled for just a moment but recovered. "We were just going about our day when a contingent of Guardians showed up, asked if you were here, and started to ransack the Coven office. Then they moved outside and began cursing anyone in the wrong place at the wrong time. Said something about orders to find Mildred or kill the entire Coven. They ambushed all the businesses along the street with curses, blighters, fire, death." His voice caught in his throat. "We didn't see it coming. I sent Dafne to tell you."

Mildred's stomach turned into a cold fist, grateful that she'd told the Coven Leaders and High Witches where she could be found. So that had been the girl who came after her. "I see. How many dead so far?"

Talbot swallowed. "Too many."

"Where are William and Lily?"

"I don't know. I haven't seen Lily. She's probably in the apothecary. William ran down the street to protect the orphanage."

Mildred sent a message to Dolph and Marten through the silenda. "I'll take care of the Guardians outside," she said. "Keep yourselves safe in here. Don't leave for any reason."

"You can't!" Talbot gasped, rushing forward. "They're here for you. We . . . the Resistance needs you!"

"I have no intention of getting caught," she retorted. "Stay inside until I tell you to come out. I'm protecting the office with a spell so no one can transport inside."

Before they could voice another word of protest, Mildred transported to the middle of the street. Those left alive had deserted the road, leaving it empty except for two pairs of Guardians trolling from one house to the next, banging on doors, pulling witches into the street, and alternately cursing or killing them. Mildred paralyzed the patrolling Guardians, hid a crying child behind a water barrel, and took stock of the situation. At least fifteen bodies filled the dirt road, choked by curses and betrayed by their own Network. She could barely contain the rage filling her heart.

"Guardians!" she shouted, placing a powerful protective spell around herself that Marten had taught her years before. Few Guardians could get through it with their magic, and she fervently hoped these weren't the talented exceptions. "I believe you have business to address with me."

The Captain on the porch whipped around, his eyes narrowing on her.

"There she is. Get her!"

They surged forward as one but stopped, unable to press further. Roots as thick as snakes and twenty times stronger than steel sprang from the ground and clutched their ankles, anchoring them in place.

"Under whose authority do you execute witches in this Coven?" she demanded, pressing forward. "You attacked a city of innocent witches. Under the rule of the Esmelda Scrolls, which still constitutes the supreme law of the Central Network, all of you shall meet death as your punishment."

"Under the command of the High Priestess!" the Captain said, shrieking as the roots grew up his legs and wrapped around his waist. "These aren't innocents! They're supporters of the opposition. They're hiding *you!*"

Mildred's fury lent speed to the roots, which wound up their waists and over their shoulders.

"You can tell Evelyn to come after me herself if she has a problem with me. You can also tell her that I *will* make sure she pays for this."

Unable to move, the Guardians hurled curses and blighters at her, but they bounced off her shield, occasionally returning to hit the Guardian that sent them. Boils sprang up on the face of one Guardian, and another paralyzed himself. Mildred put a sleeping incantation on all of them, and they slumped against their cages of roots.

"Mildred." Marten's steady voice came from beside her. "I just arrived. What can I do?"

Her voice trembled. "I'll let you deal with these traitorous disgraces," she muttered, her eyes still on the five Guardians. Dolph, who'd transported in next to Marten, walked toward them.

Marten put a hand on her shoulder. "We'll take care of it."

As if his touch linked her back to reality, Mildred shook herself out of her rage-filled stupor and faced him. Her chest heaved up and down.

"They died because of me," she whispered, feeling as if a part of her soul had faded away in the sheer horror of the moment. "All of them did."

"No," he said. "They died for a cause that we're all fighting for. They died because Evelyn is a tyrant that fears you. This is not your fault."

Mildred swallowed, pushing aside her emotions. She'd deal with them later, when witches didn't need her. "I need to check on the rest of the city," she said. "Take these renegades away from my sight before I finish them myself. Once I take power, they'll receive punishment under the Esmelda Law."

With that, Mildred spun on her heel and started down the street, an invisibility incantation gliding down her body until nothing could be seen of her.

Despite Mildred's best efforts to save those still living, fifty-four witches died in the streets of Stilton Coven. She quietly organized aid while hidden under an invisibility incantation, moving from building to building, ensuring she saw with her own eyes every casualty of the massacre. With Lavinia's help, Mrs. F provided a hot meal. Stella found three apothecaries to treat the wounded, and after Mildred sent out a plea through the silenda, families throughout the Middle Covens and beyond brought the devastated witches into their own homes.

Mildred remained in Stilton until the last witch departed for safety. William and Lily alone remained at the office, unwilling to be frightened from their home. Dolph assigned two undercover Captains to protect them. Once her followers left, Mildred transported into

Letum Wood, where it would be safer to talk. Stella, Lavinia, and Marten followed.

"What happens now, Miss Mildred?" Lavinia asked. She stood an arm's length away, shivering. Marten leaned against a trunk and stared at the ground with a weary gaze.

"We press forward," Mildred replied. "We honor those who gave their lives by emerging victorious."

Lavinia's wide eyes seemed to glow in the fading light.

"Do you think we can do it?" she asked, her voice sounding hollow. "Can we beat a High Priestess so powerful and so frightening?"

Mildred met her gaze in the moonlight.

"That's exactly what we're going to do."

Gather the Witches

"It's an old cotton mill," Lavinia explained the next day, pressing her fists onto her hip bones and surveying the crumbling walls. "Isn't it perfect? The third floor is just one big open area where the textile machines used to run. It backs up to Letum Wood, so witches can transport to the forest, then slip inside the back doors and up the stairs."

Mildred appraised the mouldering building with a critical eye, worried it would cave in while they met inside. Nothing but forest and empty fields surrounded the decaying mill tucked deep in the Middle Covens. An old dirt road made a winding turn not far from the entrance to the mill, but it had overgrown with weeds, leaving only two faint tracks.

"I think it will be just right, Lavinia," Mildred said instead of voicing her concerns. "It's far from Chatham Castle and seems big enough for all of us. Well, as many as we could fit anywhere, I suppose. Show us the inside."

Five minutes later, Mildred, Stella, and Marten stood at the top of an open room cluttered with old ironwork machines and discarded brooms. The rusting machinery that once produced the finest textiles in the Central Network would have to be pushed aside, of course, but otherwise, the large space would be just right. Puffs of cotton sprang into the air and floated on an invisible breeze when they walked through room.

"It's perfect," Mildred said. "We'll assemble them here for the meeting tomorrow night. Since most of them haven't been here before, they won't be able to transport in the first time and will have to walk or ride horses. At any rate, this will be much safer than meeting near a town."

"Yes," Lavinia said with a wide grin. "And they'll fill the whole room. All of them want their revenge more than ever since the massacre."

"Good," Mildred said. "Call them, Lavinia. Gather the witches. We have a war to win."

The next evening, Mildred watched in astonishment as witch after witch poured into the old cotton mill. She'd never seen all her students gathered in a single space before, having always split them up into different classes. Her old Assistant Barnaby had even arrived, giving her a shy wave from the corner of the room where he stood. A few gypsies came, their bright, exotic sashes and billowing clothes drawing nearly all the eyes in the room. To the Resistors' credit, no one openly shied away from the gypsies, though they weren't overly friendly either.

"Merry meet again, Miss Mildred." Mysterious, gray-eyed Ann winked when she walked past. "It's good to see da leader fighting da darkness."

Dolph and his trusted Captains filtered through the mill, searching every hand for the silenda, noting each face present. Marten stayed close to Mildred's side, murmuring protective incantations under his breath, coating the windows and doors with spells to prevent sound from traveling. A definable tension ran through the crowd. Mildred caught whispers of the massacre everywhere she went. The thirst for justice burned in all of them.

"Let's begin," Mildred told Lavinia after the trickle of bodies slowed. "The less time we're grouped together, the better. I won't stand for a replay of earlier this week."

Lavinia bobbed an obedient curtsy and disappeared into the mass. Mildred cast her eyes around the room, lingering on a figure in the back. The hem of an ivory gown peeked out from below the blackest cloak, and a lock of blonde hair tumbled from its hooded depths.

"Marten," Mildred asked, gesturing to the unknown participant. "Who is that witch?"

"Mabel," he said. "May's granddaughter."

Mildred looked at him in surprise. "Indeed? I don't remember swearing her in with the silenda."

"She has a silenda. I checked myself. She's from the Bickers Mill Covens and looks nothing like May, so you may not have recognized her."

"But the Resistors are mostly servants from the castle."

"You accepted trusted friends and family members from your Covens, remember?"

Mildred shook her head. She didn't remember and that frightened her most of all. Was the silenda taking so much out of her now? Could she continue at this rate? She let out a long, weary breath. Since the massacre, she hadn't slept much, plagued by nightmares and a heavy conscience. It didn't matter if she thought she couldn't continue with her responsibilities; she had to.

"Can Mabel be trusted?" she asked.

He hesitated. "She swore the vow of silence."

Mildred pushed the thought from her mind, trusting in the power of the vow for the time being. The room quieted by degrees thanks to Lavinia's barking commands. With as much dignity as she could muster, Mildred lifted her hem and stepped onto a box. At least three hundred pairs of eyes stared at her, but she felt no fear.

I would lead these brave witches anywhere.

"I'm quite overwhelmed with gratitude for you, today of all days," she said. "Almost all of us have worked together for years now as a kind of family, and we welcome with open arms anyone here today. May we fight together to save our homes and avenge our dead."

A bellow rose from Todd and his kitchen friends. They whooped and shook their angry fists.

"We're here tonight to lay out our final plans," Mildred continued. "Dolph, Marten, Stella, and I have worked hard at finalizing what we'll do to overtake the Elitists before they can establish a new law."

"When do we act?" a voice called from the obscurity of the room.

"When Donovan dies," she said. "The Resistors at Ashleigh House will notify us the moment he passes. I will send you a message through the silenda so you know to go to your assigned positions. Once I give the command, we act."

Mildred conjured a cloud of a million black beads that flew into the air, hovering in a loose formation above her head for all to see.

"Now I shall review the plan for the night of the overthrow. Marten, Stella, Lavinia, and I have split you up into teams according to your magical strengths and talents."

The floating black beads divided into a vast array of groups, both large and small, over the top of Mildred's head.

"A collection of teams made up of at least four Resistance members each will be assigned a specific Council Member, Coven Leader, High Witch, or known Elitist to find and subdue during the takeover. Place them in the dungeons once you arrest them; I'll interrogate them after the takeover. Although emotions will be running high, I want no unnecessary violence. This is the Resistance, not a riot. We'll do the right thing, which means no killing unless your own life is threatened."

Swarms of black beads attacked other beads, surrounding them and separating them from the rest. "Understand?"

The group haphazardly nodded. A chunk of black beads shot off to the side and hummed above Lavinia's head, rotating around a small castle. Her chest puffed out.

"The maids, led by Lavinia, will infiltrate the entire castle through the secret passageways to keep track of Evelyn and the other Elitists without being seen and notify us of what's happening. Some Council Members may know about the secret passageways and try to use them to escape, in which case the maids will capture them. If another group needs help, they'll be a possible resource."

"*Possible* resource," Lavinia repeated with a severe glare. "We'll be very busy."

"Meanwhile," Mildred continued, gesturing to a sprawling clump of beads that had zipped over to Marten, Dale, and Jorden. "These three will work with the Guardians surrounding the castle and placed strategically throughout the Network, especially in Ashleigh City, Newberry, and Chatham City. If any discontent arises, the Guardians will reassure and subdue. We want the smoothest transition possible with as little violence as we can manage. They may use paralyzing incantations and stunning spells but will not curse anyone."

"What about Dolph?"

Mildred's eyes slid over to Dolph and caught his steely gaze. His jaw flexed, and he nodded to her. "He'll take care of Noah, the Head of Protectors," she said.

The host of beads pulled back together, formed a circle, and dissolved in a burst of falling black snowflakes. Two young teenage girls in the front, William and Lily's daughter Hazel and her friend Tabitha, giggled when the flakes fell in their hair.

"What about Evelyn?" someone called.

"Are you going to fight in a Magia against her?"

Mildred paused, her breath catching in her throat. *Yes, Mildred. What about your friend? Will you fight her in the most uncontrolled of all fights, the Magia?*

"I will," she declared with a stony voice. "Evelyn is mine."

Stella, who clung to Dale's arm not far away, nodded in resigned acceptance.

"We will distribute your individual assignments tonight. Meet with your Team Leader and begin to prepare. Time is our most precious commodity. I expect all of you to use the silenda to coordinate practice with each other between Resistance meetings so that you're ready to go when the time comes. Any questions?"

Mildred fielded questions for another twenty minutes, and when no more came, hopped off the box with Marten's assistance. A swarm of Resistors surrounded her in a chattering hoard. She addressed their concerns one at a time, conversing with unparalleled patience while the crowd ebbed away.

An hour later, she sat down on her box with an exhausted sigh. A painful pulse at the base of her neck threatened to morph into a splitting headache. The chattering voices—though gone—still persisted in her mind. She rubbed circles along her temples to allay the pain.

"More witches came than I expected," Marten said, his cheeks puffing out. He laid his hands on her shoulders and pressed into the tight muscles. "They really would follow you anywhere, wouldn't they?"

"They'd follow any leader that promised them freedom."

"No," he replied softly. "Not anyone."

"Four hundred witches showed up," Dolph said, flanked by his Captains. "We couldn't fit all of them in this room, so the rest waited in the stairwells and on the second floor. I manipulated a few incantations so all of them were able to hear."

"So many?" Mildred asked, tilting her head back. "Really?"

"Really."

"Think this plan will work?" she asked him. "No one presented any objections. I think we've covered most of . . . well, everything."

Dolph jutted his bottom lip forward but eventually nodded.

"Yes. I do."

Mildred let out a long sigh. "Good," she said. "Me too. But for now I'm going to bed. I'm exhausted."

Stella studied her with a wary eye. "You all right, Milly?"

"Yes, fine. Just tired after . . . talking to so many witches."

But Stella's acute gaze haunted Mildred as she stood, brushing her skirt until it lay straight, and avoiding eye contact with her friend. The deep weariness that permeated into Mildred's bones left her drained, leeched dry of all energy. Displaying their plan visually through magic had required most of the energy that the silenda hadn't taken, but she forced her usual calm facade. Better, she thought, to not alert them to just how heavy the silenda had become, for they needed it. It was the lifeblood of their movement, the only way to safely communicate.

"Good night, all of you," Mildred said. "I'm going to retire to the home of the kind witch who is hosting me for the night. Lavinia, thank you for your help in finding this place. It's perfect. I'll see all of you tomorrow."

Katie Cross

How About Tonight?

Mildred stood in the great room of the Stilton Coven office two weeks later, hidden by an invisibility incantation, eyes tapered in thought. The day had seemed odd to her, which was the only thing that separated it from all the others that passed before. They'd all become blurs of business, silenda messages, moving from place to place, helping the Resistors, and training team leaders. But today felt different. Thick clouds piled in the sky though nothing came from them, casting the evening into early darkness. A change seemed to ripple through the air, though she couldn't put her finger on it.

"I've just received a message from Hazel at school," Lily said, bursting into the office. William looked up from where he worked at his desk and beamed. Mildred shifted further away, feeling like an intruder even though both Lily and William knew she was there. She remained invisible nearly all the time now—yet another drain on her powers. Rumors circulated that Noah was searching for Mildred, so Dolph gave her a few spells to keep her safer. She never remained in one place for very long.

"And how is our darling girl?" William asked.

Lily frowned at the opened paper as she pulled her cloak off, sending it to a coat rack with a spell. It fluttered as it sped across the room, finally landing on a peg with a sigh.

"She said that some girls at school are hostile about the current political situation. Most of the students come from wealthy families, so they're supporting Evelyn and the Elitists. You know Hazel," Lily said with an exasperated sigh. "She can't stand the thought of lying, so she just keeps avoiding it whenever they ask her opinion. I'm worried about her."

She stood next to her husband, frowning. William wrapped an arm around her slender waist and leaned into her side. Lily chewed on her bottom lip.

"Hazel is a clever, fast girl," he said. "She'll keep herself safe."

"I just . . . I'm afraid she'll be cursed because she doesn't believe in Elitism. Perhaps we should pull her."

"She's in her final year. All she has to do is lay low, like she has been, and she'll be fine. Besides, she'll be safer out there during the takeover than here. She's in the silenda. As soon as we act, she'll hide for several hours before transporting home, as we've already discussed with her. It will be just fine."

Lily sucked in a deep breath, then let it all out in a great *whoosh*. "Yes," she murmured, running her hand through William's thick hair. "You're right. You always are."

Mildred pretended she hadn't listened to the conversation until she heard the preemptory whistle of a transportation spell. She turned around to find Marten standing near the fireplace, arms folded across his chest. Mildred removed her invisibility incantation and stepped away from the windows.

"Merry meet, Mildred," he said with a warm smile.

"Marten."

"Come, William. We have other mail to discuss," Lily said, pulling him to his feet. With a nod to both, the couple disappeared upstairs, leaving Mildred and Marten alone. Mildred felt immensely grateful. She hadn't had any time alone with Marten in the weeks following the massacre.

"Here," he said, motioning to a chair. "Have a seat, and let's talk."

She sank into the chair next to him. He sat on the armrest, and she leaned against his side.

"As soon as this is over," Mildred muttered, "I'm going to sleep until I'm forty. Would you like to nap with me?"

"Yes," he said, chuckling. "I think I'd like that."

He draped an arm around her shoulder; she closed her eyes and inhaled the musty scent of his clothes. In the midst of her frantic existence, Marten had always been the stable rock she leaned on. She'd never known love could feel so certain and secure.

"I just want this to end," she said. "But then again, I don't because . . ."

Her words hung in the air, unstated but not needed.

"How about tonight? Would that be soon enough?" he asked.

Mildred's eyes popped open, and she stared at the fire for a few seconds. When she looked up, Marten gazed down on her with concerned eyes.

"Tonight?" she whispered. He nodded.

"Donovan just died. The Guardians sent Dolph the notification, and I came right away to tell you. I think Evelyn is just finding out now as well."

Mildred snapped into action. "I need to notify Lavinia to send the maids into the secret passages and track Evelyn's every move."

"I've already contacted her." He took her arm and pulled her close. "They're on their way. She'll be here to report as soon as all the maids are in position and they find Evelyn. But before you launch into plans, I want to talk to you about how you are doing."

"Me?" she asked, eyebrows lifting. "What do you mean?"

He pulled in a deep breath and laced their fingers together. "Have you thought about what it will mean when you defeat Evelyn in the Magia tonight?"

She paused, feeling a sudden stillness spread through her body. She'd wanted to delay comprehension of her task for as long as possible, but time was no longer a luxury.

"Yes," she whispered. "Once or twice."

"Have you thought about what it means for you and me?"

Mildred closed her eyes. "No. I didn't want to. I've just thought about the fact that it has to be done."

Marten squeezed her fingers, then pressed his lips to them and met her dark eyes. "I love you, Mildred Graeme. No matter what happens tonight, I shall always belong to you."

"If I'm successful in saving the Network from Evelyn tonight, we will be forever separated. I cannot be hand fasted to you as High Priestess."

A failing smile flickered across his face. "Even if the rule that the High Priestess can't be married is a tradition, and not a law written in the Esmelda Scrolls?"

She lifted a hand to his face. "Even then. This Network has suffered through enough from its leaders. Transitioning into my leadership will already be difficult."

Marten pressed his palm to her cheek and threaded the tips of his fingers into the short hair at her temple. She leaned into it with a sigh.

"I know you wanted more," he said. "I know that you wanted a life outside of politics, but you were made for this."

Mildred swallowed. "It's the very last thing I want."

"That's why it's supposed to be yours."

He looked between her eyes, studying them for so long she feared he was trying to memorize something. It frightened her. She reached up and covered his hand with hers.

"It won't matter what level of intimacy we live with," Marten said. "I'll always be here for you. I'll always love you, Mildred. Besides, I can't lose you, not really. I never had you. Both of us love the Network too much. It's like having a mistress and a wife. You can't have both without eventually losing one."

"No," she said, touching his lightly stubbled face with the tips of her fingers. "I suppose you never did have me."

Marten kissed her softly on the lips.

"Will you promise me something?" she asked.

"Anything."

"If I take over as Highest Witch, will you always stand by me as my best friend?"

"Forever," he said, gathering her into his arms. He gripped her dress more tightly in his hands, melding their bodies as close as he could. A moment of longing passed through Mildred, stronger than physical passion and more overwhelming than love.

"Thank you," she whispered into his shoulder. "I love you."

Marten swallowed and pressed a hand to her hair. "Not as much as I love you."

A light tap sounded on the door to the Stilton Office. "It's Lavinia, Council Member. I've come to report."

"You'll be at my side?" Mildred asked.

"Forever."

When Mildred pulled away, she felt herself change. Her jaw hardened. She lifted her head just a fraction of an inch, but it made all the difference. She felt in charge and ready when Isadora's voice from so long ago drifted through her mind.

Sometimes we fight our destiny because of our fears, when what we really need to do is learn how to make destiny work for us.

Mildred wrapped the words of the Watcher in her heart and stepped back. "We have a war to win tonight, Marten. Go to your Guardians. I'll take care of Evelyn."

Assemble at your positions immediately. Best of luck, my friends.

Mildred wrote the message out on paper first, reviewed it, and finally nodded. It didn't convey the strength and power she wished to give the Resistors, but it was enough. They were strong on their own.

She closed her eyes and murmured the incantation. Sending it to the hundreds of witches within her silenda tugged at something deep inside her. She recognized the stir of magic in her chest. It fought for a second and finally departed from her, leaving an empty hole in its wake. She grabbed the edge of the desk when her knees buckled.

"Miss Mildred?" Lavinia inquired from where she stood across the room, waiting. Mildred opened her eyes and braced herself against the desk. She pulled in a deep breath.

"Yes?"

"Are you all right?"

"Yes."

"You're very pale and—"

"I'm fine."

Lavinia swallowed. "It's the silenda, isn't it? There are too many witches pulling from your magic. I've been worried about this all along! What if it kills you?"

"I'm fine," Mildred snapped. "Now tell me what you saw in the passages."

Lavinia reared back, but, accepting the determined look in Mildred's eyes, gave in. "I saw Evelyn in the Council Room meeting with a group of witches. I couldn't tell who they all were by their voices, but I recognized Grant and Gloria amongst them."

Mildred straightened, feeling a bit of strength return to her muscles. She willed her magic to grow. "Did you overhear any plans?"

"No, but it's not hard to guess what they're going to do." Lavinia glanced down at her hand. "One of the maids is contacting me now," she said. "Evelyn left the Council Room, but they can't tell where she is. She must have transported. Oh, wait, another message. Evelyn's in her office. They . . . they can't see what's happening. They said something blocked their view."

Mildred stopped. "The Esmelda Scrolls." The maids wouldn't have been able to see the scrolls when they appeared to Evelyn for the first time, as only the Highest Witch could lay eyes on them. The magic surrounding the scrolls would have prevented it.

"Are you ready for this, Council Member?" Lavinia asked. "It sounds like it's time for you to face your enemy."

"She's not just my enemy, Lavinia," Mildred whispered. "She's my best friend. And yes, I'm ready. Transport to my old office. We'll go through the secret passages from there."

It's Not Yours

A suffocating feeling permeated the secret passageway outside the High Priestess's office, nearly robbing Mildred's breath. Evelyn's low voice murmured in the background, but as the maids reported, Mildred saw nothing through the peephole in the painting.

She closed her eyes and mentally searched for her powers, worried when she found them faint and struggling. Her magic felt tenuous and weak with the Resistance communicating constantly through the silenda. Her own silenda faded into a new message every four seconds, changing so often her skin burned. Sharp tingles ran through Mildred's skin when she dropped her hand back to her side. Could she fight Evelyn and win?

Don't think about it, she told herself. *Just do it.*

Be a lioness, Marten's voice whispered in her ear though he was nowhere to be seen.

"I will always love you, Marten," she murmured, a hand pressed to her heart. No matter what, from here on out, she'd be lost to him. Either in death or in a life promised to the Network for the rest of her life. This wasn't about her anymore. This was about the Resistors, the Central Network. The future.

I am a lioness.

Her powers expanded from a fickle flame to a blooming fire in her chest. Finally ready, she drew in a breath to prepare for the biggest fight of her life, then spoke an incantation. The painting that acted as a door into the High Priestess's office disappeared, exploding across the room and skewering itself on a statue.

"Merry meet, Evelyn," Mildred called, stepping out of the passageway. "I've come to congratulate you in person."

Evelyn's eyes narrowed. She stood over a small, carved wooden box lined with gold. A shuffle of movement caught Mildred's eye. May stood off to the side, arms folded across her chest.

No doubt the box held the Esmelda Scrolls. What else would be so old? But Mildred saw no sign of the famed law, which meant Evelyn hadn't removed the scrolls from the box yet. If she had, she'd replaced them to speak with May. Or she may have already destroyed them, and Mildred was too late.

"Mildred," Evelyn said, eyes flashing like bolts of lightning in a storm. Her presence crackled with power. "How kind of you to think of congratulating me at such an opportune moment. You haven't been around in a while."

"I've been busy," Mildred said, moving carefully into the room. "Trying to save the Network from the plans of a tyrant."

Evelyn smiled. "How noble of you. Wasteful, but noble. What are you really here for, old friend? I don't have time for chitchat, you know. A Network to rule as Highest Witch, and all. Is this one last attempt to get me to see the light of your ways?"

The cold tone of Evelyn's voice sent a chill through Mildred's spine.

"Evelyn Ringer," she called with a voice of strength and steel, "I'm here to challenge you to a Magia."

An explosion of light blew apart in the middle of the room. Mildred ducked and covered her face, turning away from the blinding flash. It threw her back into the wall, stealing her breath. Glimmering swirls of light bloomed in the air, encircling Evelyn and Mildred at waist height. If Mildred or Evelyn cast any purposeful magic inside the Magia circle, they would forfeit the fight and die.

May had been thrown against the wall, her hair singed and smoking from the explosion. Her eyes flickered as she edged toward the door, fear swimming in their icy blue depths.

"You think you're stronger than me, Milly?" Evelyn asked, hissing her name.

"I don't think it, old friend," Mildred replied. "I know it."

Evelyn laughed, letting it build on itself until what little sanity she had seemed to possess fell in shreds. Her black irises burned as hot as a bed of coals against her pale skin. Mildred didn't even recognize her anymore.

"You who couldn't even defend yourself as a child?" she asked. "Who couldn't render enough magic to levitate a feather?"

"We were friends once, Evie," Mildred said, thinking of her empty pinky finger where the Witches' Oath once lay. "Do you remember that? Do you remember our oath, our sleepovers, our times together? Or have you chosen to forget?"

"Friends?" Evelyn sneered. "That's what you think, is it? That I would be a friend to one as unsupportive as you? That I'd care what you think of me? All of this fighting is because of you, Mildred. We could have been great together, but you chose to break us."

"Your greed wouldn't allow it."

"You didn't trust me!"

"No," Mildred said. "Eventually, I didn't."

Evelyn snarled. "Then let's do this Magia right, *friend*."

They released magic at the same moment. Two waves of power collided, thunder hurling them off their feet as if they were rag dolls. Evelyn slammed into a bookshelf, Mildred, the wall. The windows shattered in a spray of glass, admitting a wind into the office that swept a stack of papers into the air like a flock of creamy white birds. Mildred forced herself to her feet, black dots swimming in her vision.

"I'm improving the Network, Milly!" Evelyn cried, clutching a shoulder. "I'm fixing all her flaws, don't you see? Just like Esmelda in the ancient days. She wrote a new law. She fixed the problems. Why can't I? Don't you see I want the best for the Network? I've given up everything to serve these ungrateful witches."

A wild gust of sultry wind stormed through the room. Mildred stiffened, finding her balance again. Her power struggled to rebuild itself like a dying flame. She forced her concentration on it, willing it to grow.

"You're not fixing anything. You're oppressing your citizens."

"You would coddle all their faults."

"No, but I wouldn't oppress the poor just to support an Elitist lifestyle."

Sparks rose from the fireplace, ripping through the office like a tornado. They spun past Mildred on a rampage of fire, burning hot and red.

"I'll set the poor free!" Evelyn yelled. "No more murders of innocent witches in uprisings. No more riots, no more misplaced currency."

Mildred released magic again, scattering away the scalding particles on her skin by sheer force. Books soared off the shelves. Evelyn ducked away from the shower of heavy tomes.

"Getting your revenge on the poor won't bring your mother back!" Mildred shouted over a burst of wind. "She's gone! Just like Nell! May left you as well. All of them are gone except for me and Stella."

"You don't know anything!" Evelyn shrieked. "*Nothing!*"

"It's not too late! Stop this madness."

"I've given my life to this, Mildred. I won't let it go now."

"You can't control the Network. The poor rise up in rebellion against you right now. They're following my commands. We will win!" Mildred stumbled to her knees when the floor vibrated and bucked. A fresh wave of magic sent her flying into the wall. Her ribs cracked against a statue.

"I'll never allow a rebellion!" Evelyn screamed. "You and those rats are going to die tonight. You brought it to this."

"You can't stop us!" Mildred yelled into the howling wind, gasping for breath. She put a hand to her side, feeling a sticky dampness. "We're taking over the castle. The Council Members will be thrown into the dungeons, and you will die."

Evelyn cackled.

"You'll never kill me. You don't have the power. I'm the Highest Witch! Donovan is gone. My law will reign supreme, and all of you shall see the truth of my ways. I'm right, Mildred. I know I'm right!"

Mildred sought for her magic again, but it had shriveled inside her. Her very bones ached. Her heart stuttered in exhaustion.

"The poor must be led," Evelyn said, her eyes alight. "Don't you see? I'm the new Esmelda. I'm here to change the world!"

Mildred leaned into a mighty gust of wind to keep from falling over. Evelyn released her magic so frequently that it collided with itself. The fire flared. The wind swelled. Everything scattered into a blinding chaos.

"You're losing control, Evelyn! You're going to kill yourself if you keep this up."

Evelyn tipped her head back and threw her arms wide. The edges of her ebony dress flapped in a mad dance around her ankles, the long skirt billowing in blooms of darkest silk.

"I've done it, don't you see? I'm Highest Witch. I possess the scrolls. I'll destroy them and finish the job I started fifteen years ago: saving the Network."

Magic left Mildred of its own accord, and she was too exhausted to prevent it. A blaze of heat ballooned into the room from the fireplace, forcing her to shrink away from a wall of flames. Wind caught the fire and carried it higher. An inferno raced across the bookshelves, burning the hairs on the back of her arms. Paintings melted into rivers of ink in the waving heat.

"Everything is ready for the New Central Network. Everything except for you." Evelyn's hysteria calmed for just a moment, betraying a flash of sadness that made her appear even more out of control. "And now you must die at my hands for the good of the Network."

Smoke and ash fell into Mildred's eyes. She tried to release magic again, but nothing happened. Her muscles twitched when she attempted to stand. "No!" she whispered frantically, stumbling. "No!"

A muggy wall of hot air knocked both of them to the ground. Mildred lay on her side, trying to catch her breath through broken ribs. Evelyn leapt back to her feet, her skin glowing as she levitated off the floor, flying far above Mildred. The ground shivered, drawing chunks of stone and dust from the rafters. A rock pelted Mildred on the crown of her head, and blood leaked from the gash.

"Don't do this, Evelyn," Mildred cried, climbing to her hands and knees. Her arms trembled with the effort. "You'll destroy yourself and the castle. Rein your magic back in! You'll break the Network, not save it."

A cyclone spun around Evelyn's floating body. Chairs groaned as they slid across the floor, and the pages of unburned books fluttered in the air as the wind caught them up. Mildred crawled into the eye of the storm, not strong enough to do more.

"I am the Highest Witch in all of the New Central Network," Evelyn bellowed, her voice booming through the torrent. "I have prevailed!"

A fissure cracked the ceiling, freeing a slab of rock. The ground rippled under the crash, knocking Mildred off her knees. Blurry images whipped past her in the storm. She lay trapped in the heart of Evelyn's deranged frenzy, gripping the cracks between the floorboards as an anchor.

Her body begged for darkness, for silence. She had no more power left for herself. Burrowing deep inside herself, she turned to the things that strengthened her. She saw Marten's face. Then Stella, and Jorden, and Mother, and all the Resistance. Perhaps her burgeoning power originated not inside herself, but in the influence so many witches had on her life. For herself, Mildred could not muster the power. But for many she could.

Be a lioness.

Oh, Marten. The magic in her heart expanded once again. *I shall love you forever.* Another chunk of stone fell from the ceiling, smashing Evelyn's desk into splinters that fluttered into the storm. Mother's voice rose from the innermost chambers of her heart.

You'll change the world. You're made of steel, you know.

The last of Mildred's power flared to life.

I am a lioness.

Tingles flooded her skin and legs.

I will not fail.

Mildred grabbed onto a flare of magic and forced it to grow. It bloomed, pulling the last of her physical strength. Her vision dimmed. Her left hand slipped from between the cracks, and she nearly fell into the screaming whirlwind.

"Are you ready to die, Mildred?" Evelyn called, her hair forming a red halo around her head. "Are you ready to die for the Network?"

The wind tunnel tightened around Mildred, yanking off one of her shoes. The fingers of her right hand cracked as if they were about to break off.

"No," Mildred cried, a sob in her throat. The magic inside had built so quickly she couldn't hold it in. "I'm ready to live for my Network."

With a final breath, Mildred released the last power that tied her to consciousness. A great rending split the air, followed by an ear-splitting crack and then a groan. Boulders rained from the sky in a sudden deluge. She crumbled into darkness and knew no more.

The Esmelda Scrolls

Mildred woke to a whisper.

The wind had settled into an occasional caress, blowing thick black clouds past the castle and revealing glimpses of stars in the night sky. Papers fluttered to the floor. Smoke steamed out of the scorched wall behind the fireplace, but the flames lived no more. Mildred blinked to clear the dust from her eyes. Her hand burned; her side ached. She gingerly shook her head, surprised to be alive. Several rocks tumbled off her back in poofs of dust when she straightened onto trembling feet.

Stones and broken rafter beams littered the floor. The oblong area where she had lain remained free of debris. Somehow her own magic had protected her from itself.

"Blessed be."

Sitting within arm's reach was a square wooden box with metal corners, the same box that had sat on Evelyn's desk. An ornate pattern of words inscribed the top and sides. Hints of soot dusted the top, filling the claw feet at each corner. Mildred looked past it, to the enormous pile of stones, and Evelyn's ghostly white hand sticking out of her makeshift tomb.

Mildred's heart stuttered. "Oh, Evie," she whispered, tears in her eyes. "I'm so sorry."

A *ting* broke the silence. The High Priestess bracelet dropped from Evelyn's wrist and rolled across the floor, landing a breath away from Mildred's feet. She stared at it in quiet disbelief.

SAC ERO DOS SUM MUS

The gentle whisper that woke Mildred returned on the wind. Sparkling fragments of a deep yellow cloud formed around the abandoned bracelet, lifting it into the air. She struggled to keep her feet as the glittering mist surrounded her.

It's a far greater sacrifice than any will ever know, an ancient voice sang in her ear, *but it is yours to make.*

"I didn't ask for this," she whispered, staring at the bright silver bracelet rotating in the cloud. "I didn't want it."

That is why it is yours.

"What if I don't accept?"

You already have.

Mildred drew in a deep breath. "Yes. I have."

The bracelet widened, slipped over her extended hand, and shrank to the size of her wrist. The cool metal dropped onto her skin, and a suffocating weight fell with it. It seemed to press through Mildred's skin, into her muscles, crushing the very marrow of her bones. She fell to her knees, struggling to bear the unexpected burden.

Her ribs would not expand. Her mind could not comprehend. Darkness played at the edges of her vision, threatening to pull her away into the welcoming maw of nothingness, free of the pain she had just escaped. When she could bear it no longer, the merciless weight slackened. Her muscles released. Mildred pulled in a giant gasp of air, and a surge of strength followed.

Evelyn tried to come to power through control. She grieved and never let go. Because you understood what she did not, you have won.

The top of the wooden box flipped open. Nestled in a bed of sapphire silk lay two scrolls sealed with Donovan's stamp. Mildred started at the sight of them, her heart in her throat.

"Would she have been able to destroy them?" she asked in a hoarse whisper. "Would she have broken the Central Network?"

No magic is infallible.

Mildred glanced at the bracelet. Her entire body hummed with new life, prickling underneath her fingernails and consuming her skin. A distant shout of voices in the hall drew her gaze to the doorway. The box holding the Esmelda Scrolls closed.

Be true to the Central Network, and the Esmelda Scrolls will be true to you. The scrolls will return when you are alone and able to compre-hend their words and the power they bestow. The whisper began to fade. *Under the blessing and empowerment of Esmelda, you are now the leader of the scrolls, and the Highest Witch of the Central Network.*

The final words faded in a dissipation of yellow cloud.

So mote it be.

A scuffle of shoes announced Marten and Stella. They skidded to a stop in the doorway. Their eyes skimmed the field of boulders, Evelyn's hand, and finally the bracelet glinting off Mildred's arm.

"Mildred," Stella said.

"Evelyn and I had a little disagreement about her ruling style," Mildred said, clearing her throat and glancing askance at the room. "I won."

Marten fell to one knee, his hand over his heart. "High Priestess," he whispered, head bowed. "Allow me to be the first to pledge my life to your service."

"Stand up," she muttered, rolling her eyes. "You don't bow to me, Marten."

"I bow to you forever."

"But Mildred, y-you've given up everything," Stella said in a breathy voice, rushing forward. She stopped an arm's length away, as if she were frightened to touch her. "You—"

"Have a mess to clean up," Mildred said, ignoring Stella's tears. "What's happening with the Resistance?"

Marten paused, blinking. He swallowed. "Thanks to Lavinia and her maids, we control the castle, Your Highness," he said, ris-ing. "Guardians maintain the peace, and four Council Members have been locked in the dungeons. Eddy's dead—at Evelyn's hand, I might add—so there are only nine more to track down. The gypsies control most of Chatham City, but Jorden is struggling to claim Ashleigh. We just sent a group of fifty Guardian reinforcements. Most smaller villages report no problems, although a few High Witches have aban-doned their post, and rioting has overtaken the bigger cities."

"Any idea how many we've lost?"

Stella shook her head. "At least twenty from the castle takeover."

"Thirty gypsies so far."

Mildred received the news with little change in expression, though her heart felt heavy.

"And rioting?"

"Newberry is the worst," Stella said. "Dale just left with his Guardians to try to subdue it, but it sounds ugly. Ten Guardians have already died. More of the injured are transporting into the High Bailey as we speak."

"I see," Mildred murmured. "It's time I addressed the Network as her new leader. I'll leave for the worst places immediately. Perhaps we can frustrate the violence."

Marten motioned to several shifting shadows in the hall at his back. "Since the castle is secure, we came to ask for your orders."

A group of ragged Resistors appeared behind him. Lavinia walked in first, eyes dazed, face burned on one side, bearing an injured maid on one arm. Witches limped into the open space along the wall with broken legs, burned skin, and torn flesh. If they had looked haggard before, they were downright ugly now.

Tears filled Mildred's eyes.

So many missing, she thought, her heart clenching, wondering where Todd had gone. Mrs. F? Lavinia's sister, Leslee? Had they all fought and died for her? Once they'd all gathered in a mass of sweaty, bloodstained bodies, Mildred climbed on a boulder and held Marten's shoulder for stability, for he stood ever at her side.

"Donovan and Evelyn are dead," Mildred said, her voice cracking. "You've won it for the Network, by the heavens. The good gods know that *you have done it!*"

A deep, guttural sound erupted. Witches fell to their knees, weeping. Hoarse cries filled the air, disappearing into sobs and weak exclamations of relief. Lavinia ducked her head and wept. Two kitchen workers clung to each other near the door.

"To the Highest Witch that dispelled the dark days!" Marten cried, his voice breaking. "Mildred Graeme!"

One by one, the witches of the Resistance lowered to a knee, their filthy, tear-streaked faces tilted high with pride.

"To our High Priestess!" they called. "Mildred, the Lioness of the Central Network!"

Mercy and Justice

The first month of Mildred's reign passed in a blur that she later couldn't recall. Whatever busy times she'd had as an Assistant didn't compare with her first weeks as High Priestess.

Ten Coven Leaders and three Council Members remained at large for the first two weeks. With steady tracking by Marten and Dolph, the Elitists answered for their deeds. Those unwilling to swear allegiance to Mildred with a binding to never act in any traitorous manner again were executed. Most capitulated to Mildred's authority once they saw the remains of their leader, for as she suspected, they hadn't really loved Evelyn.

Mildred replaced the Council, who called new Coven Leaders, and all the cobwebs and shadows of the Dark Days faded away. Lavinia, who promptly took over as Head Housekeeper in place of the one who had died saving a younger maid, ensured that a statue modeled after her deceased sister, Leslee, stood in the gardens, dedicated to the brave maids that saved the castle.

Those who hadn't survived the takeover—Porter, Terry, Alfred, Mrs. Quinten, Tom, Mrs. F, Bart, and too many Resistance members and Guardians, were honored by an eternal arbor in the main gardens. With a heavy heart, Mildred struck Evelyn from all records and buried her in a lone grave deep in Letum Wood.

Burdened by a collapsed economy and more problems than she could hope to fix in ten years, Mildred interviewed what remained of Evelyn and Donovan's Council, beginning with Grant, to put all the pieces together.

"May was lethal in her motivation," Grant said from across her desk. A rope, woven with thin strings of steel, wound around his hands. He appeared oddly calm and expressionless, still well-kept and manicured despite two months in the dungeons. Lavinia sat off to the side, scribbling his responses, believing that *someone should record everything that happened.*

"I thought May and Evelyn were quite close," Mildred said with surprise.

Grant scoffed. "May didn't care about anyone but herself. She used Evelyn the whole time. Her plan from the very beginning was to climb into the political sphere on Evelyn's back, then defeat her in a Magia once she instituted her own law. She figured Evelyn was weak enough."

"Then what would she have done?" Mildred asked in surprise. "No one liked May."

Grant shrugged. "No one really liked Evelyn either, but they did what she told them." Mildred conceded to the point with a slight nod. "I told May I didn't think it would work," he continued, "but she said that didn't matter. She had a plan that didn't require anyone's good opinion."

The execution of May had been particularly sad, as no one came to attend her or keep her company in her final hours. No one showed remorse at her passing. Any attempt to contact her daughter or granddaughter was futile. They both rejected the messages. Mildred couldn't shake the awkward feeling that something wasn't right.

"Why did you join with May?" she asked next, pushing her thoughts aside to review later with Marten. He always helped her see from a different perspective. "I thought you loved Evelyn. Why would you want to kill her?"

"I did enjoy her for a while," Grant said wistfully. "As much as I could appreciate anyone that wasn't myself, anyway. She became too demanding, annoying even. Our infatuation didn't last long. In the end, May seemed likely to win, and I wanted to be on the winning side."

Mildred leaned over her desk while a scroll unrolled itself in front of him.

"This is a rather complicated binding, Grant," she explained, gesturing to the first paragraph. "You've answered all my questions and helped us locate Council Member Wayne. If you sign this binding, which details every act of treason you may not take, and promise your total allegiance to the Central Network and the Esmelda Law, you are free to live your life."

He glanced at her in disbelief. "I thought it would be the dungeons."

"That's still an option, if you want," she said, waving a quill at him. "I'm not without mercy. Neither am I without justice. You'll have eyes on you for the rest of your life. You cannot hold a position of power. If you take a job, it must be approved by Dolph or me. If you move to a different Coven, we must be notified. What life you do lead outside the dungeons will be controlled and regulated because I shall never trust you. Trying to wiggle out of this binding will only result in your death."

Grant raised an amused eyebrow and lifted his bound hands.

"Where do I sign?"

Later that afternoon, Mildred's new Assistant Neesa, whose hazel eyes gave her a serious bearing, strode into the room. She hated small talk as much as Mildred did, which meant her interview had only taken ten minutes. Neesa's favorite thing to do was sort through and answer messages and paperwork, so Mildred gratefully left her to it.

"Stella sent word from the Southern Covens," Neesa said, plucking a letter off the top of a pile. "She's training her new Coven Leaders how to report during the Esbat and will be there tonight."

Mildred's forehead furrowed. Stella's new appointment as Council Member to the Southern Covens provided plenty of distraction while she mourned the loss of Dale, who fought bravely to quell the riots in Newberry, but ultimately sacrificed his life while subduing the violence. Stella had lost so much in the past year but pushed on.

"Thank you, Neesa," Mildred said, jerking out of her thoughts. "Most of the Council Members have been retraining Coven Leaders for the Esbat. It's been years since Donovan allowed them in, so they don't even know how to do a proper report."

Neesa shifted to the next letter. "Your brother requested you bring a dessert with you for your weekly dinner tomorrow night. He said to remind you that Imogen loves chocolate, and to bring a few things to put in your room at their new house in Ashleigh City."

"Notify the new cook, Fina, please. Tell her to make a chocolate cherry cake with extra cherries and no coconut, the way her mother used to. Is Marten going with me?"

"Yes, but he can't meet you for dinner tonight. He's meeting with the Ambassador to the Eastern Network because Donovan hadn't appointed an Ambassador for ten years now." Neesa consulted an organized list of notes in her hand. "Also, William and Lily responded to your letter, and he agreed to remain Coven Leader over Stilton. Their daughter Hazel experienced some kind of shock recently and hasn't spoken a word since. They pulled her from Miss Mabel's School for Girls and want to remain at home until she has recovered."

Mildred's forehead furrowed in concern. "Is she all right?"

"I don't know, High Priestess. Hazel won't speak. They've asked Mabel, but she says she doesn't know anything. Hazel's friend, Tabitha, doesn't know what happened to her either, but she heard May speaking with Hazel in the hallway late one night right before the takeover. She said Hazel's been acting funny ever since."

"Tell William and Lily that it's quite all right," Mildred said. "I'll follow up with them on it later."

"Speaking of Mabel, she's outside your office at your request, High Priestess," Neesa said. "That's all I have for now."

"Oh, yes," Mildred said, setting aside a list of Covens that needed food until the farms recovered. "Let her in. Thank you, Neesa."

The door closed behind Mabel as she entered the office with an unusual feline grace. Her blonde hair gleamed in a bun at the nape of her long, pearly neck. Her sapphire blue eyes shone with a confidence that Mildred hadn't seen in witches twice her age. She wondered where it came from in someone raised by a horrid witch like May.

"Your Highness," Mabel said, bowing her head. Mildred let the lack of respectful curtsy slide, discomfited to realize they were the same age. Mabel seemed so much younger.

"Thank you for coming today, Mabel," she said, motioning to a chair behind her. "Please, have a seat."

"No, thank you."

Mildred remained standing herself, irritated by her inability to get a good grasp on Mabel's elusive personality.

"I saw you at a couple of Resistance meetings," Mildred said. "You hid in the back beneath a dark blue cloak most of the time, didn't you?"

"Yes. I was an avid supporter."

"Stella tells me you asked to take charge of capturing your grandmother. You can understand why I didn't give you that job, of course."

Mabel shook her head innocently. "No, High Priestess. I can't imagine why you didn't."

"Whether you swore allegiance to the Resistance or not, I didn't expect you'd go through with the capture of a family member."

"If I didn't get rid of May, she would have gotten rid of me. It's a common thing in our family."

Mildred thought back to May's cutting gaze and didn't doubt Mabel's statement for a moment.

"Is that why you turned her in?" Mildred asked, glancing down at a note she'd received from Mabel detailing May's whereabouts.

"Yes."

A bundle of letters from Evelyn had come with Mabel's letter; further testament to May's devious plans, providing sufficient evidence for her execution. Mabel had done everything possible to ensure her grandmother's demise. May had left the final fight, leaving Evelyn to battle Mildred alone. Mildred studied her, haunted by an uneasy instinct that told her Mabel was far from innocent herself. She had no proof that Mabel aided Evelyn and May in their thwarted takeover, but she suspected something was off.

"As I understand the events," Mildred continued, "May fled back to the school once the Magia between Evelyn and me began. While there, she packed and left to hide in Letum Wood, where she remained until you reported her."

"Yes, that's right."

"How did you know she was there?"

"I spoke with her before she fled. It wasn't difficult to figure out. I know May better than anyone. She may have had great expectations for her own success, but she was a coward. She had a selfish soul beneath all that beauty."

"Did she ever try to involve you in her plans?"

Mabel laughed. "The good gods! May didn't trust me. She feared that I would gain power of my own and destroy her."

Mildred couldn't help but notice that Mabel blithely avoided the question. "Would you have destroyed her?"

Mabel smiled in a slow, easy manner that didn't reach her cool blue eyes.

"In a heartbeat."

"How am I to trust that you didn't betray the Resistance? You lived and worked with the enemy, after all."

"Several Resistance witnesses have spoken in my name. I know you've already heard their testimonies."

"That doesn't convince me of your loyalty. Other Resistance members have spoken against you. They said you didn't attend all their meetings, you were seen with several Elitist sympathizers, and you disappeared the night of the takeover."

"I took the vow of silence, did I not?"

"You may have found a way around it."

"Was your vow so poorly constructed?" Mabel asked, and Mildred's annoyance deepened.

"I also brought you here to discuss your grandmother's school," she said, turning back to the steady, safe point of business. "You want to keep it running."

"Yes," Mabel said. "I'm partial to the manor and the job."

Mildred hesitated to trust Mabel with any kind of power, but she lacked a logical reason to prevent her running the school. It had been the premiere Network school for years, and a handful of trustworthy Resistance members had spoken for her.

"I've decided that you may remain as Head Witch in place of your deceased grandmother," she said. "Effective immediately."

A delighted smirk played at the corners of Mabel's lips. "That's excellent news."

"There will be a few changes, of course. The Head of Education must approve every teacher you appoint. Isadora will live on school grounds to protect the students and report to me. The Network will place a teacher of our choosing on staff at every Network school from here on out. I'll allow you to run it," Mildred said with her usual severe gaze. "But that doesn't mean I trust you."

Miss Mabel's eyebrow lifted, but her expression didn't waver. "I'm at your disposal, High Priestess."

"That's all I have for you today, Mabel. I expect to see you at the meeting with Network teachers before the school year begins. Let me know if you have any questions. You may go."

Mabel bowed her head. "Merry part, Your Highness. I do look forward to our time getting to know each other."

She left without a curtsy, departing as silently as the wind. Marten slipped inside before the door closed and smiled.

"Do you think you could spare a few minutes for lunch with an old friend?" he asked. "I'm sorry to miss dinner tonight, but the Eastern Network Ambassador awaits. I shouldn't miss the first meeting in my new job as Ambassador, should I? It's been a few years since Donovan actually *sent* an Ambassador, so relations are a bit strained."

She grinned. "I'll have lunch with my *best* friend, you mean."

A flicker of pain shot through his eyes, but he hid it with a smile. Instinctively, he reached out to hold her hand, but stopped and tucked his fingers into his pocket instead.

"What's wrong?" he asked, gazing on her sudden frown. She shook her head in frustration.

"I have a terrible feeling that something isn't right. Mabel knows something about her grandmother that she isn't admitting. I can sense it. And I can't stop thinking of what Grant told me about May's plan."

"Do you have an inkling?" Marten asked.

A ridiculous thought flittered through her mind. She almost let it go, dismissing it without saying a word, but a growing nervousness prevented it. She met Marten's concerned gaze with great hesitation.

"I've been thinking about the rumors of the Almorran *Book of Spells*. Do you remember?"

"There are always rumors about the *Book of Spells*. Witches have been terrified that it will resurface ever since Esmelda formed the Network thousands of years ago."

Mildred couldn't find any facts to back up her hunch, which made her uncomfortable. "Perhaps," she muttered. "But I can't help . . . I wonder—"

"If May had found the *Book of Spells* and planned to use Almorran magic to kill Evelyn?" His eyes went distant for a moment, then refocused. "Is that what you're worried about?"

She nodded, grateful that he didn't laugh.

"If her plan had been to use the black magic of the Almorrans to take over, it doesn't matter," Marten said. "She's gone."

"I know," Mildred said. "But her granddaughter isn't, which means the *Book of Spells* could be right under our very noses."

She let that sink in, and Marten's face elongated into a frown. "What are you going to do?" he asked.

"Watch and wait. I've asked Isadora to live on the school grounds. I figure if Mabel uses Almorran magic, Isadora will detect it right away. I'm going to send Dolph to the school when Mabel is at a meeting to investigate further. If she has the *Book of Spells*, I'll find it."

"If you don't find it?"

"I don't know," she whispered. "If she's not actively using it, we probably shouldn't fear too much."

Marten motioned to the door. "Let us think of pleasanter things for now. Fina has lunch waiting for us in the dining room, at our table. It's blocked off now, so no one shall bother us."

Mildred smiled. "That sounds lovely. Thank you, Marten."

The sun fell through the windows in long, warm beams. A gentle fall breeze drifted through the hallways, rustling her short, auburn hair. She nodded to two maids—surviving Resistance members—who smiled and curtsied. Marten remained at her side, talking about his plans for the meeting with the Ambassador. A feeling of contented joy settled in Mildred's chest. *I will make this a good life.*

She continued down the hall with Marten at her side, where he'd always been, and where she imagined he always would be.

Printed in Great Britain
by Amazon

44736324R10217